About the Author

One of Britain's most prolific authors, Michael J H Taylor began his meteoric writing career at the remarkably young age of 19, when a major publisher gave him the opportunity to contribute to a world-famous yearbook. Soon he was writing two, three and even four books a year under his own name, allowing his work to reach a much wider audience. This prestigious output of aero-space and other books exceeded 100 titles by the year 2000, gaining him five-star reviews and multi-million sales, with many translations to satisfy worldwide demand.

In a major shift, and after producing three internationally acclaimed one-million-word books, in 2003 he gave up his previous writing genre to become a full-time novelist. His home, a converted Victorian school in a picturesque Somerset village, gave him initial inspiration to write historical novels based on areas of the West Country made famous in Thomas Hardy classics. Then, after completing his third historical novel in 2009 to form a trilogy, he changed to modern storylines for his later novels.

His new book for 2018 publication, *The Boy Caught in the Starlight*, is to be the first in a series of adventure novels.

Dedication

To my wonderful daughters, who would definitely give me their last Rolos… or so they say! Also to my good friend 'Horace', who brandished a metaphorical stick until I completed a children's novel which would, in his words, 'rival the best of the rest'.

Michael J H Taylor

THE BOY CAUGHT IN THE STARLIGHT

AUSTIN MACAULEY PUBLISHERS™

LONDON • CAMBRIDGE • NEW YORK • SHARJAH

A CIP catalogue record for this title is available from the British Library.

ISBN 9781788489461 (Paperback)
ISBN 9781788489478 (Hardback)
ISBN 9781788489614 (E-Book)

www.austinmacauley.com

First Published (2018)
Austin Macauley Publishers Ltd™
25 Canada Square
Canary Wharf
London
E14 5LQ

Acknowledgements

The cover illustration is based on an original concept painting by renowned artist Peter Hodges.

Chapter 1
The Drowning Sailor

Having been persuaded to tell the true story of my amazing starlight adventure—holding nothing back, even at the risk of terrifying the readers—I will first reveal the circumstances that brought me into contact with the inventor of the Starlight Machine, the crusty old Professor Septimus Kneebone.

The professor was, and remains, a very strange man with many eccentricities, who prefers his own intelligent company to that of others who he casually dismisses as *muddleheads*. I remember the day I first saw him when he was red with fury and ready to burst, thumping his fists and shouting something rude at the top of his stuttering voice. To my astonishment, he wore what looked like a giant baby's nappy instead of trousers, with creepy spiders crawling in and out of the creases. He told me the spiders were his indoor pets. I later discovered the proper name for the nappy garment was a *dhoti*, a type of loincloth normally worn by Hindus.

Just as strange was the old man's hair, a dirty chocolate brown at the sides but with pure white spikes on top. The spikes were caused by frequent electric shocks to his head. These hurt, and to lessen the impact of others he knew would follow he had taken to wearing rubber boots to insulate himself from the ground, with holes cut out where his toes poked through for ventilation.

And yet, despite his odd appearance and short temper, it was obvious from the beginning he was a man of considerable intellect, whose experiments with starlight would later, and quite unintentionally, lead Dad and me into fearful danger. Of course, we have forgiven him and are now firm friends. For the horrifying ordeal which followed our first meeting taught us both trust and companionship, two things that are precious beyond measure when forged from adversity.

Thinking back, I find it hard to believe it was only a year ago when it all began and I was a typical bored teenager, perhaps too bored to even realise I was bored, and hating every moment. Boring life, boring dad, very bossy mother. My thrills came from watching swashbuckling action movies, which fleetingly brought fantastic excitement into my life. But once the entertainments ended, my room always returned to the usual deathly silence and my spirits sank with it.

I had only one thought: *Why do others have all the fun?*

I too wished to be at the centre of great sea battles with cannonballs ripping through the masts of old wooden warships, or uncover mutinous treachery by spies and villains. And there had to be treasure to find—lots of it—enough gold and silver to satisfy the greed of even the most murderous blackguards.

Looking around the living room for inspiration, the dreadful truth was plain to see. My home at number 21b Rosemount Rise could never be a hot-spot of adventure. Nobody had ever been murdered there or frightened to death by a malevolent ghost, or trembled in the middle of the night as burglars attempted to break in using secret underground tunnels. Once, fire-fighters had rushed the front door with a large hose in their hands, but even this was a hoax. We had no chimney and therefore no chimney fire. They left without a squirt of water leaving the fire engine.

It seemed impossible for anything really exciting to happen in Rosemount Rise, like…

"999. What service do you require?"

"The Police. Quick, there's been a terrible atrocity. What did you say? Yes, of course they are dead. Everyone's lying on the floor with their throats torn out, and the paw prints of a large wild cat are smeared on the wall in blood."

"Calm down, sir, while I write this down. First things first. What number Rosemount Rise are you phoning from? Did you say 21b? Stop wasting police time, young man. Nothing ever happens in the vicinity of 21b."

No, the situation had to be faced. Only in my imagination could I be snatched from my dull existence and thrust into a world of rip-roaring danger, where peril lurked around every corner and life hung by a thread. There would never be a gang of desperate thieves hiding next door, just old Mrs Boswick and her tatty cat sitting by the television. The only gold she had filled the holes in her decaying teeth. It would take a desperate robber to want those!

Boring... that was my life and it was likely to stay that way, or so I thought until I met the professor, a self-proclaimed genius and inventor of many wondrous things. At once everything changed, and I had an adventure even greater than my imagination, filled with gunk, terror and treasure.

Here's what happened.

* * *

My dad, whose name is Oscar Trotter, had taken me to the professor's home which stood deep in woodland on the outskirts of town. This impromptu visit was only to check the old man was okay after a violent storm had caused local flooding. A long, pot-holed drive branched off the main road and led to a simple cottage which was not exactly derelict but certainly neglected. It suited a man who hated crowds, or maybe company of any sort. Tiles were missing from the roof, the paint was peeling, and the window in the front door was boarded over with a wooden panel roughly cut from an old tea chest. Visitors were greeted by the words '*Fine blend tea from India*' nailed crookedly across the cracked glass.

I became intrigued from the outset, as it was so different from my own modern terrace house in a treeless suburban street.

Dad knocked, and when there was no reply he tugged at one corner of the wooden panel until a nail pulled free, allowing him to squint through a wedge of old glass. His head moved from side to side to catch any inside light, but it was soon clear from his expression that he could see very little and the panel was allowed to snap back against the door. A sash window to the side was completely blanked off by a crumpled sheet.

Near the cottage stood a truly enormous shed, almost the size of a small aircraft hangar, and it was there Dad led me next. I recollect approaching with caution as I could hear angry voices. Some spoke severely and others not so, and whether the perpetrators jostled among themselves to be heard or spoke in fright I could not easily tell. But once Dad also heard shouting he took to his heels and ran towards the wide shed door, leaving me to catch up. He flung the door open. I peered into the shed from behind his back, hardly daring to believe my eyes.

Oh my gosh! I will never forget what we saw. Intense light burst into our faces, almost blinding us. Within the light moved the ghostly figures of a ragged band of seamen who looked just like characters from *the Pirates of the Caribbean* or *Treasure Island*. Yet, as I later discovered, they were not actors but men who had actually lived three hundred years ago and later died, and who would now be buried in naval graveyards or lie undisturbed as bones at the bottom of the ocean, their flesh picked away by scavenging fish. Their captured images, so lifelike despite being slightly reduced in size, were not projected on a screen or wall but were seen as complete three-dimensional, holographic figures standing barefoot on the quarterdeck of a large wooden warship, which rolled unsteadily through high seas. The action filled most of the shed's inside space.

Because of a violent sea swell, the ship's tall masts were leaning out over the water, sometimes to port and then to starboard, leaving nothing below but open ocean for other men working high in the rigging. Disaster awaited a careless slip or fall.

Those on the quarterdeck stared over the sides of the ship, but whether they looked for a fallen comrade or for some other reason was as yet unclear. Nevertheless, whatever the cause, they were willing to brave the ferocious waves which constantly pounded the hull and sent sea-spray high over their heads.

I watched as many times drenched sailors lost their balance and were washed across the deck on their backs, crashing into hatches or capstans until their bones crunched and teeth rattled. But even after injury they still crawled back on their hands and knees, with bleeding fingernails fighting for grip. And soon they were joined by more sailors from the lower gun deck who jostled for a view, although it was no place for the faint-hearted.

With all this unfolding before my eyes, I looked on with wretched curiosity, mixed with abject horror, unsure what was going on or how it could be happening. I was mesmerised, spellbound, which at first subdued any hesitancy. I knew it couldn't be real, yet it was undeniably authentic. Of course, I felt incredibly unsafe, my young legs turning to marshmallow. Yet I stood affixed, unable to leave and, in truth, at that point I don't think I wanted to.

Within this fevered scene the sailors suddenly parted, as eight other men stomped past, their wet feet thumping the deck in unison. They were hunched forward, straining every muscle to pull a thick rope which dragged a condemned sailor beneath the ship as a punishment. Thrown into the water with his legs tied to stop him swimming and his body weighted, his survival depended on being pulled under the entire length before his breath ran out.

Throughout the chaos and drama, the merciless sea never relented, making the task both grim and futile.

"Keep heaving, men," came a weary voice from within the images. *"Tucker's lungs must be as empty as a drunkard's glass. Pull for all ye are worth. The keel-hauling must be quickly done."*

"Aye, boatswain, but we must keep the rope long," shouted another, shaking his head after being lashed by a wave. *"Better he drowns than we drag him against the barnacles on the hull. I've seen a corpse with his head ripped clean off from rasping along the bottom of a ship."*

"The weight he carries should keep him clear of the barnacles. Pull harder, me boys."

With dripping hair hanging limply over his eyes, the boatswain squinted towards the onlookers. *"Will none of ye lend a hand to help an old sea salt?"* he pleaded. *"We can't save him alone!"*

None moved, for all feared the commodore's revenge. A boy stood at the front. He looked no more than twelve and yet already had the complexion of a seasoned sailor. The boatswain's stare fell hard upon him.

"Not even you, lad, who he treated like a son?"

The boy turned to the others, who shook their heads as a warning not to get involved.

"No, upon my oath I dare not," he said, stepping backwards into the crowd.

Watching from the poop deck was a young non-commissioned officer, who stood by the commodore.

"Tucker will be dead by now, sir. No man can hold his breath that long, God rest his unworthy soul. Shall I stand the men down? They are done-for."

The commodore, who never said ten words when a hundred was possible, looked at the men below. *"Let them sweat a little longer, Mr Fairbrother, and learn the consequence of disobeying my orders."* His voice was cold and cruel. He turned to walk away, certain his duty was being done.

"But the weather is violent," challenged Fairbrother while still peering down. *"Surely, everyone is punished enough?"*

The commodore froze. Then, thunderously, he turned. Fairbrother could feel the commodore's stare piercing the back of his neck.

"No disrespect intended, sir," he continued unwisely, *"but regulations demand punishments are conducted according to the laws of the sea. What chance did the keel-haulers have to save Tucker's life when the deck and rope are so slippery? Maybe the lesser punishment of keel-hauling port to starboard was more appropriate under the conditions."*

The commodore's grip tightened on the handrail. *"You would have me wait 'til the sea calms just to save the men from shivering? No, mister, not I. That would not do at all. I alone interpret the law on board this ship. Do you question my authority?"*

"No, sir," he replied weakly, *"only..."*

"Only, only? Blast you with a cannon if you don't still try to give me a lesson in seamanship. The Navy is released of another rum-drinking dirty scoundrel and I, for one, will shed no tears. It is the example made to those left on deck that matters now."

"What's going on, Dad?" I remember screaming at the top of my voice, my trembling hand squeezing his arm. "Who are these horrible people?"

"I don't know, Son," he replied, giving me no courage. "They aren't real people, that's for certain."

"Are they ghosts?"

"Of course not. I think it's some kind of clever trick using cameras. If only the old..." He suddenly paused, turning towards a faint sound that appeared separate from the rest. He listened intently, wiggling a finger into his ear to clear any wax. "There he is," he pointed. "There's the old man we've come to see. He's inside the car I've bought from him."

I recall how hard it was to squint through the light, but finally I too saw him in all his strange glory. "Is that him?" I yelled in a startled way, trying to make out what he was doing. "I think he's shouting something to you, Dad. He'll burst a gut if he gets any redder." I remember feeling genuinely concerned for the strange old guy, although I had never met him before and wasn't at all sure I wanted to now.

"We'd better get him out, and quickly," Dad had barked with urgency.

With the perilous sea adventure unfolding around him, the old man was thrashing about the inside of the strangest little car I had ever seen. Dad called it a Bubble. I later discovered this was the professor's Starlight Machine, but at first glance it looked totally rubbish. Pipes, aerials and satellite dishes stuck out from the bodywork.

Anyway, the old man had stupidly trapped himself inside the machine and was frantically trying to get out, stuttering as he cursed his bad luck for being so careless. He banged his fists against the car door to show all exits were blocked.

"Don't leave me," I had begged Dad as he pulled his arm free of my grip. But he did anyway.

Edging closer and closer, Dad broke through the light to rescue the old man. Somehow, and I don't know how, he managed to summon the strength to push the little car backwards. I admit to being too scared to help. The car door suddenly flew open.

Without a word of thanks, the old man scrambled free and lunged for some kind of electronic box on a table-top, which I later discovered he called the Receptor. Then, with a flick of a switch, the entire swashbuckling adventure disappeared—the violent waves which had crashed against the ship and the men in their gruesome duty vanishing in the blink of an eye.

The shed suddenly, bewitchingly, became silent and still which, as I recall, shocked me nearly as much as the naval drama in its full fury.

I don't know what I expected to happen next but the old man still managed to surprise us by running out of the shed and into the garden, from where a loud grinding noise momentarily shattered the newly-won peace. Minutes later he returned with a cheeky grin across his face, as if everything was completely normal.

It was then I had my first proper look at Professor Septimus Kneebone. I was transfixed. Perhaps I shouldn't say it, but he was… well… totally scary.

Now, let me tell you something. The stupendous adventure which followed this, our first meeting, was the stuff of dreams and nightmares in equal measure—haunting and strange—and rather more than a little frightening to anyone who months later had the courage to listen to the professor recounting episodes from what had taken place. I was told of grown men and women shrieking with terror as the professor described the desperate times we witnessed in language so vivid that they spilled their drinks and eventually went home in the darkness of night shivering to their bones.

Locally, the professor became well-known for his storytelling, and even now I can't quite decide whether people listened to be scared or thrilled. Certainly, the professor couldn't disguise his own enthusiasm. Indeed, every pat on the back and shake of his hand gave him the heart to think he was being taken seriously as an inventor and adventurer. That is until one day a stranger challenged the authenticity of the events so dramatically described.

"Leave the old boy alone," replied a woman who jumped to the professor's rescue. "The mad, old scoundrel is doing nobody any harm." Sadly, she thought she was helping, but she was not.

On hearing this, I was told the professor had broken down in tears, realising for the first time—and in a most painful way—that nobody ever believed a single word he said. The wicked men of his tales were merely seen as the objects of a tormented imagination.

My father, having also been keen to tell of his part in the adventure, became similarly depressed.

At long last, the penny dropped. Despite the truth of everything the professor and Dad said, the stories had been viewed as nothing more than far-fetched fairy tales.

Consequently, a little while later, Dad suggested I should chronicle the entire story of the Starlight Machine before small details were forgotten.

At first I refused, having been shocked to hear that both he and the professor had let our guarded secrets out of the bag. I feared I would suffer ridicule from the bullies at school if they knew.

Of course, I should have realised my reply would upset him and it did in a big way. Therefore, after a bit more thought, I gave in, but on the strict condition it would be written as a novel for people to believe as fact or dismiss as fantasy fiction. No harm could come from that. After all, it would at least ensure no more of the story would be leaked piecemeal by the professor, allowing gossips to ridicule the claims or embellish the facts until every aspect was held in contempt.

* * *

And so, here we have it, my complete story as *the boy caught in the starlight* and what took place over several weeks, when I saw things almost too incredible to describe and when I had to fight for my life against a band of desperate villains who would stop at nothing to gain the secrets stored in the professor's machines. Nothing has been left out except for the location of the shed, which I am not revealing to anyone who doesn't already know, however much that upsets Dad and Gracie. This is because the *Starlight Machine* remains hidden there in full working condition and would be dangerous to anyone who could not control its mighty power.

So, read on with anticipation as I describe the full adventure which turned my life from ordinary to extraordinary. It begins by looking back to when Dad restored vintage cars, I was ordinary John Striker aged 13¼ (my mother's best—and only—boy!) and I knew of the professor only as 'the old man'.

Oh, and in case you are wondering, I was given my mother's surname... I think I prefer Striker to Trotter anyway. Come to think of it, I'll call myself *Jake* in the story as it has a certain daredevil ring about it, don't you agree?

Yes, Jake Striker it is—soon to be a boy hero!

I will now start the novel at the very beginning, just before the adventure itself began, with my very annoying mother. After all, it was her fussing that made me rebel into becoming the leader of our little band of heroes.

Jake's Novel

Chapter 2
Parents Are So Embarrassing

I mean, all boys love their mothers, don't they?

Jake loved his mother, and his mother loved him. She was always telling him so. Unfortunately, she was always telling everybody else too. Jake loved his mother loving him, but he just wished she would do it... well... quietly.

The trouble was, Jake's mother also believed him to be no ordinary child and had a cupboard full of awards and trophies to prove it. And so she missed no opportunity to tell the world of Jake's fine character, adventurous spirit and high intellect, believing to the depth of her heart that all other parents had the misfortune of being lumbered with quite ordinary children who were probably best ignored.

This made Muriel Striker an exceedingly tedious person, whose company everyone avoided.

"Poor Jake, having to put up with Muriel as his mother. I don't invite him over to play with my kids in case she brings him," was a typical comment.

Fortunately, Jake was quite different to his mother, probably because he really did have the intelligence to know what to say and when, or more importantly, what not to say. This side of his character proved vital when he later learned a secret. It was not a small secret but a stomping great big one, so fantastic that he thought few people outside his family would believe it.

This would not be the first secret he kept from his mother but by far the greatest. Once, to stop her talking about him during a school Sports Day, he had deliberately lost a running race by slowing down before the ribbon, dropped the baton during the relay and clipped the high-jump pole with his heel. These tricks had worked well and his mother's wagging tongue had been temporarily halted. Naturally, he didn't like losing as he knew he would disappoint her and, anyway, he liked to win, but it was a small price to pay for anonymity.

"Poor Jake, he used to be so good at sport. I was thinking of inviting him over, but I'm afraid my children will tease him for letting down the Red Team. He lost every event he was in. Reds missed out on winning the trophy by just 2 points," said a parent.

The same ploy was also used to good effect for Parents' Evening, when the day before he deliberately got his spellings wrong and made a nuisance of himself in front of the teacher, making it certain his mother would be greeted with a frosty look from the headmaster.

Beaming with pride, Muriel had entered the headmaster's office and said: "I suppose you want to tell me how well Jake is doing?"

The reply was not as she expected.

"Not very well, I'm afraid. His teacher is not at all pleased. He is disruptive in class, he sometimes forgets to do his homework, and Jake is complacent."

Muriel did not know what 'complacent' meant until she got home and looked it up in a dictionary.

"Ah, here it is. Oh! Self-satisfied," she said to herself. She sat back in a chair, puzzled. "Self-satisfied. Now, is that good or bad?" She looked again at the dictionary. "It also means 'smug'.

24

Oh, dearie me." She thought hard. Then her frown suddenly dropped and her lips began to curl. "Of course, it's the headmaster's way of telling me that Jake is clever and he knows it. Nothing wrong with that." She clapped her hands with joy. "A very nice thing to be called... complacent. Yes, it has a ring to it. I'll telephone his father and give him the good news." She lifted the receiver and dialled the number.

It should be understood that Muriel Striker nearly always called Jake's dad 'your father', or 'him' or 'he'. She almost never used his actual name, even when calling Jake 'her little man about the house' and instructing him on the safe way to change a light bulb or some other small household task as "*your father* isn't here to do it for us".

Well, *he* has a name, and that name is Dad to Jake and Oscar to others.

"03535. Oscar Trotter speaking."

"It's me," she said without further introduction.

His voice dropped with disappointment. "Before you start, Muriel, I should warn you that I'm due at the club in thirty minutes for a dart's match, so please make it quick. What's Jake done now?"

"He's complacent! Isn't that jolly good? The headmaster said so."

Raucous laughter burst down the telephone and into Muriel's ear. She held the receiver away and stared into the earpiece. Only when the laughing stopped did she raise it again, asking: "What's so funny?"

"You daft thing. Complacent isn't good. Far from it. It means he's not really trying. Good old Jake. Boys will be boys."

Muriel ended the call without another word passing her lips.

It is a common fact that some children have both their mother and father living with them, while other children live with just one parent in the house. In Jake's class at school there were twenty-six children, both boys and girls, of which nine lived with their mothers. Archie, Jake's best friend, was the exception. He lived with his father, who he teased rather a lot for being scrawny and bald and not at all like the Superman his dad pretended to be when he effortlessly swung Archie around in the garden. Of course, nobody cared much whether they lived with one parent or both as all the children were equally loved.

Jake's father lived many miles away; he needed lots of space to collect and restore old cars, or at least that was his excuse. He often found them as rusty wrecks in farmyard barns, covered in straw and with chickens running in and out of broken windows, or abandoned in the corners of fields. But the distance between his home and Jake's never stopped Oscar Trotter from loving his son just as much as if he lived with him. It was just that he could not face a lifetime listening to Muriel talking on, and on, and on. That's why they never married.

Oscar Trotter really looked forward to seeing Jake as often as he could, and it was on one such occasion that Jake's life changed from ordinary to extraordinary.

Chapter 3
The Bubble Car

The astonishing events began on what seemed a quite ordinary day, the 1st of May, a day that was to finish in a most extraordinary way.

The early morning was overcast and disappointing, particularly as the school was holding a Spring Fair with maypole dancing, wobbly bicycle riding, a coconut shy, a talent contest, a historical fancy dress competition and lots, lots more. Jake was particularly excited at the prospect of spending a pound at a stall where wet sponges could be thrown at the headmaster's face. Just imagine, three throws at the headmaster's 'mush' for just fifty pence, and he had enough for six.

Jake threw back the bedroom curtains with relish, only to look up at a blackened sky. He then looked down at his fancy dress costume. It was made from cardboard covered in aluminium foil to look like a Roman soldier. He felt pretty stupid wearing it, but his mother insisted he should take part and win the competition. But his anxiety went further than looking silly in front of the girls. He wondered whether the sticky tape and glue would hold the cardboard together if it became saturated by rain. Or, as he feared, could he be left standing in the middle of the playground in his vest and pants, with his friends laughing as the soggy costume fell in pieces around his ankles.

In the room below, Muriel was also peeping through the curtains, tutting as the first clap of thunder shook the windows.

She had already cleared a space in the display cabinet for the new trophy Jake was bound to win. Then lightning struck again, this time as a more furious jagged fork of electricity piercing the sky towards the far side of town. The resulting thunder sent Jake's cat scurrying from the window-sill until only its tail stuck out beneath the settee.

The telephone rang and Muriel answered. She called up coldly.

"It's your father, Jake. He wants to speak to you."

Jake slid down the banister rail, which was still his favourite way of getting from upstairs to downstairs. Indeed, Jake rarely walked anywhere, but ran, slid, hopped, danced or skipped, his thick hair bobbing up and down with every movement, his grin wide enough to light a street.

His mother waited at the bottom with the receiver in her outstretched hand. She didn't mind his unusual method of coming down as it showed that Jake possessed exceptional balance. He never fell off, as she often told the neighbours with pride.

"Hi, Dad!"

"Hello, Jake. Ready for the fair? I'll be leaving in ten minutes. Where shall we meet? How about by the hotdog stand?"

"It's going to rain here, Dad. The sky is as black as... as..."

"Coal?" interrupted Oscar.

"I was going to say... as a witch's cat. And Mum's seen lightning."

"Strange," Oscar replied, carrying his mobile phone into his garden, "the weather here is great. No sign of rain at all, although I've seen a bit of lightning, which I suppose is a little odd. Perhaps I ought to speak to Mum again."

Jake handed the phone to his mother.

"Yes, what do you want?" she grunted.

"Is the weather really as awful as Jake says?"

"Worse. The rain has started and is coming down in... in..."

"Sheets?" Oscar replied.

"No, in…"

"Bucket loads?"

"Stop butting in. It's coming down the road in a torrent, like a river."

"Do you think the fair will be cancelled?"

"Almost certainly. Anything else?"

"Yes, I'd better have another quick word with Jake."

Muriel left the receiver on the window-sill and walked away, leaving Jake to grab it eagerly.

"It's me again, Dad."

"Look, Jake, I've something I want to show you, something I found in an old man's shed not far from my house. I've already paid him £100 for it. I can collect it anytime I like. If you think the fair is definitely going to be cancelled, would you like me to pick you up and bring you back here for the weekend? We can have fun collecting it together after you settle in and then do other stuff. I know you get bored at home. Anyway, another pair of strong hands will be useful."

Jake was excited and said so.

"Great, then I'd better square it with your mother. Can I have another chat with the old drag…" He coughed rather deliberately. "Sorry, Jake, I swallowed down the wrong hole. I meant to say, I'd like another chat with your dear old…"

Jake smiled at his father's awkwardness. "It's okay, Dad, we both know you call her a dragon when nobody can hear. I know you only mean to be funny. I'll get her."

Jake's mother was already rearranging the cabinet, sighing as the space cleared for Jake's expected trophy was back filled. Anyway, she knew exactly what Oscar was likely to be asking. And so, instead of taking the receiver, she merely waved her hand and said it was fine so long as Jake was back in time for school on Monday.

"Fab! See you in an hour, Jake. Bye."

"Bye, Dad."

Jake's mother locked the cabinet doors and stood back, staring at the place where Jake's latest triumph would have been displayed.

"You'd better start packing a few things."

Jake turned to leave, but his mother called after him.

"By the way, did your father call me a dragon again? He usually does when he thinks I can't hear."

The question put Jake in an awkward position. He had been taught never to lie unless the truth was likely to hurt somebody's feelings. The fine line between 'a little white fib' and an 'outright lie' was sometimes hard to judge. His father had helped with this confusing problem by giving him clear examples of right and wrong.

"If a fat lady is going to a party in a new dress," Oscar had once said to Jake, "and that lady asks if she looks nice, it is perfectly all right to say she does, even if she actually looks like a beached whale on two piano legs. It is the kind and thoughtful thing to do. However, if by telling a lie someone else suffers, then that is entirely wrong."

So, with his father's advice in mind, Jake faced his mother and said: "He did, but I was not supposed to hear. He never means it, you know. It's all part of Dad's peculiar sense of humour. One day he'll grow up!"

What Oscar hadn't said on the telephone was that the lightning Muriel had seen had actually struck the ground somewhere close to the old man's cottage. Yet, curiously, the sky above his head was blue and turning brighter by the minute, not at all the right weather conditions for lightning. And, he had not felt a drop of rain either. It was all very strange indeed.

Jake's excitement for the outing was obvious from the way he ran to his father's car, threw a case into the back and plonked himself on the passenger seat, all the time grinning. His hair was dripping wet. Oscar nodded towards the glove box.

"Look inside," he urged. "Tell me what you make of it."

Jake pulled the handle and the courtesy light went on. Inside, among the toffee wrappers and petrol receipts, was an oval object with no noticeable opening or switches. It was the size and shape of a medium Easter egg, but heavier and silver in colour.

"What is it?" asked Jake, spinning it around in his hands.

"I was rather hoping you could tell me," replied his father, while glancing skyward through the windscreen. "I thought it might be an electronic game or something else you would know about."

They drove quickly out of the rain and into the clear sky. The suddenness of the change perplexed Oscar, as the drenching downpour had not faded gradually but ended instantly, as if driving through a waterfall and out the other side. It had been the same on his way to Jake's.

"Well, I'll be... how odd," he murmured, as he switched the windscreen wipers off.

"Where did you get it, Dad?"

The question snapped Oscar out of his confused thoughts. "Oh, I found it in the pocket of a raincoat in the old man's shed. He asked if I would clear some rubbish for him. I couldn't refuse as he seemed such a sweet but strange old chap. There wasn't a lot I could clear at such short notice, just a few garden pots, tools and the coat. I did that straight away, leaving the heavy stuff like the machine I've bought and a mirror for another day. He wanted a table with all sorts of weird electronic stuff on it and a chair left behind. Apparently, they aren't rubbish. Looked like rubbish to me, but, hey, one man's rubbish is other man's valuables."

Now, there is nothing more likely to gain the attention of a boy than the word 'machine'. It hardly matters what the machine is for. The mere fact that it does 'something' is enough to make it an exciting and mysterious treasure. And so, as expected, Jake's eyes lit up.

"A machine? Is it working? What does it do?"

"How would I know," replied Oscar, distracted by a short fork of lightning that suddenly appeared from nowhere and crossed the sky. He listened for the sound of thunder that usually followed. "Did you see that, Jake? The lightning is close to where the old man lives. That's the second time today. Do you mind if we go there first? I ought to see if he's okay. He could be flooded out."

Jake liked the idea.

"I should warn you, Jake, he's not someone you would call conventional. I think he must've lived in the Far East for a while, judging by his clothes, and picked up some strange habits. He hardly speaks, but when he does he stutters and jumps about like a man walking on hot coals."

"But what does the machine do?" persisted Jake, caring nothing for the old man's travels.

"I've told you, I don't know. It clearly started life as an ordinary and tiny Bubble Car built in the 1950s or 1960s, but now has pipes, wires and satellite dishes sticking out all over the place. I was hoping it would be easy and cheap to restore back to its original condition, but I'm beginning to have second thoughts. I'll need to know what it's been used for before taking it apart for restoration. It could be a problem, or even dangerous."

The answer intrigued Jake and he became impatient to get to the old man's home. They turned off the main road and onto a pot-holed drive.

Then, finding the cottage unoccupied and with the windows covered, they followed the path on foot to a huge and well-built shed which stood in a clearing. Surrounded by trees and bushes, it was ideally sited for secrecy. Yet, despite its remoteness, the outside appeared well maintained, as if it took pre-eminence over the cottage.

To a critical eye, the shed had undoubtedly sunk on its foundations at some time in the past, but the wide door and window remained square within their frames, with no sign of force having been needed to open them. Even the climbing wisteria plant spreading unchecked over one side seemed vigorous and healthy, a sure sign of permanence, though carefully trimmed from the roof. The conclusion was simple. Only the floor had ever moved, but not recently.

Ever since the first lightning struck, the old man so vividly described by Oscar had been searching high and low in both the cottage and shed for a small electronic device he had constructed but now mislaid. The hunt had finally moved to the last place he could think of, and the last place he wanted to look, that being the tiny interior of the Bubble Car. For he alone knew the particular hazard posed by the onset of lightning to anyone in close vicinity of the car. But there was nowhere else, and the device just had to be found. It was even more dangerous to leave it unattended.

With the flash of the second lightning bolt, the rummage had turned from hurried to frenzied. And while things were already looking bad, his squirming inside the car was about to make the situation far, far worse.

With his fingers desperately probing every inch of the upholstery and all other nooks and crannies, and his legs folded awkwardly within the confined space, a foot clipped the well-worn handbrake. At once the car rolled silently forward with the slight slope of the floor, the soft 'clonk' as it bumped against the shed wall concealing the full gravity of what this meant.

The shocked expression on the old man's face showed he understood the problem all too well.

In that moment of carelessness he had made himself a prisoner, trapped inside a car with only one door, and this was at the front where it could no longer be swung open. But there was more to confound the situation. A protruding headlight had brushed against a switch on the front of an electronic box as the car drifted past the table, triggering a chain of events which the old man had no immediate means of stopping.

Even before the car bumped the wall, the space within the shed had burst into an intense and startling light show, with breathtaking spectres filling most of the available room.

It was then Jake and Oscar reached the shed, where they froze at the extraordinary scene of naval punishment and seamanship playing out before them. The car itself had become virtually invisible, buried within the changing seascape.

"What's going on, Dad?" Jake screamed at the top of his voice, his trembling hand squeezing Oscar's arm. "Who are these horrible people?"

The unexpected appearance of Oscar and Jake framed in the sun-lit doorway came as a huge relief to the old man, but, try as he might to attract their attention, his gestures remained hidden among the events unfolding all around. Frustrated, he hammered his clenched fists against the door, snivelling "p-p-poo-bum-wee-head". The strange words were immediately repeated as a mechanical-sounding echo, without any natural variation in tone. And yet, despite the first cry and the phantom echo which followed, he could still barely be heard above the forlorn conversations of the despondent sailors as they pounded the soaking deck of a wooden warship.

Gawping open-mouthed into the light, Oscar stood paralysed until his concentration was interrupted by the sound of the old man's sob. Unlike all other voices, which were heard as powerful conversations in monotone, his was timid and incoherent, its high-pitch stutter making it the only voice to sound real.

As yet Jake heard nothing beyond the sailors' cries, and at first he thought only of running away. What couldn't be understood, he felt, had to be feared. Perhaps he should have said as much to his father, but, as dangerous and perplexing as the situation appeared, very gradually his curiosity grew stronger than his fear, leaving him strangely drawn to continue looking.

Oscar's narrowed eyes searched for the source, finally fixing on an area of the naval scene where the constantly changing light and moving figures stretched strangely out of shape as they fell upon the unique silhouette of the little car.

"There," he pointed. "It's the old man we've come to see. He's inside the car I've bought from him."

Initially Jake found it hard to squint through the light, but eventually his eyes adjusted and he too caught sight of the old man. He looked ready to explode.

"We'd better get him out, and quickly," declared Oscar, though the hairs on the back of his neck stood up at the prospect of plunging into the unknown.

"How?" asked Jake in a cold sweat, still squeezing his father's arm for security. "It could be harmful to enter the light."

"I don't think so," replied Oscar dauntlessly. "The old man seems fit enough, so I guess there's no radiation or any other hazardous stuff. I'm pretty sure he wants my help, rather than ordering us to leave the shed because it's risky to stay. Anyway, it's a chance I must take."

Despite Jake's pleas to stay together, Oscar faced-up to his duty and pulled free of his son's restraining grip. Then, resolutely walking forward, he broke through the dazzling light to where the old man stared out of the car's side window, gesturing with his hands what needed to be done. Oscar had passed through objects which appeared solid without feeling any sensations upon his skin, as if transmuted from human to ghost. Even the thick wooden planks of the ship's hull were as nothing.

From Jake's perspective, his father disappeared from view the moment he entered the light, and this frightened him. As far as he could tell, his father had been swallowed whole within the images, which danced over his body to render him invisible. Jake half expected him to suddenly reappear as a separate figure among the crew, but of course that couldn't really happen.

Oscar pressed up against the car window. The old man was clearly sweating, his handprints left on the glass as slippery reminders of his predicament.

"Slide the window open," suggested Oscar.

"Slide the window open," was repeated, though not in Oscar's own voice.

"What the heck…"

"What the heck," followed another eerie echo.

The old man tapped the glass. "Face the other w-w-way when you speak, Mr Trotter," he stuttered, loosely holding a hand over his own mouth. "Everything we say is b-b-being electronically mimicked by my Lip Reader m-m-machine. Turn away or cover your m-m-mouth if you don't want your lip movements d-d-detected."

Oscar turned, understanding nothing.

"And in answer to your s-s-suggestion, I glued the windows sh-sh-shut for security. Didn't want anyone stealing m-m-my invention."

"Tell me what to do," pleaded Oscar.

"P-p-push the car back, and do it quickly. I can't g-g-get out unless the door is s-s-swung open, and that requires space. I n-n-need to get out right now!"

Oscar stared at where the car touched the wall.

"I'll never squeeze in there."

"Then f-f-find another way, for g-g-goodness sake," barked the old man. "Stand on top if you m-m-must."

Oscar tested his left foot on a bumper. It proved a convenient shape to gain a solid foothold, and soon he felt sufficiently assured to stretch his right leg across. And in this straddled position he leaned back against the shed wall, pushing forward with all the strength he could muster. But the angle was shallow, and after much grunting the Bubble Car still stubbornly refused to budge.

Inside, the old man was becoming overwrought, his expression changing from worry to mortal terror. He feared a dappled grey sky might be forming over the shed roof.

Oscar flopped forward to take a breath, his hands outstretched on the windscreen. He looked down at the old man, whose screwed-up face had turned an alarming shade of purple. Horrified a heart attack or stroke was imminent, he forced himself back upright for another push, though his aching back resisted.

"Raise one f-f-foot further up the door," shouted the old man. "You'll be able to apply g-g-greater forward pressure if you do. It's a question of geometry and p-p-physics. But, I beg you, please h-h-hurry. And mind the trailing w-w-wire."

Although it risked damaging the fragile bodywork, Oscar did as he was told. Through gritted teeth, he again pushed until his leg shook and his skin burned.

At first, nothing happened. Then, just as he was ready to give up, he felt an almost imperceptibly small movement, as if the tiny car was becoming unstuck from the wall. It was the reassurance needed to continue, and suddenly the wheels began to rotate more easily. Soon Oscar was holding the car away from the wall at full stretch, his locked leg quivering under the pressure, his muscles tight and throbbing.

"For pity's sake, Mr Trotter, how am I s-s-supposed to open the door with your enormous w-w-weight on it?" spluttered the old man cruelly, in a voice suddenly made ugly by disappointment.

Oscar could hardly believe the ingratitude. "It was your flipping idea!" he retorted severely.

"The s-s-situation requires someone with b-b-brains, which clearly isn't you. Can't the b-b-boy help?"

Oscar twisted the best he could to see Jake still standing anxiously in the doorway. "He's afraid. It's me or nobody."

"Oh dear! Very well, but try to do b-b-better!" came the muffled reply. "You must always think b-b-before acting."

Oscar felt a renewed flush of anger at the barely veiled insult. "Like you did when you got yourself stuck inside the blasted car?" he parried.

"Quite d-d-different. Anyway, are you g-g-getting me out or st-st-starting an argument?"

Oscar looked around for new inspiration.

"Act decisively, Mr T-T-Trotter. Think and act. M-m-much longer and none of us will have a care in the w-w-world to worry about."

Oscar grumbled to himself.

"Silly old duffer. Serve you right if I leave you to stew in your own juice," returned the echo of his words, much to Oscar's embarrassment.

"Charming! Thought I wouldn't h-h-hear, did you?" chided the old man. "You really can't get to g-g-grips with Lip Reader technology, can you, Mr Trotter? Even if you whisper, the Lip Reader will repeat things at full volume by recognising the movements of your mouth."

"I've an idea," panted Oscar, this time careful not to speak in the wrong direction. "I'll bring my legs together on the hinge side of the door. Then, if we coordinate our efforts, you should be able to force the door open the very moment I jump clear."

"How will that h-h-help?" rebuked the old man. "The car will roll f-f-forward before I get out."

"Don't try to."

"No?"

"Absolutely not! You must hold the door open at ninety degrees as the car rolls forward. You'll have enough time to do that. The edge of the door will then impact against the shed wall, stopping the car and giving you room to exit safely. I don't suppose it will cause too much damage."

"Then g-g-get on with it," shouted the old man desperately. "Every m-m-moment matters."

Oscar slowly shuffled his left leg across, while maintaining the required pressure. It made balancing more difficult, but at least the car didn't move.

"Okay," shouted Oscar through the windscreen, having first checked there was nothing preventing him from leaping off. "Grab the door handle on the left... sorry, I mean *your* right. When I count to three, swing the door wide open. I'll jump at the same time."

The old man nodded.

"Are you ready?" boomed Oscar. "I can't hold the car a minute longer. It's going, I can feel it!"

"No, w-w-wait, Mr Trotter, we've overlooked s-s-something obvious."

But Oscar wasn't listening. "It's now or never. On the count of Three…"

"What? Did you s-s-say Three?"

Instantly the old man threw open the door and jumped out with dexterity. Oscar, who was unprepared, tumbled sideways off the car, crashing awkwardly onto the hard floor. He cowered for the inevitable 'crunch' of metal, but the only sound was of footsteps running towards the control switch. Then the amazing light show suddenly vanished, the boat and all its crew gone in the blink of an eye.

"Oi," shouted Oscar, lying flat on his back, "did I say three?" He looked around. "Hey, where are you when I'm moaning?"

There was no reply and no echo either, the old man having fled the building to pull a lever attached to an outside wall. A loud and sustained grinding noise resulted, as if something huge was being mechanically lowered.

"That was a c-c-close one," the old man stuttered on his return, his face once more a withered shade of pink. "A jolly close shave indeedi-deedi-do. God save the Q-Q-Queen and God save you too, m-m-my dear Mr Trotter. Now, you were s-s-saying?"

"You're a blithering idiot," winced Oscar, cradling his shoulder as he inspected the car for damage.

The old man noticed the strange angle of Oscar's arm and knew at once it meant a dislocated shoulder. Slyly, he slithered to Oscar's side where, after a few moments pretending to look at the same scratches, he lunged for Oscar's damaged arm and wrenched it violently.

"Ouch! You idiot, what the devil are you playing at?" Oscar cried, dancing around the room. "You've broken it."

"On the contrary, Mr Trotter, I've reset the b-b-ball into its socket. It will f-f-feel completely better in a minute or two."

And, as predicted, it did.

"I suppose I should thank you, even though you caused the accident." He stretched his arm and twisted his shoulder. Both appeared normal, though sore. "What possessed you to exit the car before I was ready?"

"Again you didn't think matters through b-b-before acting irrationally. As a genius, it didn't take me more than a n-n-nanosecond to realise all that One, Two, Three stuff was totally un-un-unnecessary. And as for falling off cars, w-w-well, most theatrical but utterly p-p-pointless. I only had to reapply the h-h-handbrake to stop the car from moving forward."

Oscar flared. "You're blinking kidding me! Why didn't you say the handbrake still functioned?"

"I wasn't s-s-sure it would. The thought just p-p-popped into my head at the last possible moment. I tried to w-w-warn you, but as usual you weren't in any m-m-mood to listen. I was very n-n-nearly late, late for a very important d-d-date," he cheeped musically, much to Oscar's astonishment.

"You what?"

"Forget I s-s-sang anything."

It wasn't hard to do.

Oscar rubbed a wet fingertip across the worst scratches. "If I need to buy paint to repair the marks, it'll come from the money I've already paid you. None of this is my fault."

The old man shrugged, knowing Oscar had more chance of getting blood from a stone.

"I warn you, it won't be cheap to do the job properly. What colours are these? The shades are unusual."

"I've always thought m-m-metallic vomit with a flash of orange," giggled the old man, "or possibly r-r-raspberry puke and yellow. Just as you say, they're not f-f-factory standard."

"Sick!" said Jake as his first word to the old man, the end of the light show giving him the courage to approach.

"You're still a blithering idiot," cried Oscar.

"Face it, Mr Trotter, you became h-h-hysterical," taunted the old man, winking wickedly towards Jake.

"That's rich. Is that all the thanks I get for freeing you?"

"More than you deserve. I was about to f-f-free myself when you blundered in. As usual, you misread the s-s-situation. I had the means of extraction at h-h-hand."

"That can't be true."

He nodded triumphantly.

Oscar wondered how it was possible. His eyes glanced over the car for clues. "Don't tell me you had fuel in the tank to start the engine?"

"I won't, because I haven't. Anyway, a litre of petrol wouldn't h-h-help in the least."

"Why ever not?"

"I r-r-removed the engine years ago."

"You did what? You let me buy a car without an engine?"

"You're supposed to be the ex-ex-expert when it comes to cars, Mr Trotter. I merely went along w-w-with your enthusiasm and valuation."

"Then tell me, clever dick, how you proposed to get out?"

"You of all p-p-people should know m-m-most Bubble Cars were built with sunroofs. I merely had to squeeze out the top."

Jake examined the roof. "Excuse me, sir, there might have been a sunroof once but not anymore. A metal plate has replaced it, which has your paraphernalia attached."

"Ah, so the boy does s-s-speak more than one word at a time. Then answer me this, y-y-young man. How do you know I haven't fitted quick-release b-b-bolts?"

"Did you?" asked Jake.

The old man twitched before leaning inside the car to continue the search he had started before Jake arrived.

"He's spinning another yarn," sighed Oscar, irritated at the unpleasant sight of the old man's wiggling bottom.

"Perhaps you should ask him what's going on," suggested Jake in an inquisitive voice, expecting to be overheard.

"Going on?" replied the old man, replacing the padded seat.

"My son means all that fantastic film stuff."

He crawled out, his face showing disappointment. "Film?" he said contemptuously, glimpsing once more into the car before giving up the search. "That was n-n-no film. It was r-r-real... well... sort of. Anyway, it's none of your b-b-business. You wouldn't understand the t-t-technology involved even if I told you."

But Oscar was not ready to dismiss the experience so lightly. Above all, he needed reassurance the car was safe for restoration and there was no better time to find out its true worth than now.

"Try us," he said. "How did you achieve those wonderful effects? I've never seen anything like it."

"Of course you haven't, and n-n-nor will you again," snapped the old man, straightening to regain his full height.

Oscar stood his ground.

"Oh, very well, but if I t-t-tell you it must stay within these walls. Is that a solemn p-p-promise?"

Oscar and Jake agreed.

"Th-th-think of it as a way of seeing historical events as they happened, using the s-s-speed of light as the means. Or, to p-p-put it another way, reliving the p-p-past without the fictional bunkum of time travel. That, my friends, is the p-p-process in a nutshell."

"Did you just say *time travel*?" flustered Jake, at once launched into high excitement. "It's getting better and better."

"No, boy, I didn't, so c-c-curb your runaway enthusiasm. But I can recreate the next b-b-best thing."

"Using the Bubble Car?" probed Oscar.

"It's central to the p-p-procedure, Mr Trotter, but not exclusively."

They nodded politely, even expressively, but in truth neither had a clue what this meant. The old man turned away, sure he had already said far too much.

"That's it?" rounded Oscar in shock. He grabbed the old man's arm. "Aren't you going to explain properly?"

"Nope."

"Not even give us a hint as to where the light originates from."

"The electronic apparatus on the t-t-table gathers, processes and p-p-projects the light."

"Yes, but you don't say where the light comes from before it's *processed* and *projected*? Is it the Bubble Car?"

"Kind of," replied the old man dismissively, before removing Oscar's hand and walking away. Then he stopped and turned, as if realising only a better explanation would put an end to their curiosity. "There's an awful lot m-m-more to it, which you could n-n-never understand. The Bubble Car is m-m-merely the most vital link in a c-c-chain of ingenious apparatus."

"You've lost me!"

"Deliberately, Mr Trotter, entirely d-d-deliberately! Think of it l-l-like this. A gun f-f-fires a bullet, but only the bullet kills. That analogy d-d-demonstrates the importance of b-b-both the gun and the bullet, but the deadly n-n-nature of just one. Understand where I'm h-h-headed?"

"Not really. Are you implying the Bubble Car is like a gun?"

"You c-c-could say that."

"And fires a bullet?"

"No, of course n-n-not."

"But fires something?"

"I s-s-suppose it does, in a way."

Oscar's patience at having to extract information a bit at a time was turning harsh. "Enough! Now I have to know what I'm getting myself into." With that said, he sprang the short distance separating the two men. "Answer me straight, without any more digression or half-truths. Is the car dangerous or not?"

"Only to those w-w-who are inexperienced in its use," replied the old man, perfectly calmly. "Its p-p-purpose is peaceful, but that doesn't m-m-make its operation risk-free."

"Meaning what?"

"R-r-really, Mr Trotter, you ask too m-m-much."

"Very well, if you want to play cat and mouse over the car, tell me what caused the grinding noise we heard? Is that part of the chain?"

And as if to emphasise the importance of knowing, Oscar placed a persuasive hand on the old man's shoulder. With the grasp held firm and close, he leaned his weight forward, pinning the old man against the wall. He could feel the gentle rise and fall of bones beneath a thin layer of old flesh.

The threat, as much as it was, left a clear meaning.

Slowly, the old man's head pivoted until his raised eyes locked squarely onto his tormentor's face.

"You may try to f-f-force me to reveal more, Mr T-T-Trotter, but since you have n-n-nothing intelligent to ask, the time for foolish q-q-questions must end. Until we are better acquainted and you earn my t-t-trust, the p-p-process you have inadvertently witnessed will s-s-stay my secret. As for the grinding, you should have no c-c-concern."

"I need to know if Jake and I will be safe if we trailer the car away."

"As long as your curiosity goes no f-f-further than thinking of my machine as a car made of saleable component parts, then you will be p-p-perfectly safe. Danger could only come f-f-from unwarranted curiosity into the way I've used it. Getting it away from the s-s-shed is, I am p-p-pleased to say, the first step in rendering it h-h-harmless."

"Which brings us full-circle back to the light show."

"Mr Trotter, separate in your m-m-mind the sale of the car and my ex-ex-experiments with light. The former involves you, the latter most c-c-certainly does not."

"Not so fast," beseeched Oscar. "I'm a businessman, a salesman and entrepreneur, always on the lookout for money-making ventures. As such, when I spot an opportunity I seize it."

"And have you?"

"Don't be stupid! Of course I have. If you've come up with something radical which supersedes 3-D and 4-D cinema, why, I want to be part of it. And, from what I witnessed, you could be onto something tremendously exciting. With proper commercial handling, your invention could make millions, or even billions, for both of us. What do you say to that?"

"Even if it was t-t-true, why would I s-s-share my invention with you?"

"Because I now own the car, and you said it's the main component of the process. That entitles me to a piece of the action."

The old man laughed.

"No, really, I'm serious," continued Oscar. "You will need proper representation to market it successfully. I could be that man. What do you say?"

Jake tugged at his father's arm.

"I say no more q-q-questions or propositions, Mr Trotter!" and with that he pushed Oscar away. "It seems only the boy l-l-listens with open ears. I suggest you both p-p-pretend you saw nothing unusual. After all, it would s-s-still be under wraps if you hadn't stumbled into my s-s-shed unannounced."

"Lucky for you we did," commented Oscar snidely.

There was a short pause as that truth sank in. "Oh, very well, I concede what you s-s-say contains a tiny e-e-element of fact," the old man muttered ungenerously, "but luck really didn't c-c-come into it. I always knew you wouldn't wait long to g-g-get your hands on m-m-my machine." He wiped his gloves on an oily rag, which he absentmindedly handed to Oscar.

"Actually," said Oscar, holding the rag with his fingertips before dropping it on the car roof, "my son and I were concerned by the unusual weather."

"And w-w-wanted to see if I was unharmed?"

"Something like that."

At long last the old man lowered his guard, his watery eyes showing emotion. He sniffed with a kind of whistling sound.

"Well, I never did! It's b-b-been a very long t-t-time since anyone worried about me. I am quite frazzle-dazzled."

Jake could only gape, thinking the poor fellow had gone quite mad in his solitude.

"How old are you?" the old man asked, beckoning Jake to join him.

Jake found his legs wouldn't obey.

"He's 13," interrupted Oscar, embarrassed by the delay.

"Isn't exactly a c-c-chatter-box, is he?" and in a hop, skip and jump the old man brought his face to within a stale breath of Jake's nose. "Ten green b-b-bottles hanging in Jake's loo, ten green b-b-bottles hanging in Jake's loo, and if one green b-b-bottle should need a number two, there'd be nine clean b-b-bottles and one neck-first in poo," he sang, grinning from ear to ear. "Ha-ha, that's a g-g-good one. Remember the r-r-rhyme, boy. You can tell your school f-f-friends. You know what a 'number two' is, I suppose? It's another name for…"

"He knows," cut in Oscar.

"Of course, you can change the rhyme to f-f-fit any name. Ha-ha, ha-ha-ha… ha-ha!"

Jake shuddered at the man's strange behaviour. He *was* old, yet not so very old the brightness should have left his hollowed eyes. A smell of fustiness rose from his loose-fitting tunic, which was drawn up between his legs to form baggy shorts, or, as Jake thought, a giant once-white nappy. Creepily, a spider crawled in and out of the folds.

The man followed Jake's stare. He gently lowered a hand and the spider climbed effortlessly onto his outstretched palm.

"L-l-let me introduce Annie the arachnid or, as I c-c-call her, Annie the 38th. As you see, she's p-p-perfectly tame. Still, soon one of her offspring will have to take her p-p-place as my walkabout pet. Did you know spiders only l-l-live a year?"

"I don't like spiders," mumbled Jake.

"Shush, or she'll hear you," scolded the old man, cupping his hands together. "They're very sensitive c-c-creatures. In India, I learned to r-r-respect all living things, whatever form they take. I once took a c-c-cabbage to a fine restaurant for an evening meal. We dined by c-c-candlelight and the next day, in appreciation of the c-c-company, I ate it in a stew!" He laughed heartily, looking between the two blank faces opposite. "Oh, cheer up. I'm not so b-b-barmy as to do that. It was a j-j-joke! Come, we must be friends, g-g-good friends. I know w-w-we will be. I know these things because I'm a g-g-genius. Have you ever met a g-g-genius before, Jake?"

Jake shook his head.

"Well, now you h-h-have. Of course," he added, letting the spider return to the folds, "even those of us with amazing intellects are c-c-capable of making occasional m-m-mistakes. It was a bleak d-d-day when I accidentally sat on Annie the 37th. Still, Annie the 38th doesn't hold a g-g-grudge."

"Annie the 38th told you that?" said Jake, immediately regretting he had spoken.

"Ah, so the little s-s-sparrow has properly found his tongue." He tried to pat Jake's head, but Jake was too fast and dodged away. "My, the s-s-sparrow is timid. No, boy, English s-s-spiders can't speak."

Oscar bent down to Jake's ear. "Take no notice, Son, he's quite harmless. Normally he's a very silent man. You'll like him when he settles down."

Jake was less sure but willing to learn.

Having spoken kindly, Oscar found he could only wince as the old man kicked the car door shut. And, in this vein, Jake ignored his father's look of despair as flakes of paint fell like snow. Instead, Jake passed his attention to the curious figure of the old man himself.

His costume, for that is how Jake viewed it, was completed with an ill-fitting waistcoat over a collarless shirt, pink washing-up gloves and purple flowery rubber boots with the ends sliced-off where his toes poked through. Yet, there was one more thing which added to the general impression of absurdity. The man's hair was a tangle of brown at the sides, crowned on top by the purest white spikes. And so, in every respect, he was the most peculiar specimen of manhood Jake was ever likely to meet.

"Stop gawping, Jake, it's rude," reprimanded Oscar very softly, so as not to be overheard, but it made the old man laugh.

"Don't c-c-concern yourself, Mr Trotter," he said, having lifted the oily rag from the car. He stuffed it back into a pocket. "Let him s-s-stare if he wants to. It's what *muddleheads* do."

Oscar was amazed he heard anything.

"This time it *was* a t-t-trick. Years ago I taught m-m-myself to lip read. Comes in useful in my line of w-w-work. Simply said, I saw your reflection in the m-m-mirror and read your lip movements." He pointed to the wall.

Oscar rubbed his chin. "So, why invent a Lip Reader machine when you can do it yourself?"

"At last a s-s-sensible question from another *muddlehead*," said the old man. "Normal lip reading r-r-requires concentration on one p-p-person at a time. That r-r-restriction is what gave m-m-me the idea to invent a Lip Reader machine. With it, I can detect s-s-speech from lots of people at once."

"Ace," said Jake.

The old man smiled. "Yes, it is *ace*. And, by the way, I didn't think for one m-m-moment you were being r-r-rude, Jake. I know I h-h-have the look of an undernourished b-b-badger, but I've had a lot to w-w-worry about and many shocks. As for my c-c-clothes, which seem to fascinate you the most, I only have myself to p-p-please, so I'm not in the least c-c-concerned with what they look like. I dress for comfort over style, s-s-something I learned while travelling. You've heard of India, Jake?"

"Of course. My teacher says it's a strange country where they have lots of very poor people and yet spend zillions of money sending men and satellites into space. She says it's an enigma, but I don't know what that means."

"I s-s-suppose it is a puzzle. But India is also the l-l-land of mystics, where spiritual life for many p-p-people is more important than wealth and p-p-position, or space exploration for that m-m-matter. I learned things there that are b-b-beyond normal understanding, things you would c-c-call magic and your father would call tricks, but, in fact, are n-n-neither."

"Like what?" asked Jake with growing interest.

"Perhaps we'll have a chance to d-d-discuss them one d-d-day. As for fancy clothes," he added unashamedly, "they're such a w-w-waste of time, which can be better spent ex-ex-experimenting. If I had my w-w-way, I would wear nothing at all except for a p-p-pair of rubber boots and the occasional clean pants. But, then, I have visitors to c-c-consider, so I make a little e-e-effort to cover myself up." He tossed the pink gloves onto the table and tore open his shirt at the neck. "Ever seen anything l-l-like this?" There, dangling from a short length of grimy string was a severed monkey's foot. "Hold it if you l-l-like. Touching is supposed to b-b-bring good luck."

"Didn't bring much luck to the monkey," replied Jake with obvious repugnance.

The old man buttoned his shirt. "It was already d-d-dead when I found it, silly. Still, I understand it isn't everyone's c-c-cup of tea. Talking of which, come, follow me to t-t-the cottage. You can sit while I fetch us all a nice h-h-hot chocolate. You like h-h-hot chocolate?"

Jake nodded.

"Good, because I've invented a bolt-on g-g-gadget that makes it extra t-t-tasty. It's all a question of temperature and c-c-creaminess. It took me a whole m-m-month of work in the shed and cottage to f-f-find the best formula. If a thing is worth d-d-doing, it's worth d-d-doing well... etc."

Jake grabbed his father's sleeve as they left the shed. "Do you think the gadget is part of the machine? When you take it away, is making hot chocolate all it will do?"

"I sincerely hope not," returned Oscar, looking back suspiciously at the Bubble Car. "I think we must tread carefully. Be guarded in what we say. Now we have witnessed his experiment, he might be less inclined to give up the car."

"He may think you will now try to exploit it for more than restoration."

"If he does, he's not as daft as he looks. In fact, I can't begin to understand why he decided to sell it in the first place. He said it was fundamental to his work."

"Retirement?" suggested Jake. "Clearly he doesn't want to capitalise on its commercial value."

"No, Son, there's much more to it, and I intend to discover what that secret is. We've only dipped a toe into his world."

It was soon after this that the full extent of the old man's strange life began to open out before them, and little by little they were drawn into his world of miracles, crime and deception. And, once involved, they quickly discovered the need for bravery and cunning to fight the perils resulting from the old man's enigmatic affairs.

Chapter 4
Secrets in the Cottage

The distance between the shed and the cottage being short, Jake had expected a quick stroll along the tree-lined path. All signs of lightning had gone and the sky was clear. Yet, surprisingly, the change seemed to worry the old man as he left the shed, as if the brightness exposed his escape. He took each step with caution, peering left and right, furtively staring past several felled tree trunks to the woods beyond, his ears primed for any unexpected sounds. And when Jake tried to speak, he lifted a fingertip to his lips, all the while slipping quietly forward.

Throughout, the old man insisted Jake and Oscar matched his steps stride-for-stride, and soon their paces became so even and noiseless that all were afraid to breathe. But, whatever real or imaginary terrors lay hidden among the woods, none presented itself, and progress towards the cottage was steady.

At the front door, Oscar wiped his brow. "It's true. Cowardice *is* infectious. I'm a nervous wreck," he said to Jake in a soft voice. "What was that about? It's broad daylight, for goodness sake, and there's nobody around for miles."

The old man pulled Jake towards him, and whether this was a kind or scared gesture Jake had no means of knowing. Still, his father did nothing to prevent it, so it had to be okay.

"Before we go in, J-J-Jake, you should know I don't w-w-work to live but live to w-w-work. You will see visionary things, and afterwards you will n-n-never be the same b-b-boy again. Do you understand?"

Jake said he didn't, feeling nervous that some unmentionable horror loomed behind the door. Quivering, his imagination ran riot, thinking the old man might get him inside and then slam the door in his father's face before bewitchingly metamorphosing through sorcery into a monstrous creature intent on devouring his brain.

"Jake, he's waiting," whispered Oscar, encouraging him forward. He was surprised to feel Jake shaking. "Shush! Calm down, Son. He only means the cottage is untidy. I've been inside and it's perfectly safe. He's a bit of a crackpot. Spent far too much time living alone, I expect. He says odd things all the time. I ignore them and so must you. Just nod, smile, and go along with whatever he says until I get my hands on the car. I'll be right behind you, I promise, but I want you to see the room first. It's bizarre in an amazing kind of way."

"Cooool!" gasped Jake as the door swung open and the interior was revealed.

"Have you ever seen such a place of w-w-wonder?" beamed the old man, pointing with a thin, wiry finger.

Jake's eyes flared, awe-struck by the spectacle stretching out before him.

"Wowww!"

The room was a jumbled festival of half-completed experiments, breathtaking models, enormous piles of papers and books, and shelves stacked from floor to ceiling which sagged under the weight of grotesque creatures floating in domed pickling jars. A column of rusty biscuit tins rose beside the shelves like an ancient obelisk waiting to topple, while other tins were randomly discarded about the place. Having seen the jars, Jake had no wish to ask what was stored in the tins.

Jake's senses were in overload. Yet, despite the eye-catching extravaganza, he wondered how anyone could live among such clutter. At present, the only light came from a small kitchen window and a larger sash window covered by a thin crumpled sheet which provided an opaque haze.

The presence of two beds implied this was the only room, which explained the disorder. A tiny kitchen of sorts occupied one corner, with a pleated curtain hanging from string which could be pulled to hide the area from general view, although an abundance of cobwebs suggested the curtain was rarely used. Heaped under a sink were layers of unwashed clothes, over and through which tiny spiders scurried. The only full-height interior door opened into a cramped toilet.

"Listen, Jake," said the old man as he let Annie join the other spiders, "a h-h-house lives and breathes just like the humans occupying it, although few p-p-people have the foresight to realise. Stop for a moment and s-s-see if you agree."

Like many old houses, the place *did* have its own peculiar noises, as though the walls pulled against their foundations and the timbers expanded and contracted by the effects of heat and damp. Living in a modern house, these were unknown to Jake and he was pleasantly surprised. And now, while he stood motionless, other unusual sounds materialised, like the clawing of mice or rats. But the old man reacted differently to these and said they were to be ignored. The time had not yet come to reveal all the room's secrets.

To Jake the room was utopia, an irresistible sweet shop of curiosity and fun, where every pile of rubbish could be a mountain to climb or a fortress to defend, and every bubbling glass flask that steamed or spat liquid held a fascination in blue, red or yellow. Of course, to Oscar it was a dump and a dust trap, fit only for a bonfire, but then he viewed it through adult eyes.

Strangely, at some time in the past the room had been decorated for Christmas and then left untouched, like a museum exhibit that nobody visited.

Around the walls and shelves were the faded remains of paper-chains, mostly broken and hanging down from drawing pins; in the few places where paper-chains remained suspended across the arched ceiling, they were held up by green spikes of a gluey substance. Next to the fireplace stood the dried skeletal stump of a Christmas tree, with two presents leaning against the red metal bucket. Both were wrapped and unopened, yet brown with age.

"What's this?" asked Jake inquisitively, turning his attention to an illustrated calendar nailed to the wall. The picture showed a boy-band named Culture Club, with the male vocalist wearing makeup. The date of December 21st was ringed.

The old man returned a smile but offered no explanation. Instead, he pointed to the apex of the ceiling where, way above Jake's head, floated an enormous model of a winged Pterodactyl. It rocked slightly, disturbed by air blowing through a hole in the roof, as though the ceiling drew breath.

"How is it possible?" spluttered Jake in bewilderment, noticing there were no strings or wires holding it up.

"It's a marvel, isn't it," said the old man with pride. "From my r-r-researches, I discovered the b-b-bones of giant pre-historic flying reptiles had f-f-far larger internal cavities than would be necessary just to contain marrow. It was also evident the c-c-cavities were divided into two parts by connective tissue and b-b-blood vessels. By the way, Jake, marrow is the s-s-soft substance that fills the hollows inside b-b-bones and is made up of f-f-fat and maturing blood cells. The b-b-bone walls also drew my attention, b-b-being incredibly thin. Ideal for achieving l-l-lightness of weight. Knowing evolution rarely occurs without r-r-reason, I wondered whether the oversized and divided h-h-hollows had other purposes than the obvious."

"And?" asked Jake, wanting to believe the old man could know such things.

"One night, after I h-h-had eaten far too many p-p-prunes and f-f-found I farted rather a lot, it occurred to me as the smell rose that to h-h-help the creature lift its ample weight off the g-g-ground the largest cavities could've held a lighter-than-air g-g-gas vapour released from the smaller marrow cavities. So, I made a scale m-m-model to test my theory. I was shocked by the volume of lifting g-g-gas the bones could hold."

"Ordinary birds don't use gas to fly," suggested Jake.

"Bright boy, good boy. You're r-r-right. Modern birds have enormous muscles for their s-s-size and weight, so they don't need help. That, too, is e-e-evolution. But look at this m-m-monster, Jake. How could something as b-b-big and primitive as this fly, especially with such an enormous h-h-head and underdeveloped muscles, and thicker s-s-skin instead of lightweight feathers. And mine is only a s-s-small scale model of the real thing. A living Pterodactyl had a twelve m-m-metre span. No, it would be impossible. A n-n-naturally forming gas has to be the a-a-answer, I'm sure of it. I've seen them fly and soar in my s-s-shed."

"You've done what?" leapt Jake excitedly, barely able to contain his enthusiasm to be told more.

"Seen them f-f-fly."

"But... but... I thought they became extinct with the land dinosaurs."

"They did, many m-m-millions of years ago."

"But you just said..."

"F-f-forget I opened my mouth."

Jake turned to his father, who was peering over the old man's shoulder with his eyes crossed and a finger circling his temple, gesturing he was completely bonkers, as batty as a straight banana, a sandwich short of a picnic. Jake fought the urge to laugh.

"So," continued the old man in all innocence, "to t-t-test my theory I constructed the model and p-p-pumped helium into the hollows, the same g-g-gas as used in party balloons. And, voilà, as you see, it s-s-stays up beautifully by itself. Dinky-dinky-do! It was a q-q-question of understanding the ratio between the weight of the m-m-monster and the volume of gas needed to help it rise.

My calculations were p-p-perfect. Now tell me I'm not a g-g-genius."

"I suppose the model also stops rain from falling on your bed through the hole in the ceiling," said Jake quickly, not wanting to appear rude.

"Actually, a small t-t-tarpaulin on the roof does that. It holds rain out but not the b-b-breeze."

"What about the other bed?" said Jake quickly to divert his eyes from his father's tomfoolery, pointing to the smaller of the two. It was stripped of its mattress and covered with rows of dusty books. Next to it was a boy's bicycle resting upside down on its handlebars and saddle.

"Oh!" replied the old man sadly, suddenly turning pale and clumsy. He stepped forward, clipping the edge of a chamber pot, which tipped onto its side. "I can't t-t-talk about them."

"And these? What do they do?" continued Jake without pausing, peering into flasks of bubbling liquids.

"Enough, Jake," interrupted Oscar, wanting to focus on matters pertaining to the car. "These are private things and you shouldn't pry."

"I don't mind t-t-telling…"

"No, enough is enough. I apologise for my son's curiosity."

With a thousand unanswered questions still in his head, Jake's attention shifted to an immense blackboard occupying the centre of one entire wall. Scribbled in blue chalk were mathematical equations, chemical symbols and a long list of ingredients. At the bottom of the list—under magnesium and iron filings—the chalk had been hurriedly rubbed out. Over the smudge was written 'buy three dozen sausages, but not those horrid ones with red specks'.

"Fantastic!" cried Jake as he spun on his heels, trying to make sense of the room.

Everything was frozen in time, as if a clock had stopped many years before and everything else had stopped with it. Even the air was an unpleasant mix of damp and stale decay, a sort of tobacco and salt smell which could easily have come from sniffing a dead sailor's wooden chest dragged up from the bottom of the sea.

"Your father's right," said the old man at last. "I think you've s-s-seen quite enough for one day."

He invited the guests to sit while he made drinks, pointing to three chairs grouped around the fireplace. But reaching the chairs was difficult through so much clutter. The old man had devised his own method of getting about the room, with several small spaces left clear that corresponded to the exact length of his stride, like stepping stones in a sea of chaos.

Oscar found the challenge quite fun and was soon sitting with a broad grin of satisfaction written across his face. Not so for Jake. Having shorter legs, he struggled to cross without upsetting the delicately balanced piles. His father's outstretched hand helped him over the final hurdle.

"So, young J-J-Jake," said the old man as he passed the mugs around, the remains of a left-over sausage from an earlier meal hanging from his mouth, "would y-y-you like to know something interesting before your d-d-dad takes the m-m-machine for scrap?"

Jake nodded enthusiastically.

"Then you shall. B-b-but first, I expect you would be equally f-f-fascinated by this." He cleared a space on the floor, exposing a trap door. A large brass handle was inset into the top. Pulling the handle revealed an underground hole, deep enough for two people to stand uncomfortably. "It's m-m-my shelter."

Oscar leaned over the dark space. "From what?"

"Lightning strikes of course, but it's just as g-g-good for detaining unwelcome v-v-visitors or hiding from debt-collectors." He laughed as he slammed the door shut. A cloud of dust rose, which temporarily choked the air. "Useful, that. S-s-saved my life more th-th-than once." He sneezed, followed by Jake.

"Bless you," said Oscar kindly.

"*Gesundheit*," reiterated the old man, burying his nose into cupped hands to stop another sneeze escaping.

Oscar wolfed down the delicious hot chocolate in double-quick time. "I'm sorry if I've given you the wrong impression," he said, wiping his mouth, "but I never intended to scrap the machine. And now, having seen the light show, I'm looking forward to seeing what else it does. Then, and only then, will I decide whether it's got business potential, or should be restored back to its original use as a classic road car, or should be carefully broken up for spare parts."

Stunned by the revelation, the old man dropped his mug, which shattered into many small pieces and sent chocolate splashing over his bare toes.

"But it must be d-d-destroyed," he gasped, "and s-s-soon. You don't understand the d-d-danger that comes from owning it in its working form. I've given it up and so m-m-must you."

"My choice to make," asserted Oscar casually, leaving no room for debate.

"Then, I can't let you h-h-have it."

"It's already mine," he countered firmly. "And if you think you can persuade me to…"

A sudden and alarming gnashing of slobbering teeth and scratching of claws stopped Oscar midstream.

"S-s-shush, I'm p-p-perfectly fine," consoled the old man after twisting to face away. "The nasty p-p-person won't argue with me again."

"What was that?" jumped Oscar, sitting upright, his eyes searching for the source of the noise.

"Jorvik. And I should k-k-keep your voice down if I was you."

"What's a Jorvik?" asked Jake.

The old man pointed towards a small door to the left of the chimney breast. It was the size of an under-stairs cupboard, with a heavy lock and small metal grill for ventilation. "It's my Bloodrat. It gets extremely n-n-nasty if it thinks I'm b-b-being threatened."

"What on earth is a Bloodrat?" enquired Oscar, lifting his feet off the floor and encouraging Jake to do the same. "Is it dangerous?"

"Very much so. I keep it l-l-locked away when I have friendly visitors. It's the only Bloodrat in existence."

"Where did it come from?" pressed Oscar, relieved to hear the growl turn into a low whimper as the animal settled back.

"It didn't c-c-come from anywhere. I invented it, to solve a problem."

"Say that again."

"I invented it."

"Can I have a quick squizz through the grill?" asked Jake eagerly, already standing.

The old man thrust out an arm. "Keep back if you value your n-n-nose. I told you, Jorvik doesn't care for s-s-strangers. It's the m-m-most aggressive animal I've ever known, and believe me I've known a few. Blind from birth, it has a c-c-cruel and c-c-cold attitude to every other animal species it detects through smell."

"But not with you," added Jake sensibly.

"No, not me. I have Jorvik's t-t-trust. I was there when it was b-b-born and consequently it thinks I'm its parent. I can't say the feeling's mutual, though. It's not m-m-much to look at, but it does its job remarkably well."

"I know I'm going to regret asking," said Oscar, "but what kind of animal is it?"

"I thought I made that clear. Jorvik is not like anything you w-w-would recognise."

"Meaning?"

"Some y-y-years ago, unwelcome noises in the garden were becoming s-s-so frequent that I decided to get myself a guard d-d-dog or perhaps a guard goose for p-p-protection. But neither proved s-s-satisfactory. The goose could be bribed with b-b-bread, while the dog did nothing but b-b-bark non-stop day and night. Drove me p-p-potty."

"That I *do* believe," tittered Oscar wryly, looking very pleased with himself.

"Curiosity is not a mistake, Mr T-T-Trotter, but stupidity is when in my company. Please shut-up, unless you w-w-want to leave empty-handed."

"Oh, Dad!"

"Okay, okay, I'll sit quietly on the naughty step."

"So, to continue, when faced with t-t-two useless animals, I ate the fattened g-g-goose and gave the yapping dog to a d-d-deaf farmer. But that left the problem unresolved. That's when I had a b-b-bright idea. If the perfect g-g-guard animal didn't exist, why shouldn't I invent m-m-my own?"

"Errr… because you can't invent animals!"

"Ah, but you c-c-can, Mr Trotter, and I have the living p-p-proof. The outcome was the Bloodrat, which I n-n-named Jorvik after the Viking name for York w-w-when Eric Bloodaxe was king."

"How was it possible?"

"By taking the easy route to s-s-solve a difficult problem. Cross-breeding, of course."

"I don't understand," said Jake.

"The clue is in the w-w-word, my boy. First I decided what characteristics I wanted in a g-g-guard animal. That was the easy part. I needed a d-d-dog to sniff out intruders, c-c-crossed with an animal known for mindless aggression. The result was my Bloodrat. Pure genius. It took time, b-b-but I got there in the end."

"Are you telling me those pickled animals in jars are failed attempts at creating a Bloodrat?"

"No, Mr Trotter, but I'm glad you're p-p-paying attention. They resulted from early ex-ex-experiments to see if it was possible to cross-breed unrelated animal groups. Having read up on the s-s-subject, it was clear the so-called ex-ex-experts thought it was *not* possible. Hogwash! I showed them, or at least I would if I c-c-could tell them, which I can't, as we know, t-t-tell them that is." He drew breath. "For early trials, I used small animals with s-s-short natural lives."

"Sounds cruel."

"Not in the least. I've already t-t-told you I respect all living creatures. I would never deliberately h-h-harm anything. Indeed, m-m-many of my cross-breeds lived full and happy lives. I pickled them for future s-s-study after they died of natural causes."

"And the failures?"

"Alas, there were a f-f-few, which still troubles me. Still, each failure brought me c-c-closer to success. You see, I knew others had crossed donkeys with zebras to p-p-produce Zonkeys, Zebroids and Zebonkeys, and donkeys with horses p-p-producing Zorse foals. Donkeys, mules, horses and zebras are r-r-related and success was almost guaranteed. But d-d-dogs and cats aren't, for example."

"And so?"

"As I'm not in the least interested in s-s-sharing my home with a d-d-dirty great Zonkey, I had to look to my own genius. After several false s-s-starts, I chose to cross-breed a bloodhound d-d-dog for its good sense of smell with a wild rat having s-s-sharp teeth and a t-t-temper to match." The old man looked towards Oscar. "It wasn't easy. They don't make ideal b-b-bedfellows, if you get my meaning." He winked rather too obviously, and Jake noticed. The old man coughed. "The two species were more inclined to kill each other than make b-b-babies. However, after years of p-p-patience, I bred the world's only Bloodrat."

"My friends at school are going to love this."

"You're n-n-not to tell them anything," snapped the old man. "The Bloodrat is ex-ex-extremely aggressive. It would tear anyone to p-p-pieces it didn't recognise by smell. It's loyal only to me. That's why it became fierce when it heard raised voices, and why you can't approach it."

"What if it escapes? Could it breed in the wild?"

"Thankfully no. As the offspring of different species, it was b-b-born sterile. You see, I think of e-e-everything."

"That's what the scientists said in Jurassic Park."

"Please don't mix scientific f-f-fact with cinema fiction, Mr Trotter. A good film is just that, s-s-splendid entertainment."

"What does Jorvik look like?" enquired Jake enthusiastically.

"I told you... h-h-horrible. Imagine if you can the b-b-body, long floppy ears and n-n-nose of a bloodhound, married to the p-p-pointed head, menacing dark eyes, whiskers, c-c-claws and long leathery tail of a wild rat. There you have it. Pretty, it is not."

"A huge rat on legs! Sounds ghastly."

"Actually, Mr Trotter, it's not big at all. About the s-s-size of a cat. I'm not entirely s-s-sure why, but cross-breeding often causes dwarfism and, in this case, b-b-blindness. Now, can we forget Jorvik for a moment and get b-b-back to the important matter of the Bubble Car? I'm sure Jorvik will stay q-q-quiet if we don't raise our voices."

It was hard to dismiss the Bloodrat without seeing it first hand, but discovering Jorvik's existence was not why they came and so talk of cross-breeding abruptly ended.

"You told me earlier you decided to give up the car but didn't mention the reason. Now you insist I shouldn't have it, unless for scrap," remarked Oscar as he bent over to pick up the broken china. "I don't understand why destroying the car is so important. I realise you never expect to drive it, but why shouldn't someone else?"

"Because!"

"Because?"

"Because of what I've t-t-turned it into. It's not a car any longer b-b-but a machine built for entirely different purposes. Without being broken up, h-h-how can I be sure it won't attract the attention of criminals and thieves, p-p-putting you and Jake in danger's path."

"What thieves and criminals? Who else knows of it?"

"I c-c-can't be certain anyone does, but I have reason for s-s-suspicion."

"Tell me."

"It's a long story that doesn't c-c-concern you."

Oscar's eyes rolled. "Anyway, I thought it only worked in combination with other devices. That's what you said," he argued, wanting to establish a position of strength.

"If you u-u-understand that, Mr Trotter, why then would you insist on t-t-testing it at all?"

Oscar thought for a moment, unsure whether he had been outwitted. "Curiosity, I suppose, plus I'm not sure how much of what you say I should believe."

"Are you c-c-calling me a liar?" flared the old man.

Oscar gasped, before quickly glancing towards the cupboard. "Probably not," he replied cautiously, relieved Jorvik had not stirred, "but I can't pass up any chance to get rich. When I came here, I only wanted a car to restore back to its 1950s' condition. Now I've seen what else it can do, the profit I could make from restoration is nothing compared to its potential for entertainment."

"So, money is m-m-more important than Jake's safety?"

"NEVER!" jumped Oscar.

"Listen well, Mr Trotter. You were n-n-never expected to see my light shows. It is an unwelcome c-c-complication. But now you h-h-have, I suppose I must tell you s-s-stuff I wanted kept s-s-secret."

"Go on."

"Many, many years ago I transformed the car into a p-p-platform for harnessing unbelievable quantities of e-e-electrical energy, for release in a single shot."

"Like a ray gun?" asked Jake excitedly, thinking of his comics.

"Not at all."

"And this can be done time after time?"

"That's right, Mr Trotter, although only when the c-c-conditions are right." He turned to Jake. "And to answer you, its uses are p-p-peaceful."

Jake appeared disappointed.

"It is crucial for h-h-harvesting the type of images you've s-s-seen today," continued the old man. "But, that said, the machine by itself cannot p-p-produce any visions in light. To do that also requires the other equipment I invented, which you will n-n-never, ever, take from me. So, there is no p-p-point in testing the machine yourself, and every reason not to." He stopped to draw breath, before leaning forward with a sincere look stamped across his lined face. "Please don't test it, and don't sell it on as a project c-c-car either. If you advertise it for sale, its uniqueness will draw public attention. Just b-b-break the wretched thing up into small pieces or leave it h-h-here for me to deal with!"

"Are you truly saying it's only our welfare that concerns you?" quizzed Oscar, as he dropped the broken china into a handy box.

"Mainly, b-b-but not exclusively," tutted the old man truthfully, taking the box from Oscar to place among other detritus on the shelves. He followed Jake's eyes. "Some use can be f-f-found for the crocks. Even b-b-broken things can have future value."

"So, there are other issues for consideration?" interrogated Oscar, raising an arm to help the old man reach a higher shelf. One slight push and the box disappeared from view.

"Yes."

"Tell me what they are. Do they include interest from thieves and criminals? I need to know if I'm to forfeit making a fortune from the machine, or even a good profit as a car."

The old man looked around the room, before fixing his stare on the Christmas tree. His thoughts wandered to times long past.

"The reason for g-g-giving up the machine is easy. It successfully served its intended p-p-purpose but still failed to give me the most important r-r-result I needed." He wiped an eye. "Now I'm t-t-too old to try any m-m-more. It's taken t-t-too long to help Michael."

"MICHAEL?" they shouted in unison.

Jorvik snarled.

A chill shot through the old man. "D-d-did I let slip my son's n-n-name?" he asked coyly, jerking between the two stunned faces.

Oscar nodded vigorously.

"Is that his bicycle by the bed?" enquired Jake.

The old man twisted, his thoughts now a tempest of grief and disappointment. He took a few moments to reply.

"It was, decades ago. He will h-h-have outgrown it now."

The words were not freely spoken and ended with a loud snort.

"My mum always says a problem shared is a problem halved," offered Jake with kindness.

The old man shook his head, trying to find the right words. "Not in this case. I've let a genie out of a b-b-bottle." And with that said, he visibly shrank in stature.

"Go on," encouraged Oscar, an outstretched hand forcing the old man to look up.

"C-c-can I trust you to understand without t-t-taking advantage?" asked the old man. "A long-lasting secret is not easily s-s-shared after so many years."

"What choice do you have?" said Oscar, a hint of menace in his tone. "Convince me why I shouldn't do what I like, or I'll go home for a trailer and take the machine away today and never come back."

"A provocative s-s-situation," grumbled the old man.

"A situation of your own making," rebounded Oscar. "You took my money without conditions, and now I want the Bubble Car in the same good faith. It's a simple and legal transaction."

Again, all went silent. Then, with much to think about, the old man suddenly dropped to his knees. He reached beneath Jake's seat for two tiny chanting bells, which he held between closed fingertips. Perplexed, Jake moved aside.

"What's happening, Dad?" whispered Jake. "Why is he sitting cross-legged? What's going on?"

"Shush!" cautioned Oscar. "He's gone into a self-induced trance. I've heard of mystics doing that, but I've never seen it until now."

Over and over, the old man chanted a sweet-sounding phrase, with too few notes to be called a melody but equally not a monotonous sentence. Throughout, the bells jingled.

Jake was captivated, but Oscar viewed it as an opportunity. He wanted to creep away unnoticed.

"Where are you going?" Jake uttered nervously as his father took a backwards step.

"Just keep an eye on him. I'll be back in a flash."

"I know what you're thinking of doing, and it's dishonest."

"Not if I don't take anything from the shed. I just want a quick snoop around. See what I can find out."

It was then the old man's eyes suddenly burst open, staring blankly into the distance. "Blast your dark hearts, you thieves," he bawled, all serenity gone from his voice. "You'll not take it from me, not now, not ever."

"Blimey! Does he mean us?" reared Oscar, watching the old man's eyelids fall shut again.

The Bloodrat stirred within the cupboard.

"I'm with you, Dad. Let's make a run for it before he properly wakes." He stood.

"Not without the car. He'll never have us back. Leave this to me."

Oscar placed a soothing hand on the old man's head, but the gentle touch was enough to raise a scream and cause Jorvik to growl from behind the grill.

"Shake him, Dad. Wake him before the Bloodrat breaks out."

"Not likely. I've heard waking people from a deep trance is dangerous."

Without the assurance of a familiar voice, Jorvik's grinding of teeth against the metal grill and wild clawing became fearsome.

"Dad, it's going to get out. Can't we do anything to shut the rat-dog up?"

"Do what? It can't be approached."

"I could shove a cushion over the grill. The dark might settle it."

"You heard the old man. Jorvik is blind! No, Son, stay well clear."

"Keep away from me or I'll blow the place apart," roared the old man. "Dead men don't talk."

"Dad!"

"Okay, Son, we'll do it your way," and with that said he slapped the old man's face. The effect was slight, so he did it again—but harder this time—guilt-ridden to feel the weight of the blow against the old man's cheek.

"Bangers!" howled the old man, making Jake trip over a pile of magazines. He then spread his arms like an awakening eagle, swaying to a different ringing noise between his ears.

"I'm so sorry," said Oscar as the old man slowly revived, helping him to his feet. "I tried to be gentle. They were more slaps than bangs. I didn't know what else to do."

"And why should you," he slurred. "You weren't to know I've run out of sausages."

"Sausages?" repeated Jake with his mouth held open. "What are sausages to do with…"

"Be quiet," cautioned Oscar, not wanting to remind the old man of the recent violence.

The old man turned towards Jorvik's cupboard and spread a hand over the grill. The familiar smell of its master immediately subdued the Bloodrat's aggression.

"What just h-h-happened, Mr Trotter?"

"You were about to tell me how the machine works," he hinted artfully, hoping to profit from a lie. "Then you fell over."

"Was I? Did I? Then, why am I h-h-holding chanting bells?"

"Tell him, Jake," said Oscar, fearing he had no quick answer.

"I think you thought I would be interested. You were demonstrating how to chant when you... sort-of fell, I suppose."

Oscar approved.

"That sounds plausible. Indecisiveness is a very b-b-bad habit of mine, but I can't h-h-help myself. I once thought I was cured, but I couldn't decide if I was. So I use m-m-meditation to clear my head. I find it helps, although I must admit it's n-n-never before caused me to wake with a sore jaw," he added, rubbing his face. "What disturbed Jorvik?"

Jake shrugged innocently, which added another lie to the first.

"Perhaps it didn't like your singing," proposed Oscar, thinking off the cuff. He caught sight of Jake's disapproving glance. "By the way, you said some strange things just now. Has someone really tried to steal from you? And, more urgently, do you have explosives tucked away somewhere? Because, if you have, it's illegal and very, very dangerous."

The old man pulled the bells from his fingers and returned them to the floor. "I can charm s-s-snakes, you know, and make c-c-coiled rope fly."

"I take it that's a *no,* then?" challenged Oscar.

"You can do those things?" asked Jake with gusto, his curiosity raging. "Would you show me sometime?"

"I could s-s-show you now."

"No!" exclaimed Oscar firmly, anxious to leave the cottage in the shortest possible time. "Can we please get back to the business at hand? I've a car to take away."

The old man grunted, and all talk of snake charming and flying rope was forgotten.

"I've come to a c-c-conclusion," said the old man, taking a deep breath before continuing, as though afraid he could lose his nerve if the words caught in his throat. "As f-f-far as I'm concerned, I'd be b-b-better off *not* s-s-selling the car and *not* telling you about Michael either."

Oscar slumped back into a chair.

"And yes, Mr Trotter, I now remember what happened. If you had any decency, you'd see the hurt and mischief your prying is c-c-causing me."

"Leaving the car behind isn't an option," cautioned Oscar softly but defiantly.

"I thought as m-m-much. In that case, you m-m-must be told more or I'll lose the only chance to p-p-persuade you to completely destroy my m-m-machine before it's too late."

Oscar was furious. He could see a good opportunity disappearing.

"You keep saying *your* car and *your* machine when it's my car. I paid you £100 and the deal was struck."

"Dad!" called Jake. "That was rude."

"Stay out of it. Business is business, as you'll learn when you grow up. The car has been bought and paid for. It's how I earn a living."

"Then, I h-h-have no option. But telling comes in the form of a w-w-warning." The old man stamped his foot. "Oh, for goodness s-s-sake. This r-r-ridiculous st-st-stutter." He reached for a bottle on the fireplace. It was labelled Voice Stuff Number 8. "Just one m-m-moment." He pulled the cork. The green mixture inside began to foam. With his head tilted back and eyes firmly shut, he gulped a quarter of the liquid directly from the bottle.

At first nothing happened. Then, quite slowly to begin with, green smoke began to leach from the corners of his mouth and nose.

"Ah, that's better," he said, as the smoke thickened. "Now I can talk properly. Where was I?"

"You're on fire!" cried Oscar. "At least, I think it's fire."

"Calm yourself," begged the old man in an unflappable voice, motioning Oscar to sit back down. He blew smoke rings from puckered lips, which floated gracefully towards the ceiling, where more paper chains were coated in a green slime. "It's another little invention of mine. I call it my stutter-stopper. It works well, as you can hear."

"What about the smoke inside your throat?" shrieked Jake.

"Ah, the sparrow is also concerned." He stretched his mouth wide open. "Look, it has passed. I am, as you see, no longer a fire-spitting dragon. Even better than that, I no longer stutter. Great, isn't it?"

Oscar was flabbergasted or, as Jake would say, completely and utterly gobsmacked. "It's wonderful. No, more than that, it's a blinking miracle."

"Now, now, Mr Trotter, don't get carried away. It's a simple thing I've achieved. We'll discuss proper miracles later."

But Oscar was having none of it. He could see the potential for making lots of money. "Why haven't you tried selling it? Just think of the number of people around the world with stammers *we* could cure."

"*We*?" said the old man, shaking his head in disappointment.

"You'd need a business partner, someone who is used to buying and selling."

"Tishity-tosh. You said the same about my experiments in the shed."

"Of course. Everything you do is amazing and, if I might add, has potential for making a great deal of money."

"But I told you. Money doesn't interest me one jot."

"It interests me."

"So I have come to expect. However, in this case, the potion only lasts a few hours and then the stuttering starts all over again."

"Even better. Customers could buy top-ups," proposed Oscar brightly. "Sell it by the dozen bottles, or box load, or lorry load. The sky's the limit!"

"Alas, swallowing too much Number 8 or taking it too often turns skin green for a week. In my early experiments with formulae 1 to 5, my skin stayed green for a month. Number 6 caused only my head to go green, and Number 7 affected only my nose and ears. Number 8 works much better. Instead of turning me green, it comes out as smoke which rises, unless I take too much of the stuff." He pointed to the ceiling. "As you can see, it doesn't evaporate but forms slime or even stalactites if enough settles in one place. Moderation is the key to the correct dose. One day I'll find a use for the stalactites. Now, where was I?"

"The machine?" said Jake sensibly. "We must concentrate on one miracle at a time."

"Oh, dear me, yes! I must find a way to make you both understand. Now, where to begin?"

Chapter 5
The Wizard Stick

"Begin at the beginning?" recommended Jake.

"Good boy… sensible boy. You're entirely right. Well, now, who am I?" His forehead furrowed. "Oh, yes, I'm Professor Septimus Kneebone and I've been struck by lightning fourteen times."

"Goodness gracious," exclaimed Oscar. "Really, fourteen times?"

"I know, I know. Remarkable isn't it that I survived. My friend used to call me Septic because I was always rubbing ointment onto my sore head, but that was a long time ago."

"Doesn't lightning hurt?" asked Jake, looking for visible scars.

"Not so much after the first six. That's why I wear wellington boots, even in bed in case I get up during the night. The rubber insulates me from the ground and stops the lightning from cooking my brain. I wear them so often I had to cut the ends off to let my toes breathe. Of course, the lightning started my stammer. It was also responsible for my unusual hairstyle," he chuckled. "Strangely, my hair now grows at twice the normal rate. Now, if I understood why that happens, it really would be a money-spinner." His happy tone suddenly turned serious. "I take it you have the egg, Mr Trotter?"

"You mean this?" interrupted Jake, pulling the oval object found in the glove box from his bulging pocket.

"Ah, the very thing. How come you have it?"

"Dad found it in your raincoat."

"So that's where I left it. I've been searching everywhere. Has it done anything, you know, *weird* during the lightning?"

"No," answered Oscar. "The battery must be dead."

The old man laughed until his face turned from red to purple. "Battery indeed. Your humour kills me. I'm Professor Septimus Kneebone and I haven't needed a battery to power anything since 1959." He thrust out a hand. "Can I take it?"

Jake passed it across. The old man was noticeably relieved. He rubbed his hands over the smooth surface, checking for damage.

"Without this, my Starlight Machine is just so much junk. Anyone possessing both can…"

"WHAT!" shouted Jake in a voice pitched high by excitement. "Did you just say Starlight Machine?"

"Shush, boy, it's merely a name. Perhaps a stupid one under the circumstances. Maybe a better name would be the Machine of Broken Hearts."

"I prefer 'Starlight'."

"I'll have the egg back if you don't mind," said Oscar, sounding more demanding than courteous.

"Not so fast, Mr Trotter. Without my help it would do you no good, and possibly a great deal of harm. Would you put Jake's life at risk by not understanding what it can do?"

"Not again. You said that about the car."

"I did, and now the same applies to the egg. They are connected. So, I repeat the question."

"Of course not, but…"

"There are no 'ifs and buts', Mr Trotter. You must listen, unless you want yourself and your son to be caught up in something dangerous beyond your wildest imagination."

"Rubbish," replied Oscar, believing none of it. "You just want to keep it. Well, I'm afraid I have to insist it comes with the Bubble Car."

"Trust me, you really don't want it."

"Dad!" rebuked Jake, pulling at his outstretched arm. He had never seen his father act so forcefully. He didn't like it one bit and said so.

"Don't interfere," scolded Oscar, shaking off Jake's hold. "I paid good money for the car."

"So you did, Mr Trotter. But you didn't buy the egg. It's not part of the sale."

"Finders keepers…" challenged Oscar. "You told me to get rid of everything in the shed barring the table and the equipment on it. Otherwise, leave it empty, you said."

"That's true, except I'd lost the egg, not discarded it. Be warned, Mr Trotter, I'll not argue over it. But, if you keep it, some unlucky soul might have to scrape you off the wall with a shovel after you explode. What a shame for Jake too. Such a nice boy with a bright future."

"Explode!" howled Oscar, leaping.

"Of course. None of us will be safe if the egg finishes up in the hands of a beginner. Do you own a strong pair of rubber boots?"

"Boots?" shrilled Oscar.

"To insulate yourself from massive electrical shocks."

"Shocks! Is that a genuine possibility?"

"Distinctly, Mr Trotter. What you have to decide is whether it's worth the risk. You can see what's happened to me, and I've always known how to handle the eggs I make. What chance do you have as a novice? You don't even know what it does or how to store it safely."

"Because you haven't got round to telling me."

"If I had long enough, I could teach you the science, Mr Trotter, but you could never truly understand the dangers until you've experienced them for yourself. What the egg does, and the danger it poses, go hand in glove. Still, I survived the shocks and maybe you could be equally lucky. Do you feel lucky, Mr Trotter?"

"Oh, very well, keep the blessed thing," retracted Oscar, visibly drained by the weight of argument.

Jake was relieved.

But the old man studied Oscar's face with suspicion. His surrender had come far too easily to be genuine. In the past minutes he had seen a side to Oscar's character he mistrusted, a stubborn and selfish side which made him wonder whether the change of heart would be temporary. It was entirely possible Oscar might sneakily return for the egg once the initial shock wore off. No, there was only one way to be certain Oscar would not want it, and that required terrifying him into submission. It was a risky strategy, but worthwhile if it worked. And so he said in a disarming tone:

"Okay, have it. I've decided not to contest your claim. After all, why should I put myself at risk when you're so anxious to unburden me? No, you may take it far away, but don't blame me if something bad happens." He drew back an arm, ready to throw the egg in Oscar's direction. "Here, catch!"

"No!" screamed Oscar, thrusting his hands forward. "Don't be stupid. Keep that *thing* well away from us if it's as dangerous as you say!"

"Only in the wrong hands," replied the old man.

That was enough for Oscar. He knew the old man was eccentric, but what separated eccentric from crazy? And now, face to face with unknown danger, could a crazy man be trusted not to toss the egg? This was not the time to find out. Jumping forward, he seized Jake by the collar and bundled him towards the door.

"Get out, Son. Get out while you still can. Don't wait for me. I'll be close behind. Hurry, hurry!"

But Jake, being small, couldn't easily reach the clear spaces on the floor. In the confusion of the moment he stumbled and fell, sending piles of papers and magazines sliding.

"Calm down," shrieked the old man, mortified to see his cherished possessions being trampled underfoot as Oscar also ploughed a destructive path to the door, too panicked to bother with the stepping gaps. "There's no need to wreck my life's work just because I've rattled your cage." His gasps of horror stirred Jorvik from its cushion. "I suppose I might've overstated the case a little. Stand still, please! It's not a bomb, but it does have the power to summon enormous energy."

If the change of emphasis from 'explosion' to 'energy' was intended to calm Oscar, it failed miserably.

The old man watched as boxes and experiments were thrown aside with abandon. And, once at the door, Oscar pulled the handle with such frenzy that the screws ripped from the wood and the lock became dislodged. It could no longer be opened.

"I don't believe it!" screamed Oscar, looking at the handle in his hand. He noticed the sheet covering the sash window and ripped it down.

"For pity sake… *stop!*" called the old man at the top of his voice. "My papers, my things. You're ruining years of precious work. My calculations for a hovering bicycle are in a hundred places."

But the plea fell on deaf ears. Oscar, now drunk with hysteria, pushed hard on the sash, but it was stiff.

"Hell!" he shrieked, letting go and taking a few backward steps. "Get out the way, Jake," he waved. "Give me room to shoulder charge the blinking door. I'll soon have us out."

"No more," bellowed the old man as an ear-splitting command. "Stop immediately or face my deadliest powers." He leapt forward and in three strides reached the kitchen, where he grabbed a short multi-coloured stick. "*Kumquat, aubergine, mange-tout!*" he chanted in his best wizard's voice.

The effect was both dramatic and instant. Oscar froze in a cold sweat before suddenly crumpling to the ground like an undermined tower, helpless to protect himself or his son.

"Dad!" screamed Jake as he watched his father fall.

But the old man held him back. "Leave him. The mind is a wondrous thing. He'll be fine once he realises I haven't turned him into a pillar of salt. Auto-suggestion. It's how voodoo works. It induces a hypnotic state by the power of suggestion. Your father believed he was cursed by my spell, so he subconsciously reacted as if he had been."

"I don't get it," said Jake, still afraid for his father.

"Just wait and see."

After no more than a minute Oscar lifted his head, his eyes blank and swimming. Everything was a blur, and his ankle throbbed from the awkward collapse. Then, gradually at first, the memory of the experience returned.

The old man was by now standing over him, smouldering. He had discarded the stick. Oscar looked up, unsure what was going to happen next.

It was the deathly silence which followed that took Oscar's nerves to a crescendo. Each second was a slow torture, as if standing alone on the stage of a large theatre with the audience staring in silence to hear the opening line of a play he couldn't remember. Yet, as moment followed moment, absolutely nothing happened—no bangs, no flashes and particularly no alteration to his physical body. He allowed his eyes to drift towards Jake, who was leaning against the wall as calm as if waiting for a bus.

"Now I have your complete attention, Mr Trotter, perhaps you would get a grip on your emotions before you break my door and shatter your shoulder blade."

Oscar looked across to the stick on the floor.

"Oh, that little thing?" remarked the old man casually, following Oscar's stare. "Just a length of bamboo I use to stir paint. Completely harmless. As for the spell... well, tell him, Jake."

"Oh, Dad, as soon as he chanted the names of exotic fruit and vegetables I knew the spell was fake."

"See, that's the reasoning of a clever child. This is not a house of magic, but one of science."

Still tense, his heart pounding uncontrollably, Oscar hardly knew what to believe. He had felt within a wizard's spell of death but, there he was, none the worse for it.

"For goodness sake, Mr Trotter, you're upsetting the boy and greatly irritating me. Perhaps this will convince you to snap out of your unnecessary panic. Just watch what I can do with the egg in complete safety."

Before Oscar could stop him, the old man carelessly tossed the egg high into the air. Oscar ducked as it came down.

"Bish-bosh. Completely harmless when there's no lightning," he said with glee as he caught the egg one-handed, before stuffing the smaller end into his mouth and dancing wildly on the spot.

Oscar had never seen anything so irresponsible, enfeebling him more completely than any pain from the fall.

"I give up," groaned the old man, flopping back into his chair. "What will it take to convince you that we're not about to be blown to atoms?"

"For starters, you can put that thing down… extremely carefully if you please," whimpered Oscar nervously.

Jake approached to help him up, but Oscar grabbed him so passionately that their bodies met at speed.

The old man winced at the sound of heads colliding, but did as he was asked.

At last, Oscar released the hold. Jake, who had felt the damp from his father's sweating palms through his clothes, reeled back. He didn't want to be constrained. Even with a sore head, he was pumped with adrenaline and eager to explore the old man's world.

"Are we now safe?"

"As houses, Mr Trotter, so long as the weather stays fair. You're much more likely to give yourself a heart attack than die from anything I can do. Look, I can even bounce the egg off the wall."

"Don't you dare!" yelled Oscar. "Just leave it on the mantelpiece where I can see it."

"Oh, very well, but you must allow me to put it away safely in case lightning returns," said the old man, his job done. He tapped on the short door to reassure Jorvik. A contented growl returned. "The fact remains, however, that unless I am given a chance to explain my invention properly," he added on turning, "I can't possibly now let you have the Bubble Car either, since you know there's a miraculous connection between the egg and the car." He reached for a tea caddy where he kept money hidden. "I'm afraid I've already spent some of the £100 on humbugs and sausages. You can have the rest back, though."

After his recent experiences, the money seemed of little importance to Oscar. "I only came to see if you were okay, not to be scared to death or blown to pieces."

"Hardly likely, Mr Trotter, but you're a difficult man to convince. You must be prepared to listen with an open mind or have the £92.17p left in the caddy. Which is it to be?"

"Go on, if you must," invited Oscar with caution, resuming his seat. But Jake was kept close.

"Fine, but explaining won't be easy." He shut the lid and pushed it out of sight. "Tell me, Mr Trotter, what do you know about sausages?"

Chapter 6
Outsiders

"Sausages?" said Oscar with surprise. "What in heaven's name are you banging on about now?"

"Sorry, sorry, I was thinking about my dinner. Of course, I meant to say the speed of sound and light?"

"An easy mistake to make," returned Oscar unwisely, recovering some of his composure.

"Answer me, blast you!"

"I don't see what…"

The old man stretched towards the egg as a warning not to be trifled with.

"Oh, very well. Actually, not much, I suppose."

"How about you, Jake?"

Jake considered the question. He raised a hand as if begging for a teacher's attention. "Sound travels through the air at hundreds of miles an hour. I know that from school. But some aeroplanes can fly even faster than sound. Supersonic aeroplanes. Like jet fighters."

"Absolutely correct." The old man clapped his hands. "Goody gumdrops. Now we're getting somewhere."

"Yes, yes, that's all very interesting, but what's it got to do with the egg?" implored Oscar.

"I'm coming to that if you give me half a chance."

At this moment occurred Jake's first mysterious encounter with outsiders, who would later cause the two men and the boy to fight for their lives. And, although the initial skirmish was slight, even unseen, it was only the beginning of the matter.

Suddenly there was a stirring among the garden hedges. The old man froze, before twisting his head like an owl towards the window.

"Somebody's out there?"

A bird flew up, followed by another and then fifty more until a flock gathered low in the sky, swooping and climbing in a wonderfully fluid cloud-like formation. Then, just as quickly, the rustling stopped and the birds circled around the trees, twittering their trill songs until all were again perched on branches.

Jake stood on a chair for a better look. "I can't see anyone."

"Are you sure?" asked the old man fearfully, his hand hovering over the handle on the trap door.

Jake jumped off and made long strides to the window. "I'm certain. It's as still as a…"

"Millpond," interrupted Oscar.

"I was going to say 'graveyard', but thought better of it."

Rarely deceived, the old man remained convinced there had been a person or persons unknown disturbing the birds. Attuned to hearing even the slightest noise from years of living in this remote place, he now thought he could detect hushed voices diminishing with distance.

"They're leaving," he said.

"Who?" asked Jake. "There's nobody out there."

"Believe me, there is." His chin dropped onto his chest as he turned to cock an ear in the direction of the sound. "There it is again. A man spoke and another replied."

"Could it be Michael returning?" enquired Oscar, trusting the old man's instinct.

The suggestion seemed to hurt the old man, who, with the noises gone, recoiled into the cushions of his chair. All colour had left his face, and his voice grew weaker. "There's no chance of that. None at all." He glanced at the Christmas presents leaning against the bucket.

Oscar sensed the changed atmosphere, which had become melancholy in an instant. "Are you alright?"

"*Fiddly-foo*," he muttered into his lap, "what is past has gone. I must stay focused on my work. It always helps ease the burden of loss."

"Michael is lost?" sprang Jake with uncharacteristic boldness.

"It does no good to dwell on things that are no longer obtainable," said the old man, pulling the oily rag from his waistcoat to wipe away a tear. "Life goes on. Now, where was I?"

"I think the time has come to tell us all your secrets," said Jake compassionately.

Chapter 7
The miracle Starlight Machine

The best thing to come from the undetected noises in the garden was the old man's growing willingness to share a few of his anxieties. Yet, even now, and probably because he preferred his own intelligent company, only slowly would barriers be lowered. Nevertheless, the seeds of change had been sown and bit by bit Jake and Oscar would be let into the old man's private—and above all secretive—world.

"It boils down to this," said Oscar, grabbing the moment. "To understand who might be lurking outside and why, we must be told everything relevant. And I do mean *everything*."

Jake looked furtively between his father and the old man for signs of a breakthrough. "Dad's right, sir," he added after a brief pause.

The old man grunted and then, without a word of explanation, got up and walked to the window, where he managed to force the sash to open. He climbed out.

"What the devil's he up to this time?" said Oscar in shock, dumbstruck the old man was prepared to leave the security of the cottage.

"If I didn't know better," replied Jake, "I'd say he's deliberately making a target of himself."

"For what purpose?"

"How would I know what's going on inside his head. Maybe to flush out intruders, to bring them into the open. You must've

83

noticed he's constantly on alert. Look how we had to cross from the shed."

Several times the old man was heard asking himself if anybody was near as he paced backwards and forwards past the window, stopping once to pick a handful of wild-growing mint; the relief on his face when he then replied 'no' confirmed he was not inviting company but hoping to avoid it.

Then it happened.

Something whistled past his head, so unexpectedly that he didn't have time to duck before it struck the cottage wall. There followed the sound of running feet and arguing voices fading into the woods.

Strangely, having stuck a fingertip into the small hole left in the brickwork, the old man appeared unmoved by the experience. Whatever caused the damage had ricocheted away. And, with his curiosity satisfied and sufficient mint leaves stuffed in his pocket, he climbed back into the room and sat, as if it was the most natural pastime in the world.

"What happened?" asked Oscar, unsure how to approach the matter.

"Are you speaking to me?" replied the old man absentmindedly, as Oscar and Jake waited for an explanation.

"We heard a thud. It was quite distinct."

"And voices," added Jake. "Don't forget the voices."

"Well?" pressed Oscar.

It became obvious from his facial movements that the old man was trying to think, and that the procedure was in very slow motion.

"Well?" repeated Oscar, his irritation plain to both.

The old man did not so much as move, but eventually said in a calculated tone: "Kids playing with a sling-shot, I expect, trying to break my window. That's how the door glass became cracked." Yet it was clear from his voice that he wasn't entirely sure.

Oscar found the explanation insincere and said so.

"I can't believe you would be spooked by children. I've seen how you twitch at every noise. No, there's more to it than you're letting on."

At last, and only after a battle of stares, did the old man admit the first noises were probably not children, although, with the absence of a loud report, the recent thud was almost certainly caused by something of no importance, which indicated children's pranks.

"Which brings us back to where we started," said Oscar. "If you remember, Professor, before you jumped out of the window we were discussing Michael. Shall we continue?"

"Michael once had a sling-shot. I made it from a dead branch and plaited knicker elastic. But that was decades ago." He enjoyed the memory.

"Don't stop now. We want to hear all about Michael."

It took a little while longer for the old man to snap out of his reminiscences, but when he did he looked mistily at Jake before his stare shifted towards Oscar, when his face took on a conspicuous frown.

"Oh yes, I recall, Jake and I were discussing jet fighters." The old man's deliberate snub was obvious. "Did you know the American X-15A rocket plane flew at nearly seven times the speed of sound in the 1960s? That's over 4,500 miles per hour." He became aware of Oscar's shuffling. "And yes, Mr Trotter, I will allow you to call me professor if you pay more attention to what's being said."

"Which brings us nicely back to Michael," was Oscar's quick riposte. "Is his disappearance somehow linked to the egg and the Starlight Machine, and perhaps even the outside noises?"

"I told you," returned the professor. "Kids playing and foxes rummaging around the dustbins and scaring the wildlife are the likely causes. Anyway," he continued, "I was next going to ask what you know about the speed of light?"

"The speed of... oh, for goodness sake. I give up!" recoiled Oscar, slumping into his chair. "I ask one thing and you reply with another. I just want to know what happened to Michael, collect the car and get on with my life."

"I won't tell you yet, Mr Trotter, because you're not in a fit state of mind to understand," he replied brusquely before turning to Jake. "And before your father interrupts us again, tell me what you know about light."

"Not much, I'm afraid," admitted Jake. "All I know is light travels a million times faster than sound."

"That's right, give or take a bit. That's why in a storm people see the flash of lightning well before the sound of thunder reaches their ears. It's all a question of different speeds."

"Yes, yes, very interesting I'm sure, but where is it getting us?" protested Oscar. "If you won't talk about Michael, at least give me a clue as to the purpose of the wretched egg. Where on earth does it fit into the grand scheme of things?"

"It doesn't, on Earth that is!"

"Sorry?"

"You're not a patient man, are you, Mr Trotter? Rush, rush, rush. Well, I won't be hurried." And, to emphasise the point, he took a screwed-up paper bag from his pocket and stuffed two humbugs into his mouth. "Yummy, I can't get enough of these. I always say a humbug is the perfect remedy for gloom. Like one?"

"Now sweets!" groaned Oscar, refusing the bag. "What next, a drive through the countryside or perhaps scones and cream in a tea shop?"

"All right, all right, but humbugs help me concentrate. Now, going back to what we were discussing..." He turned to Jake. "What were we discussing?"

"The speed of light, sir."

"And humbugs," added Oscar sarcastically, "which, incidentally, don't appear to help your concentration one jot?"

The professor ignored the sneer. "Light... yes. Now then, Jake is right about the speed of light but, interestingly, it travels faster in the vacuum of outer space than in the Earth's atmosphere. Do you accept this as fact?"

Oscar and Jake nodded, although neither knew if it was true or not.

"Good. So now you'll be pleased to hear I've come to the point where I can tell you of my discovery."

"At last," huffed Oscar, adjusting his seating position.

"Be quiet, Dad."

"Everyone knows lightning is made of electricity," continued the professor. "But where does the electricity come from?"

"I don't really care."

"Well, you should, Mr Trotter." The old man grabbed the painted stick and swished it close to Oscar's face. "It's not *spookiness* or magic." He tossed the stick over his shoulder. It hit the wall, bringing down more paper chains. "Whoops... Oh well, I'll fix them later. No, Mr Trotter, there's not a hint of supernatural about it. Tell me, have you ever played with Jake on a rug made from man-made fibres and then got an electric shock when you touched your car?"

"Too right I have, and it's very painful."

"And that isn't magic either! It happened because your body created an electrical charge by rolling on the rug, which you discharged by touching the metal car. A wonderfully simple kind of lightning went between your hand and the car."

"Well, I'll be..."

"At last I've caught your interest. Now, real lightning is similar in some respects, although we see it as a flash of light in the sky. Inside a thundercloud are tiny ice crystals which bounce about and crash into each other. This crashing causes the cloud to create an electrical charge, which we call *negative*. At the same time, an opposite type of electrical charge forms on the ground, called *positive*. When the *negative* and *positive* charges are strong enough they try to meet up, and, when they do, *wham*, lightning happens."

"Wicked!" cried Jake.

"Tell me, young man, have you ever been told not to stand under trees during a thunderstorm?"

"Yes, of course. Mum is always saying that."

"Very wise. The *positive* charge on the ground likes to gather around the tallest object it can find, such as a tree or a church spire. So, stay clear of them in a storm."

"What about thunder?"

"Good question, easily answered. Lightning gives off massive heat which makes the air around the flash explode. We call the *bang* thunder. Exciting stuff, isn't it!"

"Go on," appealed Jake, "I want to hear more."

The professor hesitated, trying to decide how best to continue in a way Jake could understand. "Tell me, what shape is lightning?"

"Oh, that's easy-peasy," he replied brightly. "It zigzags up and down."

"Yes, and that's very important to remember as far as my experiments are concerned. Because, when lightning is going upward it is much faster than when it is coming downwards. So, being a genius, what I've done is to place a very tall aerial on my shed roof to attract lightning when I want to use its electrical energy. In turn, the aerial is connected to special apparatus built into the Starlight Machine. The apparatus replaced the petrol engine."

"You kept the engine, I hope?" asked Oscar as an afterthought.

"Of course. It's in storage. Anyway, more importantly, the lightning super-energises the apparatus with massive amounts of electrical power, and this power allows the Machine to fire the lightning bolt back up at a much faster speed. I call it light acceleration. It's like someone throwing a tennis ball and you hitting it back with a racquet as hard as you can. Do you understand?"

"I think so," replied Jake.

Oscar was unconvinced by the procedure. "Surely that means you have to wait for lightning to strike the shed before you can power the car—the Machine—which can't be very often. What use is a car which can only be driven once in a blue moon, even if it uses free electricity rather than petrol? After all, they say lightning never strikes in the same place twice."

The professor ran his fingers through the white spikes on top of his head. "I think my hair proves that isn't true. But, to answer your question, of course, it would make my experiments difficult if I had to wait for naturally occurring lightning. But I don't. I worked out how to encourage lightning and control where it strikes with pinpoint accuracy."

"Are you telling me the car works like some kind of old-fashioned dodgem at a fair, getting its electricity from a long overhead pole?"

"Mr Trotter," reproached the professor, "you must forget all about driving the car. It can't be driven anywhere, ever! I thought I had made myself quite clear on that point. It is used for an entirely different purpose. I could take the wheels right off and it would make no difference to me whatsoever, except I keep them on as the rubber tyres form a layer of insulation between the electrical charge and the ground, keeping the Machine safe."

"A different purpose?"

"Just so."

"And are you going to tell me what that is?"

"I may, in due course. In the meantime, I will explain how I manufacture my own lightning."

"Fiddlesticks! Don't bother. It's all ridiculous. You're wasting our time," rebuked Oscar, losing all interest in the car as a valuable vehicle to be restored for sale. Anyway, he wanted his lunch.

"Nothing is impossible for me," said the professor with pride. "In fact, it proved to be a great deal easier than I expected."

"You've done it?" asked Jake brightly.

"For sure. The special apparatus in the Machine has two uses. Before the Machine can be super-energised, obviously there has to be lightning to provide the electricity. So, the first job of the apparatus is to artificially generate massive amounts of *positive* electrical charge which is fed to the roof aerial. Remember, *positive* charge likes to gather around tall objects, and here nothing is taller than my aerial when it is raised up. Then, once the aerial has enough *positive* charge, it attracts the *negative* energy in a passing thundercloud and, *bang*, off we go. Luckily, a thundercloud doesn't even have to be directly overhead for the lightning process to kick off. *Fabulosa!*"

"Cool!"

"Yes, Jake, it is cool. The aerial is not only the focal point for the *positive* charge going up, it becomes the exact location for the resulting lightning strike coming down. Marvellously simple when you think about it."

"Is that why Mum had heavy rain over her house but lightning struck here, even though you and Dad had bright skies overhead?"

"Now you're getting the picture, although, on that occasion, my *positive* charge was still building up. Weak lightning was attracted but it didn't strike the aerial."

"It makes no sense," complained Oscar bitterly, the expression on his face becoming quite unpleasant. "You've ruined a perfectly fine vintage Bubble Car, and for what? To prove you can make lightning. Big blinking deal. Give Professor Kneebone a Nobel Prize for the world's most useless invention."

"It makes every sense, Mr Trotter, as you shall now discover. The time has come to satisfy your curiosity over the importance of the metal egg you found. It will blow your mind!"

Oscar winced. "In a safe way, I hope," he added quickly.

"An open mind, that's what I like," retorted the professor cynically. "Okay, try this for size. I use the enormous power from lightning to launch the egg into outer space."

"Wowzer!" exclaimed Jake with genuine admiration.

"Eggs in space," mocked Oscar. "Now I've heard everything! It certainly gives a fresh meaning to 'free range'."

"Are you poking fun at the great Professor Kneebone?"

"I think you're completely barmy. If I was you, and I'm glad I'm not, I would stick to hovering bicycles and leave the astronaut stuff to NASA."

The irksome scolding brought no reaction from the professor beyond a dismissive grunt, knowing the best was yet to come. "Leave the room if you wish, Mr Know-it-all, but please allow Jake this once in a lifetime opportunity to understand what I have achieved."

"Dad?" pleaded Jake, wonder in his voice.

"Oh, very well, get on with it," said Oscar, rubbing his grumbling stomach. "We'll both stay, so long as you hurry up. I have a date with a large curry."

"When I want to send an egg into space," continued the professor, "I merely place it in the cup holder on top of the Bubble Car. The lightning goes straight down the aerial and into the car's special apparatus and, *boom*, the egg is launched. It happens so quickly the egg seems to vanish before your eyes. Of course, I must first remember to open the hatch in the shed roof. If I forgot, you can imagine how much damage would be caused." He clapped excitedly. "Bingo, job well done!"

"Wicked," shrieked Jake.

"Before my son gets too carried away, tell me what happens if a completely natural bolt of lightning hits the aerial during a thunderstorm when you're not expecting it?" asked Oscar, sure he had found a glitch in the professor's thinking. "Doesn't that super-energise the car? And, if it does, what happens to all that energy if no egg is ready for launch?"

"At last a sensible question from you, Mr Trotter. Luckily, that can't happen. The aerial is lowered when I'm not experimenting. Sadly, though, sometimes my memory lets me down, especially when sausages are involved, and I accidentally leave it raised, which invites trouble."

"And then what happens?"

"I have a safety device?"

"I knew you would say that."

"It's the mark of genuine genius to be prepared. Only a fool would risk the consequences of forgetfulness which comes with old age."

"And this device is?" asked Oscar.

"The egg itself. It acts as a type of fuse. The egg is needed to complete the electrical circuit between the aerial and the apparatus in the car. If the egg isn't in its holder, lightning can't energise the car."

"And that's failsafe?"

"Very nearly."

"Ah-ha, so it's not one hundred percent safe."

"Look, Mr Trotter, this is cutting-edge science which requires some element of risk. If I forget to lower the aerial *and* I'm unlucky with the weather, natural lightning hitting the aerial can occasionally and unpredictably jump across to other nearby objects."

"Such as?"

The professor bowed. "My head, for example."

"Ouch!" exclaimed Jake.

"Ouch, indeed," repeated the professor. "The secret is not to forget to lower the aerial between experiments. But, if I realise too late that I've left it up by mistake, then I usually avoid standing close to the aerial until the storm has passed, and definitely never be caught near the egg which attracts lightning. That would be *zap*, another headache or even death!"

"That's why Dad can't keep the egg?"

The professor nodded.

"So you were actually telling me the truth," gasped Oscar.

"Thank goodness for rubber boots," offered Jake sympathetically.

"Indeed, young man, but this is only the beginning of my amazing invention. I haven't told you what the egg does in space, which is truly astonishing."

"Then continue swiftly," said Oscar, his stomach churning.

"Yes, please do," added Jake, anticipating something really exciting.

"Very well. Stand by to be spellbound." He coughed to clear his throat. "Once powered up, the Bubble Car…"

"Starlight Machine," corrected Jake.

"Starlight Machine, if you prefer," agreed the professor, "boosts the lightning bolt skyward, carrying the egg with it like a magnet attracted to a piece of steel. By the time the egg reaches the edge of space, it is travelling many times faster than the speed of light. I call it hyperbright speed, which is a play on words derived from supersonic."

"What happens to the lightning?" enquired Jake.

"It fades away before outer space is reached."

"You said space is a vacuum, without air."

"Yes, I did, Mr Trotter, which means there is no friction to slow the egg down. Whatever speed the egg enters space, it maintains that speed forever unless a rocket motor is fired to alter speed or direction. If left alone, it would fly on past all the outer planets and beyond into new solar systems."

"Fab," exclaimed Jake with genuine admiration.

"Of course, that isn't its purpose. For my experiments, I need to turn the egg around after a calculated distance and send it hurtling back towards Earth. So, when it has flown far enough into deep space, a pre-programmed signal causes the top of the egg to fall away, exposing a tiny rocket motor. The motor fires just once to divert the egg in a huge arc. Very little speed is lost in the process. It's a marvel of my incredible intellect."

"A tall story, Professor, made up to impress Jake and put me off wanting the Bubble Car."

"It's all as true as I'm sitting here."

"Of course it is. Come on, pull the other leg! The story is as genuine as your wizard's stick and flying rope, and you know it. If what you've told us was possible, why would the Americans, Russians and others use expensive rockets to launch satellites into space and not just hitch a ride on a lightning bolt?"

"Because they're not me," thundered the professor, "and I'm the one and only Professor Septimus Kneebone... genius." He jumped up and down. "Yippee! It's not only theoretically possible, I have actually done it many times, tra-la... tra-la!"

"Smells fishy," grumbled Oscar.

"Then, Mr Trotter, I'm doubly glad I'm not you. Jake said how aeroplanes have accelerated way past the speed of sound, so where is the difference with light? After all, nobody knew what would happen when the first pilot flew a rocket-powered aeroplane through the sound barrier in 1947. Pushing through the light barrier decades later is no different. It is harder, yes, but difficulty has never held back the progress of science."

"Okay, answer this if you can. If you have done it before, how come I had the egg in my glove box? According to you, it should be somewhere past the planet Pluto or crashing towards Earth."

"Simple, my dear Trotter. I have built several eggs over the years. But it is too dangerous to have more than one ready at a time. You took the only prepared egg I have."

"I just knew you would say that. But it changes nothing. I still don't believe any of this space malarkey."

The professor shrugged. "Should I care?"

"Can you reuse an egg, or do they smash into the ground?" asked Jake, ignoring his father.

"You are, indeed, a very bright boy. No, Jake, they burn up in the Earth's atmosphere after completing their work. It's my way of ensuring a falling egg can't cause any damage."

"So, let me ask the question again," interrupted Oscar. "Was the lightning I saw today natural or made by you and this infernal Machine of yours... or rather mine?"

"I planned it, but everything got completely out of hand. I started a cycle of events which, on that occasion, I foolishly had no means of finishing."

"Ah-ha! Caught you out," mocked Oscar. "You said you only raise the aerial when you want to send an egg into space. But, as we all know, you didn't have the egg. I had it."

"To the crime of stupidity, I hold up my hands and admit it. I acted irrationally. Seeing a storm brewing over the far side of town, I raised the aerial and even began the *positive* charging process before checking where I had put the egg. Imagine my panic when I couldn't find it in its usual insulating box. I looked everywhere, leaving only the car to check."

"Is that why you were in the car when we arrived?"

"Indeed it was. And worse still, I trapped myself inside knowing the aerial was raised above my head and was beginning to receive a *positive* charge. I knew the car couldn't be super-energised, but there was every possibility a lightning strike could find my head if the lost egg was anywhere close by. Only thanks to you, Mr Trotter, did the great Septimus Kneebone avoid catastrophe. Did I mention I'm a genius?"

"You said 'stupid' and 'irrational'," countered Oscar with glee.

"Oh, yes, I did, didn't I."

"Well, I think it's marvellous, simply terrific," said Jake, throwing a scowl in his father's direction. "Thrilling."

But the professor's pleasure was short-lived.

"Golly, I've just had the most dreadful thought. When you first came into the shed today, you had the egg in your pocket. If lightning had struck the aerial, well…"

"My son would've attracted the lightning and been fried alive!" shouted Oscar. "Thanks a bundle, Professor Idiot."

"But you don't believe any of it, Dad, so where's the harm?" Jake then turned to the professor. "You weren't to know I had the egg," he said calmly, although saying the words left a shiver running down his spine.

"Not good enough," reprimanded the professor. "I should've been less careless in the first place. Imagine sticking it in my raincoat pocket. I need my head examined."

"I won't argue with that," agreed Oscar.

"I wanted one last try, you see. Just one more try before I give up."

"Give what up?" asked Jake gently.

"Oh, something completely wonderful, yet tragic in its own way."

"Wonderful *and* tragic? How can that be?"

"Oh dear! Well, having told you so much, I suppose I might as well tell you the rest. But be warned, you won't believe anything I say."

"What makes you think I believe any of it so far?" scorned Oscar, still smarting from Jake's near-death experience. "Still, carry on if you like with the fairy tale. Once upon a time there was a…"

"Stop it!" demanded the professor, before turning to Jake. "Do you want to hear, or do you share your father's misgivings?"

"Please carry on," Jake replied without hesitation.

"Very well, for your sake alone. With my machine and a space egg it is possible to look back into the past, to see history as it happened."

"Oh, come on," scolded Oscar in the strongest possible way, leaping to his feet. "This time you're stretching credibility to the

96

limit and way beyond. You've clearly been reading too much Jules Verne. *The Time Machine*, wasn't it? Come on, Jake, we're leaving this nut house."

"I said you wouldn't believe me."

"I believe it," shrieked Jake, thinking of the wonderful yet strange things that happen on screen when playing with a game's console in his bedroom. "Is it a time machine taking you to where monsters battle with giants for the inner sanctum of a mysterious castle?"

"Good heavens, no. Travelling through time is utterly impossible."

"But, you said…"

"Dear Jake, I said no such thing. I said it was possible to glimpse back into history, not journey backwards or forwards through time. Only events that have already happened can be seen from space, and nothing can be done to alter or interfere with them. There is a world of difference."

"You claim to have done that?"

"Yes, Mr Trotter, more than once."

"Epic!" cried Jake.

"Utter tripe," rebuked Oscar with an expression that looked as though he had sucked on a lemon. "That's quite enough fantasy for one day. In fact, enough for good. I don't want you filling my son's head with such rubbish." He turned to Jake, lifting him by the shoulders. "None of this can be real. It's just storytelling from an old man who has been struck on the head once too often. It has made him a bit… well, I might as well say it… dim-witted."

"Dim-witted!" roared the professor. "You dare question the sanity of Septimus Kneebone?" He waited for an apology, but Oscar stood his ground. "Well, do you, Mr Trotter, you… you…irritating blockhead?"

The Bloodrat growled.

"Dad!" censured Jake, tugging at his father's arm. "See what you've done."

"Me done? I spoke for both of us."

"No, you didn't. You have no right to put words into my mouth. Why can't you be quiet and just listen for once?"

Oscar was astonished at being blamed.

"How can we judge properly if we don't hear the rest? Please, Dad, for me. Give the professor a chance to finish."

The professor flopped, his face long with disappointment. "Oh, dear, I became angry and I never become angry. Perhaps *I am* going a little mad."

Jake raised a cautionary finger to warn his father against making another disparaging remark.

"I know my father is a bit of a pain, Professor, but I'm from a different generation. In my world miracles of technology come true every day. I can't begin to tell you all the wonderful things my new smartphone can do. Dad doesn't even know how to Google. And what about the invention of a scanner that produces 3-D models? That's a kind of miracle of sorts, isn't it? I haven't a clue how it works, but I know it does. So, please, I really do want to know how it is possible to see into the past."

The professor sunk his nose into the oily cloth, leaving a smudge across his cheek. "Gratifying, most gratifying."

Relieved the explanation had been accepted, Jake smiled so broadly it seemed his head would split in half. Oscar smiled only at the ridiculous smudge, but this time held his tongue.

"Very well, I'll carry on, but one more comment from your father and you're both out the door. Agreed?"

Jake nodded.

"Fair enough. Now, where did I get to?"

"Another humbug moment," said Oscar.

"Dad!"

"Sorry, sorry. It just slipped out. You can't teach an old dog new… I mean… I think I'll stay quiet." He sat.

"The stars we see in the night sky are an unbelievable distance away?" continued the professor with one eye firmly fixed on Oscar. "Are we all agreed on this?"

Jake nodded; Oscar shrugged, intending to offer no encouragement.

"They are, in fact, so far away that the distance to the nearest stars is 300 million, million miles, or, as scientists call it, 50 light years. And that's the nearest."

"Picture that," murmured Oscar sarcastically.

"Yes, Mr Trotter, it is mind-boggling. And, because the distance is so enormous, some of the stars we see at night shining brightly may, in fact, no longer exist. They might have exploded 50 or even 1,500 years ago and we just don't know it. This is because the light they emitted before exploding is still travelling towards Earth through outer space, giving us the impression all the stars are still there. But they're not. We see the stars as they were, not as they are now. If a star exploded today, it could take until Jake's grand or great-grandchildren are born or possibly much longer to see it disappear from the sky."

"I think I understand," said Jake.

"I hope so, because this is the basis of how my Starlight Machine works. It is *phantasmagorical*!"

"*Phanta...* whatever you said," agreed Jake.

"The point I'm making is this. Light travelling between the stars and Earth is a two-way process. Just as light comes to us from distant stars, so sunlight radiated off Earth travels out into deep space in exactly the same way."

"Monster!" exclaimed Jake. "Imagine that."

"I don't have to. I've seen it for myself, but I'll come to that later. So, and here's the clever bit, light radiated from Earth carries all the images of things that took place on our planet in the past, like a never-ending movie film. What happened on Earth yesterday is hurtling through space as a light show right now, but way behind the images of past years, centuries and millennia. Go far enough and fast enough into deep space and you can even look back at images of Earth at the time of the dinosaurs."

"You've done that?" gulped Oscar, suddenly seeing commercial value in the project.

"Just once. I saw Pterodactyls fly, as I already told you. The images came from my first-ever experiment, launched decades ago, but it took years and years for the images to reach me from space because of the vast distance they had to travel. By then I had seen other historic events from later missions. Nowadays I limit most of my experiments to the past 400 years. These images come back much quicker."

"That's amazing!"

"Yes, Jake, it is. I do this by using the egg to intercept the images from Earth and reflect them back to receiving equipment in the shed, where they are stored and held ready for viewing. It's like jumping into a stream of history, billions upon billions of miles long and picking a particular time to watch as the images of Earth flow by." He wrung his hands with glee. "Whoopee, it's so clever, yet so simple! Like having a telescope into history. There's no limit to the incredible things to be discovered. The possibilities are endless, and all because the further out into space the egg flies, the further back in time I can see."

"So you say," said Oscar doubtfully, intending to bring Jake's thoughts back to earth. "For a moment I was starting to believe you, that is until prehistoric birds came into the conversation."

"Okay, Mr Trotter, tell me this. Do you believe in flying saucers?"

"Yup, along with fairies and leprechauns."

"Oh, so you won't be interested to know I've seen images of an alien flying-disk crashing at Roswell in 1947? Of course, the public doesn't know much about it because the Roswell UFO incident was covered up by the US military, which pretended the craft was a weather balloon. The Army said the dead alien bodies found at the crash site were, in fact, just dummies used in other top-secret experiments. But I know differently. However, as a double bluff, the Army commissioned an alien body to be fabricated from rubber and meat offal, and had a film taken of surgeons dissecting it."

"Why would they do that?" asked Jake, seeing no logic.

"Because they knew sooner or later someone would uncover the film and prove it to be a hoax, and that would finally put an end to anyone thinking there had ever been a genuine alien body found."

"Surely none of this can be real," gasped Oscar, wiping his face and flattening his hair in a single upward swipe of his hand. "The Roswell stuff and the spoof film sound plausible, I grant you that, but they can't be."

"Oh, but they are. Look it up on the internet. Marvellous, sensational, *yippee-doodle-dandy*!" cried the professor as he danced a polka amongst the chaos on the floor. "It's all too wonderful. I'm a genius. Books will be written about me." He stopped. "No, I will write books about my discoveries, accurate explanations of history that will thrill and amaze in equal measure. I'll be recognised worldwide as Professor Septimus Kneebone, one of the greatest minds the world has ever known. My name will rank with da Vinci and Einstein. And, talking of time, chocolate all around, I think."

"You can't stop now," implored Oscar unexpectedly. "I want answers that will convince me to take you half seriously."

"Do I detect a chink in your defensive armour?"

"I suppose in a strange way I want to believe. It's just that…"

But already the professor's thoughts had moved on. He jumped, danced and picked his way to the kitchen, eventually returning with three mugs of piping hot drink which were even creamier and more delicious than before.

"You were going on to say?" said Oscar, after taking a sip which burned his tongue.

The professor wiped his mouth on his sleeve, leaving a blue chalky mark across his chin. "Er… at last, straight to the point, Mr Trotter. I like that. And, in answer is to your question… why, *yippee-doodle* 'yes'. It is entirely possible to see history in the way I've described. I've done it several times without leaving the shed. In fact, you've seen it too."

"The naval stuff when we arrived," cried Jake.

"Yes. A genuine glimpse into past history, as real as the day it happened."

"It wasn't a photographic trick after all," professed Oscar, the spirited admission contrasting with the fragility of his understanding.

"No, it was genuine action from the 18th century. What you saw really took place over 250 years ago."

"Brilliant," shouted Jake.

"That's what I *d-d-doodle-d-d-dandy* reckon." He hesitated. "Oh, no! My Number 8-8-8 is w-w-wearing off."

"Don't stop now, Professor, just as you're convincing my father," implored Jake.

The professor looked at Jake's earnest expression and was moved to try something he knew could be dangerous. "For you, young m-m-man, I will be completely s-s-silly." He stood and grabbed the bottle of Number 8. It was still three-quarters full. "Here g-g-goes."

Before Oscar could stop him, the professor swallowed the lot. Immediately, green smoke burst from his mouth and nose in such profusion that he began to choke. He fell to his knees, fighting for breath and holding his throat.

Jake rushed to his side but was held back by the professor's own outstretched hand. Gradually, after several frantic gasps, the involuntary contraction of his airway eased and his breathing very slowly returned to normal. When his heartbeat similarly responded, he accepted help onto a chair. And there he sat quietly for a few minutes to recover from the alarming experience, which had also shaken Jake to the core.

"Thank goodness," said the professor presently, the panic over, "no major effects from the extra dose. I'm pleased about that. Where's my pad? I'll note it down."

But Jake could see bloodshot veins creeping through the whites of the professor's eyes. His ears were also turning green.

"Something amusing you, young man?" asked the professor.

"Your ears, sir."

"Green?"

"I'm afraid so."

"Oh, dearie me. I was afraid that might happen. Dull or bright?"

"I would say bright and getting brighter."

"Has it stopped at my ears?"

"It's hard to say."

"Oh, I won't be able to go out for more sausages without ear-muffs."

"And a scarf," added Oscar. "Your nose has begun to change colour too."

"Green?"

"Practically cabbage like."

"That does it. I'm grounded for a week. It must be because I got so angry. It affected the increased potion."

"Is there anything we can do?"

"You could take a little money from the tin and buy some sausages and hens' eggs. I don't think I'll be going anywhere for a while! Tishity-tosh, I'm off to bed." He turned to Oscar. "Oh, before you go, do whatever you can with the broken door handle and lock. A temporary fix is better than none."

"Leave it to me," said Oscar through a simpering smile, which the professor misunderstood as being artificial.

"Right, where did I leave the space egg? I think I'll tuck it under my pillow tonight for safe keeping now I know the aerial is definitely down. I don't want any burglars getting hold of it while I sleep. I hope you heard that, Mr Trotter."

Chapter 8
The Green Man

It was mid-morning of the next day, Sunday, before Oscar and Jake were able to set out for the professor's cottage with a box of groceries. The storm had moved there overnight, but now the sun shone brightly over both sides of town. They expected the Professor to be in very high spirits, despite his colour, knowing he would have company for the day.

No expense had been spared purchasing food and other provisions, for neither had seen the professor eat vegetables or fruit, or, indeed, wash with soap. Oscar had paid the extra cost from his own pocket.

At the top of the box were sausages, lots of them, none with red specks. Jake also remembered the professor loved humbugs and had sneaked a small packet into his trousers. He had bought them with his own pocket money. He had also bought a sherbet dip for himself and a roll of paper to wrap Archie's birthday present, which he intended to leave in the car.

Oscar was in contemplative mood as he drove quickly to the cottage, perhaps because he had been awake for much of the night contriving ways to make money from the professor's inventions. He was now uncertain whether the stutter-stopper had commercial value in its present unpredictable form, but the light show and the matter of the professor's hair growing unnaturally quickly held immediate promise. Several times he lifted a hand to his own bald patch at the back of his head and, knowing how it distressed him, he believed even the concept of a breakthrough to restore hair might have commercial value to a pharmaceutical company.

"Has the old drag… Mum… ever made fun of my hair?" he asked as the miles sped by.

"I don't think so," Jake replied, knowing full well she had. But he remembered the story of the fat lady with piano legs and so felt enabled to fib to save his father's embarrassment.

"That's good, although I find it hard to believe she would miss the opportunity. You know women, Jake, always fussing about their appearance. They're worse still when they get together, hunting in packs through the clothes shops, comparing likes and dislikes, and all the time hoping to dissuade each other from buying anything attractive. Consequently, they are very quick to criticise others. That's why I'm surprised she doesn't make a monkey of me whenever she can."

It was a tribute to Jake's level-headed approach to life that, at the age of only thirteen and one-quarter, he was able to put his father's mind at ease.

"Here we go," said Oscar automatically as they turned off the main road and into the professor's drive. In truth, his thoughts had remained on his bald patch since it was first mentioned, with the professor scarcely entering his mind.

"Stop!" screamed Jake as the cottage came into view.

Oscar slammed on the brakes without knowing why, causing the tyres to scrunch for grip and the gravel to give off a cloud of dust.

Leaning forward to peer through the windscreen, they stared in disbelief at the cottage, which overnight had become dark and unwelcoming. The front door swung loose on its hinges, while the roof tarpaulin flapped in the wind, held from flying away by a single rope tied to the chimney.

The dust had barely settled when Jake jumped out and ran for the door, leaving Oscar to follow with the box. Both had a really bad feeling.

"Hello! Anyone about?" Jake called, gingerly holding the door open, but only enough to speak through.

He thought he heard a weak voice telling him to come in. What followed next was a severe shock to both body and mind.

Stepping forward, Jake immediately recoiled as his feet sank into freezing cold water, soaking his trainers, socks and the hem of his upturned jeans. Indeed, the whole room was awash. Boxes, papers and some of the tins floated like so many derelict boats on a still pond, only shifting when the ripples from Jake's movements reached them.

A really unpleasant smell hung over the place, a strong odour of sodden wood and damp clothes. Jake sniffed, screwing up his face like someone tasting rotten fish.

The rather pathetic figure of the professor was huddled by the fire, which burned in a raised grate. He was naked except for a large yellow blanket, a motorcycle helmet and the usual wellington boots which stood ankle deep in water. His hands that clutched the edges of the blanket and his legs were bright green, the colour of fresh peas.

Now Oscar also entered, too quickly to be warned. He buckled as the shock of cold water met his legs. How he held onto the box was anyone's guess.

"Don't ask," muttered the professor hoarsely after raising the visor, as the visitors waded towards the kitchen. "The answer is 'yes'."

"We didn't ask anything," said Jake, his back to the professor.

"What did you say?" begged the old man.

"I said we..." He twisted. "Can't you hear anything?"

"What? If you're asking me if I'm this dreadful colour all over, the answer is *yes*. My fault. I took a chance and now must accept the consequences. Still, at least I'm not yet stuttering. Got any chocolate powder? I'm dying for a hot mug full."

"What happened?" enquired Jake, drawn to the gaping hole in the ceiling. "Where's the Pterodactyl?"

"Speak up. My ears are ringing under the helmet. Face me so I can lip-read."

"What happened?" repeated Jake quietly, using wide and exaggerated mouth movements.

"No need to shout! That's the culprit," he said, pointing to the egg nestling within the creases of the mattress. "I should've put it back in the insulating box after you went. I intended to, in secrecy, but, with all the comings and goings and problems with my Number 8, I completely forgot. Last night's natural lightning found the egg all by itself. You see before you, Jake, the perfect example of why laziness never pays."

"It struck here? A direct hit on the cottage roof?" asked Jake, looking around. And when there was no reply, he turned to face the old man before repeating the question.

"It was about midnight," recalled the professor, "when I heard a tremendous crack overhead. The first lightning bolt hit the roof so hard it scattered several tiles, letting water through. Even so, I was grateful it hadn't found the hole under the plastic tarpaulin. But, I spoke too soon. Before I had a chance to move, another massive strike came straight through the hole. It knocked the wings off the Pterodactyl and went straight for the egg."

"Ouch! Were you hit?"

"What?"

"Did the lightning strike you?" he mimed.

"No. It struck the headboard, missing me by a metre or so, but I was blown off the bed by the energy. It was the worst ever. My eardrums are damaged from the thunder exploding above my head."

"You're bleeding," said Oscar, returning from the kitchen with a clean cloth.

Jake repeated the words.

"I was scratched by the Pterodactyl's claw. Not many people can claim that in the 21st century."

"Why didn't you get rid of the egg after the first strike?" asked Oscar, now aware of the need to mime.

"Believe it or not, I couldn't find it in the dark. It started beneath my pillow but had worked its way down under the blanket to my feet. That was fortunate, as it happens. Anyway, I put the helmet on in case there was more lightning, or the ceiling fell in."

"The wellies didn't help this time? *Didn't help this time?*"

"Not really, as the bed frame was standing in rainwater, and water conducts electricity. Lucky for me the mattress is made of pocketed rubber." He blushed. "I think the trauma of the lightning strike might have loosened my bladder, though."

With nothing else to be achieved before order was restored, Jake and Oscar fell upon the task of clearing up. Drying the room using buckets, mops and cloths would take hours of arduous work, but little by little the room was reclaimed. Bits of machinery and magazines which could be rescued were hauled outside to air in the sunshine, with much of the rest piled into a scrap heap. The professor insisted the Christmas tree and soggy presents had to be saved, while the shelves with their pickling jars and the tall column of rusty tins were unaffected by the flood.

The solid furniture was left where it stood, as only the legs were wet, leaving Oscar to struggle out of the door with the professor's mattress folded above his head. Jake had offered to help, but his father insisted he was too small to be of use. This was another 'little white fib', but again said for noble reasons. The mattress was old, strangely stained, damp in one place and rather smelly, and Oscar preferred Jake should not touch it. A length of string was tied between the light and the window to peg up any papers that were retrievable.

Besides the chamber pot, which had floated with Annie the 38th clinging to the rim, Jake found a sodden bag of coins that had been stored beneath the bed. He retrieved a handful, more unusual in shape and varied in design than he had ever seen before. Nestling among Victorian pennies, tiny farthings, thruppenny bits and florins, was a wide selection of foreign coins, most pressed with the heads of statesmen from the 19th and 20th centuries or different kinds of birds.

Dipping still deeper into the bottom of the bag, his fingertips recovered several sealed plastic envelopes, wet to touch but completely dry inside. They produced another fascinating hoard, this time stamps in square, rectangular, triangular and diamond forms from almost every nation of the world. But this was not the time to marvel at such a find and so, reluctantly, the coins and stamps were returned to the bag and put to one side.

The eventual conclusion to the exhausting task quite naturally led to a hearty meal. This, of course, included sausages... lots of them to raise tired spirits.

Even while eating, the professor refused to remove the helmet, the awkwardness causing most of his egg yolk to drip onto the blanket. He had asked for the mint from the previous day to be chopped coarsely and sprinkled over the sausages, and now commented favourably on the richly seasoned taste. He was less complimentary about the ceiling plaster, which still occasionally wafted down to dust the meal in a fine grey powder.

"Oh, well," he remarked after his plate was taken away, "at least the yolk matches the blanket."

Jake added how the gritty plaster reminded him of picnicking on the beach, when sand always got into the sandwiches.

The arrival of hot chocolate met with greater success, which the professor sucked through a straw. The sweet beverage had a general relaxing affect that was particularly felt by Oscar, who looked around the half-empty room with renewed dismay.

"We've done okay, but there remain one or two jobs we can't put off. I suggest Jake washes up before we sit and talk. That will give me time to fix the hole in the roof. I've got some tools in the car, so all I need from you, Professor, is a long ladder. With any luck, I should be able to reuse the old tarpaulin. It will keep the worst of the weather at bay until you have the roof properly mended. Does that meet with your approval?"

The professor was pleased but felt he was becoming too dependent on the others, which coloured his reply.

"If you can be bothered with such trifles, who am I to stop you."

Even as the words left his lips, he regretted sounding ungrateful, especially as the help had been offered willingly. And so, with a warm heart and cheerful smile, he held out a hand.

"You know, Mr Trotter, we got off to a very bad start yesterday, and I apologise. Can we wipe the slate clean and begin afresh?"

Oscar shook his hand. The professor chuckled as Oscar followed Jake to the kitchen, noticing how he kept glancing awkwardly at his palm.

"It's all right, Mr Trotter," shouted the professor, "the green isn't contagious."

Later, the professor handed the bag of coins and stamps to Jake as a gift, giving him more enjoyment to sort and arrange at home than any pleasure he derived from playing computer games.

An hour later, with the sickly smell of drying floors competing with the more palatable aroma of minted sausages, bacon and eggs, the three again gathered around the fireplace. It had been stoked high with dry wood from the garden store.

Staring into the fire, they contentedly watched new flames lick and leap among the logs. None wanted to disturb the peace of the moment, although they all knew everything salvageable would have to be brought back into the cottage once the sun dried it out.

For his part, Jake wondered where all the saved magazines and machinery parts could be stacked while still keeping the floor clear to walk over with ease; the professor puzzled whether he could remember exactly where everything went as before to help blind Jorvik find its way around the room. Oscar was too fatigued to think at all.

It was the professor's eyelids which first flickered and then closed. His heavy head fell to one side, the helmet bumping against the upright of the chair. Oscar nodded to Jake, and together they giggled, but ever-so-quietly.

"Hey," whispered Jake, "we forgot to check the Bloodrat. It could've drowned in that tiny cupboard. Who's going to peep?"

They glanced towards the small door.

"Not me, and you're certainly not going to either," demanded Oscar. "The professor said we shouldn't go near it for *any* reason. I'm inclined to believe him this time."

"I've got an idea," said Jake, and in a trice he grabbed the paint-stirring stick which he had earlier placed on the mantelpiece. At arm's length, he scrapped it across the metal grill.

Jorvik leapt angrily at the door, its exposed needle-sharp teeth stabbing through the holes in the grill. Jake jumped. The professor turned but remained asleep.

"Phew," flinched Oscar, pulling Jake back. "Not only alive but as aggressive as ever."

"Won't the poor thing be hungry?" pleaded Jake, pleased to feel his father's protection.

"If it is, it's not having my fingers for a snack," he replied. "It certainly won't be short of water."

"What do we do?"

"I'll leave a note by the clock to remind the professor to feed it after it wakes."

"Won't it be frightened?"

"It's a rat, Jake, and rats like damp and airless sewers. Don't forget it's blind. Now, please, put all thoughts of the Bloodrat out of your head."

Jake's sigh was of an agreeable nature. "We ought to get on, Dad. There's such a lot to do."

The same unhappy thought had crossed Oscar's mind, but he had a different solution. "Look, Son, to tell the truth, I've had enough for one day. There's a second tarpaulin in the store. I came across it when I looked for the ladder. We could use it to cover the stuff outside and then go home."

"Should we?"

"I can't see why not. I could add to my note that I'll come back in a few days to bring everything in." He began to rise but froze in a half-standing position as the professor violently twitched in his sleep.

"Leave it alone, Michael. Run for the shelter," blustered the Professor, his eyes closed but his face contorted with torment. "I've cut the big man down but he's not dead. His gun is smoking but he may have another ready for firing. Run, boy, run. The others will return once they realise he's alive." A sustained squeak came from under the blanket. "Man the guns and send them packing if they do!"

"Did the professor just fart?" asked Jake, hardly able to control his merriment.

"Shush, you'll wake him from the nightmare. And the expression is 'blow-off' or 'bottom sneeze', not fart! I bet you wouldn't say fart in front of your mother."

Jake tried hard to hold himself in check as a series of abrupt squeaks followed the first. This woke the professor, who sat up in the chair.

"Incoming shells—gas masks on!" he screamed, his tired eyes only slowly focusing on the visitors. "Are you here to help? Are you armed?"

113

"Only with sausages," laughed Jake. "We brought you food and then cleaned the place. Don't you remember?"

The professor looked around the room. "Is this my room? Doesn't look much like it."

"It was flooded and we had to get rid of the rubbish," said Oscar. "And I'm pleased your hearing is gradually getting back to normal."

"*Rubbish!*" shouted the professor.

"We saved most of your work," added Jake quickly.

"Did you? Yes, jolly good. Are you sure? Of course you did, I remember. I'm Professor Septimus Kneebone and I'm a…a…"

"Genius?" offered Oscar contritely, feeling guilty for waking him.

"Quite right. Glad you think the same." With difficulty, he removed the helmet, exposing his hair which had now turned completely white. "Where are the Christmas presents? Michael will want them when he returns."

"It's time for another reviving hot chocolate," huffed Oscar, walking to the kitchen.

"You were dreaming," said Jake gently, rearranging the blanket.

"Perfectly natural thing to do," replied the professor, poking his ears with his fingertips. He tried to rise, but his body was weak. "Did I talk?"

"You farted rather a lot."

"Ah, that's the mint. Has a terrible effect on my bowels," he said without embarrassment. "Better out than in, as my mother used to say."

"Not from where I was standing," added Jake humorously, strangely surprised to hear the professor ever had a mother in the normal way of things.

"Yes, yes, but enough of that. The thing is, did I talk?"

"You said Michael should leave something alone and run to the shelter."

The professor's expression suddenly hardened to one of deathly sickness. "I said that? How irritating. I clearly need to control my sleep-talking as well as my bowels. I suppose you want an explanation?"

"Not really. Your farting is your concern."

"About Michael, silly!"

"It's really none of my business."

Oscar was heard opening and shutting cupboards and clanking pans.

"Your father won't know how to make good chocolate. You mark my words."

Oscar came back with three mugs, all steaming hot.

"Oh well, here goes," said the professor, taking a sip. "Oh, I was right. Yuk!"

Jake also took a sip. "Double yuk!"

The mugs were put aside.

"So, Professor, what was all that about Michael?" asked Oscar.

"Are you sure Jake's your son? He had the courtesy not to ask."

Oscar was taken aback. "Actually, in all honesty, I can take or leave the bit about Michael, but thinking about yesterday's conversation kept me awake for most of the night. Among other things, I really want to know more about how it is possible to see into the past from inside the shed. You were about to tell us when you turned green."

"Was I?" His eyes glanced towards Jake. "Is that true?"

The boy nodded.

"Then I suppose I should." He paused to think. "Have I said how I send an egg into space?"

Jake replied he had.

"Good, good. Now comes the exciting bit. Once the egg has corrected its course for the return journey towards Earth, remaining sections of the hard skin fold outward to look a bit like a

TV satellite dish. Of course, by now the rocket motor has also guided the egg to the correct position in space to pick up light from the exact spot on Earth I want to examine next. Without doing this, I wouldn't know what I was going to see. It could be anything from a passenger airship flying over the Atlantic to a tank battle in Africa."

"No good to you."

"That's right, Jake. I seek exact science, not pot luck. Interestingly, like a military spy satellite of today, I can command the egg to observe a large area of land or sea, or, if I prefer, pick out individual targets such as a house, a palace, a street or a town. Naturally, I usually decide on a small target, which then allows me to discover the truth about a particular historical event. You'd be amazed how incorrect respected historians have been in their learned books. But, then, they don't have a first-hand glimpse as I do."

"How can you make such precise calculations? It seems impossible, even for you, Professor."

"I don't. I first decide what I want to see and then programme into my equipment the exact date in history when it occurred and the geographic coordinates of the location. I call the equipment my Receptor Box. It stays on the table in the shed. All the hard calculations are then done electronically for me. It isn't as difficult as it sounds, as light from Earth travels at a constant speed through deep space."

"Providing flight calculations to allow the egg to intercept both the exact time and place on Earth you want to see," said Jake. "That's very clever."

"Absolutely right."

"And then?"

"Then, Jake, the dish reflects the images back to the shed as a high-speed compressed beam. The Receptor does the rest."

"What rest?" enquired Oscar.

"As well as making the pre-launch calculations and pre-programming the egg, the Receptor also collects and stores the light images when they arrive back here from space. Hence its name. The images are held in the Receptor's electronic memory, allowing them to be played back any time I choose as a 3-D holographic light show. Of course, first, the images have to be recalibrated to normal speed."

"Recalibrated? What the heck does that mean?"

"That's simple, Mr Trotter. Think of two speeding cars coming towards each other from opposite directions, each travelling at 70 miles per hour. The actual speed they pass is not 70 miles per hour but twice that, 140 miles per hour. With me so far?"

He nodded.

"Excellent! Now, the same happens to the egg in space. As the egg flies back towards Earth, it races through the light coming from Earth in the opposite direction. So, as you can imagine, they pass each other at a truly astonishing speed. Once the reflected images are received back here, the Receptor Box slows the images down to the normal speed of everyday life. I call this process *recalibrating*. Without recalibration, it would be like watching a fast-forwarding film. In fact, it would be so fast the images would be invisible to the naked eye." His mouth twitched with glee. "As you have seen from your glimpse into 18th century naval life, once the process has taken place it is impossible to tell the difference between my images from space and real life... or, rather, as it once was. Equally amazing is that it is even possible to walk around and through the images, seeing them from all directions."

"Without sound, I suppose," said Oscar. "A silent movie."

"Mr Trotter, you really are the most annoying person, with an incredibly short memory. Didn't you hear the sailors talking when you first burst into the shed?"

Oscar blushed.

"Of course you did, but I will answer you all the same. When I first started my experiments, silent images were all I could manage because the light emitted from Earth carries no sound. However, being a genius, I invented another electronic device which I fitted to the top of the Receptor. You have already experienced its marvels."

"You mean the gismo which read my lips and reproduced what I said when I first freed you from the Bubble Car?"

"The very same. It sounded to you like an echo. It's my Lip Reader. Well, there was no point in thinking up a more original name. But you also experienced its real purpose. Amazingly, it can lip-read the images of people seen in the light show, providing lost speech. Regretfully, though, my device has one or two imperfections. The greatest problem is that, for my Lip Reader to work, the people in the images have to be facing the device. The Lip Reader can't detect and reproduce speech without seeing lips move."

"Unbelievable," gasped Jake.

"Yes, it is."

"And the second flaw?" asked Oscar.

"Surely I don't have to tell you."

Oscar twisted towards Jake for help.

"Oh, very well. The Lip Reader cannot distinguish individual voices. Everyone sounds the same. A tiny variation in tone is possible, between men and women mostly, but you need a trained ear to notice even that."

"So, that's why the echo of my voice was in monotone?"

"Quite so, Mr Trotter. You see, the technology used is quite basic. I merely borrowed the idea from others and adapted it for my own experiments."

"I'll be blowed! Maybe, just maybe, you *are* a genius after all," complimented Oscar.

"Oh, Dad, you believe him at last."

"Heaven knows why, but I'm beginning to. Come to think of it, I remember reading about the American Voyager satellite which sent images of planets back to mission control at the speed of light from the farthest edges of our solar system. It took only fifteen hours for NASA to receive them. So, I guess this light travel stuff must be real."

"In that case," said the professor, "as a convert you should come back tomorrow and, if the weather is good and stormy, I'll demonstrate launching the egg."

"But what about me?" jumped Jake. "I have school."

"Can he bunk off?" pleaded the professor.

"Of course not," replied Oscar, leaving no room for debate.

"Then we must wait for next weekend. What do you say?"

Oscar looked at Jake, who nodded enthusiastically. "I have an inset day on Friday. The weekend could start a day early."

"Great. It looks like we're on," said the professor.

Oscar pulled the Professor to one side. "Launching will be safe, won't it? His mother will want him back unharmed and in one piece."

"Oh yes, Mr Trotter, safe as houses."

Oscar stared at the devastation in the room. "As *my* house, anyway."

With that reassurance, Oscar gathered his son and moved towards the door. The professor called after him.

"What about my stuff? It can't be left outside."

"Oh," replied Oscar, sighing heavily. "I suppose not. Come on Jake, we have more work to do after all."

"What can I do?" asked the professor.

"Feed the blinking Bloodrat."

"And count your fingers after," suggested Jake. "The poor thing has become rather worked up."

Chapter 9
Horatio, the Wily Fish

The following Thursday night, Jake could not sleep. Neither could his father many miles away in his own house. Both were lying on their backs listening for signs of a storm which never came. It was 2 o'clock before Jake's eyes finally closed and he drifted off, followed half an hour later by Oscar.

It was the sound of the dawn chorus at daybreak that woke Oscar first. He pulled the duvet over his head, but there was no going back to sleep. Wearily he dressed and drove to the Striker household, where Muriel reluctantly let him in at the early hour.

Oscar's *thump* on the bedroom door was the first noise Jake heard on an otherwise perfect spring morning. He tore back the curtains. Bright light streamed in. Outside, birds sang sweetly in the trees.

"I surprised you're not up, lazybones."

Jake turned over and stared through the window, disappointed at the blue sky. "It's rubbish out there, Dad."

"I know. No point in hoping it will change either. The weather forecast is for sunshine all weekend. I suggest we go fishing instead."

"Should we tell the professor?"

"The weather has done it for us. Come on, Son, get dressed and I'll ask Mum to put eggs on the stove. We must hurry. Mum will want to spend some of the afternoon with you once we tell her we are postponing our plans for a longer outing. She'll show you off to the new neighbours, I expect. I hear they have young children to impress."

"Two girls under four and a pet lizard," he replied sarcastically. "Can't wait."

Jake had fished with his father many times and become quite skilled at the sport. He had even learned how to 'tickle', requiring no rod or net to tease a fish out of the water.

The nearby river was a popular spot for anglers, but, being May, the river fishing season had yet to start. Oscar suggested a trip to the canal, where he knew the very best places to set up. His favourite of all was by a hollow on a gentle bend, where the water ran steadily over large submerged coping stones which had fallen in from the embankment. Here, wild-growing vegetation cast shadows over the water's edge. It was where Horatio could be found, the name Oscar had given to a large wily fish which had made the hollow its home. Many times he had nearly caught Horatio, only to see it wriggle off the end of his line when tantalisingly close to the landing-net, its large eyes almost twinkling with glee as it dropped with a splash to swim away like a phantom under the surface.

Oscar and Jake arrived at the canal to find both banks teaming with anglers, all sitting quietly on stools staring at tiny floats which bobbed up and down when the light breeze caused ripples on the water's surface. A single angler sat by the hollow pouring cold tea from a large flask, his rod on the ground and his keep-net empty.

"Can we join you?" asked Oscar politely.

"You can have it all to yourself," he replied, throwing the flask into a canvas bag. "Been here all night and caught nothing but a cold."

By the time Oscar had assembled his fishing rod and baited the hook with sweet corn, the man had packed his equipment and was ready to leave.

"Best of luck, mate," he said to Oscar. "I think the canal's been fished out." He looked at Jake, who was now laying on his stomach many metres away, his arm in the water. He strolled over. "What are you up to, lad?"

Jake twisted to speak, still running his fingers over and between the stones. "Tickling for Horatio."

"Oh," acknowledged the man, lifting the rod case over his shoulder, "you won't find a fish there."

Jake smiled before turning back, reaching even deeper into the cold canal. His fingertips gently moved along and around the surfaces, trying to distinguish the slimy stones from the cold flesh of a large fish. Then, all of a sudden, he felt movement—the slightest twitch. He froze, his heart pounding as he moved a hand slowly and carefully towards the head, all the time preparing to hook a finger into the fish's gill.

It was then Oscar cast his float. The *plop* as it entered the water sent shock waves in all directions. Jake felt the fish flex its tail as he tried to grab it. But it was too late. The fish rubbed past his fingers and darted away. As Jake lay on the embankment cursing his bad luck the fish jumped, its eyes dark and gleaming. Once again, victory belonged to Horatio.

"Tough tomatoes," came a nearby voice, catching Jake by surprise. A head popped up from behind a ragged bush. It was the professor wearing a hat and swimming goggles, holding what looked like a fishing pole with no line. His hearing had fully returned. "Lovely day for it."

"Gosh, I didn't see you there," replied Jake as he raised himself onto his elbows.

"I know, I know, my green face blends nicely into the foliage. Anyway, a man's shadow on the water scares fish away, so hiding is the best policy all around." He reached into a bag. "Want a cold sausage?"

Jake declined and pointed towards his father, who was fully occupied staring at the joyless float.

"I saw him when he set up. He won't catch anything there. I've already caught everything worth having. What's left is too small to bother with." He pointed to the far side of the canal. "Watch this, Jake."

The professor tapped his fingers on a keypad at the base of the pole. To Jake's amazement, a stream of bubbles suddenly broke the water's surface as a large, grey model boat appeared from nowhere.

"It's a submarine," shouted Jake excitedly. "Is that a remote control aerial you're holding?"

"Of course... is there any other way to fish?" He pressed another button and the submarine turned and motored towards them. Finally breaking cover, the professor stretched down and awkwardly lifted the boat from the water. Behind the model hung a dripping net, full to bursting with fish. "See, I got the lot." He pulled a release string and the fish tumbled from the net and fell harmlessly back into the water. "Fish aren't stupid, Jake. They won't be caught twice in one day." He looked at the water as it settled. "See you next Wednesday?"

"Next Wednesday?"

"I was talking to the fish," said the professor, throwing breadcrumbs into the canal. At once the water boiled with feeding fish, causing hundreds of tiny rings to appear. "Now, that's what I call good sport. No winners and no losers, just a bit of recreational fun."

"I doubt the fish know it's a sport."

"You think so, Jake?"

The professor dipped his fingers into the canal, just enough to wet the tips. Almost at once the shadow of a large fish could be seen circling below the surface. He clicked his fingers and then sank his hand fully into the water, palm upwards. The fish swam over and stopped directly above his hand, allowing the professor to lift it clear.

"It's Horatio," yelled Jake. "Dad, quickly, it's Horatio."

123

"Well, I'll be dashed," is all Oscar could say as he watched the professor effortlessly hold the fish. "Can I take it?"

The fish flexed its tail.

"It says 'no'."

The professor gently lowered the fish back into the water.

"Off you go, old friend," said the professor softly.

Freed, the fish again flexed its tail and swam into the murky depths of the canal.

"Remarkable," said Oscar, staring at the spot where Horatio had disappeared. "One of the most wonderful things I've ever seen."

"Not so remarkable," returned the professor. "It's all about harmony with nature. Remember I told you that before? We all live on the same planet and we share the same resources. There is empathy between animals that humans have forgotten. Creatures, even lowly fish, know when they are in safe company. Let this be a lesson to you both. Respect all that surrounds you in nature, and nature will provide all your needs."

"Here endeth the first lesson."

"An unfortunate sarcasm, Mr Trotter, but not uncommon among city folk bent on making money at any price."

Oscar felt foolish and apologised.

"Think no more of it. See you in a week."

"Will it rain then?" enquired Jake.

"Let's find out, shall we?" The professor again reached into his bag, this time pulling out a large folded balloon, which he inflated using a small capsule of gas no bigger than a thumb. "I'll soon tell you." He let go and the balloon rose skyward, drifting smoothly at first but, then, becoming erratic in the upper current.

"Ah-ha!"

"Ah-ha what?" asked Oscar, his neck straining.

"The air is stirring." He stared at the sky in all directions. "It isn't yet time for a storm, but, believe me, one is coming in a few days. Maybe it will hang fire until next weekend if we're lucky."

"How can you tell?" asked Jake. "Is it magic or a mystic gift learned in India?"

"Actually I listened to the long-term weather forecast on the radio." He smiled with delight.

"Oh!"

The release of the balloon caught the interest of passers-by, who flocked around the professor until they noticed his face and hands. This sent them scurrying with horror. All, that is, except for one fat boy of about nine who held an ice cream in one hand and a burger in the other, and who never let the feelings of others interfere with his own amusement. Having pressed his nose close to the professor's face and stamped on his foot, a broad ketchup and chocolate-coated grin developed across his mouth.

"Look, Mum, I've discovered an alien."

His mother, who was struggling with his bicycle while also manoeuvring a pram, at last caught up. She looked embarrassed, astonished and then scared, in that order. The bicycle fell from her grasp.

"Don't get too near him, Willy darling. The man might be infectious." She smiled sympathetically before pulling the boy away.

"But, Mum, he's green. I've never seen a green man before."

"Then you should look more closely at your father after he's been out on a boat." She pulled him harder. "Come on, Willy dear, do as mummy says."

"But, Mum, he's properly green."

"I know. I saw him. Perhaps he comes from Greenland."

"Are people green in Greenland?"

"I expect they must be."

"Then, I must be from Hungary!"

"All right, Willy darling, you can have a pizza when you finish the burger. Now, hurry along."

The professor turned to Jake as the two wobbled away. "I think it's time to head off home before anyone else sees me.

Maybe I should stay indoors until the green fades. See you soon if the weather is good... I mean bad! Oh, and take my spare key. I can't risk opening the front door to a stranger."

"Bye, Professor," said Jake as the old man left by taking the longer scrub route away from the open path. Jake then turned to his father. "Let's try fishing further up the canal, Dad. We might get lucky there."

By mid-afternoon Muriel was fretting for the return of her favourite son, drumming her fingers on the arm of the settee. Of course, Jake was also her *only* son, but that hardly mattered in her estimation. Jake was better than a whole gaggle of children and certainly less trouble, that is unless his father led him astray.

"Isn't it time we told Mum about the professor?" said Jake as he sat in the car outside his house. "I don't like doing things behind her back."

"Not sure it's wise," replied Oscar. "What would she say?"

Jake thought hard. "She probably wouldn't believe any of it, even if we told her. But what if she did and then stopped me ever going to the professor's cottage? That would ruin everything. We mustn't let it happen."

It was now Oscar's turn to be cunning. "Right, here's the plan. You mustn't tell Mum any lies but, on the other hand, you could avoid saying too much. It's called being economical with the truth. After all's said and done, we've only cleaned an old man's cottage, bought him food and gone fishing. Nothing wrong with that."

The plan seemed a good one and Jake got out.

"Next week, then, Dad?"

"It's a date," said Oscar through the car window.

Muriel was by now standing at the door, waiting to kiss her beloved boy.

"Isn't your father coming in?" she asked as she hugged Jake to within an inch of his life.

"No Mum," he replied, getting his breath back and placing his rod by the stairs. "He has jobs to do."

"Couldn't get rid of you quick enough, I suppose?"

"Hardly, Mum. We've had a great time."

"Doing what exactly with *him*?"

"Oh, this and that… the usual stuff. We did a bit of fishing and larking around. That sort of thing."

"I hope you stayed out of the water, what with your delicate chest."

"My chest isn't delicate in the least and, yes, we stayed dry… well, mostly. Dad wondered if it would be okay if I stayed with him next weekend."

"I suppose so, but only if you win the school Chess Club tournament on Tuesday."

"I'll do my best, Mum."

"That's settled, then. I'll clear a space in the cupboard for the trophy. Pity I bothered to rearrange the shelves after the May fair was cancelled. I should've known it wouldn't be long before my little boy came first in something else."

"For crying out loud, Mum!"

Chapter 10
The Professor's Bigger Secret

Over the next few days—being alone and housebound—the professor had plenty of time to sit, eat sausages and think. Often with his head cupped in his hands and elbows dug into the flesh of his thighs, his thoughts turned dark, for he was not a man used to idleness and it brought on a bad case of the doldrums. He called these dark moments his 'black menace'. Even his 'inside' experiments, which had previously bubbled in glass flasks, had mostly been lost in the flood.

Eating vegetables and fruit had not helped either, as he detested both but had promised Jake to improve his diet by consuming everything provided in the box. And so, with every crunch of celery and swallow of peas, life appeared to be at its lowest ebb.

He brooded long and hard over his long list of troubles, finding it difficult to imagine he had any future to look forward to. Uppermost was the sale of the Bubble Car, which had not gone according to plan. Worse still, he remained bright green, his supply of humbugs was running dangerously low, the Pterodactyl lay in pieces on the scrap heap, and his notes and sketches for a hovering bicycle had only survived the flood in tatters. Even Annie the 38th had died while curled up in a cotton-wool lined matchbox on the mantelpiece. Annie the 39th, still to be trained, had scurried away for hours at a time. Calamitously, without knowing where she was, he had sat on her, forcing another new start with Annie the 40th.

And now, to add to the many other problems, he was pretty certain unknown people were again sniffing around the cottage. He had not heard them since Oscar left, but the hairs on the back of his neck—and Jorvik's clawing—alerted him to their presence. Who they were and what they wanted were questions giving him many sleepless hours. And, as if that wasn't enough to endure, the influence of 'black menace' made him mistakenly believe Oscar had been told far too much about his experiments and was likely to blab to others.

"Blood and guts," cried the professor, imagining the worse. He had even foolishly introduced the name 'Michael' to Oscar, and *that man* was likely to gnaw like a dog on a bone until the painful truth was revealed in its awful entirety.

In his present confused state, the professor was also of no use as a guard to his own property. True, he had locked the shed after Jake and Oscar left, but, apart from the occasional glance through the window, he gave home security little consideration. Indeed, one evening he had even forgotten to release Jorvik from the cupboard, and in the morning thought nothing of the oversight. Anyway, he believed almost everything of value in the cottage had been destroyed in the flood, and what remained could not possibly be of benefit to an outsider.

On another occasion he had retired to bed without checking the window was properly closed, allowing Jorvik to escape and roam free through the garden in the blackness of night. Jorvik had returned bloodied, leaving the professor to wonder whether he had caught a rabbit or even attacked a human.

Then, on Tuesday morning, having woken to the usual dark thoughts, he realised he could no longer stand the affliction. Something had to be done to end 'black menace', and that required willpower to start various positive actions. At least the first was easy, and he felt the beginnings of a smile curling his lips as he threw the last of the hated vegetables into the bin. And, from that small beginning, he became enthused to revisit one of his earlier inventions which he kept in a recess behind a large painting of a rather ugly woman.

The effect of working again was extraordinary, and his spirits quickly soared. Re-mixing the ingredients to strengthen the sticking power of the special glue he had invented as it boiled in an old blackened pot was like a reviving tonic, and quickly he began to feel his old self. There even returned a spring to his step. Little did he know how this work would later help save his life.

With 'black menace' giving way to chemistry, other problems miraculously diminished in importance. He was, as he joyfully told Annie the 40th, firmly back in the saddle. By Wednesday, after managing to glue a chair to the wall for several hours before it fell off, 'black menace' had completely vanished, and with the change came the realisation that Jake and Oscar were not the cause of his troubles but part of the solution. They were not strangers to be shunned, but new friends he could trust. After all, they had helped him in so many ways and not once asked for anything in return except for the hand-over of the Bubble Car, which Oscar had a right to expect.

This simple but belated thought cheered him enormously. For, if there was one thing the professor had learned from the experience, it was that he actually missed the company of others. Annie the 40th and earlier walkabout pet spiders were all very well, and Jorvik was often curled up close by, but they lacked a certain something when it came to meaningful conversation.

He looked around the room and sniffed. A lingering odour of damp still hung in the air, and, yes, much had changed since Oscar and Jake entered his life, but the Christmas tree was back where it belonged and that was like a beacon of hope towards his greatest wish of all, to be reunited with Michael. What was more, the two unopened presents had been carefully salvaged by Jake who, without being asked, had used Archie's gift wrap to cover the old water-stained Christmas paper with something cheerful and new.

Now, they leaned in perfect splendour against the bare tree. It was, without question, the act of a dear friend.

And so Thursday came around. The professor woke very early and looked skyward through the window, but the sun had not yet risen and the glass remained pitch black. Staring at his own reflection, a green face looked back.

"Oh, darn, surely the green should've worn off by now," he said in a weary tone. "And you should stop talking to yourself, Septimus. It's a sign of madness." He shrugged and the reflection shrugged back.

By the glow from the soft flickers of a dying fire, he encouraged Jorvik back into its cupboard and then strolled casually towards the kitchen to cook the last sausage. He was alert for the sound of unwelcome voices now Jorvik was caged, but no longer expected them. The frying pan was crawling with long-legged spiders, which he gently blew away.

And that's when he saw it, causing the pan to drop from his fingers and hit the floor with an almighty clatter.

There, in the middle of the worktop, was a large handprint, deliberately left to be seen. The rest of the worktop was spotlessly clean, just as he had left it the previous evening. Hesitantly he glanced around, but nothing else had been disturbed except for a cupboard door, which was partly open. Beneath lay a bag of flour, split at the top and with some of the contents spilled across the floor.

It seemed in that moment of shock that there was only one plausible explanation. Someone had broken into the cottage while he slept and had wanted him to know it. He quickly turned towards the front door, which was alarmingly hanging ajar. Yet, he remembered, Jorvik had remained inside the cottage. What did it mean? How was that possible?

The thought of an intruder panicked the old man, and for the first time in two days he felt anxiety returning. Nervously, he bent down to have a closer look at the handprint. It was very strange. The print was bold, mysteriously made by the intruder flattening a hand onto the worktop and then sprinkling flour around the palm and fingers to leave a clear outline after the hand was lifted away. The spilled packet pointed to a hurried escape.

"My sainted aunt!" he choked in horror, noticing a detail which rocked him to the core. The index finger of the impression was cut short. This had meaning to the old man. His mind raced back to an accident when Michael was sixteen, when his son had lost a fingertip while poking a stick into the revolving wheel of his upside-down bicycle. He had been sulking after being refused a motorbike.

"My son," he called out as a pitiful cry. "Are you here?"

The desperate plea went unanswered.

Although the possibilities were few, he searched the cottage for potential hiding places.

"Come out, I beg you. Let me see you again after so long. Everything is forgiven, I promise."

The stillness as seconds ticked by was hard to bear, crushing his spirit as expectations turned to despair. And with it returned the 'black menace'.

It was then he remembered giving Oscar a key. That had to be the answer. Angrily, he stomped to the kitchen to find a make-shift weapon.

"It's you in here, isn't it, Oscar Trotter, playing stupid mind games," he shouted caustically, brandishing a pink washing-up brush. "If you think frightening me will persuade me to give you the car, you are very much mistaken. Be warned, I'm holding a deadly weapon and I'm in the mood to use it. Face me at your peril!"

"Um?" finally came a garbled reply.

The professor twisted to confront the trespasser. There in the doorway stood a man with a bunch of car keys held between clenched teeth, silhouetted against the approaching dawn. He held two full bags.

The keys fell from the intruder's mouth as the professor lunged forward, his arm raised high.

"Watch it! What are you going to do, scrub me to death?"

The professor instantly recognised Oscar's voice, which remained so calm that it cowed him into ending the attack.

"It is you," said the old man, his teeth still gritted.

"Of course it's me, unless I'm a ghost."

The professor, whose heart had skipped a beat or two, glanced between the handprint and Oscar, and Oscar and the handprint.

"How long have you been standing there?"

"About ten seconds?" Oscar replied, stepping forward to take the shopping bags to the kitchen. "Thought you might be running short of groceries. Sorry it's incredibly early, but I've got a lot of work on today," he continued, now speaking over his shoulder in the same gentle tone. "I popped into a 24-hour supermarket. I was going to leave the bags outside, but when I saw the door was open I let myself in." He noticed the spilt flour. "Oh, dear. Looks like you've had a bit of an accident. I'll clear it up before I go."

The professor stared as the shopping was put away, never letting his eyes drift from Oscar's back.

"Something wrong?" asked Oscar innocently, sensing he was being watched.

"Got my key?"

"Oh, sorry, no. I left it with Jake for safe keeping."

"Show me your hands."

Now used to the professor's strange ways, Oscar turned and held out both hands without asking why. There were no traces of flour and, of course, every finger was of regular length. "Like to tell me what this is about?"

"I will, once I've eaten. I can't think straight on an empty stomach. Can you spare me a minute or two?"

It took longer than expected for the professor to cook five sausages, place them onto slices of bread and smear generous coatings of sauce, which threw Oscar's plan to leave quickly into disarray. He had already eaten breakfast and now brooded as time ticked by.

Oscar had arranged for a pick-up lorry to meet him in Somerset, where an old Jaguar XJS sports car had been left to rust and rot over many years in a disused car lot. The owner had agreed to a derisory £200 to take it away and Oscar didn't want to jeopardise the deal. As the cost of hiring the lorry was greater than the worth of the car, Oscar was determined to get there on schedule. Nevertheless, he graciously took a hotdog and nibbled the end while the professor explained the discovery of the handprint and the significance of the short index finger.

The story visibly alarmed Oscar. He had convinced himself the professor could be relied upon to arrange for the door handle and lock to be fixed. And, as if to underline this belief, the old man had even given him a spare key to the door. It hadn't occurred to him the professor would forget the lock needed urgent attention. Now he felt ashamed for not having taken charge of the repairs himself, causing this major lax in security.

"I'm surprised Jorvik didn't take a bite out of whoever it was," remarked Oscar as an afterthought. "Didn't it growl either?"

"No, and that's surprising. Still, I'm much more interested in the print than what Jorvik did or failed to do as a guard animal."

"I suppose," said Oscar, walking to the kitchen for another look, where he furtively dropped the unwanted hotdog into a rubbish bag. "It's definitely the hand of an adult male. Do you want it left as evidence?"

The professor shrugged.

"Very puzzling," added Oscar, holding a brush. "Why Michael, or anyone else for that matter, would deliberately leave a calling card but not want to be seen doing it is a proper riddle. Still, first things first, we must get the door handle and lock properly repaired or replaced. We don't want anyone else strolling in uninvited. Will you be here if I send a locksmith over this afternoon?"

The professor gave him a very green look.

"Oh, yes, quite. You'll not be going anywhere looking like that. But how do I explain your colour to a locksmith? We don't want him frightened away before he does the job."

"You'll think of a plausible excuse, I'm sure. After all, you are a car salesman."

Oscar said goodbye and hurried off, hoping the weather would be right for meeting up the next day. "Oh, and don't forget to let Jorvik out tonight once the handle is fixed."

Soon the glue pot was brought back to the boil.

Back at the Striker household, the week had not gone at all well. Muriel was furious with the headmaster at Jake's school for not allowing him to miss a double lesson of numeracy before the chess tournament, a decision which she thought had robbed her son of a proper chance to practise. In Muriel's opinion, this and this alone was why Jake had won only a bronze medal. The fact that Jake was very happy with bronze had nothing to do with it. It merely showed Jake possessed 'outstanding tolerance', another praiseworthy quality.

Jake had not known what was written in the letter Muriel had asked him to give to his form teacher the following morning. Consequently, he had been surprised by the frosty looks he received from staff as he walked between classrooms. Still, by the afternoon the looks had become fewer and, once home, Jake could only chuckle to himself as his mother had rearranged the trophy cabinet to push the bronze medal to the very back—a 'travesty' among so much gold and silver.

But there was another cloud looming over the horizon which could spoil Jake's chances of seeing his father at the weekend, and it had nothing to do with the weather.

Two days after the tournament, while still angry at Muriel's letter, the headmaster had singled Jake out to stand patrol at the entrance to the school toilets. Someone had been stuffing paper down the pans to block them, and the headmaster wanted a scapegoat. It was a duty Jake wished someone else had been given. It was not that he minded missing Art, but he hated becoming the laughing stock of the class bullies. He quickly earned the nickname Pee-Man Jake, and suddenly all the other boys except Archie begun pretending his clothes smelled of dirty toilets. If they were not sniffing around him with disgust, like flies around a dustbin, they avoided him altogether.

For sticking by Jake, Archie too was given a nickname— Stinky Smithers. But Jake and Archie were not like the bullies and knew the troublemakers were themselves cowardly. Together, Jake and Archie laughed off the names with complete indifference, and soon other children who had been picked on in the past began to see the bullies for what they were. One by one, the children rallied around Jake and Archie until the playground became quite empty of games.

Seeing his power diminish, Pip Taylor, the largest of the bullies, kicked a ball as hard as he could at Jake. It struck him on the shoulder, rebounded and shattered a toilet window, covering the inside with tiny shards of glass.

Hearing the glass break, the headmaster rushed out of school and pounded across the playground. He was furious.

"Who is responsible for this outrage?" he bawled, pushing his way to the centre of the crowd.

"It was Jake Striker," pointed Pip Taylor spitefully, as the other children stepped back.

The headmaster towered over Jake. "Well, Master Striker, what have you to say for yourself?"

Jake stared up in disbelief. "I'm sorry, sir, but…"

The headmaster took his part-apology as an immediate admission of guilt, although Jake had wanted to add: "but… it really wasn't my fault." At once the headmaster blew the whistle to signal the end of break, commanding Jake to stay behind while all the other girls and boys lined up and paraded inside.

"I shall be telephoning your parents, Jake Striker. I will not tolerate vandalism in school, especially from you."

By now Jake's form teacher had arrived on the scene. She stood at Jake's side, a hand resting reassuringly on his shoulder. "He lives with his mother, Headmaster."

"Then I shall call her in to explain her son's dreadful behaviour."

That was a big, big mistake.

Having received the call, Muriel thundered into the school, ready to do battle. She knocked on the headmaster's door, fairly politely at first, but, when no voice told her to *enter*, she burst in anyway. The headmaster looked up from his desk.

"And you are?"

"I am Muriel Striker, mother of the chess tournament *bronze* medal winner!"

The headmaster blushed red. "Oh!"

"Oh indeed," she boomed, plonking herself on the chair opposite. "I wanted a word with you anyway about my letter."

By the time she left, not only had her son been vindicated of vandalism, Jake had been promised a re-run of the chess tournament.

"That isn't fair," pleaded Jake, when his mother gave him the good news. "I lost because the other two players were better than me. I won't play again to fiddle the results."

Muriel was amazed. "Surely, Jake, the other two can't be better than you? Were you being bullied to lose?"

He wondered how to answer. "The school doesn't tolerate bullying, Mum. No, I won't play because I was beaten fair and square. I came in third and that's that."

Muriel said no more, but stormed off to prepare Jake's tea. The telephone rang. It was his father.

"All ready for tomorrow, Son?"

"I'm not sure, Dad," was his honest reply.

"Has the second inset day been cancelled?"

"No, the school's still off."

"Having second thoughts, then?"

"No, Dad, not at all. I've been looking forward to it. No, it's Mum."

"Oh dear, what's the old dragon been saying this time?"

"I came third in the chess tournament."

"Excellent," he said brightly. "Well done, my boy."

"Mum isn't as pleased as you, Dad."

"Oh, now I'm beginning to get the picture. Third wasn't good enough?"

"It was for me, Dad, but I've disappointed Mum."

"Let me have a quick word with her."

Jake placed the telephone receiver on the window-sill. "Dad wants a chat."

"What does *he* want?" she asked as she took the receiver, knowing he could overhear.

By the time the long call ended the potatoes on the cooker were boiling over, with water spitting and spluttering on the hot ring. Jake was sure this would make her mood even worse. But how wrong he was. She smiled as Jake quietly closed to her side, his hands clasped behind his back.

"I have to apologise, Jake. I've acted rather foolishly and it took *him* to make me realise. Coming third might not be what I expected, but it's still a fine result. So, your father and I have come to a decision. I'll be baking you a special celebration cake tonight and you can take it to your father's tomorrow. What do you think about that?"

Jake's smile was the biggest ever. "That's great, Mum. Can I stay with Dad all of Saturday and Sunday too?"

"Of course you can. You deserve it. And while I think of it, I'll be moving the bronze medal to the front of the cabinet."

"No need to do that," replied Jake shyly. "I rather like the gold and silver more."

Chapter 11
Kidnapped

The journey to the professor's cottage began slowly, but soon the crawl through the Friday traffic in the centre of town became a distant memory as the open spaces of the countryside came into view. It was like a breath of fresh air, the overnight damp making the grass smell particularly fresh. Above, the sky was overcast, just as the professor predicted, but as yet there was no sign of a storm brewing.

"Rubbish weather again, Dad," remarked Jake as he peered up through the windscreen.

"I know. I can't believe how much we hope for thunder and lightning these days."

"What do you think the professor will show us?"

"No point in second-guessing, Jake. Oh, and talking of the professor, something happened yesterday I should tell you about."

Oscar explained the handprint.

"Michael had the end of a finger chopped off?" squirmed Jake, horrified at the thought.

"In a freak accident."

"Is that why the professor left the bike by the bed?"

"I suppose so—didn't want to touch it. If it was me, I would've got rid of it straight away."

"You believe his interpretation of the handprint?"

"Not altogether. It's true there had been an intruder, but I doubt it had anything to do with his son. Wishful thinking on his part. It's just as likely the flour was spilled by accident when the intruder riffled through the cupboards and found nothing worth taking."

"Where's Michael now? Did the professor say anything?"

"I think he might've, if I hadn't been so preoccupied with the front door lock and getting away to Somerset. I could kick myself for not listening properly."

But Oscar need not have worried. As the car pulled into the drive, the professor was already waiting anxiously outside. He was now only partially green—sort of camouflaged—and jumped from one foot to the other to keep warm. He was in a most agitated state.

"Whatever's up this time?" called Oscar as he hurried from the car, noticing tears running down the professor's cheeks.

"It's Michael. I was right. He is here, and yet he isn't. Help me please, I beg you!"

After checking Jorvik was safely locked in the cupboard, Oscar led the professor back into the cottage, holding him by the shoulders to stop him shaking. The professor was dripping wet and shuffled forward as if he had aged ten years overnight. He stood, hunched and withered.

Jake, who had followed them in, pulled the newly repaired door shut and made for the kitchen. Several uncooked sausages remained on the draining board. He sniffed them. The cold room had kept them unexpectedly fresh.

"Fancy a bite of breakfast?" he called, hoping to cheer the professor.

The old man shook his head. "Not for me, dear boy. I couldn't eat a thing?"

Oscar, who had left the professor's side to find him a warm coat, was dismayed. "How about a nice mug of hot chocolate? Now, I know you would enjoy that."

"With a nice big slice of Mum's special celebration cake?" suggested Jake. "I've left it in the car, but it won't take a sec' to get it."

"No thanks to both."

"Humbugs perhaps?"

"Not even a humbug," came the sorry reply.

Jake returned the frying pan to the cupboard. The atmosphere was dismal, with none of the fantasy and expectations he envisaged.

"Look on the bright side, Professor," said Oscar through a half-smile as he held the coat open. "Whatever else is wrong, at least your stuttering hasn't returned. That must be some kind of record."

"It will return, and at the most inconvenient time," lamented the professor as he pushed his arms into the sleeves.

Oscar waited patiently as the old man pulled the coat tightly across his chest and then sat. He looked drained and panicky, but his lips wouldn't speak the words that troubled him.

Oscar sat opposite, encouraging him to talk. But when he didn't, Oscar stoked the fire and then fetched a rather large glass of rum with only a tiny splash of water. This was received with gratitude, more so when another followed the first.

"You mentioned Michael," said Oscar gently to break the deadlock, finally taking away the empty glass. "Does that mean you have news?"

The professor nodded.

Oscar's jaw dropped. "Will you tell me?" he asked eagerly.

The old man's look remained plaintive, full of fear and sorrow. "I desperately need your help, Mr Trotter. I'm in such trouble." He reached across to take Oscar's hand, which he held in a tight grip. "Can you help me? Both of you, I mean," he added, glancing grim-faced between father and son.

"We will if we can," assured Jake, much to his father's approval. "But how, and by doing what?"

The professor stood, dropping his arms to let the coat fall to the floor. He bent down, and with much effort lifted the trap door.

Oscar's eyes widened. "Goodness gracious, the hole is full of water!"

"In there, believe it or not, is where I spent last night."

"There? Standing up to your waist in wet?"

He nodded.

"Little wonder you're so miserable."

"Freezing cold," replied the professor. "It must've filled during the flood, and wasn't emptied during the tidy up. I hadn't thought of that possibility before I jumped in. You can imagine my surprise. I couldn't breathe at first. The shock nearly caused my heart to stop."

Oscar took the handle from the professor's thin fingers and lowered the trap door until it closed with a soft thud. "What on earth was so awful that you were willing to spend hours down there?"

The professor's terrified expression was almost an answer in itself. "There's something very bad going on here."

"Meaning?" enquired Jake attentively, a cold shiver running down his spine.

"It was about eleven o'clock last night. I had worked all afternoon in the shed preparing the Starlight Machine for your visit when I heard a rustling noise outside. I looked around, but all I could see was a fox sniffing between the dustbins. A dustbin lid lay on the ground, so I assumed the fox had knocked it off. Anyway, I went indoors to make supper and let Jorvik out, after which I fell asleep."

"Then you heard the noise again?" suggested Oscar impatiently, trying to move the story along.

"No, Jorvik did. He woke me with his snarling. So I looked, and right enough I saw a crouched man running between the trees and the shed. I think another man remained hidden among the shrubs. That's when I decided to hide in the underground hole."

143

"Gosh! But are you absolutely certain? It must've been very dark outside."

"I wouldn't have jumped in the hole and stayed there if I wasn't, Mr Trotter," returned the professor sharply. "You see, I've seen the crouching man once or twice before."

"What! You never mentioned it."

"No. Well, I had my reasons."

"Why didn't you get the police and have them arrested for trespass?"

"Would you have your own son arrested, especially if he had been missing for years and years?"

"MICHAEL?" exclaimed Jake and Oscar in unison.

"My lost boy. I thought of calling out his name, to see how he reacted, but then realised the other man made it dangerous for both of us."

"Wait," cried Oscar, unsure where the conversation was heading. "I don't understand any of what you're saying. Please help me out. For starters, how long has it been since you last saw Michael, close up I mean?"

"He vanished decades ago. He was a teenager, big for his age and very independent in his actions, but still only 16."

"On December 21st," exclaimed Jake, pointing to the calendar.

"Yes, in 1983."

"1983? That would make Michael only fifteen years younger than Dad is now. Dad's a bit of an oldie to have a child of 13."

"I am not!" exclaimed Oscar. "Thousands of Dads my age have young children, and many are a lot older too I might add."

Jake laughed. "It's okay. You act and play like a five-year-old. Nobody cares, and my friends really like you."

But the diversion had no effect on the professor's mood.

"Michael is not a boy," he emphasised. "I don't even know if I would recognise him any longer. In my head he remains 16, but my gut tells me it was him."

Oscar turned towards the Christmas tree. "Are you telling us those presents are from Christmas 1983?"

"A Transformer and a Mattel Intellivision electronic game for Michael, still in their boxes. Anyway, I told you, I now think the man I've seen skulking around the garden in the past, and again last night, could be him! It finally fits."

"I'm bewildered," admitted Oscar, forcing the professor to put the coat back on. "You've never seen the man in the garden clearly and you've not seen Michael since he was a child, yet now you're sure they're one of the same person."

The professor rolled his eyes. "Oh, do keep up, Mr Trotter! The handprint I showed you. Nobody else could've left it. It was a sign, a warning only I would understand."

"Like a secret agent's message?" jumped in Jake.

"Kind of. I believe he's trying to let me know he's alive and close by, but can't make direct contact because of the terrible trouble he's got himself into. Maybe I'm in danger too."

"What terrible trouble? Running away from home is serious, but something only you and Michael can resolve as father and son. It's nobody else's business," said Oscar. "So why wouldn't he show himself?"

"There's more to it than that. I'm sure it has something to do with the Starlight Machine and the knowledge it provides."

"There are simpler ways to communicate than leaving handprints, even if he's too ashamed or concerned to face you man to man. A letter, for instance. That's what I would do. None of this skulduggery nonsense."

"Not if he's being held hostage."

"*Hostage*! Where on earth did that idea come from?"

"It's a terrible thing, but I've often had to face the fact that my dear boy could be dead. But, joy upon joy, the handprint tells me he isn't, although sadly it probably comes as a warning of danger, not reconciliation. So now I can properly ask myself the question—why hasn't he ever come home?"

145

"And from that you make the wild assumption he was taken hostage and remains so years later. I'm sorry, Professor, but at the risk of upsetting you I have to say the idea is absurd."

"It's a possibility."

"Show me the ransom note asking for money in exchange for his release?"

"There hasn't ever been one."

"In that case, he's definitely not a hostage. Anyway, if you saw him, he can't be tied up or confined to a locked room."

"He still could be a hostage, if his captors want something only he can provide or do."

"Such as?"

"Operate the Starlight Machine in secret, or provide the knowledge of how it works, for the benefit of the gang."

"Can the Machine make money?"

"Not in the way you're thinking, Mr Trotter. It's not a jackpot fruit machine or a printing press for bank notes. But, if used deviously, it could be the source of enormous wealth."

Oscar's ears pricked up.

"Consider this," he continued. "If images from space showed where pirates had buried treasure in the past or where money was stashed from a bank robbery, why, there would be a fortune waiting to be dug up. The criminals would only have to locate the site using the Starlight Machine and bingo, the cash rolls in. The possibilities are boundless."

Oscar's mind raced at the prospect. "Why couldn't *we*... I mean *you*... do that? It would be like winning the lottery. Just think what you could do with the money."

The professor shook his head. "I thought you knew me better. I thirst for knowledge, not to become drunk on wealth."

Oscar knew this was true, but he was different. "It occurs to me," he followed, "that if the criminals and Michael have used the Machine for that purpose, they would need to do it in secrecy to avoid police involvement in the recovery of stolen goods."

146

"That's what I just said."

"Has the Machine ever been used without your knowledge? There must be ways of knowing."

"I don't know, Mr Trotter," was his unexpected reply. "Michael used it by himself once when he was 16. That much is certain. After that, well, maybe."

"But surely you can tell," challenged Oscar. "For a start, space eggs would be missing."

"Not even then, I'm afraid. I can be awfully forgetful where I put them. I have mislaid several eggs over the years."

"Oh, come now, Professor," continued Oscar harshly, "be consistent with your reasoning. If, for the sake of argument, we accept the notion of a criminal gang, we also have to face the fact that the space eggs were stolen and not mislaid."

"It's highly possible."

"What's more, no hostage is ever left to walk about by themselves. Which means, like it or not, Michael is helping them willingly."

"That, I won't accept. Without some freedom of action, Mr Trotter, how could Michael operate the Machine for his captors? No, I reckon they keep him under constant surveillance while he does their bidding."

"Which would explain why you saw two men outside. One Michael and the other his guard," said Jake.

"Held hostage all his adult life? Implausible," cried Oscar. "Blessed hard to believe."

"Nothing is impossible," pressed the professor. "Think about it. It would be the perfect crime, without a known victim or any chance of discovery. And now they've come back for another go."

"You're forgetting one thing," offered Jake. "Dad took away the only usable space egg."

"The criminals wouldn't know that, and nor would Michael," he replied.

Oscar struggled to accept the chain of events. "So you're suggesting Michael broke into the cottage because he was ordered to search for the egg, but instead he risked everything to alert you of his presence?"

"Perhaps things are changing within the gang, causing my personal safety to be at risk."

"Was Jorvik out of the cupboard on Wednesday night?"

"Yes."

"Then why didn't it bite the intruder?"

"I wondered about that too, and I think I have an answer. Being blind, Jorvik does everything by the sense of smell. Michael is my flesh and blood. Our scents could be similar. It's another proof of Michael's presence."

Oscar was far from convinced and said so.

"I know, I know," continued the professor, "it does seem a long shot. But, just because we don't have all the answers, it doesn't mean it's not true. A handprint doesn't make itself. And Michael's handprint is unique, like an autograph."

"Even if you're right," said Oscar, "where would the criminals stay unobserved while hanging around for the right time to use the Machine? They could hardly check into a hotel with a hostage. And yet, they would need to remain fairly close by in case a storm brewed up."

"I've been thinking about that too," said the professor. "As they would also need to travel unobserved all over the country to dig up their fortunes, they might use a caravan as a mobile base."

"We passed one this morning, Dad, in the lay-by just up the road," added Jake excitedly.

"A clapped-out old white and blue thing, with green algae on the roof?" asked the professor.

Jake nodded.

"Oh, don't worry about that. It's been there on and off for donkey's years. Someone's holiday home, I expect."

"Parked up in a public lay-by?" said Oscar. "I don't think so."

"We could check it out," suggested Jake bravely.

"Let's not get ahead of ourselves, Son. Leastways, we should re-examine the evidence before spying on someone's private property."

The professor walked away, returning with a box-file. After a quick search, he handed a photograph to Oscar. "That was Michael at 15. I hardly ever look at it now. It causes me sorrow to remember how things were."

"A fine lad," remarked Oscar kindly, "but it hardly helps us."

"I suppose not. I just thought if you saw it you would understand why a foolish old man would never give up on his son. What father would? Only, I'm now too old to carry on much longer. That's why I wanted to use the last remaining egg. It was to be my final attempt to discover what happened to Michael on the day he disappeared, before I sell the Bubble Car."

"That's it!" exclaimed Oscar, leaping to his feet. "Stupid of me not to think of it before." He gave the photograph back. "I'm not saying I believe any of this hostage mumbo-jumbo, but, for the sake of argument, what if your advert to sell the Bubble Car was seen by the bad guys? If they did, they would realise they had only one chance left to use the Starlight Machine for their own profit, and it would have to be soon. Afterwards, they would need to destroy all evidence that implicates them."

"But, Dad, they could've bought the car themselves if they wanted it," returned Jake. "After all, you said it was cheap."

"Did I?" grumbled Oscar under his breath.

"Cheap?" scolded the professor. "Should I have asked for more? I only paid £100 for the car second-hand in 1963. Has it gained value?"

"It's a wreck, Professor. A lot of cash is needed to restore it. Now, can we get on," snapped Oscar, embarrassed by the amazingly good deal. "A car is only worth the money someone is willing to pay for it. Did you get other offers?"

"None," replied the professor.

"Well, there we are then."

"But why didn't they buy it?" niggled Jake, wanting an answer.

"I think that's pretty obvious, Son. We all know the Machine doesn't work without the aerial, an egg, and other equipment in the shed. The car alone is of no use whatsoever." His eyes scanned the room. "Talking of which, where is our egg?"

"*My* egg, Mr Trotter, is safely hidden from everyone."

"Which puts us in grave danger. The criminals, if they exist, might stop at nothing to get their hands on it. Ransack the place or even rough us up to talk. Perhaps that's why Michael took such a gamble to warn you. Quick, secure the door and windows."

"Why keep it at all?" said Jake nervously as he lunged for the door handle. The sharp click as the key turned in the lock and the rattle of a bolt being slipped into place heightened the atmosphere of threat. "We could destroy the egg and throw the pieces outside. That would stop them from bothering us. Without an egg to find, surely they would go away."

"I can't destroy the only egg I have," protested the professor. "Don't ask me to."

"No, Jake's right. It could be a way out of this mess."

Frightened as he was, the old man stood his ground. "I kept it for one final mission into space. It's been my work over the last decade to discover what happened on 21st December 1983. I can't risk not ever knowing, especially as we have no firm evidence Michael is here or the gangsters exist."

"You've changed your tune," said Oscar in astonishment.

"Adapted to a changing situation."

Oscar sensed there was nothing to be gained from arguing. "Very well, but if things get dangerous we must reconsider the possibility. I won't put Jake's life in the firing-line. I shall be judge and jury in deciding. Is that understood?"

"As a last resort," conceded the professor. "I'll agree to that." He grabbed the pink washing-up brush. "Until we think otherwise, I'll defend the egg using all means at my disposal."

Preparing a defence like a ninja assassin, but brandishing a weapon no deadlier than candyfloss, was not quite what Oscar had in mind, but he let it go for the sake of unity.

"Can you remember anything about that day in 1983?" asked Oscar to quell the professor's belligerence.

"Not much," he answered, tucking the brush into his waistband. "I'd taken a train to London to buy exciting new microcomputer chips to replace the printed circuit boards and integrated-circuit microchips I used in my electronic equipment, returning home late in the pouring rain to find the Machine had been used in my absence. I knew this because the aerial was raised and the only completed egg had gone from its box. I was younger then and less forgetful, so I knew with certainty it had vanished. What's more, the Receptor was red hot, although switched off. Only Michael could have launched an egg. That was when I received the first lightning strike to my head."

"But why have you waited until now to look back at 1983?" asked Jake. "It seems such an obvious thing to do."

"Of course I've tried before, but not during the first two decades of Michael's disappearance, as strange as that might seem. My only excuse is that for a very long time I remained utterly convinced Michael would come home of his own free will. So, I immersed myself in experiments and the years just flew by. Of course, he was in my thoughts, but I imagined him to be a happy-go-lucky sailor travelling the world, always in some exotic far off place and out of contact. That gave me a great deal of comfort. Only after celebrating his 35th birthday—by myself—did it finally hit home that he was never coming back and that I was alone in the world. As I said, I couldn't even be sure he was still alive. So, belatedly, I decided to find out what he had been up to on the day he left, and, of course, I had the perfect means of doing so."

"But you didn't manage it. What went wrong?"

"For a long time I couldn't understand why nothing seemed to work anymore. I had launched plenty of eggs perfectly successfully for my historic researches, but now each time I planned a mission to 1983 something went amiss or, just as stupidly, I mislaid the prepared egg and had to spend months constructing a replacement. However, it now seems likely some eggs were not mislaid but stolen by Michael and the gangsters."

"How about the eggs you managed to launch? What happened to those?"

"Oh, don't remind me. Mission failure was caused by a simple oversight on my part. Such a waste of thoroughly good lightning too. You see, in my eagerness, I didn't appreciate the computer memory in the Receptor Box was already heavily overloaded with old stuff. There wasn't enough memory capacity left to hold the new images beamed from space, and so none was stored. I really can't imagine why it took me until recently to realise such a fundamental oversight, but there it is."

"Overloading the memory. We've all done it on our computers."

"I suppose. In my defence, although I upgraded the computing capacity of the Receptor in the 1980s, the memory is severely limited by modern standards. I could kick myself for taking so long to realise. Last month I reluctantly cleared a lot of the old images from the memory to make room for one final launch before the Bubble Car is sold."

"So you never found out what Michael was doing on the day he disappeared?"

"No, Jake. But it must have been something significant to give him the confidence to leave home."

"To seek his fortune?"

"Or sell his discovery to someone who would pay good money for the information?" suggested Oscar.

"That, Mr Trotter, is my greatest nightmare. He had been pestering me endlessly for the cash to buy a motorbike. We often argued over it. Still, I can't believe Michael would deliberately hurt me by telling outsiders about the Starlight Machine. No, I have to conclude he only wanted to raise a bit of money and then come home, but it all got way out of hand when he approached the wrong people."

"This makes some sense," said Oscar thoughtfully, strolling around the room. "If he really did discover something big, and saw it as a way to fund a motorbike, he probably would've been blind to the danger of approaching complete strangers with the information. Perhaps, at last, the bits of the puzzle are coming together."

"I wish I'd bought him the wretched thing. But I thought if I completed my experiments for a hovering bicycle, he would forget all about the motorbike and enjoy something unique." He lowered his head. "I neglected his needs because of my thirst for knowledge. The world is topsy-turvy. Old people have most money when they don't need it, whereas young people need money when they haven't got any. Someone once said youth is wasted on the young. It's not true. Wisdom is wasted on the old."

Oscar waited patiently for the professor to finish his reminiscences before interrupting.

"Recapping, you think Michael's first secret use of the Starlight Machine might've been for nothing more than to fund the purchase of a motorbike, but this may have led him into unknown danger."

"It's plausible," acceded the professor. "And knowing Michael had the power to discover other great riches, why would criminals then let him go after gathering the fruits from one mission when by holding him they had a never-ending source of renewable wealth."

"That has to be it! It explains why the eggs were stolen and not mislaid as you first thought, and why you occasionally saw the caravan in the lay-by and people in the garden," cried Oscar. "As a hypothesis, it works. Now we must…"

"Stop," called the professor brightly. "It's even better than that. Just think. If the Starlight Machine was used without my knowledge, it would explain why the memory in my Receptor Box became unexpectedly full. It wasn't me overloading it, but them."

"Oh dear!"

"What now, Dad?"

"I can see a problem with that reasoning," said Oscar timidly, not wanting to put a spanner in the works but having no choice. "Other than recently, did you ever delete old images from the memory, Professor?"

"I had no reason to. I wanted to keep everything as proof of my work and discoveries."

"Then tell me how Michael found memory capacity in recent years when you couldn't?"

"Oh, Dad, that's easy to answer," said Jake intelligently. "The gang wouldn't want to leave any clues behind to incriminate them. So, once a job was over and the treasure found, they were bound to eventually wipe the images from the Receptor before starting another caper. That alone provided space. Without realising, they probably used and reused the last bit of the Receptor's memory, leaving nothing for the professor."

"Which means the handprint *is* Michael's. There's too much evidence to think otherwise. It's marvellous, simply marvellous!" The professor leapt about the room, waving his arms and leaping from foot to foot. "*Yippee-doodle-dandy*! The Great Professor Kneebone does it again."

"Does what?" asked Oscar, astounded by the old man's foolishness.

"Don't you see? We don't need to wait for lightning or use the egg. In fact, I can agree to the egg being destroyed. If Michael and the gang are nearby, as I suspect they are, we can mount a rescue mission to free him. On the other hand, if the gang is elsewhere, all we need do is turn the Receptor Box on and, with any luck, it will show us Michael's latest escapade. Somewhere in the images will be the all-important clues as to what they're up to and where they are."

"Unless they have already wiped it from the memory to stop the police finding out what they've done," suggested Oscar. "After all, we think they want another egg to launch, which indicates a new project."

"No! What you previously said was right," contradicted the professor. "I too think it was my advert to sell the Bubble Car that has brought them back here earlier than they wanted. Things are definitely looking up."

"Oh blimey!" exclaimed Oscar darkly as another thought popped into his head, and at once all colour drained from his face.

The professor froze in mid-dance. "What now?"

For a brief time Oscar said nothing, as he considered how to deliver the bad news. "You just said *you* recently wiped the memory. Don't you understand the implication of that? *You've* probably, but accidentally, erased the gang's images along with your own, and any clues they held. We are back to square one."

The professor slumped, and if there had not been a chair at hand it is probable he would have ended on the floor. One thing was certain, the revelation had flushed the rum from his body to leave him stone cold sober.

"Oh, no! It appears I'm no genius after all, but a foolish old fossil."

Jake looked between the dazed adults. "I can't believe you two, and how easily you give up." He turned to the professor. "How did you go about clearing the Receptor's memory?"

The old man raised his stare. "I started by deleting the oldest stuff first and working my way forward. I sacrificed the dinosaurs and a lot more for Michael. My evidence of many wonders has vanished forever."

"Pity we didn't know you before," said Oscar glumly. "Jake could've introduced you to the wonders of a Flash Drive."

"Oh, buck up you two. I've never known such a pair of whingers and windbags. For goodness sake, don't you realise what I'm getting at?" He waited, but neither spoke. "Professor, you said you cleared a lot of the old images." The professor nodded. "That isn't the same as saying you cleared the lot. Well, which is it?"

"A lot, but not all."

"That's wonderful! Can't you see why? The old stuff *has* gone, but the most recent definitely hasn't."

"You know that?" said Oscar shortly.

"We all do, Dad, because we've seen part of the images ourselves."

"By George, Jake's right," sprang the professor, suddenly leaping like a frog. "Come to think of it, I don't remember ever researching 18th century naval life. It merely appeared around me while trapped in the Bubble Car."

Oscar vigorously shook the professor's hand. "All might still be well. And what's more, the fact that the images have not been erased by the gang suggests they haven't yet managed to extract sufficient information from them to get their sticky little hands on any valuables of the period. That's really great news for me… I mean us, all of us. And if the gang is panicking to launch a new egg before the car is sold, I'm sure we can cook up quite a surprise. They'll not get their hands on the professor's egg. The hunt is back on! To the shed. Come on, Professor."

"I'm right behind you, but there's something I must do first." He marched towards Jorvik's cupboard.

"What are you doing?" shouted Oscar, grabbing the professor's hand before he had time to open the door. "Don't let the rat-thing loose while we're here."

"But it's where I normally keep the insulating box for the egg. Getting past Jorvik wouldn't be easy. It's the perfect hiding place.

Anyway, as we don't need it, I'm going to bust the wretched egg with a hammer. Now, let go of me, Mr Trotter."

"No," screamed Jake, "we may still want it."

"Jake's right again," cautioned Oscar, glad there was another good reason for not releasing the Bloodrat. "We must stop being so gung-ho and think before we act. It's what you told me to do. Remember? What we need is a proper plan, none of this rushing around stuff. Who knows what dangers might be facing us? Let's do it properly from now on. But, where to begin?"

"Sausages," suggested Jake brightly.

"The boy's a genius, the little captain of our enterprise," agreed the professor. "We should plan our next move over a delicious meal. Lead the way to the kitchen, Captain Jake."

Chapter 12
Lost Images from Space

The afternoon temperature suddenly and unexpectedly plummeted, becoming the coldest of any day in May Oscar could·remember. The sky, which had been pale grey, was now brewing darker, while the trees suddenly appeared to lose their lustre. It was a depth of cold that pierced to the marrow and threw spring back to winter.

"This is more like it," said Jake with glee, staring out the window. "I think the weather's turning properly rotten at last."

Gathering around the fire, the three talked while tucking into hot sausages that had been sizzling in the pan just moments before. Each bite was too hot to chew until it cooled between clenched teeth, yet as soon as one piece was swallowed so another irresistibly followed, such was the succulent flavour of the meat and its warming effect on their spirits. Even Jorvik enjoyed a sausage pushed through the grill.

"Wouldn't want to be skulking around the garden," remarked Oscar absentmindedly.

"Hope Michael isn't out there," replied the professor, rubbing his eyes. "He never did like wearing a vest."

Jake put his plate on the floor and dealt the professor the last sausage from the pan. "Don't worry, we'll find him. But even if we don't, you mustn't think the worst. There's a strong chance we've got everything wrong. He could be sunning himself in the

Bahamas for all we know. He might even have children of his own."

"I'm a Granddad? Wow!" cheered the professor.

"Calm down. Jake didn't say that. He merely meant we've made an awful lot of assumptions from very few facts. We could be right, but equally, we could be horribly wrong. It remains to be discovered. And we will. But we must show patience. Take it one step at a time. Do you have anything to add, Professor, that doesn't include disembowelling the intruders with a washing-up brush?"

"It was jolly painful," remarked the old man, while looking contentedly at his green hands which were becoming lighter by the hour.

"What was?" asked Oscar.

"Erasing years of work. I had unlocked so many of history's enduring mysteries."

"Such as?"

"Oh, little trifles like discovering what caused King Henry VIII's *Mary Rose* warship to sink in Tudor times, the identity of the murderous *Jack the Ripper*, and whether unicorns and dragons existed. These were among my wondrous discoveries."

"Sick!" gulped Jake. "Unicorns and dragons. Did they?"

"Dragons did, but they were not the huge fire-breathing creatures of modern myths. The last real dragons were timid little creatures, half lizard and half flightless bird."

"Cross-breeds, like Jorvik," said Jake.

"And dwarfed," added Oscar.

"I suppose they were. Now, why didn't I think of that when I started the Bloodrat experiments?"

Jake patted himself on the head.

"They lived in Welsh caves but were hunted to extinction by wild wolves in the Dark Ages," continued the professor. "Their only defence was a case of very bad breath, which I observed sent even the most aggressive packs of wolves scurrying for fresh air. But hunger made the wolves return, and so another breed of animals became extinct. As for unicorns, sadly the answer is 'no'. The nearest I found was a horse fitted with a head-harness to hold the spiral tusk of a narwhal mammal. It was part of a Victorian circus freak act, led by a so-called bearded lady and tethered to a two-headed sheep. You see, I had in my possession irrefutable visual evidence of all these things and much more besides. But, alas, I can no longer prove any of them."

"I've been to Hampton Court Palace and Portsmouth Historic Dockyard with the school as part of our history lessons into Tudor times. I know all about the *Mary Rose*."

"Not all, Jake."

"Who was Jack the Ripper?" asked Oscar with a blood-thirsty tone to his voice.

"I know that too, but it will remain my secret. The truth would harm important people."

"But…"

"There are no 'ifs and buts', Mr Trotter. I will take the information to the grave."

"This is astonishing. The implications are unbelievable. I could see the winner of a horse race and then place a bet before the race has taken place."

"What?" cried the professor. "Have you listened to absolutely nothing I said? The equipment only shows events that have already happened. It cannot see into the future, dumbhead."

Oscar's face turned red with embarrassment.

But the professor's thoughts had already moved on. "Please, Jake, please, Mr Trotter, help an old man discover what has happened to his son. I know I'm asking an awful lot of you. It could be fraught with danger, but equally, it could be the greatest adventure of our lives."

"Count me in," said Oscar, regaining his composure, "but I don't think Jake's mother would approve of us putting him into difficulties."

"She doesn't need to know," pleaded Jake. "This is a job for all three fearless superheroes. The Three Musketeers: Professor Septimus Kneebone, The Amazing Oscar Trotter, and Captain Jake—boy hero!"

"Oh, Jake, if Mum only knew what we are planning."

Jake's eyes flared. "I'm needed, aren't I Professor?"

"I believe you are, my brave Captain Jake."

"Well then," added Jake, "it seems it's all for one and one for…"

"Hot chocolate!" yelled the professor. "Well, for you two at least. I'm having an extremely large whisky. Even superheroes need a bit of Dutch courage when they're my age. We can't have an amazing adventure on dry throats!"

"When can we get going?" asked Jake with all the enthusiasm of youth, as his father walked away to make another attempt at preparing good hot chocolate.

"Soon, my boy. Very soon," said the professor, slapping the chair with his hand. "A great adventure awaits us." He took the whisky from Oscar's hand. "Up the heroes!" he toasted, drinking the lot in one gulp, whereupon he fell asleep.

Oscar took the empty glass from the professor's dangling hand. The rousing build-up had, just as suddenly, flopped to a standstill.

Jake slipped a soft pillow behind the professor's head.

"What do we do with ourselves for the rest of the day, Dad?" he whispered, walking away from the professor. "He might be spark out for hours."

Oscar shook his head. "I doubt he'll come around 'till early morning. He's old, and he had no sleep last night. We should leave him to rest, as much as that dampens our immediate plans."

"I know what," announced Jake enthusiastically. "We could use the washing up bowl and chamber pot to empty the water out of the under-floor hideaway, then pour it down the sink. That way we don't have to go outside. It could be a right laugh."

Oscar failed to see any fun in the plan, viewing the prospect through adult eyes. He looked at the professor. "I don't think we'll need to tip-toe about. He's going to have quite a headache in the morning."

Chapter 13
The Glue Gun

On Saturday morning Jake rose early from the professor's bed. He had shared it with his father and had not slept well. Oscar, used to sleeping alone in a king size bed, had revealed some very annoying habits, including mumbling, stretching, kicking, snoring, scratching and... well...let's just say making unfortunate smells!

The old man was already out of his chair, staring attentively through the window. Only minutes before he had unlocked the front door and taken Jorvik for a walk along the path. Now the Bloodrat was back in its cupboard, gnawing contentedly on a dead bird found by the dustbins.

"Did you sleep okay, Jake?"

"Not at first. It was Dad's snoring." He decided not to mention the other things.

"I know. He woke me too. Still, I made sure it didn't last too long. I put a few drops of my Number 5 Snore-Stopper up his nostrils. That did the trick. Only, it isn't quite perfected yet, but I don't suppose that matters."

"What do you mean?" asked Jake with some concern.

"Morning campers," yawned Oscar, wiggling his bare feet and stretching his arms above his head. "I can't remember when I last slept so well. The quiet around here is total."

Jake looked alarmingly at his father. "Professor, is that meant to happen?"

"Ah," he replied, "yes, it can cause shrinking."

Oscar looked at the others looking at him. "Something wrong?" he said in a shrill, pinched voice.

"Nothing at all, my dear Mr Trotter, at least nothing a little time won't cure."

"What?" he squeaked. "Someone find me a mirror?"

"I wouldn't do that if I was you, Dad."

But it was too late.

"Ohhhhh!"

"Now, now, Mr Trotter, things are never as bad as they first appear."

Oscar looked again at his reflection. "Ohhhhh! What have you done to my nose?"

"It could be worse, Dad."

"How?"

Jake had no idea, but it sounded the right thing to say.

"Mr Trotter, I assure you the affliction is temporary. My Number 5 doesn't last long once the recipient is standing upright. It sort-of travels downwards to your…"

"What! You stuck some witches' brew up my nose?"

"We needed a good night's rest and you were making the most dreadful racket."

"I don't snore."

Jake laughed.

"What's so funny about disfiguring my face?"

"I was just thinking, Dad. You could have a great career imitating Pinky and Perky."

"Actually, Mr Trotter, the new nose suits you. The old one was, well, rather large, if you don't mind me saying."

"Big?" cried Oscar. "It wasn't in the slightest bit big. It was…" He again caught sight of himself in the mirror. "Oh, yes, well, I see what you mean. A smaller nose does look rather fetching." He moved his head from side to side. "Hum! Rather handsome actually."

Almost at once the skin over his nose erupted like cooking popcorn, then burst to its normal size."

"There," said the professor contentedly, "you are completely restored to your old self."

"Thanks a lot," replied Oscar in a disappointed tone. "I don't suppose…"

"No, Mr Trotter, before you ask, I can't give you more of my Number 5 to make it permanent. It doesn't work like that. You'll just have to fall in love with your old nose again."

Oscar ran his fingers over the contours of his face.

"Honestly, Dad, you look fine… for an elephant." He backed away, laughing.

"Wait till I catch you," scalded Oscar playfully, chasing Jake around the room, for there was something quite reassuring about having his old nose back.

But the professor noticed his Number 5 potion had travelled down to Oscar's toes, which were now shrinking.

"Sit down, Mr Trotter, before you fall down. Anyway, breakfast is almost ready. You'll feel normal afterwards."

"I will?" said Oscar, suddenly feeling rather wobbly.

"Right," said Oscar an hour later, assuming control, "this is it. The adventure starts here. What's first on the agenda?"

Oscar smiled blankly at Jake, and Jake grinned vacantly at the professor. Obviously making a plan was going to be harder than merely talking about it.

The professor, whose legs still felt cramped from a night in the chair, got up to stretch his muscles, returning a short while later with a wicker basket. Inside were a coiled rope and a musical pipe. He placed them at his feet. Soon he was playing music in a most mysterious way, running his fingers quickly and melodically over the row of small holes.

Almost at once the end of the rope began to rise from the basket, snaking its way towards the ceiling. Jake stared open-mouthed, for he was still young enough to think magic was possible. Oscar, who had long given up believing such things, leapt onto a chair and waved his arm above the rope to see what was pulling it up. To his amazement, there was nothing.

Then, just when it seemed impossible to astound them further, the other end of the rope lifted free of the basket to dangle in mid-air, leaving the entire rope floating unattached. Jake and Oscar stood agape, not daring to take their eyes off the rope in case they missed something else.

Neither spoke again until the professor stopped playing. As his cheeks emptied of air, so the rope wound limply down.

"Remarkable," said Oscar in an astonished tone, noticing the rope had not only landed in the basket but re-coiled itself. "I've never seen anything like it. It's the best trick ever."

"Trick!" raged the professor. He tossed the pipe carelessly into the basket before straightening to regain his composure. The pause calmed his pulse. "Oh well, think whatever you like. By the way, how are your toes?"

"My toes? Same as always." He wiggled them in full view. "Why, have you done something else to me?"

"So they are. Jolly good." The professor winked towards Jake, causing both to chuckle.

"Come on," said Jake, trying to get the plan back on track. "The first thing we should do is think up a name for our adventure. They always use a code name in films. How about Operation Shielding Michael?"

"Yes, good," agreed Oscar.

"*Doodle-dandy*," added the professor, while glancing towards the window.

Jake wrote it down in a notepad.

"Next, we should list our options," suggested Oscar. "For starters, we have an egg left, but we don't want to use it unless we have to. All agreed?"

"Ah! Well, actually we don't," interrupted the professor coyly.

166

"We don't? But I gave it back to you and you hid it."

"You did, but I decided I didn't want it after all."

"Without asking our opinion?"

The professor shrugged.

"Blimey O'Reilly! Go on, tell us what you've done," said Oscar, hardly daring to hear the answer.

"In the early hours of this morning, while you were snoring, I asked myself what it would take to encourage the gangsters not only to clear off but set Michael free. Two birds with one stone, so to speak."

"And you concluded without further discussion?"

"We had already discussed destroying the egg to stop their fiendish ambitions, but I later realised sacrificing the egg alone would never be enough. Then it came to me in a flash. Without the egg AND without the Receptor Box they had no reason to stay and no further use for Michael. So," he added proudly, "I put the egg in the oven and turned the temperature up to maximum. It was the only way of destroying it quietly. And, just as I expected, it eventually cracked and burst. I dumped the bits out of the window as the first step in my plan."

"Please tell me this is a wind-up," cried Oscar. "Another of your silly jokes."

"It's not, and I'm pleased I did. There's no going back. It would take months to construct a new egg."

"And the Receptor?" appealed Oscar, his foreboding rising.

"Next on my hit list."

"OMG, don't touch it!" bawled Jake. "Didn't you realise there's a flaw in your plan? You really should've talked it over with us first."

"Flaw? What flaw?"

"Oh, Professor! The egg might be destroyed and thrown out, but has Michael walked through the front door a free man?"

"Give it time, dear boy. I still have the Receptor to smash."

"And if the gang isn't camping nearby, how can we find them without the Receptor providing clues as to their whereabouts?"

For several minutes the old man could not speak. Instead, while thinking, he drew comfort from burying his face in the oily rag and blowing his nose like a fog-horn. When eventually he did look up, he was sullen and frail.

"Oh dear, I forgot we might need it ourselves."

"Even then Michael could never be set free," added Oscar to emphasise the point. "Think about it. They couldn't release him in case he identified them to the police. He would be a traitor in their mist and probably better dead!"

"Dead! Now I'm properly scared," jumped the professor, his face hardening to the awful possibility. "But only yesterday you were in favour of destroying the egg."

"For purely selfish reasons," admitted Oscar, though his tone for once conveyed pity. "I wanted to keep Jake safe. I'm ashamed to say I hadn't properly considered Michael's welfare." He looked between the professor and Jake. "Up to now, Michael has only been a name. Even after seeing his photo, I can't imagine him as a real person. Forgive me."

"What have I done? I've made matters worse," the saddened old man said through a hangdog expression.

"We have to hope they only want to use the Receptor," said Jake, attempting to smooth over the cracks.

"And Plan B is?" petitioned Oscar. "I'll be blowed if I know what we should…"

"Right," interrupted Jake, scrubbing through the heading in the notepad. "We must move on quickly from Operation Shielding Michael to Operation Storming Michael. And the first thing to do is check out the caravan in the lay-by. Let's call it Plan C for Caravan."

"We do *still* have a Plan B," said the professor weakly, hardly daring to suggest it.

"Do we?" asked Oscar, scratching his head. "Let's hear it."

"It's what you said before. We should re-examine the images of the 18ᵗʰ century warship. See if we can determine what interests the gang."

"If there is a gang."

"Naturally."

"Very well!" exclaimed Jake. "As we still have a working Receptor, we can do that. So, it seems we have two possible lines of enquiry, as long as the professor's hammer is tucked safely away in a drawer. What needs to be decided is which comes first, looking at the images or attack the caravan in force like Superman would in the face of danger."

"Sneak up to the caravan for a discreet peep through the windows gets my vote," said Oscar, choosing his words carefully to quell Jake's thirst for the dramatic. "If Michael really is there, and if by chance he's also unguarded, we might be able to release him without any heroics. After all, we don't know how long the caravan will remain parked up, so speed might be essential. But, if we do, it has to be done peaceably. There's nothing to be gained by violence of any kind, particularly if the caravan is being used by gangsters who could be armed and desperate."

"Cool," said Jake.

Oscar tugged him to one side. "No, Son, not cool in the least but potentially dangerous. Take the situation seriously. We're no match for criminals, so no heroics of any kind, whatever we find."

"Oh, is that all that worries you?" said the professor as he skipped to the hinged wall painting, where he removed a massive gun and a black pan of thick liquid from the hidden recess. His courage had returned. "I've always wanted to try this invention on a moving target, but the ammunition wasn't strong enough. Now I think it might be. It's my Number 1 glue gun."

"Awesome!" shrieked Jake. "What does it do?"

"One squeeze of the trigger releases a spray of super-tight glue, leaving all door locks, keyholes and windows stuck as tight as a drum for a few hours. For a little while, it can turn a room into a prison or a fortress. The glue sticks to plaster, cloth, wood and metal. I wouldn't mind meeting any troublemakers along a dark alley while armed with this little beauty."

"It works on people too?" asked Jake.

"I've never tried it on a human target. The glue wasn't formulated for that purpose. However, I'm hoping it will," replied the Professor with glee, "although humans have a natural body heat which might affect the glue's ability to set. On the other hand, it might set even harder and for longer. I really don't know."

"Can the gun be trusted to work properly?" asked Oscar. "Or is it another one of your *jobs in progress*? After all, doesn't Number 1 indicate the first prototype?"

"It requires a little more development to be perfect, but it's almost operational. However, we must treat the trigger with caution. It has a tendency to… Oh!"

Before he could complete the sentence, the professor tripped over Oscar's shoes which had been carelessly left by the bed. The gun slipped out of his hands and flew high into the air before cartwheeling across the floor, all the while spraying a stream of purple gunk.

"Duck," screamed Oscar, throwing Jake to the ground as a jet of spray blasted over their heads.

The quantity of ammunition seemed endless, streaking two walls and part of the ceiling in a sticky syrup which followed an irregular course, like the trail left by a snail.

"Where's the professor? Did he dodge in time?" asked Jake as he lifted himself to his knees.

"I'm over here," came a muffled, yet joyful reply from a mound of glue attached to the wall. "I was going to say, the trigger has a tendency to stick open. However, I think you both know that now."

As he hung with his feet off the ground, the professor uttered no words of complaint, apprehension or despair. Instead, he found the experience profitable from a scientific viewpoint and, perhaps, even darn-right exhilarating.

"Are you all right?" enquired Jake, trying his best not to laugh.

"Fine, in a clingy kind of way. Please don't come too near while it's setting. It's enough that I can't move for an hour or two. There's no point in you being stuck to me."

"How can we help?"

"Some water, if you would."

"To loosen the glue?"

"No, I'm thirsty. I'll drink it through a straw."

"One other good thing has come from the experience," said Oscar, suppressing a smirk.

"Really? What would that be?"

"It answers the question about human targets, even bony ones like you."

At the sink, Jake attempted to turn the tap. "It won't budge, Professor. It's stuck solid."

"Oh, jolly good. It really does work well on metal, just as I hoped."

"Yes, yes, but what about you?" asked Oscar.

"Oh, don't mind me. I'll nod off until the glue molecules break down. Do whatever you like to amuse yourselves. I'm fine if left alone."

The professor's pluck brought a tear to Jake's eye. He nodded appreciatively, which he needed to do to stop himself crying like a baby. If only he had some humbugs to offer the brave old man.

Oscar retrieved the gun using a rag. "Well, I know what I'm going to do. For starters, this thing can go back behind the painting where it belongs. It's of no use to us."

Hearing criticism of his invention, the professor's calm attitude suddenly changed. He began to wriggle. "Pack away our advantage? No, sir, not me."

"Obviously I didn't mean you, Professor. Lending a hand is not something you'll be doing for a while."

"No, Dad, the professor is right. The gun will give us courage. Besides, if there is a gang, it will show them we mean business."

"Or make them think we're spoiling for a fight. No, it has to be put away."

"For another occasion, perhaps?" suggested the professor, realising he could do nothing to prevent it.

Oscar walked away, which actually said it all.

Chapter 14
Michael is Seen

It was afternoon before the glue fractured and the professor dropped unhurt to the floor. He had woken minutes before to the sound of Jake and Oscar discussing tactics and, finding he had increased movement in his arms and legs, had prepared himself both mentally and physically for the fall. When it came it was little more than an awkward inconvenience, particularly as his loose clothes had remained stuck to the wall to leave him standing naked except for a pair of rubber boots.

Jake and Oscar blushed at the sight, but the professor thought nothing of it until they emphatically turned their backs.

"Look at this," said the professor fifteen minutes later, having changed into the only normal clothes Jake ever saw him wear. He moved uneasily in trousers and a knitted jumper. "The gangsters didn't come last night, or this morning. The broken egg remains exactly where I left it. I wonder if we've misread the situation after all."

"There's only one way to find out," said Oscar, and soon the door to the cottage closed as they put Plan C into action.

The three slipped stealthily along the drive that divided the cottage from the garden and into the wood beyond, moving quickly and with very little noise. The sun was still high, but, where its warming rays were unable to penetrate the foliage, the undergrowth remained damp and soft.

For safety they decided to approach the lay-by in a wide circle, using the trees as cover. The diversion meant a steep and difficult climb, and it was not long before the effort caused the professor's head to thump from the earlier excess of whisky. At the brow of the hill, he flopped onto the trunk of a fallen oak, sweating and pulling at his jumper to cool off.

The elevated position provided a commanding view over the treetops. To the south was the professor's home and shed, with Oscar's car parked on the drive. To the north the wood descended as a gentler slope, and here trees both tall and short grew irregularly as nature intended, obscuring much of the main road which fringed the edge. The lay-by was entirely hidden.

On the far side of the road was a second wood, this time densely planted with fast-growing conifers. The ground there was generally level, less rugged, and stretched into the distance before the landscape changed again into an expanse of cultivated farmland where the tiny black and white shapes of cattle could be seen grazing. Then, in the farthest distance the eye could see, was the grey-blue of the coast. From their vantage point, it was just possible to make out white breakers rolling towards the beach, but only imagination could add the sound of seafoam creeping over the sand.

Oscar joined the professor on the trunk, leaving Jake to pace over the plateau. The boy was too excited to sit still, and used the time to work out the shortest route between the road and the cottage should they need a fast escape. He judged the lay-by occupied a curve in the road where a line of silver birches and wild-growing bushes obscured its presence.

The professor, who had meditated to control his headache and was now beginning to enjoy himself as he looked around with fascination at the changing landscape, was suddenly grabbed by Oscar and pulled backwards over the trunk. It was the first and only time the old man ever managed a backward roll.

Oscar had heard a noise coming from the opposite side to where Jake stood. And, right on cue, a figure appeared out of the trees, humming an unrecognisable tune.

The stranger strolled with his head down, passing in front of, but slightly below, where they hid. He wandered from side to side collecting twigs and small branches, which he stuffed under his arm as an ever-growing bundle. He was evidently in no hurry and probably had no use for the firewood either, but merely needed to occupy his free time.

"That bloke could be one of the gang," whispered Oscar so softly that it barely interrupted the sound of the stranger's tune.

Slowly the humming ebbed as the man wandered away until it disappeared completely. But, just as the professor dared raise his head above the trunk, the same voice boomed urgently in a high pitch which echoed through the trees: "He comes. It's time."

"Blimey!" panicked the professor, "I'm sure he saw me."

Oscar wrapped his arm around the professor's neck to keep him low. "I don't think so. He's calling someone else. Stay down and keep as quiet as a mouse!"

Heavy footsteps could now be heard as the man ran down the slope, the bundle of firewood abandoned in the undergrowth. Oscar and the professor remained hidden until they were sure he had gone.

"Where's Jake?" asked Oscar as a dreadful afterthought, unable to see him anywhere on the plateau. "That boy should stop running away."

The professor peered down the slope and shrugged. He was nowhere to be seen.

"What the devil's he up to? He's only thirteen. We must find him."

"Give him a few more minutes," suggested the professor in a tone so calm that it irritated Oscar. "He seems to be the kind of lad who can look after himself."

"Hardly! He's my son and my responsibility."

But the advice was good, for moments later Jake came running up the slope.

"I was right, Dad. The lay-by is dead ahead. I followed the man until he led me to it. I stayed well hidden. It's not far. The caravan's there too, just as we thought it might be. The bloke yelled in a scared way as he approached it, so there must be other men about. Come on, let's go and see what's happening."

"Now listen to me," reprimanded Oscar to curb Jake's runaway enthusiasm. "That's the last time you go off by yourself. Do you understand? There could be danger out there and we *must* stay together at all times. Have I made myself clear?"

Jake nodded apologetically.

Confirmation of the caravan being occupied by men, rather than a young family on holiday, strangely unnerved the professor.

"I've been thinking. Are we getting ourselves into something we can't handle?"

"A bit late to decide that now," replied Oscar over his shoulder, already looking for the easiest way down the slope. "It's today or never. Make up your mind, Professor. Are you determined to find Michael or not? Face it, Jake and I can walk away anytime and it wouldn't alter our lives one jot. We are taking risks for you, so it falls on your head alone to decide whether we press on or go back."

The professor strolled about a little, speaking no audible words but with his incoherent mumbling becoming ever louder. This worried Jake, fearing he was to be robbed of a great adventure at the very moment it could begin.

"Well, which will it be?" demanded Oscar. "The three musketeers or the three blind mice?"

"Come on, Professor," urged Jake. "Michael could be so close. He needs us. Don't let him get away."

It was extraordinary how quickly courage returned to the professor's face, reviving his colour and consuming his fear.

"All for one and one for all," he cried as he set off charging headlong down the slope.

Jake and Oscar stood amazed.

"Well, come on," he called back. "What are you waiting for? Michael... Ahhh!"

Jake winced as he watched the professor run headlong into a low-hanging branch, which struck him so completely across the face that his legs buckled and he was instantly cut down. He was left sprawled across the ground.

"Now that had to hurt," gasped Oscar, though a wry smile formed on his lips.

"On second thoughts," added the professor as he brushed specks of bark from his forehead, "I vote we take it steadily. My headache is back."

Just as Jake said, the caravan was in the lay-by, hooked up to a Range Rover that had its doors flung open. A small camping table stood in front, with half-empty glasses and the wrappings from several packets of sandwiches.

The professor and Jake crouched behind Oscar, who was himself screened from view by a large bush and the shadow it cast.

Two men were standing nearby, checking their watches and talking. One was the wood-collector who, judging by his behaviour, had left his light-hearted spirit amongst the trees and was now quite agitated. The other man appeared more demanding, pressing his views forcefully. They were too far away for Oscar and the others to hear much of the conversation, but, judging by their animated gestures, it was not at all pleasant.

The wood-collector listened with his arms outstretched, shaking his head defiantly. Clearly, these expressions had meaning, for, having exchanged sour looks, he stomped away to rattle the caravan door, checking it was properly locked.

"They aren't exactly buddies," whispered Oscar. "We can rule out holiday-makers. I think we might be on to something here."

Now alone, the other man turned and ran to the bend in the road, staring impatiently into the distance.

"They're frightened," added Oscar. "Of what, I wonder."

While the professor and Oscar watched with heightened interest, Jake detected a slight movement of the caravan on its wheels, as if someone inside had moved. He then fancied he caught a fleeting glimpse of the upper half of a face peering out of a window, seen so briefly that he couldn't be certain it had happened at all.

"Dad," said Jake excitedly while keeping his voice soft, stretching forward and shaking Oscar's shoulder. But Oscar leaned away to stop him talking. "Dad, listen, I…"

"Shush! One more peep out of you, boy, and we'll send you home," avowed the professor testily, his own nerves balancing on a knife-edge.

"Fine. If you're not going to listen, I'll do it myself." And with that said he lifted himself onto the balls of his feet, enough to raise his head to a gap in the upper sprigs. This provided a better view of the lay-by and all that surrounded it. To the left was a large tree with several low branches, not ten metres from the caravan. It offered good cover and could easily be climbed to see straight into the caravan windows without straining.

With his mind made up, Jake squatted behind the professor, hoping to crawl to an unobstructed space from where he could dash across the road. But the professor had been watching him suspiciously out of the corner of his eye and grabbed his trouser belt the very moment he passed, dragging him back with considerable strength.

"Get off," complained Jake, twisting to get free. "I had a perfect chance too…"

"…get us all caught. Trust me and listen to what's coming."

A split-second later the men from the lay-by turned to the sound of a battered parcel van approaching from the opposite direction, its broken exhaust pipe making the most dreadful racket.

It stopped behind the caravan. A man got out, rubbing his buttock where a patch of quite different material had been roughly sewn onto the back of his trousers. He was wild with anger, slamming the door with such force that the whole van shook and a cracked side window shattered into a hundred tiny pieces.

The very presence of the newcomer was sufficient to darken the mood on both sides of the road, and it was likely all who stared at him felt tremors through their backs. For, there was nothing pleasant about his appearance or bearing. He was thick-set, unshaven, with heavily weathered features. At first he hobbled in a hunched, almost deformed manner, yet he was not old, weak or crippled. Then, as the three men met, he straightened to the full height of a short man. Jake thought he looked a lot like a fisherman or dock worker.

Although Oscar and Jake could hear little of what passed between the men—and the distance made lip-reading by the professor impossible—the van driver made no effort to suppress his feelings, which Oscar read like a book. Clearly, there was no unity among the gang, and it was probably only the prospect of ill-gotten money that kept them together.

"What's the meaning of this letter?" raged the van driver in a voice as biting as a cracking whip, his heavy black eyebrows brought low by temper. "Don't you ever, ever post anything again to my home address, you idiot. I was only away for a couple of days. Anything you have to say could've waited 'till I came back." He held a screwed-up piece of paper in his clenched fist. "I should've scooped your eyes out with a pencil the first time I caught you spying on my private business."

"It's over," said the wood-collector in a broken foreign accent. "I want no more helping you."

"It's only over when I say so," returned his tormentor fiercely, poking a straight finger into his chest. "I'll slit any throat as quick as take a knife to a chicken's gizzard, and think no more of it. Understand?"

Shaken but determined, the wood-collector stood his ground.

"You said I get rich, but I not see any money. I only get empty pockets, empty promises, and a belly full of greasy food which gives me diarrhoea."

"I house you, don't I?" said the van driver coldly. "Without me, mate, you would've been deported back to your own country long ago, and good riddance. It is only cowardice that's kept you here, plus the fact you've got nowhere else to run to. I am, you could say, your benefactor."

"I live in cramped caravan and we eat nothing but fried meat and chips, but still I put up with discomfort because of money promised."

"Your discomfort? That's a good one. What about our discomfort when we try to use the chemical toilet after you've been?"

"You make me empty bucket in toilet each day, so what's problem? It's horrible job. I don't like carrying poo sloshing in stinky wee."

"Someone has to do it, and you do most of the filling."

"My stomach can't take much more rubbish food. I need vegetables and fruit, and clove of garlic sometimes."

"Garlic! Did you hear that, Pete?"

The third man sniggered, but only to appease.

"Anyway, you fool, we have money. Lots of it."

"No, you have money. I never see any."

"Of course you don't. You've not earned it."

"I help, don't I?"

"That's not how the system works. Money comes at the end from jobs completed."

"Then shared?"

Harry pursed his lips. "Not exactly. Someone has to fence the booty and hide the proceeds from the coppers until the heat dies down. That's my job. I take all the big risks."

"Money has been very long time in hiding, I think. Have you ever shared with anyone, Harry?"

"Did you catch that, Professor?" said Jake from across the road. "I think I just heard the new bloke being called Harry. That's our first clue."

"Second," corrected Oscar. "Haven't you noticed? The tall man is wearing a Manchester United football shirt. It has 'Pete' printed on the back. I can't recall a current player named Pete, so it has to be his own name."

"You'll get a share when I say so," snapped Harry belittlingly. "Perhaps after this job is over."

"Only perhaps? What about men helping you before I joined gang. Did any get rich?"

"They got exactly what was coming to them," replied Harry through a wicked laugh. "Strange," he added, digging a small hole in the crumbling tarmac with the toe of his boot, "they also argued with me over money but then disappeared before I could give 'em what was owed. Can't possibly say where they went, either. But, nobody can call me unfair. I invested their shares in a big house, swimming pool and a Ferrari to launder the cash, and they can have it whenever they *ask for it* face to face. You might say I've invested it for them."

"For you to enjoy."

"I have to act natural to avoid suspicion. A lot of money attracts snoopers, but not if they think I'm already rich."

The reference to murderous deaths was not lost on the wood-collector, yet the thought of freedom now overcame any fear of the present.

"Not good enough. I no longer stay. Give me some money or I go to police to confess everything."

Harry's stare burned deeply.

"Threaten me with the coppers, would you?" he shouted with aggression, brutishly kicking the camping table high into the air. It broke where it landed. Then, cursing like a madman, his nostrils

181

flaring, he grabbed the wood-collector by his shirt collar and in one sickening heave threw him hard against the Range Rover, pinning him to the open door.

The frenzied violence caused Pete to gasp, but Harry's dreadful scowl warned him not to interfere.

"Ask anyone who knows me, Miguel, and they'll tell you what happens to people who double-cross me. There's too much profit to come from this job to stop now, and I won't let you rob me of the richest picking we've ever chased. It'll be the worse for you if you try."

"The wood-collector's name is Miguel," murmured Oscar. "I distinctly heard him say Miguel. Now we know them all. Shame we can't make out everything they're talking about."

"Was it more bad for them, the old gang members?" asked Miguel courageously.

The effect was immediate and completely unexpected.

"Oh, come on, mate," said Harry, releasing his grip and brushing Miguel's collar with the back of his hand. "All this talk of past troubles is no good. Mates stick together through thick and thin. We need each other. That's a fact."

Again Miguel shook his head. "It is end. We tried, but job not working good. And there are no more jobs after this. We all saw advertisement in paper to sell Bubble Car. Without little car machine, no finding of treasure. You must call it end and be satisfied to divide wealth. A little money must come my way. It only fair."

"No, Miguel, I've been to the shed and looked for myself, and I can assure you the car is still there. I have an injured bum to prove it," said Harry, rubbing his wound. "Next time I'll be armed and ready if that horrible creature attacks me."

"But for how much longer will car be in shed?"

"Probably not long. So we must use it again, and soon, if we're to find the gold and other stuff we know once existed."

"How long can we stay here not noticed?"

"The plan can't proceed without another space egg. The last one didn't provide all the information we need. We must break in again to find another egg to launch. After that, just a few days at most if the weather allows. Anyway, we've never been hassled before."

"Too long!" returned Miguel. "I want escape from Britain now."

"And what if I agree to the gang breaking up? Have you thought what happens then?" said Harry, adding to the tension. "I would need to burn the caravan with everything inside. Leave nothing for the coppers to find."

"No!" followed Miguel's panicked reply, "not that. Policemen would hunt us like the bad dogs. We would not reach coast, and I not care to rot in jail with keys thrown away just for you to have yacht."

"You're a fool, Miguel, if you think I would give you a choice. We're all in this together right up to our villainous necks. It's too risky to stop, and all because of what's inside the caravan. Either we carry on or the goose gets properly cooked."

"There is other way, for sure," pleaded Miguel. "We can all stay quiet as mouse with heads down for a while and then make safe escape. We abandon caravan near busy holiday park, where nobody nosy about for long time. When caravan found, we already escaped to another country."

"This *is* my country, where I live in luxury," demanded Harry in an unflappable tone. "I'm not giving it up for the sake of a bit of bloodshed."

"Bloodshed?" cried Miguel. "You harm other men?"

"No, no, you misunderstand the English language," corrected Harry, retracing his thoughts. "I meant ruthlessness. I relocated them, that's what I meant."

"Where?"

"Down-under."

"Australia? Or perhaps you bury in concrete under swimming pool?"

Harry stared hard before speaking. "That's for me to know and *not* you to find out."

"More I say we must get away fast."

"And I say I'll torch the caravan if you try."

Miguel turned to Pete, who had stood motionless throughout the confrontation. "You have dead men on conscience? You join gang before me."

"Leave me out of it," he replied nervously, trying to avoid his gaze.

"Go ahead, Pete, tell him what he wants to know," barked Harry. "There'll be no faint hearts in my gang—not here, not now, not ever. Make his blood boil with terror. I dare say Miguel thinks we're all mummies' boys, less wicked than we make out to be. It's time we put him straight. Go on, tell him. That's an order."

Pete scarcely knew what to do.

"The devil's choice, Pete," continued Harry coldly. "Be damned if you don't have to choose which side of the fence you sit." There was another pause, during which he snorted, drew phlegm and spat far into the air. "Well, I'm waiting for an answer."

Pete shot nervous glances between the two.

"You ever been paid?" appealed Miguel, hoping to catch him off guard.

He hesitated before replying: "Not yet, but that doesn't mean…"

"Hear that?" jumped Harry. "He expects to be paid and one day he probably will be." Again he rounded on Pete. "Now, I ask you for the last time, do you stand with me or the traitor?"

From their hiding place, Jake, the professor and Oscar watched as Pete finally stepped forward. They were shocked. It was not at all as they expected. Pete stood shoulder to shoulder with Miguel, two against one across an imaginary divide. Yet, far from being flustered, Harry stayed as cool as ever.

"So, here we have it, a foreigner and a coward in cahoots," he taunted, again kicking the tarmac, "both as soft as butter and ready for a long spell in jail. Very well, let's see if this changes anything."

Miguel winced as Harry dipped a hand into his pocket. He expected a loaded gun to be pulled out, but only a roll of banknotes appeared in Harry's palm. The roll was thrown onto the ground.

"Three hundred quid for anyone who decides to stay loyal. Call it a down-payment."

Miguel thought he could answer for both, no longer fearing a backlash through the strength of numbers.

"Your blood money not enough to bribe us. Now tell truth. You never intend to pay us, do you?" He waited for an answer, which didn't come. "So we walk away, poor but free men."

When Miguel had finished speaking, and with his own plan failing, Harry grunted, cursed and cast a wicked look.

"Just try it, sunshine! You'll get no mercy from me," he warned, proving once more he remained the boldest of the three. "I'll tear you limb from limb, and then do the same to Pete if he so much as moves a hair on his head to protect you."

Never was there such a turnaround as that now caused by these dark and sinister threats. With his nerve appearing to evaporate, Pete bent down, greedily seized the money and walked back to Harry's side. It was obvious Miguel felt physically sick at Pete's collapse.

"Ho-ho-ho! Christmas has arrived early for Pete," sniggered Harry. "Now how do you feel, Miguel, knowing your army has deserted? Alone, vulnerable, dangerously exposed—all three, perhaps? But, don't worry, I have something for you too."

Then, in the blink of an eye, it happened.

With a thunderous clash of bodies, a scuffle broke out, followed after several fearsome blows by a scream. When they parted, Miguel was left doubled-up on the tarmac, his arms folded across his stomach. He tried to stand, but Harry landed another blow to the top of his head, sending a shudder resonating through his body. Only his outstretched hand finding the car bonnet kept Miguel from fully collapsing.

"I warned you," panted Harry, towering over him with his fist raised. His knuckles were taut and white. "Don't say I didn't. Around here things are done my way or not at all. I don't go in for democracy." Again his fingers sank into a pocket, this time removing a matchbox which he rattled menacingly in Miguel's face. "Perhaps you would like to be tied to the caravan and torched along with the goose?"

"You not dare," ridiculed Miguel, blood dripping from his nostrils. The bravery of his words was in stark contrast to the feebleness of his voice. "You not so crazy."

"Oh, but I am," scorned Harry through an expression so cruel that it was impossible to believe he wouldn't actually do it if pushed further into a corner.

From the way Harry played with the matchbox, Pete could tell he was itching for that provocation.

"Enough!" Pete shouted, pulling Harry away to get between them. "Can't you see he's done for? You've proved your point. For pity sake, leave it at that."

As Harry grudgingly put the matchbox back into his pocket, Pete lifted Miguel's arm and placed it around his shoulders. Although Miguel fell unsteadily against him, Pete still managed to haul him properly onto the smooth surface of the car bonnet, where Miguel's legs hung over the front grill like a dead weight.

It was during this lift that Miguel unintentionally glanced across the road. Fleetingly, his half-closed misty eyes met Jake's. And yet, being bruised, battered and breathless, the incident was just as quickly forgotten.

"Oh no, Dad. I think he saw me," cried Jake as he ducked beneath the bush, for the possible consequences were frightening.

Oscar wrapped Jake in his arms before stretching up to take a quick glance over the top. He could see Miguel with his head down. Harry was still hovering menacingly close.

"It's all right, Son, I'm sure he didn't. We're safe if we stay hidden."

His reassurance settled Jake, although secretly Oscar knew Harry was perfectly capable of killing them all if they were discovered.

Yet, what occurred next was even more bizarre.

With perfect indifference to the pain he had inflicted, Harry left Miguel draped awkwardly on the bonnet and walked to the van where, to the sound of clinking glass, he rummaged inside until he found the only large bottle with a lid. Then, returning, he casually smashed the glass neck against the wing of the Range Rover. Beer bubbled out from the jagged end. Harry sucked the bubbles before taking a long swig, all the time keeping Miguel firmly in view.

"Want to party, Miguel?" he teased after wiping his lips across a sleeve. There was no reply. "Not talking to me?" He brought his face so close he could almost smell fear. "I'll take that to mean *yes*," he said, sneering as he callously wrenched Miguel's head back by his hair. "It's customary for everyone at a party to have a drink."

With Miguel's mouth already hanging open from the torture, Harry tipped beer down his throat until it gushed back up and he choked.

And that was how Miguel was left, conscious but convulsing, slumped, and with beer dripping unchecked from his jaw. The bottle was abandoned on the bonnet.

Across the road, the professor buried his face in his hands.

With Miguel still retching, and to Oscar's amazement, Pete now stepped across to join Harry in front of the van. Strangely, they now appeared to talk normally, as if nothing had ever come between them. The close proximity meant Miguel could hear everything they said, and yet they didn't seem to care. What did it mean? Even in his fragile state Miguel looked shocked to his boots by their unexpected fraternity.

Despite the ferocity of Harry's attack and the resulting injuries, Miguel was actually more winded than seriously hurt, and so it was not long before he could stand without assistance. And, although he still felt queasy, he quickly realised any weakness was not from the attack itself but from the quantity of alcoholic beer he had been forced to swallow.

When they finished talking, Harry patted Pete's shoulder in an amicable way. Yet, the very moment they separated, their looks changed again, bearing no obvious signs of friendship.

"Good cop—bad cop," whispered Oscar. "That's their game, to break Miguel's nerve. I'm sure they're acting enemies when all along they're collaborating. It's a way of confusing Miguel into not knowing who to trust. Of course, I could be wrong, but I bet I'm not. I wish I could hear what's being said."

"Well, and think carefully before answering," said Harry coldly as he thrust a hand to Miguel's throat and held it in an iron grip, restricting more air than he could bear, "are you still expecting to leave?"

Miguel stole a sideways glance towards Pete, whose current expression gave no sign of allegiance to either person. In his thoughts Miguel cursed Pete for his cowardice, a man he had once called a friend but whose present weakness had put him on the wrong side.

Breathless, Miguel struggled to speak. "I guess I'm…" he spluttered in a shallow manner, his eyes straining to fix on the bottle, "… *against you!*"

Impulsively, he lunged forward to tear at his attacker's grip. The speed of the move so shocked Harry that Miguel had time to snatch the bottle. Now brandishing the jagged neck uppermost, he was amazed how quickly the weapon gave him confidence.

"Stand away, you both," he demanded, shifting his position to the side of the car. "I'm going. You not follow me." His stare fixed on Harry, believing him to be the greatest threat.

But it was not going to be so easy to escape. Already Harry had noticed a length of broken pallet wood lying by the kerb. Hammered into one end were four bent and rusty nails. It was a weapon of sorts which, although out of immediate reach, was nevertheless enticingly close. Could he grab it before Miguel struck with the bottle? Harry knew it would take suicidal courage to try, but, then, his whole life ran deep with risk.

Miguel followed Harry's stare, and when their eyes met again both knew it would not end well.

In an instant Harry threw himself sideways, wailing like a banshee as he plunged down for the weapon. The wildness caught Miguel completely off guard, making his reaction an unconscious act. With his arm at full stretch, Miguel slashed the bottle in a huge involuntary arc. The jagged edge, swung only for defence and without any proper aim, nevertheless caught Harry's forehead before striking a second gash across his right thigh.

Nobody was more shocked than Miguel as the bottle ripped through flesh before flying out of his hand. It smashed close to where Harry fell awkwardly to the ground. But the wounds, which would have felled most men, did nothing to lessen Harry's determination to retaliate. And, if Harry's earlier conduct had been alarming, it now became truly terrorising as he held his own lethal weapon for use against the unarmed man.

Ignoring the blood which ran around the contours of his nose and down his leg, Harry pounced. A heavy blow from the pallet wood crashed down. Miguel ducked, which probably saved his life, the wood shattering as it struck the top edge of the car's door. Yet, he was not entirely saved. The tip of a nail had caught his shoulder, ripping through his jacket and piercing down to the bone beneath. He writhed as blood seeped between his fingers, making

Harry laugh as he pinned him to the car with more weight than Miguel could endure.

Across the road, the professor grabbed Jake and covered his eyes, as punch followed punch in the one-way battle. Finally, with his jaw dropping, Miguel lifted a hand in submission, groaning like a beaten dog.

"He's done for," whispered Oscar, who alone was still watching.

The professor turned to look for himself, amazed to notice Miguel was still capable of taking a crafty glance. "I'm not so sure."

What followed next was both astonishing and quickly done. As Harry released the hold to tie a handkerchief around the top of his leg to stem the bleeding, Miguel slid himself up to his full height and then, with tremendous force, landed a withering kick with the underside of his boot. From such a blow there was no instant recovery, and Harry fell crumpled onto the tarmac. It was the chance Miguel needed to get away.

Taking to his heels like a fox escaping the hounds, Miguel dodged furiously in and out of the conifers of the nearby wood, never daring to look back. Soon he was practically invisible amongst the thickening undergrowth, which in places had grown into imposing hedges. Yet, despite the distance between them, he could still hear Harry's deathly shouts as he recovered to begin a hot pursuit.

It was while jumping over a fallen branch at full speed, in an area of the wood where the sun cast irregular shadows through the trees to confuse the senses and dapple the light, that Miguel lost his footing and fell headlong into a hollow. He rolled to a stop at the bottom. There he froze with his shoulder burning like a branding iron, for the sound of heavy feet was getting louder by the second and any slight movement could give his position away.

How Harry had closed the distance so quickly with a wounded leg was a mystery. Yet, it was undeniable he had outrun Miguel through determination and a vengeful need for retribution, and was now uncomfortably close.

Not daring to lift his face from the mud, Miguel was left unsighted and helpless to what approached from behind. The thought of Harry creeping up undetected and viciously stamping on his spine made his heart pound within his otherwise deathly still body.

Meanwhile, back at the caravan, and with nobody to stop him, Pete now took advantage of the bewildering situation to make his own escape. For, any agreement to stay with the gang had been well and truly cast aside by Harry's excessive brutality.

Feeling little courage but much resolve, Pete jumped into the Range Rover and pushed the key into the ignition, constantly looking left and right in fear of Harry's return. Much to his relief, the car started the first time. But he had good reason to worry. The noise of the over-revving engine as it burst into mighty power was heard by Harry, who slid to a sudden stop despite the overpowering pain it caused.

It was this change of direction which saved Miguel from being discovered.

Harry turned with a ferocious glare, realising he had been double-crossed for the second time. Meanwhile, the Range Rover's spinning tyres burned rubber and smoked as they fought for grip with the weight of the caravan in tow and the speed of the escape.

Vital minutes were lost by Harry as he shuffled back out of the woods, his injured leg held straight as it was dragged behind. By the time he reached the lay-by, only skid marks on the tarmac showed where the vehicles had been.

Cursing, Harry hobbled to the van, where he sat in agony. Whether the greater pain was from his injured leg or pressure on the wound to his buttock from an earlier skirmish was impossible to tell. Both felt severe. Yet, at least the keys were still hanging in the ignition, allowing the engine to be quickly started. The chase was on.

Harry's hand, now shaking with fury, engaged the gear stick and the van leapt forward. But a terrible crunching noise brought the engine to a sudden stall. He had run over the table, which was now firmly wedged beneath the front bumper.

Slamming the door so hard the wing mirror fell off, he tore at the obstruction. Yet the effort was futile. By the time the table had been dislodged, the road ahead was empty of cars in both directions.

The professor, Oscar and Jake waited anxiously as the van was manoeuvred in a three-point turn before driving away, its exhaust rattling.

"Let's get out of here," said the professor, suffering from pins and needles.

"We should give Harry a bit longer," cautioned Oscar. "Didn't you see?"

"See what?" asked Jake.

"The idiot drove over the nails. Penny to a pound he won't get far before he has to stop to change a wheel. He might even come back here to do it."

The possibility of Harry's return was a good reason to remain crouched. The professor, by now desperately needing to stretch his legs, took Jake's arm and together they cautiously backed behind a tree. And there, in their respective places, all three listened for any sound, however slight and distant.

"So far, so good," said Oscar after a few troublesome minutes, glad when nothing disturbed the singing of birds and the quivering of branches. "He must be too far away to come back now. I think we can chance it. Come on you two."

The prospect of home brightened the three adventurers. But the ugly fight weighed heavily on their minds and for a short while nobody spoke, despite there being good reason for hope. With

Harry gone and the gang dispersed, it seemed the neighbourhood was freed of a violent gang.

Of course, nothing had been gained to help the professor in his quest to find Michael, although, as Oscar pointed out as the two walked together with Jake some distance behind, they had nonetheless achieved something from the experience; their spying had *not* linked the reckless desperados with Michael's disappearance, since he had not been seen and no mention of his name had been overheard. It was possible the gang was nothing more than opportunist thieves.

And so, for the present, the world appeared to be a slightly safer place. Perhaps it was even possible the professor's fantasy was true, and Michael really was sunning himself on some tropical beach. And with that thought uppermost, Oscar agreed to let Jake race away.

Little did he know the decision would have near fatal consequences.

Jake, being a very normal boy, viewed danger as excitement, as long as the danger was not 'too dangerous'. Now free to explore alone, he thought he would quickly circle back to the lay-by to check for clues and return before anyone missed him. It had to be done in secrecy if he was to avoid another lecture from his father.

And, just as before, the broken pallet, squashed camping table and shards of glass remained scattered over the tarmac. However, at the back of the lay-by—previously hidden by the caravan and unnoticed even after it was towed away—was a very large council waste bin on wheels. Seeing this reminded him of the letter Harry had held in his fist before the fight.

It can only be imagined the thrill Jake felt when he found the letter lying on the ground among the discarded sandwich wrappers. It was badly screwed-up and hard to read, but nothing a bit of TLC couldn't cure. Elated for being one step ahead of the adults, he pushed the letter deep into his pocket for later examination while he searched for anything else of significance.

Despite the urgency to get back, Jake's attention finally turned to the waste bin itself. There was a slim chance something of no importance to the gang but relevant to the investigations had been thrown away by the criminals, especially as they had camped over many days.

Anxiously glancing at his watch, Jake gave himself just ten minutes to rummage around. He knew it wasn't really long enough, but the bin had to be searched now in case it was emptied before he could return with the others.

With heady expectations of what might be discovered, he pushed the lid back. The rising smell of rotting food, soiled nappies and excrement from the caravan's chemical toilet was sickening.

Turning his head aside while squeezing his nose, he used a length of pallet wood to stir amongst the bags. But the arm of a thirteen-year-old was too short to allow the bottom to be reached.

What would Sherlock Holmes do, he wondered? One thing was certain, Sherlock wouldn't let a little thing like a bad smell get in the way of duty.

Bolstered by that thought, Jake threw caution to the wind and bravely scrambled inside. And, in case anyone saw him, he pulled the ill-fitting lid back over his head.

For whatever reason—perhaps the lack of fresh air combined with poor light and ammonia vapour rising from the nappies—a feeling of extreme drowsiness quickly washed over his body while sifting through the rubbish, his thoughts gradually becoming slower and confused. And within this intoxicating atmosphere, his eyes eventually closed.

There, Jake might have stayed, knocked out to the world, had it not been for a heavy kick which shook the bin and distorted the lid, allowing a blast of fresh air to rush in. He was startled into consciousness.

"Wait 'till I get my hands on him," thundered a cruel voice from the outside, groaning and swearing. "I'll cut him up proper next time. Just see if I don't. Where's the blasted paper?"

Jake instinctively knew 'the blasted paper' was the letter stuffed inside his pocket, which meant only one thing. Only a very thin wall of black plastic separated him from Harry. He stared up in horror as now the lid began to move.

"Crapping hell!" shouted Harry as the noxious smell hit his face. The lid was quickly slammed back down.

But Jake could hear Harry taking deep breaths, which meant he was likely to try again.

Desperate not to be caught, but with no means of escape, Jake had to think fast. And at such a moment of fear, even revulsion could be overcome.

Quietly, nervously, yet unflinchingly, he clawed himself deeper into the rubbish, all the time cursing his foolhardiness for returning to the lay-by and making the bin his likely grave. Squidgy nappy bags were heaped over his head to complete the deception, the desperate smell and soggy contents needed for camouflage.

It was not a moment too soon. Even before he had time to pull his shaking arm fully from view, the lid was thrown back to reveal Harry's face peering down into the dark and disgusting morass. His cheeks were round and bursting as he held his breath.

Jake froze, hoping his exposed hand would go unnoticed.

"Blood and guts," Harry cried as the last of the air left his cheeks and he let go of the lid, struggling not to be sick.

Inside the bin Jake held his nerve, unsure whether Harry would try for a third time. And for a short while there was no sound at all. But then a steady trickle beat against the side of the bin, followed by another short pause and the clip of footsteps walking away. The van door was heard to shut and the engine started. The failing exhaust sounded all too familiar.

Jake remained in the bin until all noises from the van disappeared, knowing impatience could still get him caught. Then, after cautiously raising the lid enough to see out, he climbed free. His feet dropped into a small puddle of water shimmering on the tarmac.

"Harry had a wee against the bin," he chuckled to himself, though mostly from relief after surviving the scariest moment of his young life. "He's human after all." He felt for the letter, surprised his pocket was ringing wet. "Okay, so what if I peed myself? Nothing to be ashamed of. I was scared silly." He broke into a run, glad to be heading back. "I have the letter and he doesn't. Victory goes to the boy hero," he whooped as the lay-by was left in the distance.

"That dirty scoundrel Harry is a proper nutcase and no mistake," said the professor as he increased his stride for the journey home. "Had Miguel not got the better of him, why, I'm sure I might've lost my temper and hit him myself. I was getting very steamed up."

"I didn't notice," contradicted Oscar unwisely. "In fact, I thought you seemed rather subdued."

"Self-restraint," was the professor's snappy riposte. "That's what you witnessed. Inside I was boiling like a kettle. Control is the first rule in martial arts. Did I tell you I once lived in Japan?"

Oscar said he had not, but thought he had mentioned India.

"Yes, yes, India, Japan and China. I've been all around the Far East. Of course, it was a long time ago I learned the techniques involved in martial arts, but I expect the fighting moves would soon come back to me if I needed them. Like riding a bicycle."

"Riding a bicycle? What are you talking about?" called Jake as he ran up the hill.

"Once taught, never forgotten." The professor sniffed the air. "Where have you been, Jake? You smell like… old toilets?"

"Oh, just here and there. Wait 'til you see what I've found." He felt in his pocket for the letter, which came out damp and torn. The once clearer words had become a series of pale and smeary streaks. Jake stared at the letter, now entirely illegible.

"What have you got there?" asked Oscar.

"Oh, nothing, Dad. Just rubbish to be discarded."

"And the surprise find?"

"Lost, I'm afraid!"

The temperature fell as they progressed homeward. It made the troubled walk refreshingly pleasant.

"Phew, what an afternoon," remarked Oscar, taking a quick look backwards as the others walked on. "I never want to see a clash like that again. It was proper scary."

"Did you see the bloke in the caravan?" asked Jake out of the blue, increasing the length of his strides to match the professor's.

"A man? I saw nobody."

"There was. It was when you grabbed me."

"I doubt it," said Oscar, catching them up. "We all would've noticed."

"But I did, Dad, I really did… or at least I think I did. It was the top of someone's head."

"What if the boy's right," cautioned the professor, drawing to a sudden halt. "If it's true, the person obviously wasn't trusted enough to be let outside the caravan. Meaning…"

"How can you know that?" challenged Oscar, cutting through the professor's sentence.

"Isn't it obvious? We saw Miguel check the door was locked. If someone was inside, that person was not meant to escape. I could be Michael."

"What about Harry's threats to set the caravan alight?" added Jake without thinking. "I heard snatches of that when he started shouting."

Oscar quickly put a hand to Jake's mouth. "That's enough idle speculation. We mustn't let our imaginations run amok. Besides, I only caught him talking about cooking a goose. No harm in that. Even criminals need to eat."

"Not only that," corrected Jake, not to be silenced. "He also said 'torching'. And he had matches."

"Cooking, torching, where's the difference? For goodness sake, everyone, keep calm."

"Calm!" exclaimed the professor, now taking Jake seriously. "Calm, when Michael might be in harm's way."

"Now look what you've done, Son," said Oscar bluntly. He turned to the old man. "Look, we have absolutely no proof of anything Jake claims to have seen or heard. Nothing has been set on fire, added to which I saw nobody in the caravan and nor did you. Let's face it, Jake has the imagination of a boy. Everything is circumstantial at best and complete rubbish at worst. I suggest we bear it in mind but don't become too hot and bothered unless something else occurs that substantiates the claims."

The professor appeared unconvinced.

"And we mustn't forget," resumed Oscar dispassionately, "the caravan took off in the opposite direction to that dreadful Harry bloke, so, come what may, all is well for the time being. I'm pretty sure Pete isn't half as dangerous as Harry."

"I suppose," conceded the professor.

"If Jake really did see something, it's just as possible it was the head of a large dog. Now, you must agree, that makes more sense. From a distance, a dog's head could easily be mistaken for that of a man, and they would keep a big dog locked up."

"If you're blind and stupid," remarked Jake sarcastically.

Oscar let it go.

"What do we do next?" asked the professor. "We must do something. Call the police, perhaps?"

"And say what? You can look back in time and make rope fly. Oh, and by the way, we saw two men fighting over what to do with a beaten-up old caravan. And, horror upon horror, they want to cook a goose. No, I don't think we would be taken very seriously."

"What about Miguel and Harry? They were both wounded. Now, that has to be a crime. We could at least report that?" said Jake.

"Where's the victim? The police wouldn't do a thing without a body. No, best stay out of it. In fact, truth be told, I couldn't care less about Harry, and by the looks of things Miguel wasn't too badly hurt."

"If only we could speak to Miguel," muttered the professor. "He could tell us what's going on."

"I would rather avoid them altogether."

"Has any of this helped?" asked Jake.

"Of course it has," replied Oscar reassuringly. "We now know the owners of the caravan are violent men, and very possibly criminals. What, if anything, that has to do with us only time will tell. But it's a start."

"It's not much," said the professor.

"I know, my friend, but every investigation begins with a single clue."

Soon after six o'clock that same day, Oscar chose to drive back to the lay-by, in case there were any clues left to find. He didn't know his son had already combed the area, and Jake wasn't about to tell him.

In normal circumstances Oscar would not have shown the slightest hesitation to walk beyond the lay-by, especially as the early evening sun still lit the woodland. But it was somehow different now. The thicket held a menacing atmosphere. Indeed, his fear of Miguel, who might be lurking like a wounded wild animal among the trees, was greater than his curiosity.

Had he been braver, Oscar would have discovered Miguel lying in the bracken, suffering the pain of his wound, with blood dripping down his sleeve and onto the broad green leaves.

And there, among the undergrowth, Miguel waited for darkness, intending to set off on foot towards the coast where he would smuggle himself onto a cargo boat destined for the continent. He, too, had returned for the note bearing his name and found nothing.

With much to occupy his mind, the professor sat heavily in his favourite chair awaiting Oscar's return. 'Black menace' was again rearing its ugly head, and nothing Jake said or did could lift it. And yet, the very moment Oscar walked through the door and said he had found nothing new, the professor's spirits soared.

Oscar now called for a council of war to lay new plans. Discussions would take place over a substantial meal of sausages in home-made tomato sauce, served with rice and a spoonful of green peas placed on the side.

"Random," said Jake half an hour later, as he watched the professor eagerly attack his supper. "I've never known you to willingly eat vegetables. Were they left over from the packet Dad bought?"

"Actually no. They're dried peas from a box," he replied categorically, not wishing to explain what he had done with the others. "I normally keep them for a pea-sucking game using drinking straws. Michael loved playing that. He could suck forty peas a minute." He wiped away an unexpected tear. "So, every Christmas I play it as a reminder of good times past. Of course, now I never lose."

"Well, I love them. Mum insists I eat vegetables with every main meal, and fruit at least once a day. She says it does me good."

"And so you must, young J-J-Jake."

"Oh, Professor, your voice!"

"W-w-what a time to c-c-come back." He looked at his hands. "S-s-see, all the green has gone. Still, t-t-this is no time to worry about a-a-appearances…"

"You okay, Professor?" asked Jake, noticing him wobble.

"Actually, I'm f-f-feeling a touch p-p-peculiar. It must be all that r-r-running about. The war c-c-council will have to w-w-wait."

The professor left the table for his bed, his head falling hard upon the pillow.

"Should I fetch a doctor?" asked Oscar, as he lifted the professor's head in preparation for administering a dose of Voice Stuff. He noticed the label read Number 8½. "Is this a new formula?"

The professor swallowed hard. "A s-s-slight last-minute improvement to the potion. I'm hoping it will last even l-l-longer than N-N-Number 8."

"Any side effects?"

"We'll soon f-f-find out," he said through a slight smile.

The potion was to be followed by a glass of water, which Oscar raised to the professor's mouth. The old man took a gulp without thinking.

"*Tush* to that s-s-stuff," he grumbled, having blown the water out like a fire extinguisher, along with several rings of green smoke. "I don't need a q-q-quack and I certainly don't need w-w-water. I know what does me g-g-good when I become faint, and it isn't p-p-prescribed from a medicine bag. Fetch me a w-w-whisky before my brains desert my skull. See, my lips already j-j-jitter with anticipation."

Oscar returned with a shot of whisky diluted by a large quantity of water.

"Good grief man, are you deliberately trying to d-d-drown me?" complained the professor without an ounce of gratitude. "You can do the washing up with that stuff because it's not going down my t-t-throat. Get me a brandy instead that hasn't had its face w-w-washed in H_2O."

The very moment Oscar left the bedside, the professor grabbed Jake and pulled him close.

"You're the one with young eyes, Jake, so I t-t-trust you the most. Were you imagining things or did you really see Michael?" he pleaded in a feeble voice which contrasted to the strength of his hold. "Tell me the truth, boy, before your father returns."

"I saw somebody in the caravan. I'm pretty certain I did."

The professor fell back. "That's good enough for me."

Chapter 15
Held by the Police

It was now Sunday, Jake's last day before school. The professor, who was using a boat oar to remove cobwebs from the top of the Christmas tree, was deep in thought, worrying about the impossibly short time left before his friends would leave.

"If we bring all hands to bear," he uttered dolefully, "we still haven't the crew to weather the storm."

Jake scratched his head, wondering what he meant. Oscar was less polite, having spent an uncomfortable night in a chair.

"I don't understand a thing you're talking about, Professor. Oh, and by the way, you're not stuttering."

"Forget the blinking 8½," replied the professor, equally curtly. "All I'm saying is… we're sunk. I can't save Michael without your help, yet after today you won't be here. As I said, we're done for."

He rested the oar between a shelf and the mantelpiece as an improvised clothes line.

Jake looked between the two gloomy adults. "This is no way to be, landlubbers," he said in an upbeat manner, getting into the same sea-faring role. "So what if we can't solve the riddle today. We can continue next weekend. I say we hoist the main-brace, fly the Jolly Roger, and make preparations to sail. What do you think?"

"What the devil's he on about, Mr Trotter?" asked the professor as he sat.

"How would I know? You started the nautical stuff."

"Oh, come on you two," rebuked Jake. "Let's drop the sulky faces and prepare ourselves for next time. You can sit around if you like, but I'm for getting on with the investigations. And, talking of investigations, we should start with the Receptor Box. See if anything useful has survived. By the time we return from the shed, maybe your clean loincloth thingies will be dry enough to wear, Professor. You're beginning to stink."

The thought of discarding the uncomfortable trousers and jumper for his favoured baggy dhoti and a waistcoat was just the tonic needed to revive the professor's spirits. He leapt to his feet and, with Jake barely able to keep up, hurried to the shed where he re-attached a thick wire cable between the Receptor Box and the Starlight Machine. Then, after pushing a plug into a wall socket, he sat busily turning knobs and flicking switches. A soft humming was emitted. Jake looked on in awe before sweeping the middle of the floor in case any holographic images came to life.

While the two were happily occupied in the shed, Oscar sneaked off to his car to listen to the Sunday cricket. He soon came running back.

"You won't believe what I've just heard on the local radio," he yelled, bursting into the shed. "The police have found an injured man wandering about the countryside. They've asked if anyone can help identify him, as he speaks no English and…"

"You think it's Miguel, don't you?" interrupted the professor.

"Why not? A wounded man of foreign nationality. It's certainly worth checking out."

"Where's he from?" asked Jake innocently.

"With a name like his, Spain I reckon," replied Oscar.

"But they said he doesn't speak English. We know Miguel can."

"Wouldn't you stay conveniently dumb in his place?"

"At last we have him in our clutches! *Yippee-do-da-dandy*," cried the professor. "We must go to the police station at once. The

Receptor will have to wait." He again flicked switches and the humming stopped.

Oscar was annoyed. He had not expected the news to override the excitement of seeing more images held in the Receptor's memory and said so. "We should've discussed it properly before you shut down. Everything has to be done by consensus."

"Nothing to debate, dear boy. It's obvious we have to go," the professor replied, removing the plug.

"I understand that, but does it have to be right away? Miguel—or whoever it is—is secure in police custody. Surely we could go tonight, just before I take Jake home."

But the professor was mostly thinking about Michael and insisted the police station took priority. He reminded Oscar that, of the three of them, he alone was capable of operating the Starlight Machine and Receptor Box, so there could be no argument.

For any good to come from the diversion, Oscar knew someone had to speak to Miguel face-to-face and alone, well out of police earshot. "Otherwise he won't spill the beans." The professor wanted to be that man until Oscar alluded to the 'greenness' around his face, which automatically ruled him out.

"I'll take Jake with me to hurry things along. See you later, Professor."

The high security within the police station fulfilled Oscar's worse fears. The glare of bright lights, the closed-circuit cameras recording every movement, the locked doors and iron bars made it impossible to approach Miguel confidentially, even if the duty officer allowed limited contact, which he didn't. Worst still, unless locked away in a cell, Miguel was always accompanied by a police guard, at which time he made out he could understand nothing being said in English.

To "would you like a coffee?" or "do you need a new bandage for your shoulder?", he merely shrugged, and any number of quick-fired questions by the police to catch him off guard never broke through the wall of silence.

With no realistic option, Oscar took the difficult decision to tell the police most of what he knew about the gang and the caravan, only holding back details of the professor's machines and Michael. But the omissions made his story fragmented and difficult for the police to believe. Consequently, everything he said was viewed as having no credible significance to the investigations, that is until he stressed the importance of being allowed to talk to the inmate alone. That changed everything. Suddenly the duty officer's ears pricked up. He frowned, glared, paced about the room and left briefly to seek advice, returning a short while later with a colleague who brought recording equipment to capture their conversation.

"DCI Brian Pew interviewing Oscar Samuel Trotter. Sergeant Simon Jones in attendance. The time is 11:05 am. Are you Oscar Trotter?" he asked for the sake of the recording.

"You know I am. I've already told you that."

"Answer the question."

"Yes."

"You came here of your own free will, asking to speak alone to a foreign gentleman held in cell 3?"

"Yes."

"What was the reason for this highly irregular request?"

Oscar couldn't think how to answer.

"Come along, Mr Trotter, it's simple enough."

Before Oscar had a chance to make up a believable excuse, the officer began firing a stream of other questions in a quite aggressive manner, which made Oscar feel very uncomfortable. No, more than that, he felt innocent but threatened. He started to fidget and sweat, and muddle his sentences, signs the officer took as complicity to some wrongdoing.

Thank goodness for Jake.

In a separate interview room, Jake had given his own sketchy account of events in the lay-by. And, much to Oscar's relief, the statements were compared and found to be almost identical, differing only in respect of an unknown man seen in the caravan which his father said was a dog. Still, the police were now satisfied as to Oscar's overall innocence of a crime and the interview was terminated.

But even this was not the end of the ordeal. An identification parade from behind glass, in which Miguel stood within a row of randomly-chosen men to be picked out as one of the so-called gang, wasted even more time which could have been better spent with the Receptor Box. Then, of course, there followed endless form filling. By now Oscar had learned not to protest about anything.

In the waiting room, Jake sat impatiently for his father's release, watching the hands on the wall clock turn very, very slowly.

And Jake was not alone in clock watching. Fretful for their return, the professor took the decision to restart the Receptor without them. It was a decision he would regret. Almost as soon as the Receptor came to life, red and green lights began flashing in an ever faster and totally uncontrollable sequence, which he had never seen before, while an alarming smell of overheating rose unexpectedly from the back.

It was three o'clock in the afternoon before the police finally told Oscar he was no longer needed and could go home, thanking him for his cooperation but warning him not to leave the country until the investigation was completed.

And with that cloud hanging over his head, Oscar finally walked free, scarred by the experience. He felt sure he was now a suspect in his own right, with his name added to a computer file of known criminals.

Jake also felt frustration, as the best of the day had passed for no apparent good.

And so it had, in a most hurtful way.

For, only minutes after Oscar and Jake left, Miguel also walked out of the police station a free man. He strolled casually to the main gates, where he stopped, shook hands with a stranger, and the two went off in opposite directions.

Oscar could hardly believe his eyes. He wanted to chase after Miguel, that is until Jake reminded him of the outside security cameras watching their every move. Instead, he ran back into the building.

"What on Earth's going on?" he remonstrated to the duty officer.

"We had to let him go, sir. We were obliged to find him a lawyer and that clever dick pointed out that we had no evidence against him, no scene of crime, and no reason to believe his injury was anything more than a simple accident caused by climbing under a barbed-wire fence. Once the lawyer said we breached the gentleman's Human Rights if we held him longer, we had no choice but to release him into the clever dick's care or face being sued for a ridiculously large amount of money."

"But I've just seen them part company with a handshake!" exclaimed Oscar.

"Well, I never did. It only goes to show what tricky chaps lawyers can be."

"Is there nothing you can do?"

"There most certainly is. I can go and have a nice cup of tea in the canteen. Would you like one brought up for you?"

Oscar stormed out the door, causing the officer to remark as he gathered the paperwork and dropped it into a bin for shredding: "No need to take that attitude, sir. The tea here is quite nice."

But now something else played on Oscar's mind as they drove away. By giving the professor's address to the police and identifying Miguel in the parade, and in turn the police letting Miguel go, he had possibly exposed the professor to new dangers that he might have to face alone once Jake was taken home. It was a terrible thought, but there was nothing he could do about it.

Chapter 16
The Amazing Room of Light

Meanwhile, all was panic in the shed. Smoke was emerging from the back of the Receptor Box, the earlier humming had become loud buzzing, and the coloured lights were now pulsated so rapidly that the professor struggled to flick switches in the correct sequence to slow them down. Yet, there was still more to worry him. The needle on the dial showing the amount of electricity being used was revolving wildly out of control, while the row of numbers indicating the year required for a space mission spun like a fruit machine.

It was into this chaos that Jake entered the shed.

"Professor," he gasped, one hand holding the door, "what's happening?"

The professor's face ran hot with sweat. "Everything is going crazy. It's never happened before. I can't control any of it."

Oscar, who was close behind, noticed a heat haze rising. He sniffed the bad air. "Leave this to me," he called, rushing to the Receptor and ripping out the only visible wire. At once the coloured lights vanished, the needle and numbers froze, and the buzzing stopped. The sudden quietness was astounding. He then pulled the electrical plug from the wall socket and left it on the table.

"Great!" shouted the professor angrily. "Very well done, Oscar, you simpleton."

"What have I done wrong?" begged Oscar, sure he had put a much-needed stop to a runaway situation.

"Just about everything," was the professor's grim reply. "Would you shut down your computer without first going through the correct procedures?"

"Of course not, but…"

"Then why do it with my things? Goodness knows what damage you've done to both the Receptor and Starlight Machine. I had everything under complete control before you walked in."

"I don't think so, Professor," said Jake, coming to his father's defence. "You looked very worried, as if you were trying to stop the whole thing from exploding."

"Exploding! There was no chance of an explosion, silly boy. A small fire, maybe, but never an explosion."

Just as the words left his lips, a loud *bang* shook the back of the Receptor, followed by what looked like a spray of steam. The shock knocked the professor off his seat.

"There we are," remarked Oscar smugly, helping the professor to get up. "Jake told you so."

The professor squirmed free before reaching behind the Receptor, where he felt the unmistakable shape of a fizzy-drinks can wedged under the casing. After a great deal of wriggling, he pulled it out. It was bent and buckled, with the top blown off.

"Ah, that's where I left it." He pushed the warm can into Oscar's hand. "That, Mr Trotter, is your explosion. The contents must've boiled with the heat coming from the Receptor."

"I could hardly be expected to know that," protested Oscar. "I thought I was helping." Then, dropping the can, he inspected the Receptor's casing.

"Oh well," appeased the professor, his mood swinging back after noticing the care Oscar was taking to check for signs of damage, "think nothing more of it, dear boy. A simple mistake to make. But in future, leave the clever stuff to a genius… namely me!"

"Is there any chance we can carry on today?" asked Jake hopefully.

The professor ran a finger through the sugar-sweet liquid sprayed over the Receptor's controls. It oozed around the switches and dials.

"Um, cherry flavour if I'm not mistaken," he said, sucking his finger, "with a hint of E150d colour and Acesulfame. Absolutely delicious."

"But can we continue?"

"Can't risk it, my boy. The Box needs to cool and dry off before I can repair the wire your father so recklessly ripped out."

Jake flopped, sulkily kicking the can across the floor.

The professor saw the disappointment on his face. "I'll tell you what," he continued. "Can I trust you to clean up the mess while your father and I make a spot of tea? I can't wait to hear what happened at the police station. But no fiddling with my machines, mind. I must have your promise on that."

Jake jumped to the task.

"Well, that's settled," smiled the professor, leaving the shed with Oscar.

While walking to the cottage, Oscar expressed his fears over Miguel's release. He expected the news to upset the professor, but his reaction was calm and steady. This surprised Oscar, as it greatly disturbed him. It was then he realised the professor wasn't looking around the garden for intruders as they trod the path, as he usually did, or made any effort to stay quiet.

"I had a feeling that might happen," said the professor, stopping to square-up to Oscar. "You can't tell half a story to the police and expect them to come to a correct conclusion."

"Shall I stay overnight? Once Jake is taken home I could return. You would feel safer if I did, I'm sure, and it would certainly ease my conscience for dropping you into this pickle."

"*Toshkins*!" replied the professor, jumping from one leg to the other. "If Miguel thinks he can get me, why, let him try, that's

212

what I say. If he gets into the cottage I'll tell him to *stick 'em up* and, if he doesn't, I'll stick him to the wall with my glue gun. I'll sleep with it under my pillow. I've already topped up the ammunition."

"Is that wise, given the doggy trigger?"

The professor considered the problem as they approached the cottage. "Okay, if I can't hold him up, I'll hold him out. If I hear any noises outside, anything at all, I'll use the gun to glue-up the door and windows. I'll keep it under the bed instead." He pushed the door open. "Does that make you feel happier?"

"Much," said Oscar, crossing to the kitchen to put the kettle on.

Inside the shed, Jake carefully wiped the sticky drink from around the knobs, switches, lights and dials of the Receptor Box. It took a while, but soon the Receptor appeared clean and dry. He sat back contentedly, admiring his work and wondering what the various switches did. And the more he stared, the more the controls seemed to stare back, like a row of disciplined soldiers in perfect symmetry awaiting orders.

It is hard to say what happens to boys when faced with machines and the possibility of adventure, even when forbidden to fiddle with anything that is not theirs to touch. Invariably, temptation gradually overcomes caution. And, if left unchecked, such feelings germinate into an unstoppable need to explore.

And so it was with Jake, despite his mother always telling the neighbours he was the most obedient child she had ever known, never a moment's trouble, and could be relied upon to act older than his age. Sadly, Muriel Striker did not understand older boys either.

Fostering an overwhelming urge to play at being the professor, Jake pondered over what he could do without getting into trouble. The shed door was open, but it was unlikely anyone would see. Shutting it would only raise suspicion.

Now with a sweet tingle of excitement running through his body, he fluffed his hair into a tangle and thrust his hands forward as if to turn the switches and dials. But, without touching, everything was cold and inert and the game was not in the least thrilling. It lacked the most important ingredient for fun, a true element of danger. And so, after double-checking the main power plug was disconnected from the wall socket, he picked up the broken wire and mischievously poked it into a hole in the casing. Nothing happened and, in honesty, he was relieved.

For such a small experience, Jake felt exhilarated. But it was now time to stop mucking about. And yet, as he rose from the chair, his eyes were drawn towards the electrical energy dial. The indicator needle remained jammed mid-way around the face, but the dial itself began to glow. Instinctively, he tapped the glass. That was *a big, big mistake*. The needle suddenly spun to 'full' power.

"*How*?" he shrieked, grabbing the unattached plug from the table top.

Then it happened!

Oscar was pouring milk into three mugs when a tremendous flash of light burst from the shed door, dazzling him through the kitchen window.

"What the..?" screamed the professor at the very same moment, anxious a storm was about to hit.

But Oscar was already out and running down the path.

"Professor," he shouted back on reaching the shed, "what should I do? Jake's inside and the sailors are everywhere."

"I'm coming, I'm coming," called the professor from the cottage door. "First, I need to grab some things."

The brilliant light, originating from the same tiny lens in the front of the Receptor Box, filled the shed and spilled into the garden through the open door, only gradually fading with distance. It was the same scene of seamanship as before, but the story had moved on.

"One day you might make captain if your weakness isn't too liberally spread amongst the crews who serve under you, Mister Fairbrother. Then, and only then, may you talk to me as an equal. Meanwhile, bite your tongue, sir."

So saying, the commodore slapped a heavy hand on the midshipman's back, causing him to shake so excessively with fear that he was barely able to conceal it.

"See here," continued the commodore with the stiffness of rank, *"we both know the men are the dregs of the gutter, who serve only because nobody else will have them. Cut-throats, beggars and thieves, the lot. The Navy accepts this and curtails their excesses by wielding a firm hand and a cutting whip. Take harsh punishment away and the ship would be lost to the mob. It is different in the training of officers. They are taught their trade by example. Still, if I can't make a man of you by association, the Navy will have to accept you to be a mild-mannered ninny of no real value to the fighting service."*

"Sir, that is too much."

"No, sir, it is not enough. Go ahead if you must. Give the keel-haulers a double grog of rum to steady their nerves and warm their livers after it is over, but say it is your doing, not mine. But the boatswain gets none. Not a drop I say. He asked for help with the rope, and that I won't permit. He must pay with his skin. If he becomes chilled from the cold and wet, let him fully recover and then give him a dozen lashes with the cat of nine tails. I want him well to feel the pain of every stroke. After, have plenty of salt rubbed into the wounds. You may tell him it comes with my compliments. Take good note, Mister Fairbrother—spoilt deckhands make mutineers." He pulled a double-barrelled pistol from his belt. *"Nip 'em in the bud, that's my policy."* After checking the flints, he pushed it back. *"Now, putting that behind us, it's time for more pressing matters. Are you joining me for*

luncheon? It's pork today. Cook put a knife to one of the fat hogs I was given in Canton. I reserved a juicy loin."

"I thought the Chinese Mandarin refused to supply the ship with fresh meat?"

"He did, Mister Fairbrother, that is until I told him our ship's cannon could destroy the whole port if I had the mind."

"That did it?"

"It put fear on his face, but I could tell he still wasn't willing to spend a penny of his own fortune helping us. Blast if he didn't then try to bluff me. He said the merchants of the city were loading supplies onto three warships of thirty-two guns each and a sloop with ten guns as we spoke, which could be sent against us."

"What then?"

"It came to me in a flash. I replied in a strong tone that if we had to remain at anchor because we lacked the necessary provisions to sail, the men would starve or turn to cannibalism. I added that I had already lost too many men to scurvy and could spare no more as food."

"He believed it?"

"I'm not sure he did, so I played an ace. I walked a pace and then turned, saying that our sailors would naturally prefer to eat the plump, over-fed Chinese than their emaciated comrades, and none was fatter than him."

"That did it!"

"Never seen a Chinaman move so fast to give up his pigs. So now the question remains, are you joining me for luncheon after you've finished here?"

Two armed Marines in scarlet uniforms now burst onto deck, grabbed the boatswain and took him below.

With the boatswain gone, all but one of the remaining men at the rope dropped to their knees with exhaustion; the other, with his hands around his throat, fell face-first onto the planking in some kind of seizure. The sea swell had made the unpleasant task of keel-hauling impossible.

With two men gone, the remaining haulers knew the struggle to save their shipmate was over, yet the order to stop pulling had not been given. They tried to stand just as another massive wave burst over their heads.

The power of the wave rocked the ship and again sailors were sent sprawling in all directions, sea water washing one way and then the other over the deck. The hauling rope, now loose of any grip, slid along the deck with the forward motion of the mighty ship, and Tucker's life slipped away with it.

Only the boy, agile of limb and now with the heart to save Tucker's body, ran after the disappearing rope. He flung himself forward, catching the end which he managed to tie around his waist. But it was too little, too late. The heavy rope was unstoppable as it slid away, dragging the boy over the side. Unable to swim, he sank quickly with the weight of the sodden rope, his up-stretched arms disappearing beneath the waves.

The seamen turned in panic to where the commodore had been standing moments before, knowing the loss of a rope was a punishable offence. But he had left the poop deck, and now only the midshipman towered above them.

Fairbrother could see the terror written across their faces. After glancing over his shoulder to check he stood alone, he silently waved the men back to their usual duties. Their skins would be saved… this once.

The keel-hauling was over—the crime punished—and Tucker was dead.

It had been the commodore's decision to keel-haul Tucker, a punishment the midshipman believed to be outdated in the modern 18th century Royal Navy and he wanted nothing to do with it. The ship's log would report one death by keel-hauling and another by accident during a moderate storm.

"Davy Jones' locker for the boy, too," said an old seaman, removing his hat and holding it close to his chest.

"Or shark bait," said another. *"The King will save two shillings this week."*

The older man opened his clenched fist. In the palm was a pure gold earring. *"Tucker gave me this, just in case he didn't…"* He stopped, not wanting to say the word 'survive'. *"Poor wretch. It's not much to show for a lifetime of loyal service to the crown. Still, I'll do my duty by him and make sure his widow gets it to buy bread. He's not going to need it for his own funeral, that's for sure."*

"Why not keep it? The shipmates know you never liked Tucker, that is until he drowned."

"That may be true, but it don't stop me feeling pity for his wife."

"The one I feel pity for is the boy," said the other. *"He deserved a better end. There's nothing of his to send home."*

"Dead is dead, no matter how it comes."

"I despise the commodore for what he did to Tucker," whispered the younger. *"No man can hold his breath long enough to be pulled under a big ship?"*

"Never known it to end happily. Death be as certain as hanging from the yardarm, but without the neck-stretching. At least drowning is a sailor's way to meet his maker."

"Same for the boy, I suppose."

"Take pleasure in knowing the sea has robbed the commodore of his chance to clamp the poor lad in irons."

"Hold your tongues," thundered a command from behind. They turned to find Fairbrother with his fingers wrapped around the hilt of a curved naval sword. *"You speak mutiny while the commodore is at his table eating pork, his pistol drawn and cocked by his side. Be sure of this. He knows how you feel and it don't give him one bit of indigestion. Get back to your duties and don't let me regret my leniency."*

"Where are you, Jake?" shouted Oscar desperately, unable to see him through the awesome light show.

A whimpering noise came from deep inside the shed, but exactly where was impossible to tell. For Jake had bolted at the first sight of the ship reappearing, scarcely minding the direction he took. He ended back under the table.

"For goodness sake, Son, I can't get to you if you don't call out."

Now the professor arrived, wearing a pair of specially devised sunglasses with shuttered lenses. Instantly, he could see Jake's feet, although the rest of him was masked in darkness.

"He's over there," he said, pointing. "Below the Receptor." He pressed two pairs of glasses into Oscar's hand. "Put one on and give the other to Jake."

At last Oscar could separate the wooden walls and floor of the shed from the bright images of the past.

"I see you, Son. I'm on my way."

"I can't move, Dad. I'm really frightened by these horrible men," came a cry from the darkness, Jake's back pressed hard against the shed wall. "Help me. I don't want to drown."

Oscar turned to the professor. "Can I break into the light?"

"You did last time when you rescued me," he replied. "Nothing's changed. Remember, the people, the ship and the sea are not real despite appearances. They have no substance whatsoever."

Drawing a deep breath, as if expecting to pass through water, Oscar stepped boldly but cautiously into the scene. His body immediately blocked part of the light from the lens, casting a deep shadow through the centre of the ship's deck. He edged forward one step at a time, the crew disappearing and then reappearing as he interrupted different areas of light.

On reaching the table, Oscar knelt beneath. There on the floor sat Jake, sobbing in the shadow, the sound of the sailors and the visual movement of the rocking ship making him feeble. Oscar could feel Jake trembling as he pushed the sunglasses over his eyes. He then held out a hand, but Jake refused to take it.

"How do I turn the wretched thing off, Professor?" called Oscar over his shoulder. "Jake won't move until the images stop."

"I told you before. Unplug the Receptor Box. But don't be tempted to break anything."

Jake grabbed his father's leg as he began to crawl away.

"Don't leave me, Dad. There's something terribly wrong happening. The Receptor is working all by itself. It's not connected to the electricity supply. This time the ship must be real."

"Did you hear that, Professor?" yelled Oscar over the noise. "Jake says it's not plugged in."

"Oh," considered the professor. "Yes, I suppose that could be the case."

"What, real?" winced Oscar in shock.

"No, you fool, working by itself. I must say, I wasn't expecting that to happen."

"Tell me what to do," repeated Oscar, "and quickly. Jake's shaking like a leaf."

"Let me think for a moment." The professor's eyes rolled. "Ah, yes, it's quite obvious when the possibilities are properly considered. I remember installing a back-up battery into the Receptor Box, in case of a mains power failure while images from space were streaming into its memory circuits. I fitted it during the so-called Winter of Discontent, when union strikes brought the electricity industry to a halt and everyone in the country was regularly thrown into periods of blackout. I did it by candlelight. But that was years and years ago. I've never since had cause to test it, thank goodness. I'm amazed it still works. Well, well, that explains a thing or two. There was I thinking the Receptor sometimes overheated from consuming too much electricity, when all along it was probably the old battery being overcharged every time the Box was switched on at the mains. Well I never did! The things to be discovered by accident."

"Yes, yes, but what do I do to shut it down?"

"Nothing. Keep well away," said the professor firmly. "I'll deal with this little emergency." And with that, he calmly walked over to the Receptor and pushed a button hidden under a small square panel which controlled the auxiliary battery. At once the images vanished and the shed fell dark and silent. "And that, gentlemen, is how it works," he said with pride. "You must admit, I really am a genius."

Before leaving the shed, the professor pulled the loose wire from the Receptor. "How did this get into the wrong place?" The plastic insulation was burned and unusable.

Jake, who extricated himself from under the table without help once the images disappeared, handed back the sunglasses. He said nothing, although his face radiated guilt.

"I guess this caused the fault," the professor continued, holding the end of the wire uppermost. "Fizzy drink must've got inside the Receptor through the air vents, where the liquid made a live connection between the broken wire and the lens. The battery then provided the power to kick the whole thing off. But that doesn't explain how the wire got itself inside the casing. What do you think, Jake?"

Oscar answered for him. "Leave it at that. He knows he did wrong, Professor."

"Let this be a lesson to you both. Electricity is tricky stuff. It doesn't always need wire to carry a current. Water does the job perfectly well. The important thing now is to ensure it doesn't happen again. I'll dry the inside of the Receptor properly before fitting a replacement wire into the correct hole. Now, where did I put the coil?"

There are many contradictions to being a parent, and Jake was about to witness one of them.

If a child does something mildly wrong, a parent becomes cross. But if a child does something really bad which puts their life in danger or frightens them, then a parent will kiss and cuddle, grateful no lasting harm was done. In essence, relief always outweighs anger.

And so it now was with Jake. Oscar hugged him dearly, showing his love and thankfulness for the experience being over without injury.

But not everyone was so easily soothed. The professor was turning greener, a clear indication his blood pressure was rising.

Although blame had not been directly apportioned, Jake knew the professor had every right to expect his equipment to be left alone, and duly apologised. It was sincerely meant, and the air was immediately cleared.

"We'll put the ghastly episode behind us," said the professor more cheerfully. "You must admit, though, it *was* quite exciting."

"Will there be a next time for me?" Jake asked timidly, feeling more anxious than physically shaky.

"Try stopping us," replied the professor.

Chapter 17
Return of the Songbird

"And how was your weekend, Jake?" asked Muriel Striker late that evening, noticing the pale colour of his skin as she took his bag. "Did you get up to much? Did you keep dry? Are you feeling well? Did *he* feed you properly?"

Fortunately, Jake had rehearsed the answers during the drive home and was prepared for an inquisition. He had also discussed with his father ways to approach the subject of having another weekend together. They thought it would be very tricky to arrange. Funny how things don't always work out as expected!

"Yes to everything," was Jake's ready reply. "We had a great time... but it's super-nice to be home, Mum," he added as a happy afterthought, noticing how it brought a smile to her face.

Muriel opened a kitchen cupboard where a plate of cupcakes awaited his return, these being Jake's all-time favourites. Strangely, though, she handed him the plate with apprehension, hoping the treat would soften the blow to come.

"I received a phone call from Julie this morning. Your aunt wants to bring Gracie over for the weekend while she attends a beauty spa. Your Uncle Dave can't or won't step up to look after Gracie while she's away. A typical male Trotter, always letting everyone down. So I said she could. I know you don't like Gracie very much, but what could I do? The spa voucher was my Christmas present to Aunt Julie, and I know Gracie has a soft spot for you."

Jake pictured a little girl with pigtails and glasses, cuddling a doll and asking if he would like to help change the baby's nappy. He shuddered at the thought.

"What if I'm already going out and you forgot? Would Ghoulish Gracie still want to come? Don't forget, it's the start of half term and she might ask to stay longer."

"I can't say that. It wouldn't be true. Anyway, Julie would be upset with me for spoiling her arrangements... and please stop calling your cousin that horrible name."

Jake thought again. A marvellous idea popped into his head.

"Okay, Mum, what if you say I'm already going out for a rough and tumble adventure with Dad but Gho...er...Gracie can come along too if she wants to join in. You always told me Aunt Julie doesn't like Dad and never has. That could work. After all, it isn't as if you're saying Ghoul-head can't come. Just think, we could both be spared the little brat... girl."

Muriel doubted it would work. "I don't know. After all, you don't have any plans and I won't lie."

"I could have!" said Jake with a clever hint in his voice. "Come on, Mum, it's worth a try."

"What if she decides to come here anyway and you have nowhere to go? We would look a proper pair of chumps. No, we must face it, Jake, for your plan to work it would need your father's guarantee to take you away, and maybe he has already made other arrangements?"

"I could ask him," he returned gleefully. "I'm positive he will say 'yes'."

Muriel noticed a glint in Jake's eye. "What are you up to? You're being unusually kind to Gracie."

"What?" was his stunned reply.

"Offering to take Gracie with you, if she wants to go. I can hardly believe it."

Jake was shaken by his mother's misunderstanding of the plan. "No, Mum, I didn't mean that. I thought she would be put off."

But it was too late. Muriel had already speed-dialled the number and was talking to Aunt Julie.

"I know it's a nuisance. Jake must've forgotten to tell me." She winked at Jake, who looked on with trepidation. "I know, Julie, he surprised me too." She winked again. "No, Julie, I don't think he wants a girlfriend, even if it's Gracie." A bark came down the phone. "No, dear, I didn't say Gracie is unattractive. Quite the opposite actually. Jake was the one who suggested she could join him. What do you think?" That clearly calmed the conversation. "Okay, Julie... until Friday then. Bye, bye, dear. Give my love to Gracie, oh, and tell her to bring some of her favourite dolls."

Jake already had his head in his hands when the receiver went down. "Tell me it's not happening!"

"Oh, dear," said Muriel. "Have I done something wrong?"

"What will you do with Gracie while I'm away, Mum?" he asked hopefully.

"No, Jake, you have it wrong. Julie thinks Gracie will love to join you and *him* on an adventure, as long as she keeps her nice clothes clean. What fun for you both."

"Great!" muttered Jake, returning a half-eaten cupcake to the plate.

On Tuesday Jake telephoned his father. Muriel was in the garden taking down the washing which had been hanging all day on the clothes line, so he knew he could speak freely for a few minutes.

"Not Aunt Julie's beastly child?" remarked Oscar, bursting into laughter. "Well, my boy, you have landed us in a proper mess and no mistake. Don't you have a special name for her?"

"Ghoulish Gracie."

"Yes, that's it. Well, I never did. You of all people inviting her."

"But I didn't," he protested. "As usual Mum got it all wrong. What can I do, Dad?"

"As to that..."

"Is there nothing?"

"Short of poisoning her, nothing I can think of."

"With what?" Jake replied half-heartedly.

"Don't even joke about it."

"Should we cancel seeing the professor?"

"Absolutely not. In fact, I have quite a surprise for you on that score. Just before you rang, I received a call from the professor. He was using a telephone box. He wants me to drive over to the cottage this evening. He says it's urgent. Apparently, he has something vital to show me that just can't wait."

"What?" asked Jake excitedly.

"I'll phone you tomorrow when I know more."

Jake heard the back door slam. "Mum's back. Better go. Don't forget to call, Dad!"

"I won't. Oh, and don't dream about Gracie," spluttered Oscar through his laughter.

"Nor you about Mum," he replied.

That stopped Oscar in his tracks.

The professor's news was incredible.

"I found this note pinned to the door. It's from Miguel of all people. He says he wants to *'be clean'*."

"Really?" exclaimed Oscar, taking the note. "I suppose he means he wants to *'come clean'*."

"If I agree not to inform the police, he'll return tonight and tell me everything. He says he can be trusted."

"Do you think he can?"

"That's what I wanted to ask you."

Oscar read on. "What's this? He wants you to leave the door open as a sign of goodwill."

"I know what you're thinking. It could be genuine but on the other hand…"

"It could be a trap. Agreeing is very risky."

"So what should I do, Mr Trotter? He might know where Michael is. I would never forgive myself if I lost the only opportunity to find out."

Oscar found the idea of leaving the door open very worrying and said so. "This rogue asks an awful lot of you."

"Sure," replied the professor with growing determination, "but just think what might be gained."

"I suppose."

"I was hoping you wouldn't reject the plan out of hand. I trust your judgement."

"Okay, then do it, if that's what you want. But leave the rest to me."

"To you? He says I must be alone."

"And so you will be, Professor, in the cottage at least. I'll keep a look-out from the shed. If there's any monkey business, I'll be ready. What do you say?"

"I say yes, and thank you!"

"Oh, and keep Jorvik handy on a lead."

The evening was unusually cold for the season. By the time the moon had disappeared behind a layer of cloud, Oscar was feeling the chilling effects of the unheated shed and wished he hadn't been so eager to help. Yet, the cold was only part of his discomfort.

Gazing up at the night sky, he was also finding the darkness hard to reconcile once the unlit shed and overcast garden grimly merged into a single blackness, leaving a strangely forbidding aura in whichever direction he looked. As a town-dweller he had never known such impenetrable murkiness, with no street lamps anywhere close offering even dim light. It was a wretched situation he should've anticipated, but hadn't.

In his role as guardian, Oscar was startled several times by outside movement. On each occasion, he rolled off the chair to crouch beneath the window-sill until he distinguished the call of a fox, the swoop of an owl or rats scurrying between secret hiding places from the expected footsteps of human activity. By midnight he had become quite adept at separating the animal noises, but time had passed very, very slowly and boredom threatened to dampen any remaining wish to continue.

As one o'clock approached, Oscar was nearing the end of his patience. It was obvious Miguel was not going to turn up, and there seemed little point in remaining uncomfortable for much longer. Perhaps another half-hour at most.

Standing at the window, he pressed his hands against the frame and stared towards the cottage, no longer expecting to be noticed. The cottage door remained open and all appeared tranquil, so his eyes diverted to the soft curves and cheerless silhouettes of the nearby shrubs and trees.

By now even the foraging animals had gone to ground, leaving a general stillness which added to the feeling of isolation he couldn't shake off. He dragged the chair to the door and wedged the backrest under the handle to stop any intruders entering if the lock failed… not that he expected anyone. It just made him feel… well… safer.

Little did he know the timing was perfection.

Turning away to pour out the last drops of hot tea from a vacuum flask, Oscar suddenly sensed a presence. He had heard nothing, but intuitively knew he was no longer alone. He dropped to the floor, sheltering below the sill. Spilt tea seeped through the knees of his trousers.

Then it happened. The door handle rattled, not once but twice. Although the clatter sent shivers down his spine, he still felt a heady urge to peep out of the window. Whether this was from morbid curiosity or blind panic was impossible to tell, but such recklessness had to be subdued, and after a few seconds' deliberation he decided against it. Yet, with somebody or even many people definitely outside, a dreadful thought came to mind; it was likely he was no longer the hunter but the hunted. The plan was going drastically wrong.

Feeling more cut off than ever, Oscar held his breath, anxiously straining to hear any voices. Conversation would mean there was more than one person. Then, suddenly, heavy steps pounded between the door and the window, and at long last something distinct broke the silence. It came in the form of a sharp cry, louder and higher than a command or rebuke, and tinged with rage. And after the briefest pause, the handle again rattled and the door shook, this time hard enough to cause the chair to rock.

Oscar trembled, expecting the insubstantial door to be breached at any moment. He glanced around. The gloomy shed on a gloomy night was not the place where his life should end. But if it was to be his fate, he wondered whether Jake would remember him fondly for risking so much for so little? He cursed the professor's foolhardiness for thinking Miguel could be trusted, and his own reckless stupidity for going along with it. And yet, at that moment, he also knew his life depended on what he did next. There would be no help or rescue.

With nothing at hand to beat off an assailant, the only option left was to hide, hoping whoever was out there would eventually give up and go away. Oscar knew it was cowardly, but better he survived than die a hero. Anyway, if discovered, he could still make a fist-fight of it before falling bloodied to the floor. Surely Jake would admire the way he fell with honour.

But where to hide? There was so little in the shed, and so much empty space.

The *thud* of a kick against the door, followed by a curse, sent Oscar scuttling for the table, where he slid beneath. But the open legs left him horribly exposed. The only other place was behind the Bubble Car door.

Hardly waiting to think, Oscar rolled out and made a crouched dash for the car, where he remained hidden for what seemed a breathless age but was actually less than three minutes. And only when eventually it became obvious the shed door was not going to be smashed in did he finally dare sneak a quick look over the top.

His eyes flew open in horror.

Peering through the window was the unmistakable shape of a hunched man with a large hood drawn over his head, looking alarmingly like a ghostly monk. The figure was too small to be Miguel, and immediately Harry shot to mind, with the hood covering his head wound. He quickly remembered the first time he had seen Harry in the lay-by, when he had hobbled in a hunched manner. Everything fitted, and the likelihood of it being the worst of the gang turned his legs to jelly. For, there was no getting away from the truth; he was trapped, helpless and probably as good as dead.

Once more the handle was vigorously shaken, this time with such force that it seemed the entire shed moved with it. The door lock clicked and the chair, already loose, finally fell backwards. A rush of night air flooded into the cold space as the door swung open, the dark figure filling the entrance.

The hooded man stood perfectly immobile, with vapour rising from one hand.

Oscar gasped. "Oh my lord…"

"Say that again," came a shrill reply, the figure throwing back the hood with all the drama of a horror movie. His cold eyes scanned the dim space. "Mr Trotter, for goodness sake come out. I've brought you drinking chocolate to keep you awake, although I've been outside so long it's probably no longer hot. Twice I've scalded my blessed fingers trying to get in. Where the devil are you?"

"Over here," at last mumbled Oscar in a tottering voice, his head rising so gradually from behind the car that it was reasonable to think he had only just woken from a deep sleep.

"Not a moment too soon by the looks of it. A fine watchdog you make."

The insult cut deeply. "You blithering idiot," Oscar growled as he struggled to his feet, losing any inhibitions. "Did you seriously have to scare me to death with another of your completely stupid costumes? I was expecting a dangerous stranger, not you coming here dressed for a blasted Halloween party."

"You said you'd be ready for whatever happened."

"And so I have been, all flippin' evening and half the night. You happened to come along the one time I was momentarily off guard."

"Go on, admit it, I frightened you," the accusation bringing a smile to the professor's face.

Oscar wanted to exact retribution but thought better of it. "Next time you want something, have the good grace to say who you are before bursting in. Anyway…"

Oscar was about to add 'nothing whatsoever has happened' when, for a split second, a beam of light from a distant torch caught the window panes. Then, just as quickly, the light vanished. A single figure stood at the foot of the drive.

"Someone's come," declared Oscar, pinning the professor to the wall.

"It's Miguel."

"We can't be certain it's him."

"You're hurting me," pleaded the old man. "I can't move."

"I'll let go if you promise to keep out of sight. This is the moment we've waited for. He'll go if he sees there are two of us."

"No, I really can't move. My c-c-courage has suddenly let me down."

"Oh, for goodness sake, get a grip," Oscar replied stiffly. "This isn't the time to be witless, or lose your silly voice!"

The beam reappeared, moving from side to side like a blind man's stick as the figure cautiously approached the cottage.

"How can we be s-s-sure it's Miguel? I agree it could be a set-up."

"There's only one way to find out," replied Oscar. "Whoever it is, he appears to be alone. There are two of us. Did you leave the door unlocked when you came over?"

"I think so," replied the professor, no longer sure of anything.

231

"Right, we'll never get a better chance."

By now the figure had slipped inside the cottage, from where an almighty scream rang out into the night.

"That's it," roared Oscar, not waiting for the professor. "Down on him!"

"No, Oscar, I f-f-forgot to…"

But the warning was too late. Oscar had gone and was already dashing across the path. He was pumped up with anger. He burst into the cottage.

"*Blood and guts,*" he cried, stopping with a sudden jolt.

There stood the intruder, goggle-eyed and quivering, his face blackened with mud. He was cornered by a snarling creature of a species he didn't recognise tethered to a long length of rope.

"Help me!" pleaded the man, as Jorvik bared its needle-like teeth.

"For pity's sake, stay where you are. Don't move a muscle," ordered Oscar while also standing frozen to the spot, knowing only the professor could control Jorvik.

Had the intruder listened to Oscar's advice and remained still, he might have been saved. But he didn't.

With Jorvik now sniffing around Oscar after detecting a second unfamiliar scent, the intruder chanced sliding towards the small kitchen window. And although he moved silently on tiptoes, Jorvik was not duped. The Bloodrat turned, snarled, and struck out in all its angry blindness, jumping up to sink its teeth into the intruder's trousers, ripping straight through to the soft flesh below.

The scream was terrible as Jorvik hung down from a vice-like grip, its legs swinging off the floor as the intruder ran about the room in writhing pain.

"D-d-down, brute," shouted the professor as he at last entered the cottage, jerking on the rope. Pulling Jorvik off seemed to hurt the intruder as much as the bite.

As Jorvik's paws hit the floor, Oscar leapt onto the intruder and bundled him to the ground. The pitiful man—bewildered, squashed, bitten and breathless—dropped without a struggle and fell on his side. Oscar rolled him onto his face, snatched his wrist and held him in an unbreakable arm-lock.

"I come to be helping," cried the intruder in a foreign accent which identified him as Miguel. "You get my note?"

"Fiddlesticks," replied Oscar, while watching the professor push Jorvik into the cupboard. "How do we know you can be trusted?"

"You don't call police, I think?"

"Maybe and m-m-maybe not," said the professor, now adding the pressure of his own knee to the small of Miguel's back. "One false m-m-move and you'll cop it."

"Cop it?" he repeated. "What is 'cop it'?"

"Be worse for you. Do you understand that?" said Oscar.

He nodded. "I can now have my arm back, I think? It gets, what you call, the needles and the pins."

The professor stood to fetch the glue gun and a new bottle of Voice Stuff Number 8½. "No funny business, m-m-matey, or else," he said as he walked away, eventually returning to poke the gun barrel into Miguel's side while gulping rather too much potion.

"Else I cop it?"

"You learn q-q-quickly. N-n-now, get up slowly so we can have a p-p-proper look at you. And w-w-wipe that muck off your face."

Oscar released Miguel's arm and he rose awkwardly onto his feet, his fingertips finding the rip in his trousers. A little blood stained his hand. "See, I bleed again. You help me, please. I not want rabies."

The professor lowered the gun. "No chance of that because…" The sentence was never finished.

At that moment of repose, and in a move of unbelievable agility, Miguel suddenly and unexpectedly elbowed Oscar aside and ripped the gun clean out of the professor's hand. He held it like a man used to brandishing weapons. The professor tried to grab the barrel to wrest it back from Miguel's grip, but it was hopeless.

"Oh, jolly well done, Professor," scorned Oscar, getting up. "Now we're in for it!"

"You stop talking, I think, or you cop it," demanded Miguel in a voice as loathsome as the professor had ever heard. "I have something to say and you *will* listen or be shooted."

The professor wilted under Miguel's ugly threat, but Oscar was too annoyed to be cautious.

"Oh, very well, get on with it," barked Oscar, knowing the glue gun was more of an inconvenience to the victim than a danger. "And the expression is shot, not shooted, idiot."

"You brave man, I think," said Miguel, and in a startling turn of events he lowered the barrel. "You see, I not want to hurt nobody."

"Anybody," corrected Oscar, much to the professor's annoyance, who saw no gain in inflaming the situation.

"Anybody? Okay. My English is no much good but getting better."

"For goodness sake," bawled Oscar, seizing the glue gun. "We're not here for a lesson in English grammar. Why have you come?"

"I am called Miguel. I come from Spain. I rob banks in my country. I tell you this because I want you to trust me. I am on the running away."

"On the run," said the professor without thinking, before releasing rings of green smoke from his mouth.

The sight of the rings floating to the ceiling shook Miguel to his boots. "What devilish thing is this? What happening to mouth, old man?"

"Oh, you mean this?" The professor blew more rings.

"You do it again! What is trick?"

"He's a witch doctor with great powers," tormented Oscar. "Little by little, he can turn men into green toads."

Miguel smiled insincerely. "I am not much believing such fairy tale things. It is not possible, I think."

"Show him your arm, Professor," insisted Oscar with confidence.

The professor lifted a sleeve, revealing green skin which was darkening by the second.

"Oh," exclaimed Miguel, "you really *are* magic man."

"Magic, no," said the professor as he rolled his sleeve back down, "but great powers, most certainly."

"I wouldn't cross him again if I was you, unless you too want to be turned green," continued Oscar firmly. "He can do many incredible things, including shrinking Frenchmen into frogs. I'm sure he could equally oblige a Spaniard. How do you fancy becoming an onion?"

"Turn me into Spanish onion or green toad is horrible thing," cowed Miguel with alarm. "I not wish to be anything but normal man."

"It'll be your own fault if you are."

"I understand I must obey. Old man in nappy has dark powers. He also invented little starlight car, I am told."

"WHAT!" shouted the professor excitedly. "Did you hear that, Oscar? He knows about my machine." He turned to face Miguel. "There can only be one person who could've told you about it and used that particular name. It was Michael, wasn't it?"

"One step at a time," intervened Oscar before Miguel had time to reply, wanting to shield the professor from possible disappointment. "Start from the beginning. Tell us why you're here, and no funny business or else."

The professor was angered by Oscar's interruption.

"I come to England to get away from Spanish police. I not much money."

"Not a very good bank robber, either?" sneered Oscar.

"No, not much good. In London, by chance, I see three men force another man into van. I not know whether to help him. That is when they catch me spying. I running from them, but I not know way around little streets and soon they trap me in opposite ways."

"You mean they cornered you?" asked the professor.

"Yes. Had me in corner okay. I have nowhere to run. I tell them I will not squeak, but they not believe me."

"Squeal. You wouldn't squeal."

"That is right, old man. I said I would not make the sounds of a mice to nobody."

"Mouse to anybody," snapped Oscar impatiently.

"Shush," cautioned the professor, much to Oscar's surprise. "Let him get on with it. I want to hear about Michael."

"Well! That's rich coming from you."

"Please. Very good you correct me. I want to learn English if I am to stay here. It is well known in Spain your government does not refuse immigrants from European continent, even if no space left for British people. I want to be here before last of jobs taken."

"You'll have plenty of time to brush-up your English from inside a prison cell."

"No! I help you in whatever you want if promise made not to call police or turn me green."

The mention of police made Oscar recall the possibility of having had his own name entered into criminal files.

"I'm no scholar like you, Professor, but I know when I've been spun a cock and bull story. We should hand him over to the cops. That would also clear me of any wrongdoing."

"I cop it after all," cried Miguel, "even though I try help?"

"Oh, be quiet," shouted Oscar and the professor in unison.

Yet the professor was beginning to believe Miguel could be trusted after all, especially since they shared a common enemy in Harry. Miguel desired to be safe, and he desired Michael's safe return. There was mutual interest. Persuading Oscar to grab the opportunity presented the greatest immediate difficulty.

"Let's not act in haste," said the professor, slipping off a boot to scratch his foot. "I don't particularly care how or why Miguel became involved with the gang. The fact that he knows about the Starlight Machine is highly significant and the only good lead we have."

Oscar agreed, but without enthusiasm.

"Anyway, the police have already let him go once. What makes you think they'll take any more notice this time?"

"Go on," said Oscar, aware Miguel was listening keenly to every word.

"It seems to me he can save us a great deal of time if he cooperates. Face it. We don't even know where the caravan's gone. *He* might know. Added to which, it's dangerous spying on criminals. I'm not sure my nerves can take much more. No, in my view we should pump him for information and then decide what to do next. If he doesn't willingly cooperate, I can make him talk using special potions. My son must be saved, even if it means using Miguel as an experimental guinea-pig."

"Michael is your son?" interrupted Miguel, scared by the threat of magic.

"Didn't you realise?"

"No. I thought you just want to stop us use machine."

"Do you know where he is?" begged the professor.

"I did."

"Can you lead us to him?"

"Not so fast," checked Oscar, requiring more answers. "How can we be sure it's even the same Michael? It's hardly an uncommon name."

"Well?" asked the professor, turning suspiciously to Miguel. "We need proper proof. What can you offer?"

"Michael works little car and electronic box, but I am told he sometimes presses wrong switch because of short finger. But he not where he was. Caravan gone."

"That's all the proof I need," exclaimed the professor, jumping and turning. "*Whizz-a-doodle-dandy!* Michael is safe and well."

"He is well," said Miguel, his head bowed, "but I think he needs to be running away to be safe. He tried run before, but always caught like butterfly in net."

"In London," suggested Oscar, "where you first saw him?"

"There and other places. He is held very long time by gang, including older man who comes and goes. I know, because after they corner me they make me do many bad things for them. I was much time in Michael's company."

"If one hair on Michael's head has been hurt, why I'll…"

"Not possible. Michael is, what you call, bald as a peacock."

"As a badger, you fool," scolded Oscar.

"Michael is bald?" exclaimed the professor, running fingers through his own thick hair. "Well, I never did. How about that. Bald, eh!"

"As a baby bum," repeated Miguel.

"You said one man is old," considered Oscar, rubbing his chin. "Yet we only saw younger men at the lay-by. Harry's probably the oldest, and he's hardly a pensioner. How do you explain that?"

"As I just said, older man he comes and goes. He not live with us."

"The ringleader—the big cheese—now that makes sense. Over a long period of time the gang might change members, but the overall boss would remain constant."

"Gang is only for the rough stuff, find things and guard Michael. I usually guard. Man in charge is older. We do as he says, and he give Harry money to pay us. Only, Harry keep it all and we too frightened to tell. I owe gang nothing." He looked towards the kitchen. "Can I have drink? I have nothing to eat or drink all day because I hide from gang who search for me."

"I doubt this place is safe," said the professor. "Probably the first place they would come looking."

"Maybe you right," replied Miguel anxiously, glancing towards the door. "I have quick drink, clean cloth for bottom and shoulder wounds, and then go fast. Hide somewhere else. Hurry drink, please."

Oscar pulled the professor to one side. "Why on earth did you say such a stupid thing? How can we interrogate him if he leaves? He won't come back a second time."

"Ah!" gulped the professor.

Miguel, who had silently skulked away to open the sash window, was leaning out when Oscar noticed and hauled him back in.

"Caught you red handed! Did you see that, Professor? He was signalling. How many others are out there?"

Miguel's hesitation seemed to tell its own story. An innocent man would look him in the eyes, and Miguel could not.

"Answer me, blast it," thundered Oscar, twisting Miguel's collar to draw him close. For the situation demanded speed.

"I signal nobody. I do opposite. After what you say, I look to see if I am followed. That is all."

"Come, come," said the professor, encouraging Oscar to let go, "physical violence settles nothing. Let's all have something to eat and calm down."

Oscar's irritation at the professor's liberal attitude was assuaged, however, when the professor deliberately brushed shoulders and whispered: "that will hold him here a while longer. I can cook very slowly when it suits me. See what you can find out while I'm in the kitchen."

Oscar nodded. "The window stays shut. Understand, Miguel?" he said while checking the door lock.

"Yes," Miguel replied weakly, attempting to sit on the painful wound.

"Sausages?" called the professor from the kitchen.

Miguel looked up. "Yes, thank you old man, but please make food come quick."

True to plan, the Professor took twenty minutes to prepare the sausages, during which time Oscar tried to pump Miguel for information. Yet, whatever direction the questioning took, Miguel's understanding of the English language mysteriously worsened, just as it had at the police station. The professor, who was always listening in, couldn't understand Miguel's sudden reluctance to cooperate.

Eventually, Oscar turned to the professor and shrugged, signalling the time had come for the overcooked sausages to be tipped unceremoniously onto three plates.

"Where is knife and the fork?" asked Miguel, regaining his voice.

"Use your fingers," scolded Oscar, not wanting to provide make-shift weapons.

"Okay, but food hot. I have to wait to cool before picking up."

The professor winked at Oscar.

"Why do you British call sausages *bangers*?" asked Miguel as he blew the food. "Do they explode?"

"Sometimes they pop their skins," replied the professor.

"Just eat them and shut up, unless you have something intelligent to say," said Oscar gruffly. "You're not going anywhere until we have answers, so you can stop pretending the cat's got your tongue when it suits you."

"Cat? You have cat as well as nasty doggy thing?"

"Shut up!"

"A drink to wash them down?" asked the professor with more civility than the situation deserved.

Oscar scowled.

"I think brandy, if you have, to keep out chill. In my country cold is warmer than English spring and summer."

The professor asked Oscar to pour a large measure, which Miguel swallowed in a single gulp.

"Gang not my friends. We have many disputes." He held out the glass for a refill.

"No more," cried the professor, snatching the bottle from Oscar's hand. "It's my best brandy, which I keep for special occasions. You can have water."

But Oscar saw an opportunity and grabbed it back, quickly holding the bottle over Miguel's empty glass but stopping short of pouring any out. "Brandy comes at a price. Tell us more and you'll get more. *Comprehendō?*"

As brandy trickled into the glass, so Miguel divulged a few of the gang's discoveries.

Throughout the dialogue that followed, and even during the pauses, Oscar kept the brandy available until the Professor could stand no more. He wrested the bottle from Oscar and held it up to the light, frustrated to see it was almost empty.

"I need sleep," slurred Miguel, his head flopping to one side.

"Oh no you don't," said the Professor sternly, holding Miguel's shoulders to stop him falling off the chair. "So far you've said nothing much about Michael. You owe me half a litre of answers."

Miguel's brain swirled in a haze, befogged and befuddled. "I not remember anything more."

"Do something, you fool," cried the professor, blaming Oscar for plying far too much brandy.

"What exactly? We fed him half the bottle to loosen his tongue and keep him here, and it's worked."

"Worked?" groaned the professor, finally releasing Miguel to slide effortlessly onto the floor. "He's told us zilch that will help us rescue Michael, and now he's fit for nothing."

But Oscar saw merit in the situation. "You're overlooking two things."

"Which are?"

"He's going nowhere tonight."

"And the second?" demanded the professor, unimpressed by the first.

"If anyone's outside looking for a signal, they're in for a very long wait." He then lifted the trap door. "We have him banged to rights if we shove him down there. You can even put a chair on top for good measure and sleep on it. The door won't budge with you weighing it down."

"Must get away," slurred Miguel as he was manoeuvred towards the hole, his legs and arms dangling limply.

"Don't you worry, my little drunken sailor, nobody's going to find you in there," said Oscar, rather enjoying the moment. "In a few hours it will be dawn and you can sing like a songbird."

Chapter 18
A New Ally

It was peculiar how abruptly the dramatic events of the day ended once the trap door was closed. The world suddenly seemed to pause, take a deep breath and sooth into an uneasy calm.

None felt this more than the professor, who slumped into the chair weighting the trap door. With barely another word spoken, his eyes closed and he was gone. Then, the snoring began.

Below, Miguel was also snoring, but in a nasal, drunken manner. Together they made a frightful duet, giving Oscar no chance to sleep.

Desperate for rest, Oscar considered putting several drops of Number 5 Snore-Stopper up the professor's nose. But at the very last moment, with the bottle in his hand, he decided against it as he was unsure how much to administer. He was all too aware of the consequences of getting the dosage wrong. And so, after putting the bottle back, he strolled lazily to the window to keep guard in case something unexpected happened. By five o'clock, he too was asleep.

Oscar's dream was one of fast-moving confusion, in which he only escaped the hands of the gang by leaping skyward over the professor's cottage and falling straight into Muriel's living room. There, Muriel made him far too welcome, giving him cakes before trying to kiss him on the lips.

"Get off!" he shouted, waking in a sweat.

"Hello," came an unfamiliar voice.

Oscar rubbed his eyes to focus. The chair was on its side and the trap door was open. The professor lay stretched across the floor wrapped tightly in the rug.

"Here," returned the voice.

Oscar glanced towards the kitchen. There stood Miguel, wearing an apron. He held a pan.

"I see we are of few sausages," he said, holding the bag high. "Just six left. Should I cooked eggs?"

The professor now stirred, his body aching and his arms pinned to his side.

"Good morning Michael's daddy," addressed Miguel.

"What the devil?" groaned the professor as he wriggled, finding he was unable to move. "Help me someone, I'm paralysed."

"Who cop it now?" laughed Miguel, handing the pan to Oscar. He grabbed the edge of the rug and pulled. The professor spun on the floor like a yo-yo. "There now, breakfast soon ready. One eggs or two?"

"Two, I suppose," he replied, still in dizzy confusion. But the food soon revived his equilibrium.

"Mister Professor," said Miguel much later while helping to wash up the plates, "I could be running away if I want, or letting gang in if they wait outside. You both asleep when I crawled out of dark hole in ground with one big headache. And, by the way, hole is uncomfortable and cold. I not want to sleep down hole again."

His words rang true and were greeted as a flag of truce by the professor, who said in a kindly way: "I think I can speak for Oscar in saying you have proved yourself genuine. You are perhaps a noble fellow after all, despite your past mistakes."

"And I keep you warm by wrapping you in old rug like the pancake after you fall off chair and I get out."

"So you did," replied the professor, "but, if there is a next time, please leave my arms outside the rug. I woke feeling like the sausage in a hotdog."

"You think I am not now in trouble with police?"

"Ah, that's a different matter," said the professor gently. "If you intend to live as a free man, sooner or later you'll have to confess your crimes to the police. Otherwise, you'll always be on the run, looking over your shoulder and hiding in dark corners, never knowing who to trust."

"I think I be in prison for very long time if I do," he reasoned bleakly.

"Not necessarily," added Oscar, with authority in his voice. "If we speak on your behalf, especially if you help us rescue Michael, why, you may avoid a long prison sentence altogether."

"Ah, that good. But, I mean what I say yesterday. Michael needs to be running away to be safe. I know this from what I hear and see. I also think it not possible for us to stay in cottage much longer. Bad men are bound to come back to squash me like the cockroach and use machine again."

The professor stared suspiciously. "Hang about. Are you now saying they know you're here, which isn't what you said yesterday?" he enquired with alarm.

"No, not that. I mean it won't take them long to realise it is possible if they heard news on radio that I get caught. They will check and find police let me go. I sure of that. They will think… where could I go?"

Oscar shook his head in despair. "Which means any noise we hear—the clip-clop of footsteps along the drive, the drip of a tap, the bang of a bird flying into the window—will frighten us to death. I don't like the sound of that one little bit."

"It is bad for nerves to stay."

"But equally we can't abandon the Starlight Machine and Receptor to them," observed the professor. "I won't hear of it. We might need to use them to find Michael."

"Then, you do it quickly," urged Miguel.

"Forget using the Starlight Machine quickly," countered Oscar knowingly. "It isn't possible."

"Shush, Oscar. Not everyone needs to know what I did."

Miguel looked puzzled, but couldn't ask what this meant.

"Anyway, now we have Miguel, we can pursue other leads in parallel. For starters, there must be a more permanent base for the gang to hang out than the caravan. They can't always be travelling."

"Most time Michael held in caravan, pulled by car or van. It is not long parked in one place, but many places. He never out of sight. Where they go, he go—and where he go, they follow. He could be anywhere."

"Answer the question, Miguel," demanded Oscar. "Is there a base somewhere, like a headquarters? There just has to be."

"Maybe, but I not visit."

"Oh dear," exclaimed the professor, throwing down the tea towel. "We're back to where we started."

"I've just realised, Professor. Jake was right. He really did see Michael in the lay-by."

Miguel lifted the tea towel from the floor. "Maybe not sink yet, old man. Would you tell me what machine shows?"

"Not bloomin' likely."

"You might as well, Professor," said Oscar in despair. "It's doing us no good."

"Very well, if you insist, but I'll not be held responsible if telling him turns pear-shaped." He twisted to fully face Miguel. "It shows images of an old wooden warship at sea."

"Okay! Good! We are not sinked yet and I tell you why. Gang leader never let me see machine work. But I know of sea battle that once took place. Don't ask me how, because I not say. It is probably this you see and Harry also see."

"That's not good enough," said Oscar with growing impatience. "You have to spill *all* the beans. Right away, I mean!"

"What is spilling beans?"

"Tell us *everything* you know, fool."

"I not say too much more, because some is private to my Spanish family. Trust me, knowing my private stuff not help you find Michael. I know only of old Spanish ship and what it carry. It is same ship, perhaps?"

"Ours is a British Royal Navy vessel. Not the same at all," admitted the professor darkly.

"Then, old man, forcing me to spill private beans will not help. But gang look for something to make them richer, for sure. So, if we look at same pictures we might discover more, and where gang could go for profit if it works out clues from what is seen. I really not know myself, and that is fact."

"I see a problem," said Oscar. "If we're relying on the same images telling us where the gang might take Michael, it presupposes the gang has already been capable of working out all the necessary clues for themselves. Yet, I've got a funny feeling so far they haven't got any idea where to go. Furthermore, if they *had* sussed it out, they wouldn't still be hanging around here."

"Added to which we've seen only one ship, not a battle." The professor's head drooped in weariness. "Oh, Oscar, we are getting nowhere."

"Have you seen right through?" asked Miguel.

"Well, no, but…"

"Perhaps there is more."

"I doubt it, Miguel," added the professor realistically. "As the gang has been desperate to get its hands on another egg, it can only mean they have viewed everything and the Receptor's images haven't provided sufficient clues for their task. They obviously need additional stuff that can only come from launching a new egg into space."

"So it will be no good for us, either," huffed Oscar.

"Probably not, but that's hardly the point."

"Isn't it? What is?"

"They're bound to return here, if not to get Miguel, then to steal the egg they couldn't find last time. That's really good news!"

"Are you insane?" declared Oscar.

"Of course it's good, you dim-wit. Remember what Miguel said; where they go, Michael goes. We can't rescue Michael unless we know where he's been taken. But we won't have to search for him if he's driven back here."

"Oh dear," mumbled Oscar under his breath.

"You disagree?"

"I hate to remind you, Professor, but when you broke the egg you left it in a million pieces outside the window. If they saw it, as you intended, they would know there was no egg remaining and therefore no point in coming back for one." He turned to Miguel. "Did you notice anything broken outside when you came last night?"

"Too dark."

"Either way, we must hope they still intend to return to get you."

"I not wish that!"

"And even then, there's yet another problem. We're assuming the gang is reconciled. The last time we saw Harry and Pete they drove off in different directions."

"You're a bundle of joy," remarked the professor. "But I suppose you're right."

"Okay, first things first," said Oscar as he suddenly rushed to the kitchen.

"What are you doing?" called the professor to his back.

"I'm getting a brush and pan to sweep up the wretched pieces of egg before anyone else sees them, of course. It's what dim-wits do!"

The professor apologised. "Strange, isn't it? One minute we're safer by smashing the egg, and the next we want to lure the gang back by letting them think it still exists. Are we doing the right thing this time?"

"Quite sure we are," replied Oscar, opening the front door. "But we still need a backup plan, just in case they don't come back. As far as I can see, there's only one thing left to do. We must follow Miguel's advice and find out for ourselves what the gang already knows."

"Using the Receptor Box," rejoiced the professor. "We intended to look anyway when Jake returns. But we mustn't get our hopes too high. Finding anything worthwhile is a very long shot."

"Only Box tell us anything about treasure," said Miguel. "I think Professor is better clever than Harry and Pete, and may find clues they missed."

"Treasure!" exclaimed Oscar, throwing the brush outside before slamming the door shut. "Did you say treasure? Goodness gracious, Jake will be pleased."

"*Stop*," shouted the professor with passion. "I'm not in the least bothered about treasure. I only want Michael back."

"We know that," replied Oscar, wide-eyed, "but let's not be too hasty in dismissing a golden opportunity. I say we free Michael and then find the treasure for ourselves. After all, someone should have it, and we're taking an awful lot of risks helping you. What do you say, Professor? It would be our reward."

"I suppose I can't argue with the logic."

"And I play part in rescue," said Miguel brightly.

But Oscar's elation was cut short. "Crikey, I keep forgetting. The Receptor is damaged."

"*Fiddle bum!* Nothing I can't fix."

"And in the meantime, what should I do?"

"Clear up and clear off, Mr Trotter, and tell Jake everything he's missed. Bring the boy here on Saturday. I've a feeling we'll need him."

"What if the gang comes back in the meantime?"

"I doubt," offered Miguel. "It will take time for them to make friends again."

"Are you sure they will reunite?" asked Oscar. "They looked pretty desperate when I saw you with them."

"You see us all together?" challenged Miguel.

"Yes, and we saw you getting a thumping."

Miguel looked stunned at the revelation but soon recovered composure. "They will. Pete hungry for money. Harry has money but wants more. Sooner or later they shake hands and come back raging like the angry bull. But it will take time. Until then, I protect Professor with funny gun."

"You're willing to stay without being bullied?"

"Yes, if you give me small share of treasure if found. Anyway, I like Michael and want to help him find his daddy."

"You could both sleep down the hole," proposed Oscar. It would make a strong firing position is attacked. Don't expose yourself above ground. Use the trap door as cover and fire around it."

"I am best shot, I think. I hold gun."

"No, Miguel, we don't trust you that much. You reload the gun for the professor and keep an eye open for any attack from the rear. The kitchen window will be undefended and must be observed at all times."

"I do as you say, but we must have more blankets to keep warm, I think. Hole is horrible at night."

"Take my smartphone," offered Oscar, handing it to the professor. "Call me if you need help. I have another in the car I keep solely for business. Don't answer the phone to anyone except me. My name will come up on the screen."

"How does it work? There are no buttons to press."

"Oh Professor," fumed Miguel, snatching it away. "You not worry, Mr Trotter, I know how. I live in 21st century."

"And once mended, I could temporarily disable the Starlight Machine and Receptor each night," added the professor to regain his dignity. "We can't be in two places at once. Leave it to me. After all, I am the only genius."

Oscar agreed to the plan. "Sounds good. But, please, remember to properly lock the cottage and shed, and phone me every morning and every evening. Is that a promise, Professor? You won't get a signal down the hole, so, if I hear nothing from you, I'll assume you can't leave the hole because you're under siege. If that happens, I'll rush back with the police. Sorted?"

The professor nodded absentmindedly and waved him away.

Oscar left, leaving the professor standing in the drive to sweep up the broken egg. But, before he had walked very far he turned, smiling. "Of course," he shouted, "if the gang doesn't come back for a working egg, we could always encourage them here by tying Miguel to a drainpipe. Use him as bait, like they did in King Kong."

Miguel, who immediately jumped behind the professor, pleaded not to be left outside.

"Don't worry," laughed the professor, handing him the pan, "we're a long way from needing a human sacrifice. Still, it's good to know we have a Plan D."

Miguel tried to smile, but couldn't.

Meanwhile, back at the Striker household, Jake had been waiting restlessly to hear from his father. He had expected a call the previous evening and was impatient for any news. Several voicemail messages left on Oscar's phone had gone unanswered, and now he had to go through another day at school without knowing what was going on.

The thought of the adventure continuing without him was sufficient to take Jake's mind off his work and, sure enough, it was not long before the teacher noticed and escorted him to the headmaster's office for time-wasting in class. Fortunately, the headmaster showed great reluctance to speak to Muriel Striker, and so the censure ended there.

But Wednesday turned to Thursday and still there was no news. Jake was now becoming worried, so much so that he even considered approaching his mother. What stopped him was the thought of having to give lengthy explanations about the wonderful and dangerous things at the professor's cottage. The likely outcome of disclosure was too horrible to contemplate—grounding him for the entire weekend in the company of Ghoulish Gracie. He shuddered at the thought.

The actual reason why Oscar had not contacted Jake since leaving the professor's cottage was complicated and centred around the professor failing to telephone regularly as promised. It sent alarm bells ringing in Oscar's head in case the gang was attacking. But, as Oscar also knew the professor had a tendency to be absentminded, he had not rushed back gung-ho with police sirens wailing after all. Instead, he chose to spy on the cottage from a distance. So long as he could see the professor, and he looked safe and content, there would be no need to intervene.

The decision to play it casually caused Oscar several extra journeys to and from the professor's cottage, which had the knock-on effect of placing a strain on his car restoration business. This, in turn, forced him to work long into the evenings delivering cars to customers. And so, by the time he finally relaxed, it was too late to speak to Jake. Leaving a message with Muriel was, quite obviously, out of the question.

Of course, none of this helped Jake understand the situation and slowly he became ever more anxious to hear from his father. And it was not his only concern.

Chapter 19
The Maid on the Lake

Friday held particular dread for Jake, knowing his aunt and cousin would be arriving before tea. Throughout the day he imagined his aunt standing on the doorstep waving a white flag of truce, while all the time plotting to launch an attack on his world using the most horrible weapon known to man—Ghoulish Gracie. And, as expected, Jake had only just got home from school when the doorbell rang.

"It must be Aunt Julie and Gracie," said Muriel from the kitchen, drying her hands. "Be a love and let them in."

Jake heard himself reply "*do I have to?*" but only inside his head. He opened the door.

There stood Gracie, frowning through wired teeth and holding a doll upside down by its foot which wet its nappy every time it moved. Her hair was arranged in neat bunches, tied with huge pink ribbons which matched the bow on her dress.

"Say hello, Jake," insisted Muriel, pushing him forward.

"He's shy," observed Aunt Julie. "Never mind, he'll soon get over it." She threw a small bag into the hallway. "Can't stop. The spa is waiting. What fun! Now, you two, behave yourselves and play nicely."

"They will," replied Muriel to Julie's back, as she was already halfway to her car. The door closed.

"Well, isn't this nice," said Muriel looking between the children, neither of whom seemed in the slightest bit pleased to be there. "Show Gracie to her room, Jake, and then both of you come down for tea. I have spaghetti letters on toast and cupcakes. You can make up funny words as you eat."

Gracie slumped on the bed. "Bummer! I hate spaghetti nearly as much as I detest cupcakes. What does Aunt Muriel think I am, 4 years old?" She pulled at her hair ribbons and threw them into a waste-paper basket. "Horrid, silly things. When will Mum realise I'll be 12 soon and let me dress how I want?"

Jake stood open-mouthed.

"And you can stop gawping. I warn you, Jake, call me anything but Gracie and I'll stamp on your fingers."

"Why would I?" he asked, somewhat shaken at feeling overawed by a girl.

"Because it's not my real name, stupid."

"It isn't?"

"You know full well my proper name is Carrie."

"I honestly didn't. How come?"

She looked at him with suspicion. "As long as you're not pulling my leg, I'll tell you."

Jake nodded.

"At primary school, when the boys realised Carrie Trotter sounded like Harry Potter, they made fun of me, saying I was a transgender boy. But they didn't for long, I can tell you. I gave them a proper kicking where it hurts every time it happened and threatened I would do it again if they told on me. Mum wasn't pleased when she heard I got upset in class, so she said I could use my middle name instead. Anyway, she reckons Gracie better fits my gentle nature. Ha, she should've seen me dishing out the boot. I surprised you didn't know."

"Can't say I remember you being anything other than Gracie."

"Well, now you're warned."

"You look like a Gracie," he added kindly.

"Think so? Then that can go too," she said, throwing the doll under the bed. "Got a DS or X-Box with any gruesome vampire games?"

Jake smiled. He could grow to like her after all.

At last Oscar phoned. The two had left most of their tea and were up in Jake's room playing on his DS when Muriel called up. Jake had already told Gracie a little about the professor while they played a wicked dungeon game, not all of which she believed.

"*He*'s on the phone." Muriel left the receiver on the window-sill.

As usual, Jake slid down the banister rail, followed by Gracie who yelled with delight as she crashed into Jake. Both had chocolate around their mouths, smuggled into the house inside Gracie's doll, which now lay on the bedroom floor with its head ripped off.

"Hi, Dad!"

"Jake, I have so much to tell you. Can we talk without your mother hearing?"

Jake could hear Muriel singing in the kitchen. "I guess so, but you better be quick. And talk quietly. You're very loud, you know. Oh, and by the way, Gracie is here. She is…"

"…Ghoulish?"

"I heard that, Uncle Oscar," shouted Gracie after snatching the receiver, much to Jake's delight.

"Oh! Sorry, Gracie."

"Don't worry, Dad," said Jake, retrieving the phone. "She's okay. I think I'll need a new name for her." Gracie whispered into his ear. "She says I should call her Glamorous Gracie instead."

"How old did you say she is?"

"She'll soon be 12, going on 16!" He turned towards Gracie. "She's actually quite pretty."

"Goodness, that's something coming from you."

Gracie giggled.

"Carry on, Dad," said Jake after she calmed down. "I've been waiting days to hear from you."

Gracie squeezed an ear to the phone as Oscar explained about Miguel.

"So, I was right about the man in the caravan."

"It certainly looks that way, but I still don't completely trust Miguel. I can't put a finger on it, but I'm unsettled by him. He gave up too easily, if that makes any sense. Anyway, the professor wants us at his place tomorrow. We might switch-on the Starlight Machine and the Receptor Box, see what we can find out. Are you up for it after what happened last time?"

"Try stopping me, Dad. Only…"

"Yes?"

"What about Gracie?"

Gracie grabbed the telephone from Jake's hand. "I'm coming too! I'll scream if you stop me."

The excitement generated by Oscar's phone call was understandable. Gracie and Jake imagined an adventure so great that it would be like playing a mysterious DS game with themselves as the main characters, for indeed the Receptor's holographic images were entirely life-like through which they could freely walk. Nevertheless, as a word of caution, Jake explained how the professor would not be pleased if they messed about, as he took the search for his son very seriously. Gracie said she understood, but had her fingers crossed.

And so it was that by the early light of morning the children were up and ready, their bags packed. It had not been Jake's intention to rise so early, but Gracie had crept into his room at daybreak and jumped on him every time he closed his eyes. Under this relentless assault, he gave up trying to sleep. And while he showered, Gracie had crept down to the kitchen and taken a small bottle of cochineal from a cupboard, which Muriel had for colouring cakes. This she used to dye her hair a streaky red, knowing it would wash out with shampoo. Fortunately, the experiment in colour held no horror for her. She had done something similar before, when boiled and strained blueberry juice had been used to tint her hair blue for a part in a school Christmas pantomime.

Jake couldn't take his eyes off Gracie's hairstyle as they sat in the lounge waiting, but knew better than question her motive.

"What time is Uncle Oscar due?" moaned Gracie, pulling the curtains apart for the umpteenth time.

"He didn't say, but, unlike you, he believes in sleeping when it's dark."

It was nine o'clock when Oscar finally arrived. He turned up in a wrecked MGB GT sports car he had just purchased. Gracie sat with Oscar in the front, leaving Jake to squash behind on the half-size rear seat, huddled next to the over-night bags.

With his mother waving them a fond farewell, for the first time Jake felt genuinely apprehensive. He found himself staring at his home and all the happy memories it held.

Not so Gracie, who delighted in forcing down the stiff window until the wind caught her long hair and the handle broke.

"Another thing to fix," grunted Oscar, stuffing the handle into the glove box.

Having been denied sleep, Jake cat-napped during the short journey and only woke when Gracie twisted to jab him hard in the chest. He looked up to find the car parked in front of the professor's cottage. Oscar beeped the horn.

"That's odd," said Oscar as he stared through the windscreen at the Professor's front door. "Nobody to greet us." He got out awkwardly, as the car sat low to the ground. "Where are they?" He peeped into the professor's lounge.

"What's happening, Dad?"

"I don't know. Stay in the car while I scout around the back. I'll lock you in for safety."

Yet, the moment Oscar was out of sight, Gracie released the sunroof and began to climb out.

"No," shouted Jake, trying to pull her back. "Dad said we should stay here."

"So what," she replied, one knee already on the roof, "he's not my dad."

"Oh, flippin' heck," exclaimed Jake as he struggled to manoeuvre himself over the folded front seat. "Wait for me, then."

Oscar returned, waving a note above his head. It had been pinned to the shed door. It said they should meet the professor and Miguel at the *Maid on the Lake*, a cafe a mile or so up the main road. There was a roughly drawn map but no further explanation.

Setting off on foot, the three avoided the road by following a straight path through the woods. Gracie was particularly pleased to see more of the countryside, as she lived on a housing estate where there were few trees and no grass verges or a playground. Her enthusiasm was infectious, and soon Jake was also balancing on top of fallen tree trunks, hiding in the undergrowth, and chasing squirrels until they scurried effortlessly into the uppermost branches.

The cafe itself stood in a large clearing. It was a strong-looking place built from stone and half-logs which could have come straight out of the American Wild West. Probably because of its remoteness, security shutters with small slits were hinged to the sides of the windows, which, when closed, would give the building the appearance of a military stockade. Yet, it was called *Maid on the Lake*, a serene name unsuited to its appearance, particularly as there was no lake anywhere to be seen.

As Oscar and the children entered the cafe through the front entrance, they noticed the dark silhouette of a man standing near the end of a long and windowless corridor that stretched away behind the serving counter. He was talking to someone who remained out of view when something passed between them. Then, to the voice of a third person, the man stepped inside a room, closed the door which had a plaque reading *Gas cylinders and Toxic cleaning materials—Strictly No Entry* screwed to the front, and at once a brief rumpus flared up. From the noise of falling boxes, it seemed likely several heavy blows were thrown or possibly a knife fight broke out. Yet, whatever took place, moments later the man walked away without serious injury. He left the building from a side door wearing a coat, his hands in the pockets and his shoulders hunched forward to hide his face behind a large upturned collar. Gracie watched him pass the window.

Although calm quickly returned, Gracie thought it very odd that neither Oscar nor Jake commented on the furore. Instead, they made straight for the professor, who was sitting at a round table. A mug of hot chocolate, an empty coffee cup and the remains of a cake indicated he had not been alone.

The professor couldn't hide his look of disapproval at seeing Gracie for the first time, but somehow she managed to 'accidentally' tip a bowl of sugar over his lap and this postponed the inevitable question. She was sure her winning personality would, if given a chance, make him realise she was an asset.

"Where's Miguel?" asked Oscar, pulling out a chair. He chose a black filter coffee from the menu and strawberry milkshakes for the children.

"Needed the toilet. Why do you ask?" replied the professor, still brushing sugar from the folds of his clothes.

"Oh, no reason. Why meet here?"

The professor leaned over the table. "I'll tell you, as Miguel is out of earshot. It struck me this cafe is very close to the lay-by. If the gang ever needed fast food, it would be the obvious place to get it. I wanted to see Miguel's reaction in coming here."

"And did he react?"

"He said nothing on the way to make me think he minded in the least, but when we sat at the table he kept playing with the cutlery in a very nervous fashion."

Another man now approached. The direction he came from had not been noticed. Anyway, the professor showed no curiosity, recognising him only as the person who had been sitting at the next table but had gone off just before Miguel left for the toilet. He had then worn a coat, which he no longer had.

The man was quite short, with broad shoulders and strong muscles that stretched his T-shirt to the limit. His tanned face, partially hidden below a knitted hat pulled low over his forehead, was as big as a football and yet bore small piercing eyes. But it was his teeth which caught Jake's attention, flashing so straight and white that they had to be the result of expensive cosmetic dentistry. And so, mostly because of his perfect teeth, in Jake's eyes the man exuded an air of easy living, though spoiled by dirty black nails on otherwise unscathed hands.

Over the next few minutes, while the others talked, Jake studied the man through the corner of his eye. In some respects he resembled Harry, but he had never seen Harry close up and so could not be sure it was him. He tried to imagine him unshaven and without the hat, but it was impossible. Even the T-shirt gave this man a much stronger appearance. Only if the man removed his hat to reveal a perfect forehead or the tell-tale scar from Miguel's slash could identification be made.

The drinks arrived.

"This Miguel bloke must've flushed himself down the bog," joked Gracie, sucking hard on her milkshake until only bubbles remained at the bottom of the tall glass. "You're a boy, Jake. Go and see where he is."

The man at the next table smiled into his tea, which was now stone cold.

Jake looked at his father, who offered no objection. Even so, he was unsure whether he wanted to go. He had seen Miguel only once, when he had been involved in a terrible fight, and now Jake could only visualise him as a member of a desperate gang. Nevertheless, after the professor assured him Miguel had changed his ways, Jake crossed the room and entered the toilets, holding the door open with his foot in case he needed a fast getaway.

To his relief, the toilets were empty except for a tall man drying his hands on a small sheet of green paper. The man faced the wall, but even from this disadvantaged angle Jake was positive it was not Miguel. For a start, he was very much older. Nevertheless, he had to be sure.

"Mr Miguel, sir?"

The man turned blankly. "Me? No, Sunny-Jim, I'm Tommy Brown, the cleaner. Do you want something?"

Jake did not stop to answer, but ran back to the table. "He's not there."

"Are you sure?" asked the professor with evident shock.

"Look for yourself if you don't believe me." He lifted his milkshake, surprised to find the glass empty. Gracie grinned with strawberry lips.

Oscar leaned towards the professor. "What do you make of that? Still think he's trustworthy?"

The professor placed a ten pound note on the table and got up. "Let's talk about it at home, not here."

"What about the other gentleman with you?" said the waitress politely, picking up the money. "He had an Americano. Someone has to pay for it. Ten pounds won't cover everything you've had." She turned to the man in the T-shirt. "You saw him drink it, didn't you, sir."

The stranger shrugged and left without speaking.

"That's not nice! Manners cost nothing." She took a plastic bottle from her apron and spayed the table. "We get all sorts in here."

Oscar noticed how the man fumbled in his trousers as he shuffled away, removing a curved piece of grey debris with very sharp edges. This, he wiped on a handkerchief before pushing it deeper into his pocket.

Oscar followed the waitress to the counter.

"Sorry to bother you, Miss, but I was wondering if you recognised the bloke who had the Americano from previous visits?"

"I can hardly say, sir. We get so many people passing through, although I think the foreign gent who had been sitting by the man with the funny hair popped in for takeaway dinners a week or so back. I could be wrong, of course, but I think it was him."

"Can you remember how many?"

"Weeks or dinners?"

"Dinners."

"Well now, you're asking a lot of my memory. Let me see. He might've been the person who ordered five takeaways. We don't get many orders for five."

"Four or five? It would be helpful to know."

"Yes, I'm sure it was five. I remember because whoever it was had asked for roll-mop herrings. Roll-mop herrings indeed, I said to him. You won't get anything like that around here. Fried burgers *yes*, fish fingers *yes*, chicken and chips *yes*, but not roll-mop herrings. So he left having bought five chicken dinners, all smothered in thousand-island dressing. Fancy that. Very odd behaviour, if you ask me."

"You're absolutely sure it was five?"

"Quite certain. I found a Kit-Kat box out back to put them in. They stacked very nicely, two each side and one on top."

Oscar dug into his pocket for a five-pound note. "Keep any change."

"Come to think of it," she called through a friendly smile, waving him back and leaning over the counter to whisper, "if it's of interest, the rude man at the next table was also here yesterday—or maybe it was the day before. Whichever time, he ordered four takeaway dinners with no extras. I remember because I was told by the proprietor of the cafe not to charge him anything."

"But it was definitely him?"

262

"I'm sure. I've seen him now and again, either in the cafe or walking past the counter as if he had a right to go anywhere he wanted. I never challenge him."

"How come?"

"When I started working here part-time, I was told by the boss to keep my nose out of his personal business and private spaces."

"Meaning what?"

"He uses the back rooms for storage and occasionally to meet people. As I like my job, I don't pry."

"Thank you. I'll tell the old man what you said... about the dinners, not his hair!"

It was hard to believe the professor waited until the walk home before asking who the girl was, and even harder to believe he accepted Oscar's explanation without further comment. It could mean only one thing. He now thought they were safe enough at the cottage to receive another young visitor.

Even so, Oscar still harboured lingering doubts, with Miguel's unexpected disappearance from the cafe justifying little confidence in his loyalty. But it was an occurrence the professor dismissed as "him being too chicken-livered to face you after you offered him up as a human sacrifice". And so, to find Miguel sitting happily on the cottage doorstep as they arrived home came as quite a surprise, even to the professor.

Gracie nudged Jake, whispering that she thought he was the man seen leaving the cafe via the side exit. The coat with its wide collar game him away.

"Hello," greeted Miguel, smiling at Gracie while studying her hair. "You are..?"

"Flabbergasted," said Gracie, giving him her most suspicious girl-detective look. "Didn't I see you skulking away from the cafe?"

"I do no such thing," he replied. "I was long time in toilet and came back to find Professor gone."

"Interesting. Jake said you weren't in the loo."

"He look for me?" he blustered, squinting at Jake. "Then I think silly boy should look better. I came running back through woods, the quickly way."

"That's a nice coat," lured Gracie. "Is that blood on the collar? I suppose it came from the long scratch on your cheek?"

Miguel touched his face. "I catch on branch of tree. I should look more careful where I running."

"Where did the coat come from?" asked the professor innocently, expecting a perfectly rational explanation. "I only ask because you didn't have it on when we set off. In fact, thinking about it, the coat is similar to the one the man wore who was sitting at the next table to ours, that is until he returned without it."

"Not nice coat at all. It is for short man. I find it hanging in toilet and thought I take."

"I knew there would be a perfectly simple explanation," acceded the professor.

"Then it belongs to the man in the cafe," censured Oscar, eager to keep the pressure on Miguel.

"Oh, I steal by mistake. I should take back."

"Satisfied?" said the professor, glaring Oscar's way.

But Oscar could smell a rat. "Did you know the man at the next table?"

"Course not. I not speak to him. Is coat really his? I tell you straight, I thought coat not wanted."

"It's very odd. The man didn't seem in the least concerned to lose it. Why do you think that is?"

"Perhaps Miguel's right and he actually didn't want it," suggested the professor.

"Really? So he wore it to the cafe for the sole purpose of abandoning it in a public place. Seems a lot of bother to get rid of something that could be thrown into a bin."

"Stop!" bawled Miguel. "Is this game of questions? You ask me things I cannot answer. You must ask man in red T-shirt why he left it."

"Ah-ha," jumped Oscar. "How do you know he wore a red T-shirt, unless he took the coat off in front of you? According to the professor, he was wearing it all the time you were at the table."

Miguel paused before replying. "Man had big sticky cake I much admired. He brush crumbs from T-shirt under coat." His eyes flared. "Oh, yes, under coat. You right, he did have coat. You think it his?"

"And you still claim you didn't talk to him?" pressed Oscar.

"I talk to nobody but Professor. That is fact."

Gracie nudged Jake. "He's lying."

"I know."

Despite the inconsistencies in Miguel's explanation, the professor unlocked the front door and rolled easily into his favourite chair. Jake sat on the floor at his feet. He could feel the professor absentmindedly tapping fingers on the top of his head.

"Your father won't accept Miguel is an honest man," he mumbled as Miguel walked away to bathe his cheek in the toilet basin. "I can't think why not."

"Maybe he's a better judge than you. He sees holes in Miguel's story."

"Does he? What reason would Miguel have to give himself up, then?"

"Who knows what's happening? Possibly he wants a safe place to hide. Or it could be part of a criminal master-plan."

"What do you mean?"

"You know, like the story of Troy. Get a 'Trojan horse' inside the enemy's walls by winning the defender's trust."

"It can't be to find a space egg, because Miguel knows we haven't got one."

"It's certainly a puzzle."

"Hold on!" gasped Oscar, who had been eavesdropping. "Space egg! Of course. That's what he had."

The professor and Jake turned as one.

"I'm sure the T-shirt man had a piece of our smashed space egg in his pocket. I saw him fiddle with it when leaving the table. It was only for a moment, but I reckon I'm right. Looking at Miguel's scratched face, it wouldn't surprise me one jot if he had used it as a make-shift weapon to cut Miguel. Maybe he was wiping blood off it when he walked out."

"How could he get hold of a piece?" challenged the professor. "We swept it up."

"Perhaps it came from Miguel. It would be easy for him to take a bit from the bin to show the other man."

"Why bother?"

"To prove the egg is smashed to pieces? Maybe, the other man took it and lashed out in frustration."

"Which means the man in the T-shirt is also part of the gang? How could I be so wrong when I'm a genius?"

"I'm absolutely sure he is," claimed Jake, at last telling of his suspicions about the man being none other than Harry. "Which not only puts Miguel back in the guilty frame but means the gang has reunited quicker than we expected."

"I don't like what I'm hearing," said Oscar bleakly, glancing guiltily between the children. "Tragically, though, everything fits. Just think about it. Miguel has been encouraging the professor to look for clues in the images the gang might've missed. Why would he bother if all he wants is to quickly escape from England?"

"To help us find Michael first," defended the professor, but the words were said with less tenacity than before. "The clues are to help *us* before he flees the country."

"Perhaps he wants to make some money by finding the treasure before he jumps ship," suggested Gracie. "Isn't that more likely?"

"Or pass any clues on to a spymaster, as a double-agent," said Jake with boyish enthusiasm for the dramatic.

"Oh really," dismissed the professor, throwing up his hands. "You two must stop letting your imaginations run riot. Face it, you've both got it in for Miguel. But I've lived with him over the past few days and I reckon he's genuine. You offer no proof to disappoint me in my judgement of him."

"We three!" exclaimed Gracie. "I'm in this now, and I agree with Jake."

"There must be a way to confirm our suspicions," said Oscar. "I'm sure we're missing something obvious."

The professor, seeing Oscar's sincerity, sat back to replay the evidence in his mind. He suddenly looked up. "Stupid, stupid, stupid. Of course!" He sprang forward on the seat. "I've been really thick. What we need has been staring us in the face, and sadly it proves you could be right and I could be the worst genius on record."

"Meaning?" asked Oscar, somewhat bewildered.

"Remember what you told me on the way back, Mr Trotter? You said the waitress from the cafe served a foreigner weeks ago who bought five takeaway dinners."

"She did. At the time I considered knowing that was important, but I'm not so certain it matters anymore."

"Well, Mr Trotter, you must trust your first instinct." He stood as if to deliver a speech. "We know the gang normally stays together, moving from place to place. Agreed?" They all nodded. "Good. So who was the fifth dinner for? Even counting Michael, only four dinners were ever needed. There had to be someone else eating with them, probably someone who plans each robbery but only occasionally stays at the caravan. It even fits Miguel's own account, when he said an older man ran the gang but rarely joined them."

"That's what I was first thinking when I asked her," said Oscar cautiously. "But I then realised it proves nothing."

"On the contrary. Miguel also said three men cornered him in London, yet we've only ever seen him, Pete and Harry together. So who was the other criminal? Well, now we know for sure. It's a gang of four, not three, comprising Harry, Pete, Miguel and the overall leader Jake calls the spymaster. *Yip-yip-yippee!*"

"What the heck are you doing?" cried Oscar incredulously.

The professor stopped in mid-dance. "Oh, do wake up, Mr Trotter. This is great news. The spymaster would only hang about the smelly caravan if the gang's plan remains viable. It certainly wouldn't be the luxury accommodation he's used to."

"*Did* hang about," said Jake. "Who's to say he still does?"

"The fourth dinner says so."

"What fourth dinner?"

"The fourth dinner purchased from the cafe yesterday or the day before by the T-shirt man, who you suspect is Harry. The waitress remembered him. With Miguel no longer there, who was the fourth dinner for if not your so-called spymaster? And it gets better. Don't you see? It means Michael must be somewhere close by, where we can rescue him. It's everything we hoped for."

"But what about the shard of space egg we think Miguel handed over today? Won't seeing it stop the gang in its tracks? After all, someone slashed Miguel's face out of annoyance," said Gracie.

"Not if Miguel is spying for them."

"For what purpose, if there is no egg to find?"

"To pass on any clues we discover which they missed."

"It certainly explains the coat business?" added Jake. "Miguel had to get away without us noticing him after the fight. He used the collar to hide his wound and sneaked out the cafe's back door."

"So how do we handle Miguel from now on?" asked Gracie. "He'll be back out of the loo any minute."

"You don't handle anything," barked the professor. "It must be left to the grown-ups."

"Yeah, right!" mumbled Gracie, causing Jake to smile.

268

"We must flush him out," said Oscar. "Finally find out whether he's with us or, as we now suspect, working against us."

"There's one way," suggested the professor, "but it's hardly conclusive. We must ask him who the third c-c-criminal in London was. See if he says anything believable. I bet he won't incriminate the bloke who is the boss of the gang."

"Things okay?" enquired Miguel as he shut the toilet door to a sea of suspicious faces.

Oscar asked the question, to which Miguel had a quick reply on the tip of his tongue. Too readily, Jake thought.

"Oh, him! He was Polish man who is no more."

"Allowed to leave the gang?" asked Jake.

"As I say, he is no more."

"You mean dead?"

"He had no respect among us. He was often, as you say, drunk as a duke but swore he only ever swallow water."

"As a l-l-lord," corrected the professor, irritated by the sudden return of his stutter.

"Yes, drunk as lord. He had vodka bottles hidden in strange places, not for us finding, and often had blurred eyes and the red nose. He roll about caravan, knocking into everything. Caravan too small for this, so we finding him very irritating. When we ask where he get drink, he laugh. So we watch him but not find answer. A mystery. We look hard for bottles, but it is like the magic trick. One day, when he cutting potato while drunk, he fell on knife and die. Nobody much care, and caravan became nicer place to live."

"What happened to the body?"

"Harry dump in river. Better we not ask too much—we cannot swim."

Jake tugged on the professor's sleeve. "That wasn't what I expected him to say," he whispered. "But I'm not changing my mind. It's all a question of timing. The Polish bloke could've been dumped in the river ages ago."

"Then we should ask Miguel w-w-when the Polish man d-d-died?" suggested the professor.

"He would lie," replied Jake. "Anyway, we don't need to. You told me Miguel said an older man ran the gang, who came and went? It seems the Polish bloke lived permanently in the caravan. So, to still require four dinners from the cafe only a day or two back, it would need Harry himself, Pete, Michael and one other person to eat them. It obviously wasn't the dead Pole or Miguel, which still leaves the spymaster."

"Great thinking."

"I now clean toilet," said Miguel, wanting to appear useful. "My stomach still not good. Old man is like others. He not care much for vegetables." He walked away.

Oscar crossed to Jake and pulled him aside. "The professor might like the idea of the gang continuing its rotten deeds, but the thought of Harry reuniting with the others fills me with horror. Should we cut and run while we still can? You and Gracie could be safely home with Mum in under an hour."

Jake looked at Gracie. "What, and be left unoccupied for the rest of the weekend with Mum fussing over us. No thanks, Dad, I'm not moving. Anyway, it's beginning to get exciting."

While the others plotted and Miguel scrubbed the inside of the toilet bowl, Gracie was becoming bored with her own company. She strutted idly around the room. It was not the start to the adventure she expected and eventually said so.

"We now look at film, as little girl wants?" said Miguel, putting the brush away.

"Not so little, mate, as you'll find out if you call me that again."

Miguel stepped back to the wall.

Oscar turned slyly to the professor. "We must play along with him for the moment. See what he does next," he whispered. "Give him enough rope to hang himself."

"G-G-Gracie is r-r-right," announced the professor loudly to gain everyone's attention. "It's time to forget d-d-dead bodies and takeaways. Now, w-w-where are my w-w-wellies? We have work to do and the p-p-past to visit, b-b-but only after I get rid of this blasted s-s-stutter and put on some clean clothes."

"That's more like it," cheered Gracie, watching the professor drink from a large bottle of Voice Stuff Number 8½ before entering the toilet to change.

He returned holding his nose. "You're right, Miguel. You do need to eat more fruit and vegetables," he said through a haze of green vapour escaping from his mouth. "The place absolutely stinks."

"But I clean very well."

"Don't worry. I'll leave the door open." He put the bottle of Voice Stuff into his waistcoat pocket, just in case it was needed later. "Right, the game is back on!"

Gracie pulled Jake's arm. "Does the old bloke always dress like that?"

"It's part of his charm," he replied, holding up the professor's toeless boots. "Goodness only knows how he got hold of a pair of ladies' ones with purple flowers."

The shed was exactly as Jake remembered, except the damaged wire had been neatly reattached to the Receptor.

Gracie looked around the huge empty space with disappointment. She had expected a more exciting place than this, with rows of dials, instruments and a fantastically complicated machine at its heart, more like Mission Control at NASA.

"That daft little car is your famous Starlight Machine?"

"Shush!" cautioned Jake, although he knew the Professor must have heard. "Forget what the Bubble Car looks like. Believe me, it's the most wonderful thing ever, even better than his flying rope and glue gun, and Snore-Stopper and Voice Stuff magic potions. Dad wants it after the professor has finished experimenting."

"Why would he want that? It's even got a wheel missing. And what are all those pipes, dishes and wires for?"

"No, Gracie, it's supposed to have only three wheels. As to the pipes and other stuff, I'm not entirely sure," admitted Jake. "I never asked and thought I shouldn't."

"If it was me, I would keep asking until he told me."

"I expect you would! Fortunately, I'm not so inquisitive. I've found it best to be blissfully stupid or incredibly clever in the professor's company. He doesn't tolerate foolish questions that are mid-way between the two. Out of choice, I favour stupidity. It's far easier to manage."

"We could burst the bubble when nobody's looking."

"Be quiet, you dreadful girl," snapped the professor, trying to concentrate on the switches and knobs controlling the Receptor Box.

"The car's not the kind of bubble you can burst, as you very well know," said Jake, holding a hand to her mouth.

The professor gave a loud *hurrah* as lights began to flash and the box began to hum. "This is it. Quick, Oscar, I forgot the special glasses. You'll find them in a box under my bed."

Oscar returned with five pairs, which he handed out.

"Not very fashionable," remarked Gracie as she turned them around in her hands, her nose in the air. "Haven't you got any Dolce & Gabbanas?"

"Be quiet and put them on, you silly girl," said the professor sternly. "This is science, not a catwalk."

Gracie did as she was told.

"Don't worry. His bark is worse than his bite," Jake remarked kindly. "But, you must try to stay on his right side."

"How do I do that?"

"By remaining quiet, instead of deliberately stupid!"

Chapter 20
The Fireship

Frantic activity in the shed led Jake to believe they were about to see an immediate, awe-inspiring and blinding light show that would provide the greatest possible spectacular—the very thing to shock Gracie out of her moaning. So, when the professor announced another delay, it came as a huge let-down.

Gracie, almost sulking by now, was in the process of removing her glasses when, suddenly, it happened! The Receptor's lens burst heroically into dazzling light, filling the room with the most brilliant colours which instantly became three-dimensional holographic images of soaked seamen on the deck of the same wooden ship.

The wind had strengthened. Booms creaked and masts groaned as they strained against the rope blocks, the ship one moment plunging bow-first into the hollows of the sea and then climbing out like a great whale as the next wave rolled in. High in the rigging, men balanced precariously to reduce sail-canvas to steady the ship.

"I feel sea sick," gulped Miguel. "Is all so real. If I was cat I would now lose one life, for sure."

"Wow! This time I'm not in the least scared. It's terrific!" exclaimed Jake excitedly.

"This isn't right, Professor," observed Oscar as he tried to make sense of the changes. "What happened to the keel-haulers?"

"I had to run the Receptor when I mended the wire, to check it was working. The story has moved on a bit."

"But I not see earlier stuff," complained Miguel.

"Shush," hissed the professor, "the story continues!"

Then the wind, so dramatic just moments before, suddenly died in its ferocity to leave a strong breeze from the ship's beam. The change caught the crew by surprise. The sea swell responded at a stroke and the ship began to move effortlessly through calmer water. It was a miracle. The men perched dangerously in the rigging were now ordered to increase sail-canvas once more, a sure sign of better conditions to come.

Among the band of misfit seaman of many nationalities working on deck or up the rigging was one man who stood out from the rest. The crew called him Butcher. He was new to the scene, having just come up from the commodore's quarters carrying galley slops to be thrown over the side.

He looked a feeble sort, not in the least hardened by a life at sea. A leather patch covered one eye, crudely fashioned from part of an old boot and held in place with a string lace. Yet, despite his good eye, he moved about the crowded deck tapping a curved stick carved from a sun-bleached whalebone. Strangely, once at the water's edge, he lifted the patch to peer into the distance before tipping the contents of the wooden bowl into the sea.

"Isn't this the best fun you've ever had, Gracie?" called Jake. He looked around. "Gracie?"

"Jake," she screamed, "help me," and as she spoke she reeled, only managing to steady herself by leaning against the shed wall.

"It's all right," he offered gently, propping her up. "I was scared witless the first time I saw it, that is until Dad saved me. Look, see what I can do perfectly safely." He let go and walked into the middle of the shed floor, causing part of the image to dance over his clothes. Ahead, he cast a dark shadow which cut the ship in half.

"Get out of the way, Jake," shouted Oscar, anxious not to miss anything. "Can you rewind it, Professor?"

"Afraid not. We would have to go back to the very beginning and there isn't time to revisit scenes we've already seen. Don't worry, though, I'm sure we've missed nothing important."

"The gang hold Michael hostage to see this?" complained Miguel, shifting his stare between the image and the professor. "How can they profit from this stuff?"

"No, leave it to me," said Butcher under his breath to another sailor who was scrubbing the deck on his hands and knees. *"Go quickly, before we're seen talking."*

"Leave what?" asked Oscar, as he tried to understand what was going on. "Did anyone catch anything the other man said over Miguel's incessant complaining?"

"For goodness sake," replied the professor sharply, "don't you listen to anything I say? The lip-reader only works when people are facing the device. He had his head down, and that's why we heard nothing."

"Then how can we know what was said? It might've been important."

"We can't. We have to use our imagination to fill any gaps or, failing that, rely on my genius. Did I tell you I'm a genius?"

"Yes, Professor, far too often!"

"I've an idea," said Gracie, now trying to stand without support. "It's a good one. Why don't we lean the mirror against the opposite wall? The lip-reader would then see peoples' lips move as a reflection, even when they're facing the wrong way."

"Could it work, Professor?" asked Jake.

"Why didn't I think of that? I used the mirror to lip-read your father's whispering when we first met. Remember that, Jake?"

"Maybe I'm a genius too," smirked Gracie.

Using the mirror made quite a difference to the number of voices detected, but, even so, what had begun as a thrilling adventure for Gracie soon turned boring as she witnessed everyday life on board an old warship. For her, there was none of the high drama of keel-hauling or sorrow from drowning that Jake had experienced. Instead, she watched brass cleaning and rope mending among a myriad of mundane activities. And those sailors without occupation merely crouched on deck throwing coins against the capstan as they played chuck-farthing, or amused themselves with penny whistles that produced no sound in the shed.

Even the sea had turned smooth, making the ship's progress steady and without incident. And when the guns were heaved to their ports during practice, none was fired.

For Gracie, the dullness soon became more than she could stand. Excusing herself, she strolled about the garden texting her school friends. Only after an hour had passed, when there was nobody left to contact, did she return to the shed carrying steaming mugs of hot chocolate and a plate of biscuits on a large tray.

Once again she settled in the corner, cross-legged and dipping biscuits. Nothing much had changed since she left and there seemed no immediate prospect of drama.

Fewer sailors were now on deck; the wind had stopped blowing altogether and several Jolly rowing-boats were being launched to tow the ship towards the natural harbour of a small sandy island, where a narrow passage led to a good anchorage.

As the thick ropes tightened, so the ship began to edge forward. Overseeing the manoeuvre from the poop deck were several officers, who glanced at charts and directed soundings of the water depth below the keel. Then a cannon was fired towards the interior of the island to flush out any hostile inhabitants. All eyes scanned the beaches for movement, but no natives appeared.

By the effort of the rowers, the ship was dragged to a clear blue inlet, where the great sea anchors were dropped. Meantime

Butcher, who had watched flocks of multi-coloured birds flap majestically skyward from the blast of the cannon, tapped his way off deck, only to come back five minutes later with more slops.

At last the approaching evening began to envelop the ship. As the brightness of the Receptor's images gradually dimmed, so the inside of the shed began to darken, although the outside garden still gloried in bright sunshine. Orders were given for the ship's lanterns to be lit fore and aft, port and starboard. A separate lantern was lit inside the binnacle mounted in front of the ship's helm, below the poop deck. Inside this wood and glass cabinet were housed the compasses needed for accurate navigation, although the ship was going nowhere for the night.

"We won't see much more today," said Oscar, ready for a break. "No point in watching a ship at anchor and in darkness."

"I'm surprised at you," scolded the professor. "Surely you realise the Earth rotates."

"What? Well, yes, of course I do. Everyone knows that. But what has that to do with anything?"

"Do you really think an egg in space could gather images of the ship at night on the far side of the Earth?"

Oscar shrugged.

"Oh, Dad, I see what the professor means. Our planet isn't a star. It's got no natural light of its own. It's the light from the sun—sunlight—hitting the Earth that illuminates it. As the Earth rotates, so only the area of our planet facing the sun basks in daylight, while the area away from the sun has darkness. As the Earth rotates every twenty-four hours, so we get half day and half night."

"Quite right, Jake. And it's only daylight reflected off the Earth that can be picked up by my eggs."

"You see, Dad, when it's night-time for our ship, the Earth's rotation will have taken it out of view."

"Well done, Jake. It would be half a day before the ship returned to daylight."

"You mean," said Oscar unwisely, "in an hour or so we will have to sit through twelve hours of other stuff we don't want before the ship is seen again?"

"Please don't be dim-witted, Mr Trotter. Obviously I thought of that. I built a twelve-hour 'sleep mode' into each egg, which switches the egg off. It comes back on at the appropriate time, many hours later, meaning there won't be a gap in the images projected from the Receptor Box. The only way anyone could tell the egg switched itself off and then back on again would be when the images suddenly and unexpectedly jump from late evening to early morning, with only the slightest pause. Of course, there is one problem even I can't solve."

"Which is?" enquired Oscar with hesitation.

"We won't see anything that happened on board ship overnight. Still, let's look on the bright side. It's only mid-evening on the island at the moment. Something good might still happen."

"*Sails, south-south-west,*" shouted the lookout from the fighting-top platform high up on the warship's main mast. He stood as stiff as a pole, keeping the telescope steady as he scanned the rest of the horizon.

"That man, Butcher," said Gracie in a moment of inspiration, "he's back on deck for the third time. There's something funny going on."

"How would you know?" replied Oscar impatiently. "You've hardly spent a minute in the shed since you got here. I hope you've turned your mobile off?"

She reddened with embarrassment.

"Something funny?" enquired the professor.

"Yes. It's what he's holding. When he threw stuff overboard before, he used a wooden bowl. Now look what he's got. It's a leather bucket with the gold letters GR on the side. He grabbed the bucket and then threw the bowl away. I saw him do it."

"George Rex," said the professor. "King George II. Nothing odd about that."

"For carrying kitchen waste?"

"A bucket is a bucket," remarked Oscar scathingly.

"Actually, Mr Trotter, she may be onto something," insisted the professor.

"And that's not all. Earlier I noticed there were three monogrammed leather buckets hanging on one side of the poop deck and two on the other," she continued with authority. "I distinctly remember because I was bored and started trying to find bits of the ship matching the letters of the alphabet. A, B. C and so on. B was for bucket. Actually, so was L. Now look, there are only four. Butcher is holding one."

"And?" asked Oscar.

"I get your drift," sprang the professor. "Who on board a Royal Navy ship would disrespect the King of England by carrying kitchen slops in a monogrammed bucket? It would be a flogging offence for certain. Leather buckets were used only to hold water or sand in case of fire, and nothing else. Fire posed a dreadful risk to wooden ships because they were built using inflammable pitch to seal the deck timbers, while tar soaked the rigging. Gracie is right to point it out. We must all be more vigilant if we are to find clues and solve the riddle. Well done, my girl."

Gracie cocked her nose at Uncle Oscar, who chose to ignore it.

Now quickly tapping his way towards the edge of the deck, Butcher again lifted his eye-patch before pouring away some of the sand contained in the bucket. Then, after checking nobody was watching, he took several small pieces of tarred cloth from his pocket and placed them irregularly inside the bucket, followed by a burning taper. Almost at once the cloth began to smoulder. Barely a splash was made as the bucket was dropped overboard, the weight of the remaining sand being enough to keep it upright in the sea.

The bucket bobbed on the surface of the water, gradually drifting out to sea with the motion of the shoreline waves, while slowly but surely the cloth inside blossomed into a highly visible glow.

"It's a signal," exclaimed the professor. "That devil's up to no good and there's nothing we can do to warn the commodore."

"Lights on the horizon off the port stern," yelled the lookout, *"and another I can't make out."*

"What other?" called Fairbrother.

"Makes no sense. Seems to be nearby, very small and floating low in the water."

"A boat?"

"Too small."

"And what is on the horizon?"

"A tall ship."

"This requires the commodore on deck," decided Fairbrother hesitatingly. *"Meantime, put our lanterns out."*

"Should we raise the anchors and get the ship turned about?" asked a sailor who had stepped up to his side, knowing the midshipman to be inexperienced in the ways of battle.

"Not yet. It could be a ship from our own squadron."

"Beg pardon, sir…" he persisted, touching his forelock with a knuckle as a salute, *"but…"*

"I said wait until we know more. We mustn't risk drifting towards the sand for no reason."

Fairbrother could sense the men watching his every move. His hand instinctively felt for the sword hanging from his waist. He lifted the hilt to check it parted easily from the scabbard, for he had heard of mutiny among common sailors when they felt threatened by the actions of their officers.

"What do you see now?" hailed Fairbrother, lifting his hat in order to wipe his brow.

"Hard to make out," came the reply from the fighting-top. *"The ship's a man of war, but ours or an enemy's is too early to say."*

"How's it rigged?"

The lookout leaned forward, struggling to make out the shape at such a long distance and in the dimming light.

"Well?" demanded Fairbrother with impatience.

"I think it has high bows and flat sails. Yes, it could be rigged the French or Spanish way. Only, I've never seen anything like it. I see too many fore and mizzen masts. It's certainly big."

The commodore, who had noted Fairbrother's spiritless command of the men as he strode briskly onto the poop, cast a critical eye over his ship. Not a single man seemed to be at action quarters. *"What's been sighted?"* he boomed.

"Not sure," Fairbrother replied weakly. *"Could be an enemy ship headed our way. I'm waiting for a proper sighting before giving the men instructions."*

"Waiting, blast your eyes! Waiting! Why, Mister, you do nothing at all. We might be moments from battle with our breeches around our ankles and you think the right action is to wait? Prepare, man, prepare for the worst and hope for the best, that's what we do. What intelligence do we have on French movements?"

"None that I know of."

"That you know of! Haven't you checked with Collins? As the officer on watch, you must know everything. Are the brass monkeys fully loaded with cannonballs?"

"I'll find out." A message was passed back. *"Balls being loaded and powder distributed, sir."*

"That's more like it," responded the commodore. *"You know, it's times like this when I regret not being in command of a seventy-four gunner."*

"The ship's thirty-eight cannon have smashed many enemy timbers, sir," replied Fairbrother with uncharacteristic vigour, glad to feel the weight of command lifted from his shoulders.

"Lambs to the slaughter if we face a major French battleship while cooped up in harbour, with no room to manoeuvre. We must make room and find speed, or we'll be a sitting duck to enemy guns. You've ordered the Jolly boats back out to hold the ship steady while the anchors are raised?"

"Not exactly, sir, but it will be done at once."

"Time, Mister Fairbrother, is not on our side. Look to it! By heaven, a Frenchy isn't what I expected."

The commodore's words stopped Fairbrother in his tracks. *"You were expecting an enemy vessel?"*

"Yes, by George, but not a heavily-armed French ship of the first line, if that's what it is. Still, as I have led us into the bear pit, it is now incumbent upon me to get us back out."

"You have a plan?"

"I have a duty, Mister Fairbrother. Duty first, riches after."

"Riches, sir?"

"We'll talk about that later. A curse is upon us, and now we must prepare to fight for our lives, yet equally ready ourselves to make a tactical retreat if we are out-fought and heavily damaged. We will do nobody any good at the bottom of the sea. Who's the lookout?"

"Morgan, sir, a first-rate man."

"I know, Mister Fairbrother. I chose him to sail with us."

Right on cue, Morgan called down from the fighting-top. *"A strange thing. I can make out more than one set of sails, but not two complete. It could be two ships astern at very close quarter."*

"Two," gasped Fairbrother. *"We are done for."*

Morgan rubbed his eye before lifting the telescope for another look. *"Spanish. Yes, now I can see. Both are definitely Spanish."*

The Commodore slapped Fairbrother's shoulder. *"That's more like it. This may be a good day after all. Hurry, there's no time to* lose. Order the Jolly boats to turn the ship around and tow us into open water. A guinea for each oarsman if it is done in under thirty minutes, and another guinea for each man hauling the anchors if done in five. Once we find wind, see to it that the Jolly boats are cast adrift. Then have all sails fully rigged for action."

"What about the men in the Jolly boats?"

"Let them row ashore. We'll come back for them after the battle is fought."

"And won...?"

"Of course. Now, gather all the men on deck who aren't otherwise occupied. Oh, and Fairbrother, wipe your brow. Panic is unbecoming of an officer."

It took less than a minute for the remaining sailors to assemble.

"Men, you might wonder why I brought you south to the Philippine Islands. Now I can tell you. I came for one purpose and one purpose only, and that is to intercept an armed Spanish treasure ship making the annual Manila-Acapulco trade run. However, it now seems there are two Spanish ships awaiting plunder." The men roared. "But, before you get carried away, two ships double the risk to us from twice the number of enemy cannon. What I have to decide is, are we up to the challenge?" He stepped back, basking in the spontaneous cheering. "Ah, so you want an uneven fight? I thought as much. Now, if I have kept the secret of our mission well and we keep our nerve in battle, we will all finish the day rich men. You know the rules, for it is written in Royal Navy law that everyone on board ship will share in the value of captured enemy vessels plus their cargoes, which in this case is gold beyond imagination."

The commodore looked on with pride as elation erupted into a frenzied cheer.

"You see, Fairbrother," adopting a friendlier tone, "here we are and here we stay until the job is done or we lay wrecked on the ocean bed."

"Three cheers for the commodore," raised a voice.

The commodore, who had briefly leant against a rail, leapt forward to the sound. *"Shush, my lads, shush, or you will wake the Spaniards from their siesta."* The men laughed. He turned to Fairbrother. *"Hearts of oak. But, avast, what's that black look on your face? Speak up, man. My skill as commodore has saved the lives of the crew on many occasions and I am not about to let you forfeit yours now."*

Fairbrother, who had never knowingly disobeyed an order, reluctantly said what was on his mind. *"I was wondering whether the Admiralty would see wisdom in risking our one ship against two, merely for a pot of gold. We might be better hiding here until the danger passes."*

The commodore listened with a deadpan face, and when done he slapped a hand on Fairbrother's shoulder. *"I hear what you say, but be of good spirit, Fairbrother, for it's less of a gamble than you think. I trained the men vigorously as we sailed south, and now I warrant there is not a crew anywhere in the world which can load cannon so rapidly or fire as accurately as ours."* He turned back to the men, now wearing a serious expression. *"The midshipman here believes it is folly to fight when outgunned. I gave him leave to express his doubts and that is his opinion. And so, having told you of the riches, I now supplant avarice with a grave warning. The Spanish have arrived earlier than I had been led to believe was usual, and there are two ships. And here we are, trying to get out of a bottleneck by the strength of the oarsmen. That is the fate of the situation. So, I can no longer plan an ambush. Instead, to win the day we will have to improvise, deceive the enemy of our ability, and blast iron into the Spanish so rapidly that it falls like hail from the sky. Are you ready for such a one-sided action?"*

"We are," shouted a sailor.

"Aye, bring them on," said another, rubbing his hands together. *"I can almost smell Spanish gold in me nostrils."*

"*Are there objectors?*" asked the commodore. "*Speak up without fear, for it is your lives I risk as much as mine.*"

An old 'sea dog', who had sat quietly on a coiled rope cutting raw meat, bent his head to spit tobacco onto the deck before raising a hand. His skin was thickly lined and weathered like leather.

"*Who is that?*" asked the commodore, not recognising his face.

"*Chicot, sir,*" replied Fairbrother. "*One of the stowaways. Keeps himself mostly in the galley. Should we give him a voice?*"

"*I will listen to any man about to face death,*" replied the commodore. "*You have something to say, Chicot?*" he called, leaning over the rail.

The man grumbled before spitting again.

"*Speak up,*" bawled Fairbrother. "*Say what you will, and be quick about it.*"

"*And get up, damn you,*" added the commodore. "*Do you deliberately irritate me?*"

"*I've seen it before,*" said Chicot, struggling to stand. "*I had a ship blown from under me feet and I can tell you this, the water is no friend to a drowning man. Them who are lucky are killed outright in battle. By thunder and lightning, I pledge I'll take a pistol to me own head before letting the sea grab me alive again. Dead is as dead does, but fish feed I'll not be while breathing. A shark took a bite from me leg as a snack. I'll not be the main course too.*"

"*Your meaning?*" demanded the commodore.

"*Before two hours have passed we'll all be dead as mutton. I hear told fifty good sailors were lost to scurvy on the outward journey, and the handful of strangers and boys taken on board since can't replace them in skill or strength. Now we lose more men to the Jolly boats. With so many crew gone, how can we make an even fight of it? We can't even put a full complement to each*

285

cannon. We are doomed men if we fight. We should return to anchor and await our fate."

"Give up? Never!" shouted a sailor.

"Belay that," cried the commodore, as the crew closed around Chicot brandishing handspikes. "It's a point fairly made, and I gave him sway to say as he pleased. But, equal to his worries, I have answers. It is true scurvy sent many of your comrades to Davy Jones' locker. And, yes, we are outnumbered. The Spanish will have five hundred men on each boat and many more cannon to fire. But what the Spanish don't have is me, and I can be as tricky as a barrel load of eels! I don't think we can drub the Spanish... I know we can."

As the crew cheered the rousing speech, he took a clay pipe from his pocket and began filling the bowl with coarsely-ground tobacco.

"Tell me your plan quickly, sir, so I can have the men prepare," said Fairbrother nervously, realising the Spanish ships could now be seen as tiny distant shapes without the need of a telescope. Morgan's eyes had not been deceived. The rear ship indeed had masts missing.

"Panic never won a battle, Fairbrother," remarked the commodore as he lifted a burning taper to the tobacco. "Remember Drake and the Spanish Armada." The thin stem of the pipe suddenly snapped in his unsteady hand, and he threw the lot overboard. "Tell me you didn't see my hand shake, Fairbrother."

"I saw nothing to indicate nerves, sir."

"Quite right, Mister. And if I appear to falter as I address the men, you have permission to jab the point of your dirk into the small of my back. For I wish to die no more than you, but my rank forbids signs of weakness."

"Oh!" said Fairbrother quite loudly, offering his hand, which the commodore rejected by pushing him aside.

"Now pay heed men," declared the commodore, and at once Fairbrother noticed his shaking had passed. "We all know the odds *are against us, but I still warrant we will look back on today's scrap as glorious. Not glorious dead, but glorious rich and most of us very much alive to enjoy the spoils. Remember this, me lads. Taking Spanish gold not only fills our pockets but diminishes our enemies' ability to fight a war, so it's a patriotic cause we follow as well as a greedy one."*

"Answer about the guns," snarled Chicot as their eyes met in a fearsome glare. His tone was so coarse it caused Fairbrother to draw, cock and aim a loaded pistol. But the commodore restrained Fairbrother before speaking.

"An open backbone will teach you to show proper respect for the uniform, Chicot. But this is not the time to fight amongst ourselves. I can spare nobody, not even your sorry liver. Yet, think on this. You may still be lucky and escape the pain of the cat… that is if you die today in the service of the King."

"Or you in my place," returned Chicot wilfully, wrapping an arm around a deck cannon.

Chicot's omen brought a moment of stunned silence to all those standing on deck, when suddenly only the splash of oars and the strained voices of the men in the Jolly boats could be heard. The shocked crew looked anxiously among themselves, wondering how the commodore would react to such an insult.

It was then Fairbrother noticed Chicot glancing towards the short open stairway leading up to the poop deck, his hand hovering over his knife. Whether Chicot intended to mount the poop in the hope of cornering the commodore against the guardrail to run him through, or throw the knife, Fairbrother dared not imagine.

"This isn't over," whispered Fairbrother, hoping it wouldn't be his duty to jump in front of the commodore to receive into his own chest the whole length of Chicot's meat-bloodied blade should he attack.

"Don't worry. I too see him," mumbled the commodore out of the corner of his mouth. *"Don't provoke the situation. We are not*

in immediate danger. Chicot can barely walk, let alone rush us. I doubt the men will let him use me as a pincushion."

Fairbrother lowered the pistol's hammer with his thumb. He felt relieved, remembering he had neglected the weapon during the storm and expected neither the flint nor the sea-soaked powder to spark a shot.

"This will demoralise the men," he said.

Yet the commodore's steadfast resolve triggered quite a different reaction among the crew, who aggressively disarmed Chicot.

If Chicot imagined the commodore would be humbled by the experience, he was quite wrong. For, in seconds the miscreant himself was heavily restrained in a headlock, with the commodore looking down from above.

"Rope him to a capstan," ordered the commodore, and quickly this was done. "We cannot suffer a Judas loose among us in the midst of battle, but equally I will not have him escape danger from enemy fire." He spread his arms along the rail. "Men, we have just witnessed the trouble a misunderstanding can cause. And if my lack of openness has been a curse to morale, it shall not continue. For I am sure the problem of crew numbers weighs heavily on all of you, whether spoken or not. So hear this and be unafraid of the battle awaiting us. It is my intention to have only the upper deck cannon fully manned to fire the usual broadsides. Below deck, just two men will be assigned to each cannon."

"Not enough," shouted Chicot, violently shaking his head to avoid a gag being tied across his mouth.

"Hear me out, and never again disrespect my opinion. One more gesture of any sort from you, Chicot, and I will be less merciful and have you thrown overboard to save the weight of your sour body slowing the ship down. I gave you leave and you spoke, but now you listen to me." He watched Chicot slump, the fight gone from his body.

"Gallant men of the Royal Navy, our position is not as hopeless as it first appears, and I will tell you why. The job of each two-man team will be restricted to loading their cannon with powder and ball, and signal when it's primed and ready. Nothing more and nothing less. Independent of this, roving groups of men—'firing crews'—will rush between primed cannon, haul them out through the gun-ports and fire the blessed things. After hauling back, the firing crews will move to the next primed cannon as reloading takes place, and so on. This tactic will spring a rather unpleasant surprise on the enemy, and I'll tell you why. It is customary for the Spanish to fall flat on their bellies when they know a broadside is coming, only to stand when the danger has passed. So, once the upper deck guns fire a volley, the Spanish on all decks will stand, only to be met by cannonballs from the lower guns that will fire randomly, without a break. The enemy won't know what's hit it, or when to stand and when to crawl. Yet, this is not all the tactics I will employ. We can do more to equal the odds. Any Spaniards left standing on the open decks will be met by withering shot from our well-trained sharp-shooters stationed aloft in the rigging." He looked among the sea of faces, gladdened by the powerful effect of his words. *"That is my battle plan. Now, men, the talking is over, for I can almost smell the baccy on the Spaniards' breath. Come to action and the day will be ours."*

"I see flames," screamed Morgan from the fighting-top. *"The back ship has been set alight and is burning fiercely. It's a..."*

"...fireship!" choked the commodore. *"Glory, that changes everything. They're expecting to ram us to set our tar ablaze."*

"You mean, it's not two treasure ships after all but one ship towing a flaming wreck?" implored Fairbrother. *"That can only mean one thing—the Spanish knew we would be here!"*

"The missing bucket," exclaimed Oscar. "Butcher was leading the Spanish straight to our ship using the floating fire-bucket as a beacon. I bet his name wasn't Butcher at all, but Boucher, the French for butcher. He's a snake in the grass."

"And so is the other man, Chicot, first seen scrubbing the deck and now tied up," added Gracie. "Fairbrother said he was a stowaway, so he must've been caught hiding. It's likely he too is a rotten spy."

"Why didn't the commodore realise?"

"It's obvious to us in hindsight, Dad, but he had no reason to think it at the time," advanced Jake. "After all, nothing had gone wrong with the voyage up to this point involving the stowaways."

"Yes, yes. All very well," said Oscar, "but how could the Spanish know the commodore's plans? That's what I can't figure. The commodore kept his plans secret, even from his own officers."

"Of course, what fools we are," cried the professor. "The answer is staring us in the face. When our ship sailed south towards a region of the world usually neglected by the Royal Navy, the Spanish must've guessed it was to intercept the only vessel of real importance and value in the area, namely their rich treasure ship making the Manila-Acapulco trade run. And so, protecting their ship became a priority, as the loss of a huge amount of gold and silver would diminish Spain's funds for war. And you know what they say, attack is often the best form of defence."

"Even if that's true, how could the Spanish work out where the British would be waiting in ambush?" said Oscar. "The ocean is absolutely vast. It would make finding a needle in a haystack look positively simple."

"Yet we know they managed," added Jake.

"Surely a Spanish gold ship would always sail the most direct route, wouldn't it?" suggested Gracie. "To get its precious cargo from A to B in the shortest possible time."

"Of course," agreed the professor, "that has to be it. Well done Gracie. The Spanish would follow a narrow trade route across the sea, anywhere along which the Royal Navy could be waiting to pounce. It was knowing where and when that mattered, and the fire-bucket alerted them to both."

"You're all forgetting one thing," interrupted Oscar. "That silly little fire-bucket couldn't possibly be spotted over hundreds of miles of ocean. Yet, we think it played a major part in bringing the ships together. How's that possible?"

"Wait!" exclaimed the professor with conviction. "Maybe we've got it all upside-down. What if the spies on the Royal Navy ship had entirely different ideas?"

"Like what?" asked Gracie.

"I'm beginning to think the fire-bucket was never intended to lead the Spanish towards the Royal Navy ship. Mr Trotter is right, it could never be expected to work. But, what if the fire-bucket was to be lit by the spies *only if* the Spanish were blindly sailing into a Royal Navy ambush? You know, using it like an early warning system. That would give the Spanish time to prepare their greatest defence of all, the fireship? Don't forget, only after Spanish sails were spotted by Morgan was the fire-bucket thrown overboard. Morgan's sharp eyes as a lookout were used against his own ship. Ironic!"

"It's a bit far-fetched?" challenged Oscar. "Spies and early warning systems. We *are* talking about the 18th century."

"It's a question of intelligence."

"You mean *my* intelligence? Because if you do…"

"Not yours," replied the professor. "I mean intelligence gathering. People nowadays forget how much spying on the enemy, its preparations and movements went on at seaports in past centuries. In our modern world we tend to think information gathering on an enemy using spies and double agents is something new, like James Bond, but it isn't. French and Spanish spies kept watch on all our naval deployments, as we did on theirs." He turned. "I bet I could find a few answers in a reference book I have on Royal Navy history. Do we know the name of our ship?"

Gracie looked hard into the image. The commodore's leather telescope tube was embossed with large gold lettering. "I think it says *HMS Audacious*."

The professor ran from the shed, returning quickly with a large and dusty volume. He flicked the pages.

"HMS *Audacious*… blah, blah, blah—ah-ha, here is it. In 1743 the great warship moored at the port of Macao, where the sick and depleted crew was boosted by twenty-one fresh sailors, mostly Indian and Dutch. While there, *Audacious* attracted such interest from civilians (some known to be Spanish and French sympathisers) that armed English marines had to be posted along the quay. As a further measure to keep the ship's plans secret, covered wagons were later employed to hide the quantity and type of stores being loaded on board ship, but it is thought foreign agents rewarded the merchants with gold coins to divulge what goods they had brought to the dock. Later, the timing and direction of *Audacious's* departure caused further speculation. In addition to the twenty-one new crew, two stowaways were subsequently discovered. They remained hidden until the ship approached the Philippines. When found, they claimed to be Belgians but subsequently confessed to being French. The stowaways, who were both partially lame and thereby seemingly of no military threat, avoided hanging by serving as unpaid galley cooks." He looked up at Oscar. "Gracie is right. These were the spies. They probably rowed out under cover of darkness to board *Audacious* while the ship was at anchor."

"Anything else?" asked Oscar, looking over the Professor's shoulder.

"I still not understand what gang want with this old stuff," said Miguel, having remained quiet up to now. "It offers no profit. I say we give up as bad job. It is, what you call, a false rope."

"False lead, you twit," barked Oscar. "And we are not stopping now, just as the battle is about to begin."

"Listen to this," added the professor excitedly. "The War of Jenkin's Ear."

"Jenkin's what?" cried Jake.

"Ear. It has a bearing on the situation. Apparently, in 1731 the Spanish coastguard boarded a British merchant ship and severed an ear from the commodore in charge. The ear was later exhibited in Parliament and this caused the British to retaliate in a conflict that lasted from 1739 to 1748."

"Does this mean the spies weren't French, but Spanish after all?" asked Oscar.

"No. At that time the British were in conflict with both France and Spain. It's quite reasonable, therefore, to expect Frenchmen to help the Spanish attack the Royal Navy."

"Where does it all get us?"

The professor scanned the paragraphs. His eyes lit up. "Ho-ho. *Yippee-doodle-dandy.*"

"Well?" cried Oscar. "Don't keep us in suspense."

"According to this, Commodore Bowfinger of *HMS Audacious* sailed a vast distance to intercept a Spanish treasure ship off Cape Espiritu Santo in the Philippine Islands."

"We know that much," exclaimed Oscar.

"Be patient. There's more. During the long voyage south, Bowfinger made landfall where he intended to replenish the fresh water supply, positioning the ship well away from the Cape to remain unseen. Jolly boats were to be used to transport the barrels. However, a violent storm and strong tide carried the vessel closer to shore, where it was spotted."

"Another place where Butcher and Chicot could've boarded," offered Oscar.

"So," considered the professor, "although the Spanish might've worried about *Audacious* heading south, they knew they had spies planted on board in case the ship became a problem. This gave them the confidence to make the gold run in spite of the perceived danger, added to which they took the precaution of having an ace up their sleeve with the fireship. Being pre-warned by Butcher's flaming bucket meant they could catch the British with their pants down. In those days there was little protection against a fireship."

"You mean *Audacious* is about to be sunk?"

"I don't know, Jake. I haven't got to that," answered the professor, scanning down the page for answers.

"It's a dodgy plan," said Gracie. "To work it needs the fire-bucket to be seen? But what if the circumstances were different and the British and Spanish ships closed together in full daylight?"

"But they didn't," argued Oscar. "We have seen for ourselves it was getting dark."

"I know, Uncle Oscar, but you're missing the point. How could they be prepared for such an eventuality? It would ruin their plans."

"Not in the least, my dear," replied the professor. "The fire-bucket was useful, but not entirely essential. The Spanish still had the fireship ready for lighting, something the Royal Navy wouldn't expect in the middle of an ocean. Either way, the Spanish must have believed they had the upper hand or they would've cancelled the voyage to keep the gold safe. It's probable they also knew of *Audacious'* depleted crew."

"So, it was a pretty good plan," agreed Jake. "If no contact between the British and Spanish was made during the entire trade crossing, all the better. The gold would merely make the sea crossing unscathed. It was a win-win situation for the Spanish."

"Let's carry on watching," said Gracie excitedly. "At last it's getting really good!"

"Can you identify the lead vessel, Morgan?"

"I believe… yes… it's carrying the flag of Captain General Antonio Galvez."

"Galvez, be blowed," pondered the commodore. *"That makes the ship the Nuestra Cristo Rosa, with forty-four large cannon plus*

a further twenty-eight small cannon on its gunwales, tops and quarters. One of Spain's latest and most deadly warships."

"Should we make a run for it after all?" asked Fairbrother. "We are out of the harbour mouth, the sails have been rigged and the Jolly boats are being cut free as we speak."

"Certainly not!"

"But surely we haven't a moment to lose. We are outgunned, and then there is the fireship to worry about."

The fact that *Rosa* outgunned his ship had not been lost on the commodore.

"Before you wet your breeches, Fairbrother, you should know we don't carry enough sail to outrun a capital ship from a standing start. Rosa would merely cut the fireship loose and give chase, hauling eight knots to our six even in this light breeze. We would be caught in under an hour and lose the only advantage we have... that of guile."

"Can we win a straight fight?"

"I remind you, Mister Fairbrother, we remain a frigate of His Majesty's Navy."

"Then we surrender with dignity, sir?"

The commodore turned ferociously. "Nor does the Royal Navy surrender without a fight, even with a ninny like you on board. No, Mister, we win the day through cunning or take a beating in the process. That is our duty." He could see Fairbrother lacked the conviction for an uneven fight. "Speak your mind, midshipman, but be double quick about it."

"Well, sir, just a moment ago you said we would do nobody any good at the bottom of the sea?"

"No, Fairbrother, I said we could attempt a tactical retreat if we are out-manoeuvred and heavily damaged. We have not, as yet, sustained the slightest scratch to our pitch or paint."

"Your orders, sir?" he asked with trepidation, fearing he was in the wrong place at the wrong time but had no means to alter the situation.

"I view deception as our best hope. We must make it look as though we've lost the breeze and stood the crew down. Let the Spanish think we are unprepared and that they approach us unseen. Relight the lanterns. Then lower the anchors, but only to a depth just below the waterline to give the impression we are fully at rest and off guard. That way, we can drag them up quickly on my command. Furl the sails, topsails and gallants, but have them loose-tied for quick release. The topriggers must stay aloft at all times, ready to haul the mainsails at a moment's notice. Oh, and give them guns."

"Fore, main and mizzens, sir?"

"All, Mister Fairbrother. This is a one-chance gamble. Make sure the cannon are primed and ready. The gun crews must be divided between decks as I previously directed. But, for heaven sake, keep the gun ports closed until I give the order. Oh, and only the men below deck may strip to the waist for action. We don't want to alert the Spanish lookouts of our readiness."

"Aye, sir."

"And another thing. Get lots of men on deck, as many as can be spared. Include the cooks and boys. Tell them to make one hell of a racket and act drunk. Sing a few sea shanties, that sort of thing. You might as well launch my little boat too. Let the enemy think I've gone fishing. This is a game of cat and mouse, Mister Fairbrother, and we may very well be the mouse."

"Shall I also send a few marksmen aloft? They will be better shots than the topriggers."

"Now you're thinking like an officer. Yes, Fairbrother, we will see what the men have learned from all the exercising in quick loading and shooting at targets hung from the yard-arm. I want them armed with both ball and grape-shot."

Soon the ship was brightly lit and seemingly helpless.

"Look," cried Gracie, "Butcher is back on deck."

"The commodore asked for the cooks to join in," pointed out Jake. "Only, he has unintentionally brought a spy back up. I wish we could warn him!"

"I don't think I can watch," howled Gracie, closing her eyes. "Our ship is falling into a trap set by a well-armed enemy."

"Maybe so," nodded Oscar, "but equally the Spanish don't know the commodore is setting his own snare. What does your book say about the outcome of the battle, Professor? Professor!"

But the professor was too busy watching the action unfold to spoil it by sticking his nose into the pages. Oscar let it go.

Fairbrother returned to the poop deck. *"All done, sir. But I still don't know what you are planning."*

"Lanterns gone out or burning dim and dusky on the Rosa," shouted Morgan from above. He loaded two pistols with fresh powder.

The commodore lifted his own telescope. *"Ah-ha, just as I thought. He's creeping in for the kill."*

"Rosa will be hard to target as the light fades."

"Not so, Fairbrother. Look, the fool has lit the fireship far too early. Until it is cut loose, the gathering flames will illuminate Rosa as brightly as a thousand lanterns. It's his first mistake. So, soon comes the interesting bit, which determines our response."

"We're going to miss the battle?" cried Oscar, spellbound and anxious. "The rotation of the Earth will take the ships to the far side and out of view."

"We have an hour or so left, I think," replied the professor. "We can only hope it's enough."

Fairbrother watched nervously as the Spanish ships sailed ever closer. Fire now enveloped the wreck from stern to bow and yet it was still under tow. Without fully knowing the commodore's intentions, he believed an already dangerous situation was becoming catastrophic, yet he was too frightened to say anything.

"Stop shaking, ninny," ordered the commodore in a steady voice. "You must lead the men into battle by example. Good grief, you're more of a wreck than that blessed fireship! Take a look at the men at their guns. Do they tremble like children? Damn fine fellows when it comes to a scrap. Pull yourself together. That's an order."

"Apologies, sir," replied Fairbrother, lifting a telescope to one eye. "The Spanish are getting extremely close."

"Then we will soon know if Galvez has taken the bait. Meantime, we must hold our nerve. Until we feel the heat from the fireship's burning timbers, we must do nothing to show our hand."

"Do nothing, sir, yes, sir," replied Fairbrother, now able to see the tiny figures of distant Spaniards on board the Rosa.

"Galvez's usual method of attack is to release a fireship on a collision course just as Rosa needs to gain maximum speed for its own assault. It is a sound tactic. The closer a fireship comes before release, the more likely it is to hit its target. Remember that, Fairbrother. You may use the same tactic one day if you survive this encounter. As the fireship poses the greatest threat to our survival, Galvez will expect our attention to be diverted away from Rosa. He will then fire Rosa's chase cannon mounted in the bow before turning hard to port or starboard in order to bring the ship's heavy broadside cannon into play."

"My God," whimpered Fairbrother, "we're in for an almighty pounding. How do you stay so calm, sir?"

"Because, on this occasion, I'm sure our tomfoolery will encourage him not to destroy us. It's a gamble, but time will tell if I'm right."

"You mean, we do nothing until Galvez makes the first move?" replied Fairbrother with eyes wide. "Just bob in the water like a sitting duck?"

"No, Mister, what we do is hope with all our strength that Galvez believes we are as helpless as we pretend to be. And..."

"...And?"

"And hope he is accurate in aiming the fireship."

"You want him to be accurate?"

"Don't be shocked. It's simple enough to understand. I'm gambling on Galvez thinking he is approaching a smaller unprepared ship, unable to defend itself. Our lack of sail, dropped anchors, launched Jolly boat, drunken crew and general state of chaos will soon be noticed by his lookouts. Believe me, Galvez will greet the news with much pleasure. Then, if I'm correct, he will at once change his battle plan to suit the revised situation. Instead of sinking us, he will choose to capture our ship intact as a valuable prize of war. He's a greedy man and will hunger after the reward that comes from taking a British man-of-war."

"And if you're wrong, sir?"

"Can you swim, mister?"

"Not a stroke!"

"Nor I," replied the commodore, *"so we must ensure our feet don't get wet. You see, Fairbrother, I'll only properly know Galvez's intentions at the very last moment, possibly not before the fireship has been set on its evil course. There will be signs to recognise, I assure you. If we are to be sunk, the fireship will sail straight and true into us. But if we are to be captured, he will set the fireship on a course to narrowly miss us as a distraction. That is why I want his aim to be accurate. And while we panic, he will manoeuvre Rosa alongside to allow his men to board us with overwhelming force."*

"I don't understand. Surely Audacious will be lost either way," said Fairbrother with surprising indignation. *"That cannot be your intention."*

"Of course not, and it won't happen. What Galvez does, and what he thinks my response will be, are two very different things. But, first, I'm most anxious to see if Galvez removes Rosa's anti-boarding nets. That will tell me much."

"Sir?"

"Goodness, Fairbrother, you have an awful lot to learn about naval warfare. Anti-boarding nets are only needed for defence. If Galvez thinks there is any danger of his ship being boarded by us, he will keep the nets up to stop us swinging across. But—and this is the critical point—the nets will be in the way if he is planning to board Audacious. So, if the nets are removed, it's a sure sign he intends to board us with pistols and swords at the ready. You see, little things give away an enemy's tactics. So, we must continue to do everything possible to maintain the appearance of helplessness."

"And if he isn't deceived?"

"We lift our gun ports at the last minute and blow the fireship out of the water before it hits. Of course, saving our ship from fire would make us vulnerable to Rosa's guns, and the battle would almost certainly be lost. However," the commodore added gleefully, "if all goes our way and my plan succeeds, Galvez will get the shock of his life. It's the gold and silver carried in Rosa I want. I care little if we damage Rosa itself. But Rosa must not be sunk or the gold sinks with it."

"If the bait is taken, how do we overwhelm Rosa to get at the gold and silver? We haven't the men to overpower the Spanish crew."

"Simple, Mister Fairbrother. It is my intention to catch Rosa at its most vulnerable moment and kill as many Spaniards as we can before boarding. Just think what a feather in our cap it will be to capture the treasure and Galvez."

"I still don't understand how?"

"By being bolder than the Spanish, of course. If we survive the fireship, I will give the order to 'Ready About' as Rosa slows. In the wink of an eye, we will deploy our sails and raise the anchor. Immediately Galvez will realise he has been sucked into a trap and order full sail, and Rosa will cross our bows. Once it has passed and is unable to fire its main guns towards us, we will blast Rosa's weak stern timbers with all the power we have. Our shot will

300

punch straight through the Spanish gun decks, from end to end, sending jagged splinters of wood flying through the air to disable the crew. Any top deck crew who then dare to stand will be picked off by our marksmen and topriggers." He paused at the thought of the inevitable slaughter. "Of course, Galvez will then try to circle around to bring to bear any big guns remaining operational. But, with any luck, Rosa's sails will flutter and sag as the ship loses the wind during tacking and we can rapidly lay alongside and let loose our cannon for the second time, leaving Galvez to lick his wounds and count his dead."

"Success relies entirely on Rosa not firing its own broadsides as it crosses in front of us. It's a very big gamble, sir."

"Of course it is, but I told you, I know Galvez. We are old adversaries. He will not waste a single cannonball if he thinks we are about to surrender. With any luck he won't even have his big cannon primed. No, once he passes by and we finally raise our gun ports and let loose our cannon, it will be too late to stop us from wrecking his ship. Now, Fairbrother, get about your work."

"The Spanish are turning," shouted Morgan.

"This is it," hastened the commodore. "Galvez is about to release the fireship. Off you go, Fairbrother. You know what is required of you."

"Sir?"

"Remind me to have you replaced once this is over." He put the telescope back inside its leather case. "Your battle station as a midshipman is in the area of the main mast."

"Aye, sir." He started to walk away but stopped.

"Another problem understanding my orders, Fairbrother?"

"Merely a thought, sir. Earlier, the lookout said he saw a small floating light. Could it have come from our ship, to give our position away?"

"If so, there is your mission after the battle is over, Midshipman. Find me the traitor who did it and I will make him dance from the end of the yardarm."

"Fireship approaching," screamed Morgan. *"It's heavily aflame."*

Just as tension in the shed reached fever pitch, a startling *'pop'* froze the images. Then, the complete hologram vanished along with the sound of the sailors' voices and at once everywhere was cast in alarming silence and darkness.

"What happened?" screamed Gracie, throwing off her sunglasses before grabbing the door to let the daylight pour in.

The brightness lit up the interior, allowing Oscar's worst thoughts to be confirmed. Only Miguel stood anywhere near the Receptor Box.

"What?" pleaded Miguel, returning Oscar's accusing look.

"Did you touch it?"

"Me?"

"Yes, you. Someone's tampered with the Receptor?"

Miguel turned to the professor. "I do nothing, I promise. I am as surprised by stopping as you."

The professor strode briskly to the Receptor. "Same wire as before. It's come unattached again."

"Deliberately pulled out?" asked Oscar with understandable annoyance.

"Whatever or whoever caused it to come away," remarked the professor more calmly to quell accusations, "I assure you it can be easily fixed. I suggest we have lunch and try again later."

"Won't we miss the battle?" complained Gracie.

"Nope," said Jake, picking up Grace's sunglasses. "The images have ground to a halt." He stopped. "Or have they? Professor, why hasn't the battery kicked-in like last time?"

"Entirely different situation, not involving the power supply. Anyway, I removed the battery. I couldn't afford to take chances with the precious images or allow the Receptor to overheat."

"Not my doing," moaned Miguel as they walked to the cottage. "I make lunch now to show I help in many different ways. I not bad man."

"Can we trust him not to poison us, Professor?" remarked Oscar some minutes later, watching Miguel spread peanut butter onto slices of bread.

"Why do you never give him a chance to repent?"

"I would, if I thought he was repentant."

"I've heard enough! Leave me alone to think."

The professor walked over to Michael's bed and sat among the books, staring at the Christmas tree.

Jake eventually joined him. "Has Dad upset you again?"

"Not really. I wanted space to replay events in my mind. I hate to say it, but your father is probably right. I know I wired the cable properly."

"You mean, Miguel ripped…?"

"Shush! I'll slip away in a minute to mend it. Give me half an hour before bringing the others over. I'm taking the glue gun, just in case."

Chapter 21
The Shed is Defended

True to his word, when nobody was looking the professor crept from the cottage and hurried to the shed, where he began work repairing the Receptor. It gave him a warm feeling, knowing he was seeing the same images as Michael had in the recent past. But elation was, nevertheless, tinged with darker thoughts, as his belief in Miguel had taken another severe dent.

He had left Oscar talking candidly to the youngsters. Miguel, on the other hand, having cleared the plates, idled away the minutes lamenting his misfortune. Several times he glanced across at the others, but they remained on distant terms and turned away every time they caught him looking. With nothing more to do, he plucked a book from the bed and started reading a chapter on the mating habits of the common mayfly. It appeared, with just a few hours of life, the adult males forced themselves on the females of the species before dropping dead. He closed the book, regarding his own life as being nearly as pointless as theirs.

"What the heck's going on?" cried Oscar gruffly when eventually he strolled into the shed, cutting through the bright light. "I thought I heard talking as we walked over. Who gave you permission to start the images?"

"Nothing I could do to stop it," replied the professor without apology, winking at Jake who had followed with the others. "Like your son, I assumed the images had stopped, but we were wrong. The broken wire disconnected the light behind the lens, but the stored images continued running in darkness because I forgot to remove the wall plug providing electrical power. As soon as I reconnected the wire the pictures shot back to life and with it came the voices. Sadly, I think we've missed some of the action."

Jake sidled to him. "Is that true?" he whispered. "Only, I can't believe you would try repairing the wire without first turning the power off. You don't want more electric shocks."

The professor pulled him close. "Shush! Of course I did. I just wanted a little time to myself to look at what Miguel is afraid of us seeing, without him knowing. So, having mended the wire, I switched the plug back on. I'm surprised your dad and Gracie didn't see through my little ruse."

"And did you see anything?"

"Nothing obvious so far. Time-wise, I've viewed a lot less than the others think has passed by."

"Why the hushed voices?" enquired Miguel as he approached, said rather too firmly to be a casual enquiry. "What you see, old man?"

"What's it to you?" questioned Gracie from behind.

"I ask from interest. That is all."

"How would I know what passed in our absence," retorted the professor. "Except the fireship missed, just as the commodore predicted. I saw that. It was a near thing, though. You all should've seen it."

"I wish I had," replied Oscar in a disappointed tone.

"Flames everywhere, all along the deck and up the masts, and barrels of tar lashed to the hatches were blazing away. It was quite a sight. The fireship came so close that one sail fell in flames across *Audacious's* poop. But Bowfinger's crew heaved it overboard before the fire spread. That happened just before you entered."

Their acceptance of the situation relieved the Professor, although Oscar clearly remained angry.

"Don't keep on, Dad," said Jake, pulling his father to one side. "The professor knows what he's doing. He's having his own doubts about Miguel. Be patient with him."

"Really? And there I was thinking they were bosom pals."

A violent scream from Morgan on board *Audacious* now put the group on alert, as an iron ball from one of *Rosa's* manoeuvrable gunwale cannon cut through the maintopsail. It fractured the mainmast, causing the upper half to snap as it bent under the weight of sagging ropes and cloth, bringing Morgan down from a great height. He fell onto the deck with tremendous force, although the sickening sound of crunching bones went unheard.

"I wasn't expecting that," shouted the commodore through the chaos. *"It was a damn fine shot."*

The fallen mast unsteadied the ship, which listed to starboard, allowing sea swell to wash over the deck. The slapping water brought movement to Morgan's limbs as he lay on the deck, as if still alive. Then, as the water flowed back overboard, Morgan's body settled again in its shattered and unnatural position.

"His job is done," said the commodore. *"Have him wrapped in the Union Jack and taken below. The rest of you, cut the mast loose and get rid of it. We must right ourselves if we are to fire the cannon with effect."*

Morgan was Fairbrother's first fatal casualty of war and the shock visibly distressed him.

"No need to take on so," cautioned the commodore from above. *"His duty to me, the ship and the King is done and done well. There is no fear for his soul."*

Another cannonball from *Rosa* quickly followed the first, lacerating the foresail, shattering the boom and tearing away a long splinter which pierced a sailor's chest like an arrow. He fell back, dying. Almost immediately a third fearsome ball struck the side, causing three cannons to rip free of their mountings and roll indiscriminately past the last of the sailors still singing on deck. Again *Audacious* listed with the unequal distribution of weight.

"*Upend the blasted things and push them over the side, and be quick about it,*" bawled the commodore. "*And you lot can stop making that frightful noise! I think they know we see them.*"

Small groups of sailors grabbed anything at hand to arrest the runaway cannon and manhandle them towards the shattered side. One-by-one the guns were tipped through the gap, each dropping dramatically into the sea with a huge splash. The ship righted.

"*Will the other masts hold?*" called the commodore.

Fairbrother, who had rushed to the fallen sailor to stem the flow of blood, was too preoccupied to hear.

"*Blast your eyes, Midshipman. Look at me when I address you. We are at war, not running a nursery.*"

With tears running down his reddened cheeks, Fairbrother stared up at the commodore.

"*I will have your answer now, ninny,*" the commodore declared firmly. "*For goodness sake, man, get control of yourself. The battle has hardly begun. There will be more fallen before the day is out. You can't weep like a woman over each corpse.*"

Fairbrother glanced at the mainmast and foremast, both heavily damaged. He swallowed hard to gain his voice. "*What's left of the mainmast holds the mainsail steady, sir, but maintopsail and topgallant are gone. The foremast holds its foresail, foretopsail and topgallant. The mizzen and jib are untouched.*"

"*Then prepare for more balls now they have our range. And for goodness sake, Fairbrother, get yourself up here. That man is done for.*"

The commodore was right on every score. Scarcely had the sailor died than another cannonball pierced a sail. Repeat after repeat from Spanish light cannon then blasted away rails and ropes, and left holes in the hatches.

"*Anyone else hurt?*" shouted the commodore through the chaos.

"*Chicot is dead. His head has been blown clean off.*"

"*I meant any real men. I don't count that rascal among them.*"

"*Not a one,*" returned Fairbrother, climbing onto the poop at the very moment a length of chain was fired from a Spanish cannon.

"*My God, man!*" screamed the commodore, watching the midshipman fall forwards over the rail and onto the deck below, his arm lying limply across the dead sailor's leg.

The boatswain threw down his weapon and rushed to Fairbrother's side. It was a dreadful sight. He could hardly speak the words the commodore demanded to hear: "*Both legs gone below the knees.*"

"*Is he breathing?*" begged the commodore, showing the first sign of compassion.

"*Barely conscious, I would say.*"

"*I can speak for myself,*" gasped Fairbrother, his breathing shallow and fast. He slightly lifted his head, enough to be appalled at the sight of his own wounds. "*I'm not going to see England again, am I Boatswain?*" he croaked.

"*I fear you won't, friend. But fret not. You'll not be going to heaven alone.*"

The commodore raced down the steps to where Fairbrother laid in a fresh pool of blood.

"*Please, sir, stick me in a pickle barrel and tie me to the mizzen so I might remain at my station to the last.*"

"*See to it, Boatswain,*" ordered the commodore as he took hold of Fairbrother's hand. "*At last, Midshipman, you show proper courage. I'll enter your name in the ship's log and pin a medal on your gallant chest.*"

"*You may nail it to the barrel, sir, for I fear it will also be my coffin,*" and, with the slightest curl of his lips, Fairbrother died.

"*He's gone,*" said the boatswain.

The commodore rose, straightened his jacket and aligned his hat. *"Revoke the barrel!"*

A cannonball tore a hole through the staysail, but otherwise pitched long.

"Sir," shouted the boatswain, *"the Spanish are removing their anti-boarding nets. They tack starboard."*

"Right, by George, we have them. We have taken their best shots and survived the experience. Now it's time we taught them a thing or two. They will lose our range as they turn."

"I can hardly watch," said Oscar, so deeply involved in the action that he ducked with every cannonball fired. He was ready to stand shoulder-to-shoulder against the Spanish.

"Sir, I cannot believe it. The Spanish are reducing sail. Look, they're lowering a boat," shouted the boatswain.

"So they are," agreed the commodore. *"That's not what I expected either. Typical Galvez to play a wild card. Penny to a pound he thinks we intend to surrender without a fight as we haven't returned fire."* He allowed himself a short derisory laugh. *"We've fooled them, good and true. Right, stand by to lift the gun ports, raise the sea anchors and prepare to make sail when the piper signals. We'll cripple Rosa above the waterline to keep it afloat!"*

"Sir, the Spanish are hailing us," interrupted a lieutenant.

"Hail back... 'we can't hear'. And, Lieutenant, make ready the battle ensign, but don't raise it yet. They'll know soon enough we mean business. The fight-back begins!"

The word 'fight' echoed around the crew, raising a spontaneous and rousing cheer.

"Good grief, that's given the game away," thundered the commodore. *"Right, lads, time to show them a bit of Royal Navy iron. Open the gun ports, unfurl the battle ensign and let's have all the sail we can muster, if you please."*

"The Spanish are signalling again."

"What now?"

"They say, stand by to be boarded or we sink you. Your orders, sir?"

"Hail back, 'suck a banana'."

"Banana, sir? Will they understand?"

"Oh, yes, Galvez will. He'll think I'm making a monkey of him and become extremely angry. That's when a commander makes his biggest mistakes."

"And after I deliver your message?"

"Why, Lieutenant, rain death and destruction into the enemy's stern timbers. The moment is upon us. Now we'll see who has the mettle to win."

The message was passed. A cannonball from *Rosa* formed the reply, piercing a staysail before splashing harmlessly into the ocean.

"Ah-ha," greeted the commodore with satisfaction, noticing panic on *Rosa's* deck. *"I was right. See, only now are they pitching overboard any spare timber and cattle that clutter the deck. A sure sign they were not expecting a battle."*

"The enemy is re-attaching its anti-boarding netting," shouted the boatswain. *"The officers are helping."*

"Then, they make our task that much easier. Tell the marksmen to sweep Rosa's deck with grape-shot."

Plumes from musket fire immediately rose from the rigging, the grape-shot causing havoc right across *Rosa's* deck. Galvez and all but one of the officers fell dead or wounded among the many ordinary sailors writhing in agony. At once *Rosa's* cannon fell silent, the gunners in disarray.

In the shed, Miguel shut his eyes to the carnage.

"We have them," exclaimed the commodore in bullish tone, *"and not a single cannonball fired by us. Pass a message to Rosa*

310

that we are sending an armed boarding party to guard our gold. Tell them to remove the netting immediately, or suffer the consequences."

"What do you want done with Rosa's crew?" asked the lieutenant.

"Any not seriously wounded must be seen to throw down their weapons and come across as prisoners. As it is undamaged, I'll claim Rosa as part of my reward."

A message came back. The commodore stamped his foot.

"Damn if the Spanish don't play with me."

"What do they say?"

"They have many wounded who cannot make the crossing." He paced the deck. *"Fine, let's do it another way. Tell them the wounded can stay on Rosa, but we demand all cannonballs, muskets and swords are thrown overboard where we can see them sink. After, I will send across a small boat with two armed marines to check they fully complied with our demands. Meantime, keep the cannon loaded and trained on Rosa. Is there anyone amongst us who speaks Spanish?"*

"Butcher has both French and Spanish."

"Good, he can join the boarding party. Arm him with a brace of pistols."

Now from the professor's garden, where the trees were at their closest, suddenly and unexpectedly came the lurching whine of a car engine revving. It was loud and uneven, as if struggling over rough ground. Then, just as quickly, it stopped and doors could be heard slamming.

"What was that?" jumped Gracie, looking among the group. "Who else heard a noise?"

"I did," exclaimed Jake. "What do you think it is, Dad?"

Oscar raced to the window. He thought he detected movement among the bushes. "Oh no, we may have unwanted company. Quick, turn the Receptor off, Professor."

311

The bright images abruptly disappeared, too quickly to be by the Professor's hand. Everyone turned to Miguel, who stood frozen like a rabbit caught in headlights. He held a wire.

"What?" he asked, looking at their accusing faces. "You want machine stop. I stop it quick."

"We wanted it stopped, not broken again," challenged the professor. "There's a perfectly good switch to use."

Miguel squirmed as he timidly placed the lead on the table.

"It's exactly the same wire as last time," remarked Oscar smugly. "You see, I was right to have my suspicions about him. Don't tell me you still think he's on our side."

"I here to help," pleaded Miguel.

"Okay, Miguel, you've overstepped the mark this time. Exactly what's going on?" demanded the professor, flicking the wall plug. "Honesty would be nice for once."

"Me? I know nothing, except I am in great danger. Don't you see, bad men come to capture me. They want to shut me up. We better off hiding in darkness."

"What do you think, Professor?" asked Oscar, knowing he was the most easily swayed. "It could be true, I suppose, although I still don't trust him one little bit."

But the professor wasn't listening. From the corner of his eye he had seen a dark figure leap between trees. And scarcely had that figure disappeared than another jumped in and out of the bushes. He stared, and by waiting he saw a head pop back into view, only to withdraw just as quickly.

"Jeepers, we'll discuss this later. Right now there are more pressing matters. We must protect ourselves and the shed at all costs."

"Using what exactly?" said Jake, looking around. "We don't have any weapons."

"That's where you're wrong," smirked the professor, reaching behind the table to produce the glue gun.

312

With only one door and one window to defend, the professor was sure the outsiders could be held at bay should they try to break in. Yet, one door in full view of the garden also meant there was no escaping. They were alone, effectively cut off from the outside world, as much prisoners as defenders.

"I don't like this, Uncle. It's no longer fun," said Gracie dolefully, cowering behind Jake. Her tone was one of genuine distress.

Already feeling guilty for leading the youngsters into danger, Oscar found Gracie's plea tore at his heartstrings. He had expected her to cope better than this, especially as nothing had yet happened to seriously threaten them. He then looked across to Jake, who had already witnessed a terrible fight among the gang. If he was similarly anxious, he wasn't showing it.

For a few seconds Oscar stood still and silent, and strangely breathless. The others stared like so many sheep, waiting to be ordered this way or that. But Gracie's words had been like a moment of epiphany that changed everything, and in a flash Oscar decided he needed to regain control of the situation for all their sakes.

"I know what I'm going to do," he said, grabbing Miguel and forcing him to the floor. "This is not the time to have a cuckoo in the nest. Anyone got rope?"

The professor gestured towards the table, where a ball of thick sisal string was found in a drawer.

With Miguel tied, hands and feet, Oscar glanced at Gracie, thinking she would now be a little happier. But the sight of a fully-grown man tied up in such a forcible manner only increased her fear, as it made the crisis a reality.

"I'm really frightened," she said, her mouth trembling as she spoke. "We need proper help. We need the police."

"Still got your mobile?" asked the professor from the window.

Gracie reached into her pocket. "Always." The screen illuminated. There was plenty of battery power but no signal.

"Keep trying," said Oscar. "It's worked around here before, so it's only a question of time before a signal returns. The moment you get through to the police, hand it over. I'll do the speaking. Okay?"

Gracie nodded and set 999 into her contact list.

"Meantime, I'll try the phone you loaned to Miguel," added Jake, "although I doubt it will be any better as it uses the same network."

With Gracie staring at her phone and Jake occupied in walking around the shed with his hand held high searching for a signal, Oscar strolled to the window. "How many people do you see, Prof?"

"Two I think. But we must be prepared for more."

"Okay, I'll take over as lookout. My eyes are younger than yours."

"What should I do?"

"You'll find something, I'm sure."

For what seemed an age but was, in fact, only an hour, nothing significant happened inside the shed or out. Since Oscar's phone had not been recharged for days, it quickly drained of battery power, leaving Jake without a job. Gracie had also stopped redialling at Oscar's suggestion to conserve her battery and now sat quietly in a corner secretly reading old text messages to calm her nerves.

On the opposite side of the shed, the professor was asleep. His head had fallen awkwardly and now rested on Jake's shoulder. The boy didn't mind as it allowed him to play with Annie the 40th, which had crawled out of the professor's clothes. He still didn't like spiders much but was fascinated when it didn't try to scamper away. Even Miguel had stopped moaning as he lay trussed on the shed floor.

Oscar, who had held his own feelings in check to give an air of steadfastness for the sake of the youngsters, was himself tiring of staring single-mindedly into the garden. Not long before he thought he had seen a man crawling on all-fours towards the shed, and the possibility bucked him into action. But when a head with narrow green-yellow eyes pushed through the leaves, it confirmed only a foraging fox was on the hunt. Strangely, he had felt disappointment rather than relief. And since then not a thing had happened, making it an opportune moment to hand over the job of lookout to someone else.

With this thought in mind he twisted from the window, only to be shocked by everyone's lack of enterprise. Not one person was usefully employed. It was the only time Jake ever saw his father properly angry. For, although nothing serious stirred among the trees and shrubs, Oscar realised idleness would spawn complacency, and the dangerous situation demanded better.

"Are you all going to lie around peeing in your pants, or are you intending to do something remotely useful?"

The sharp rebuke roused the professor, who released a rather loud snore before immediately dropping back into deep sleep.

"I'm doubly surprised at you, Professor," said Oscar as he vigorously shook him, speaking in a voice so cutting that it finally broke into the old man's dream.

The professor slowly opened one eye and then the other.

"Good heavens, man. You've invented a hundred things and know a thousand magic tricks, yet not one beyond the glue gun is of the slightest help to us now in defending the greatest invention of the lot, the Starlight Machine. Come on, get your thinking cap on." He then nudged Jake with his foot. "And that applies to you kids too. You should be looking for ways to strengthen our position. We'll be absolutely fine if we pull together. We only have to remain vigilant until the police are contacted."

"At least we're sheltered," said the professor drowsily, finally stirring from a dream in which he was being eaten as a giant sausage roll. He yawned, stretched his arms and looked towards the window. "They aren't so lucky outside."

Oscar was affronted. "Who cares how they feel."

"I only meant we have three solid walls, which means they can only attack from the front. One glue gun should be enough to hold them at bay, so I don't see any point in getting too agitated."

"Blood and thunder," returned Oscar irritably, although he knew the professor was right. "This waiting for something to happen is doing my head in."

"We don't have a choice, Dad. What happens next is in their hands."

"I had expected them to go by now. After all, they haven't seen Miguel."

"Does that mean they intend to attack anyway, Uncle?"

Oscar considered the consequences of answering truthfully, deciding instead to ignore the question. "There's always a choice, Jake." He stomped to the table. "Darn it. I'm going to put an end to this right now. I'm taking the glue gun. It's time to confront the blighters. Find out what they actually want."

"No, Dad, it's not safe. Tell him, Professor."

"The boy's right. The glue gun is more of a toy than a serious weapon."

"We know that, but they don't. To anyone else, it would look pretty fearsome." He grabbed the gun without further argument and stood by the door. "Right, Professor, this has to be done quickly. When I say, open the door to let me out. But be sure to lock it behind me. And for goodness sake, don't wait to see if I'm safe."

The professor nodded as he joined Oscar at the door, but was afraid for him.

"If you're captured," he whispered to keep the possibility away from Jake's ears, "what do we do? Should we surrender?"

"Only you can judge," Oscar replied, balancing the gun between his hands to feel the weight. "Your first priority must be to keep Gracie and Jake safe in whichever way you can. I mean that. If Miguel has to be sacrificed, don't hesitate. He's not our concern. However, if you get the chance to retrieve the gun, let them have it good and wet!"

"Understood. Take care, dear friend," said the professor kindly, reaching for the door handle. "Here, wear my old hat for luck. Be our Indiana Jones for Jake's sake. It'll make you look more determined."

"Who?"

"Oh, for goodness sake, Mr Trotter, how can you not know your son's favourite adventurer?" Oscar returned a blank expression. "The intrepid hero played in films by Harrison Ford. He stares danger in the face."

"Dad!" called Jake, not so sure the advice was good. "Please be careful. Don't do anything stupid or take chances. Don't leave me alone in the world with Mum."

Oscar smiled, turned, and in a blink sprang through the narrow gap made by the professor. The door slammed shut behind him. He heard the 'click' of the latch being engaged.

Outside, Oscar remained close to the door, alert for the slightest movement. He commanded all the open approaches to the shed.

"He's got a rifle," came a voice from the trees, giving away the enemy's position.

Oscar spun on his heel, aiming the barrel directly towards the sound. His finger reached for the trigger but stopped short, knowing it to be erratic.

"Hear that, Jake? We were right. There are at least two of them," said Gracie from inside, her old grit returning after noticing her mobile showed a brief signal, before flicking off again.

Like a startled hare, a man in a red shirt suddenly flitted from behind a tree and made a determined dash for a shrub to Oscar's left. Then, a moment later, a second man broke cover, taking a wide circle to the right before concealing himself behind a large evergreen. The crack of a snapped twig made Oscar turn for a third time, his eyes glancing furtively between possible hiding places.

"Surrounded by three!" he thought, his heart now pounding like a sledgehammer. Yet, holding the heavy gun helped him control his fear.

"You okay, Dad?" said Jake softly through the closed door.

Oscar replied that he was, but needed an urgent word with the professor.

"Yes?" asked the professor, having left Jake to guard the window.

"Listen to me. I can't look in all directions at once. You must keep an eye on the bloke to the right and tell me if he so much as breathes."

The professor tapped the door three times to show he understood. But in the event, he was too pre-occupied wondering who could be guarding Michael to be of the slightest use as a lookout. Fortunately, Jake noticed and stayed put as the window sentry.

Oscar now took a backward step until he stood erect against the shed, where nobody could sneak up behind him. He raised the gun to waist height, straining to hear any conversations between the gang. The silence was deafening.

"Okay, you lot. This stops now. Come out of your hiding places or I'll fire!" he warned with impatience. "I know you're there. Show yourselves, or else."

He waited, and when nobody appeared he repeated the threat in a louder and more aggressive voice. At last, the man in the red shirt emerged from his hiding place, wildly waving a white handkerchief.

"Halt!" demanded Oscar, wanting to maintain a safe distance. The man stopped abruptly. "Now, when I say, take six slow steps forward so I can see your face."

The man hesitated at the sight of the gun. He shuffled awkwardly before obeying, constantly looking to his left and right.

The professor again tapped the shed door. Oscar cranked his head to listen, all the time keeping an eye on the intruder.

"Jake says, tell him to take his hat off. He's the bloke in the cafe."

"Right," agreed Oscar, turning back with gritted teeth. "You there, remove your hat and no funny business."

Now away from the shading trees, the bright light confirmed his identity.

"It's him," cried Jake, looking through the window. "The scar's a dead giveaway. It was Harry all along."

With his worst fear confirmed, Oscar lifted the glue gun into a more threatening position. The effect was extraordinary. Harry suddenly dropped to his knees, pleading not to be shot. Whether his contrition was genuine or false was impossible to tell, but it gave Oscar the courage to advance towards him.

"Watch it," called the professor. "It might be a filthy trick."

"Call the others out where I can see them," insisted Oscar, keeping the gun straight and steady.

Two other men emerged from hiding, their hands also raised. One was Pete and the other someone he did not recognise.

"Him!" gasped Jake, seeing the stranger was older, tall, and broad in proportion to his height. His eyebrows were black and unruly, producing an irritable look as he scowled.

"What comes next?" laughed Harry out of the blue, letting the handkerchief fall through his fingers before jumping to his feet with vigour. "You didn't really think I'm bothered by anything you can do? I was play-acting. There are three of us and we have the means to squash you like a fly."

From Harry's expression, Oscar could see this was no idle bluff.

"If you don't want to negotiate," said Oscar, "why approach under a flag of truce? Speak plainly. What do you want here?"

"I'll answer that," interrupted the tall stranger, and in a stride he stood ahead of Harry, who recoiled now that his authority had been usurped. The tall man's bearing was upright and stiff, and at that moment Oscar knew this was a person of intelligence.

319

"There's no need for anyone to get hurt, whatever Harry threatens," he added in a voice held calm and steady. "We only require a few hours alone with the old bloke in the shed. Then, if we are satisfied with his cooperation, we'll let him go."

"You would free him unharmed?"

"Sure, but only if you swear to give us a full day to get away after. No police and no following."

Oscar was disarmed by the offer, which was spoken with reason. It suggested a way out of the predicament without violence. Yet, he remained strangely pensive.

"Can I trust you?"

"Do you have a choice?"

"And if I decide the risk is too great?"

"Look here, mister," interrupted Harry, pushing forward with his arms. "*We* want to pick his brains and *you* want to save your lives. That's the situation in a nutshell. So just get the old fart out before my patience snaps."

"Stand firm for a few minutes longer, Uncle Oscar. I had a mobile signal a moment ago," came a young and deliberately loud voice from the shed, intended to intimidate the gang into leaving her uncle alone.

"Did you hear that, Pete," sniggered Harry, snubbing the tall man for being weak. "A little girl is calling the shots. I wonder when she became leader?" He glared at the ammunition reservoir on top of the glue gun. "What *is* that thing? A water rifle? Oh, no… please don't wet my shirt!"

Pete roared with laughter.

"Enough!" bawled Harry, the single word spoken so spitefully that it immediately silenced Pete and left Oscar in no doubt of his sincerity to inflict harm. "Your ten seconds of heroism are up. Throw the gun away or I'll come over and ram it down your throat."

What happened next was as unexpected as foolhardy. Quickly shaking Annie the 40th from his clothes, the professor, who had listened to everything, selflessly threw open the door and leapt out from the protection of the shed. Jake rushed to pull him back, but it was too late.

"Ah-ha! So we've winkled you out of the shell," chuckled Harry, closing the gap with a swagger. He pulled an automatic pistol from the back of his belt and a bottle of whisky from a pocket. "Well, here we have it, and a proper rag-tag bunch you make. One puny man, a boy, a girl and an ancient fossil guarding the machine." He took a long swig before carelessly throwing the bottle over his shoulder. "As you see, we have the firepower to back up our demands." He reached for the glue gun but Oscar pulled away. "Oh, go on then, keep it if it makes you feel a big man. After all, it's no match for this."

With a squeeze of the trigger, Harry fired a rapid burst of bullets into the still air. Oscar leapt sideways to hide the professor's thin frame behind his own body. The heroism amused Harry, yet still he forced them apart with the barrel of the pistol. He then closed towards the professor until their faces nearly touched.

"*Boo!*" roared Harry, the whoop so startling the professor that he slipped and struck his head hard against the shed door. Oscar watched in horror as he dropped senseless to the ground, finishing in a crumpled heap. "Well, that was easier than I imagined," laughed Harry. "We'll take him away now."

Oscar's stare seemed to lift in slow motion. "Did you just call me *puny*?" he snarled, enraged by Harry's calculated coldness.

It is difficult to say what came over Oscar at this moment, but his jaw clenched as he raised a leg and slammed the sole of his shoe hard into Harry's chest, knocking him backwards. And, as Harry tumbled, Oscar squeezed the glue gun's delicate trigger. At once a stream of gunk burst from the barrel, sending Harry sprawling and sticking him to the stump of a felled pine.

The sight of the glue rapidly hardening was enough to send the others racing in different directions. Pete headed straight for the trees, his heavy boots pounding so erratically through the undergrowth that bouquets of pheasants leapt skyward with a high-pitched *kok kok kok* until the air hung thickly with birds flapping in screaming circles. The other man fled along the path, past the cottage and into the woods beyond.

Oscar gave immediate chase, howling like a banshee and firing wildly at Pete's back. But the glue fell short. And when Pete finally disappeared from view, he gave up and turned for the shed, where Jake held the door ajar. He was pleased to see the professor had already been helped inside and was receiving medical attention.

"Enough fussing over me, Gracie," groaned the professor as Oscar walked in. "Mr Trotter is the man of the moment. I did nothing but fall over. Still, I did notice Harry's trousers. Good old Jorvik. The creature must've also taken a chunk out of his bum-skin sometime in the recent past. That's two of the so-and-so's he's chewed."

"Bolster the door, Jake," ordered Oscar fiercely, and at once the chair was wedged under the handle. "Phew, that was close. I was terrified."

"You didn't seem it, Dad," said Jake proudly. "You showed them what cowards they really are."

Gracie asked the professor to bend down so she could look again at his wound. "Only a small cut," she declared brightly, using her fingers to straighten his hair. "At least we know more than we did."

"Do we?" asked Jake.

"Of course, silly. They only talked about the machine and the professor. I reckon that means they have no idea Miguel is here."

"Or maybe they already knew," proposed the professor, and at once he noticed how their faces turned long.

"Then confronting them outside gained nothing."

"On the contrary, Son, we now know their strength," claimed Oscar in an upbeat manner. "That has to be useful. It is Harry and Pete, and another guy we haven't seen before."

"I have," said Jake, already back at the window as lookout but spending too much time listening to the others to be fully attentive.

"Where?"

"At the cafe. You sent me to the toilets to find Miguel, and that's where he spoke to me. He said he was the cleaner."

"Are you sure?"

"One hundred percent. His name is Tommy Brown."

"If he's really the rich boss, the ringleader, the spymaster, why pose as a cleaner I wonder?"

"It's obvious, Dad. To remain undercover. He might even own the place for all we know. The cafe could be his stronghold. It's certainly built to withstand a siege."

"It's possible, but unlikely."

"For goodness sake, you two," said Gracie. "It hardly matters. The important thing is we know all the gang members by sight."

"And they know our strength, or lack of it," bemoaned the professor, "which might encourage them to launch an attack to get me or the Starlight Machine, or Miguel, or all three. Still, cheers to you, Mr Trotter. You glued Harry good and proper, although I suppose even that's given away the secret of the gun's limited power. Let's face facts, it's no defence against an automatic pistol."

"Really?" objected Jake. "Ask Harry if he still thinks it's a water pistol. Who's having the last laugh now?"

"But what if they have more fearsome weapons in the boot of their car?" mumbled Oscar without thinking. "Like American gangsters with a trunk load of illegal stuff. Shouldn't we consider that?"

"Dad!" pitched Jake firmly, glancing towards Gracie.

"No, Jake, your father's quite right to mention it. We must all face the truth, however much it frightens us," said the professor. "That possibility must be considered in every action we take."

"Overall, it's not looking too clever, is it Uncle Oscar?"

"Try not to worry too much," he replied, looking around for somewhere to sit now that the chair was securing the door. "We still have a phone with plenty of charge."

The careless mention of more guns *did* set the children's anxiety racing, leaving Oscar angry with himself for introducing the idea. For several minutes he tried to convince them the gang was unlikely to hang about once Harry was rescued from the glue. But the seeds had been sown and, anyway, he knew this was a long way from reality.

"Don't forget," added the professor kindly as an afterthought, "even if they stay close, Harry will be stuck for hours, giving us plenty of breathing time. Pete and the other guy are hardly likely to act without his say-so. That gives us the advantage."

"Police not come quick," croaked Miguel from the floor, much to Oscar's annoyance. "Untie me. I stand arm to arm and fight. Please, let me!"

"Shoulder to shoulder, fool!" reproved Oscar, in no mood to play games. "And you can forget that preposterous suggestion. We're holding you secure where we can keep an eye on you, so live with it. We don't want any accidents, like the lights suddenly being turned on 'by mistake' to make us clear targets."

"You were right, Jake," admitted the professor in a moment of unusual veracity. "You really are extremely clever. Five takeaway dinners did mean four criminals plus Michael."

"I not criminal any longer," pleaded Miguel.

"Oh, shut up!" said Gracie. "If you don't, we can always glue you to the ceiling."

Miguel looked up before murmuring a prayer.

"You know, that isn't the only thing Jake is almost certainly right about. It seems to me it makes a lot of sense if the Big Cheese is this Tommy Brown bloke," said Oscar, letting the edge of the table take his weight. "Michael has been gone for decades, so the boss would be much older than the rest. And he is." He turned to Miguel. "Are we right?"

Miguel bowed his head.

"Well, that confirms a thing or two. Miguel's not here to cooperate."

"Go on, Uncle Oscar, let me glue him?"

"No, Gracie," said Jake, holding her back. "We should keep the ammunition for when it's needed. He's not going anywhere."

Gracie pulled at the string, ensuring it was good and tight.

"With a spy in our midst, there's even more reason to make this place a fortress," proffered the professor. "I only wish I had felled more trees when I had the chance. If I had, there would be fewer places left for the villains to hide."

"Dad, we can't stay here indefinitely without food and water. Apart from Gracie trying to phone the police, what else can we do? It's no use just sitting on our hands waiting for trouble to knock."

Oscar sensed the sombre atmosphere was deepening. He reminded everyone they had convincingly won the first round and there was every chance they would come out on top again if put to the test. "Everything will turn out fine if we remain brave a little longer, and that especially applies to you, Jake, who I am putting in charge of Gracie's safety."

But Gracie had other ideas. "They don't call me Gallant Gracie at school for nothing," she said with conviction. "I don't need anyone looking after me, especially a boy!"

"Has anyone ever really called you that?" asked Jake unwisely.

"Just try me, mate, that's all. I'll land a fist on ya nose quicker than you can say Jack Frost. Nobody bullies me and gets away with it."

Jake turned to his father and shrugged. "You know, Dad, we could all take a lesson from Gracie. Do you remember you once called me Captain Jake? We were to be the Three Musketeers: Professor Septimus Kneebone, the Amazing Oscar Trotter and Captain Jake—boy hero. To be honest, I don't much feel like a hero cooped up in here. It's time to go on the offensive. Attack! That's what real heroes do!"

"Don't forget Gallant Gracie—girl heroine," called the professor.

Jake looked at the girl, every bit as ready to play her part. "How could we?" he said smiling. "She would never let us."

Chapter 22
Gunfire from the Trees

Despite the rhetoric, intended to keep spirits high and minds occupied, Oscar was aware—indeed, they were all aware—of the likelihood the gang would overrun the shed in a single heavy assault once Harry was free, fearsome in their weaponry and resolve.

And so, rising to the task, Oscar again took charge of reorganising the group into a more effective force. The options were limited, but the need was greater than ever. Despite Jake's wish to attack first, the advantage of operating from a shelter where their preparations remained unobserved would not be given up lightly, particularly as they were outnumbered by both adults and guns.

"I think you'll agree I'm the best shot, so I'll guard the door with the glue gun," announced Oscar. "It's our weakest point. If I sit a few metres back, I can surprise anyone who forces their way through."

Gracie reminded her uncle that, to sit, he would first have to remove the chair bolstering the door.

"Good thinking," he replied, offering instead to squat on the floor. "And you, Professor, go back to the window as lookout, but stay out of sight and don't expose yourself to any danger. And, please, stay awake. I'll find you something to lean on. It might be a long night. Now, Jake, you keep a close eye on Miguel, and, Gracie, you must keep trying the police. I suggest we tip the table onto its side. The youngsters can hide behind it. I'm pretty sure it's thick enough to resist handgun bullets."

"That's all I do?" moaned Gracie. "I suppose it's because I'm a girl."

"Not at all," replied Oscar with merit. "It's by far the most important job."

This hardly persuaded Gracie, who had her own ideas. "I'll do the phoning, but only if I can sit on Miguel's head to stop him moving."

"I not move," cried Miguel, alarmed at the prospect.

"Okay," conceded Oscar, "but one false move, or one shout to the men outside, and Gracie will use your head as a trampoline."

He accepted the terms and slumped limply across the floor.

"I have another idea," said Gracie smugly.

Miguel looked up. "Not squashing me?"

"You hold your tongue," she returned. "No, Uncle, I have a great plan."

Everyone listened but expected something rather silly.

"We have electricity, don't we? So let's use it as a weapon. The professor could remove the long wire joining the Starlight Machine to the Receptor, add a wall plug, and connect the other end to the metal door handle. Anyone grabbing the handle will get 240 volts of electricity and the shock of their life. Good, eh!"

It was a great idea and everyone said so. Gracie, at last, felt she had proved her worth. It was now the Four Musketeers, or at least 3½.

At once, Gracie's plan was put into action. It had an immediate and remarkable effect on the morale of the group, making it much harder for the gang to breach the shed's defences. Oscar, the professor, Jake and Gracie, all suitably encouraged, took up their positions, the professor straining his eyes and ears as the only defender with a clear view of the garden.

But as the evening darkened and night crept in, nothing happened. Expectations of a quick and decisive victory which had emboldened the defenders were replaced by sighs of tedium. Just the cry of Harry glued to the tree stump broke the jaded silence. And yet, despite his threats to scoop out their livers with a spoon if he was not helped, his colleagues remained firmly hidden within the bushes.

Two hours later and still at his post, the professor's thoughts turned to food, wondering how long he could last without eating. He remembered an unopened packet of ten sausages left in the kitchen, which lay tantalisingly close but, nonetheless, inaccessible.

It was also becoming chilly, so Oscar suggested Jake and Gracie should take turns snuggling inside the draught-free Starlight Machine. However, this was rejected by the professor, who could not be sure whether the aerial on the shed roof was up or down. It was safest not to take a chance. Instead, and after saying he was quite warm enough, Oscar removed his jumper and gave it to Gracie, her clothes being the thinnest.

Meanwhile, in the garden, the red and yellow glow of an open fire burning warmly had suddenly appeared amongst the trees. Two men were huddled close to the flames, the fragmented light dancing on their faces. Both were drinking but were not yet drunk. Then one went off, returning barely three minutes later with a small package. He resumed his former place and busied himself stripping the bark off several long twigs.

"Ruddy cheek," moaned the professor as the aroma of cooking food wafted towards his keen nose. "The blighters have only broken into the cottage and taken my sausages. There're cooking them on sticks like a troop of Boy Scouts. They'll be singing camp songs next, I shouldn't wonder."

Jake considered the fire to be a good sign, as it was probable the two criminals still at liberty were more concerned with keeping warm and eating than safeguarding the secret of their position. An imminent attack, it seemed, was unlikely. And with that thought in his head, his mind wandered to home, where he pictured his mother sleeping peacefully, blissfully unaware of the trouble he was in. For the first time in the adventure he felt a little tearful… but it soon passed.

Having shown leadership qualities that surprised even himself, and with another hour dragging by, Oscar left the door to inspect the defenders at close quarters. And, just as he thought likely, they were once again degrading into a flagging and dispirited lot, not alert or panicked but lazy and dull, slowly but surely losing their ability to react sharply to a crisis, should one occur. It was a dangerous situation he could not allow to continue "as it was likely to lead to depression and anguish", he thought. The easiest remedy was to rotate the various duties to regularly introduce a fresh challenge to each defender, and soon Jake was again guarding the window. It was a job he liked, as it took his mind off home. He even offered to take a double shift to let Gracie sleep longer and leave the professor holding the phone.

Then, at last, the sun slowly and gloriously rose above the trees as a new day began, casting light and warmth over the garden. It took a while for the shed to benefit from the rise in temperature, there being only one window to capture the rays.

For longer than she should have, Gracie had slept wedged between the table and the professor, restless at first as the cold nipped the air but later sleeping deeply after Oscar found a pair of oily overalls which he gently spread over her. But now, encouraged by a slight shake from Jake, she opened her eyes.

"I haven't been asleep," she protested at the friendly smiles. "I was just resting my eyes."

Nobody cared, and nothing more was said on the matter.

Wearily, Oscar handed the glue gun to the professor, whose bones ached. The old man was relieved to stand, and ambled to the window. Gracie became guardian of the door, but without the gun for Miguel's sake. She was given the phone to hold.

"The glue's melted," said the professor. "Harry's escaped from the stump."

"I know," replied Jake, who was ordered to sleep but couldn't. "He must've broken free in the dark. At sunrise, I saw him chasing Pete around the garden with a knife."

"What do we do now?" asked Gracie. "There's still no phone signal and all three men are at large."

It needed no reply. To a loud *'ya-hoo'*, Harry suddenly sprang from the trees and ran headlong for the shed door, his bold run covered by the *crack crack crack* of automatic pistol fire that whipped through the air from the east side. The professor and Oscar dropped to the floor, just as Harry rattled the door handle. His cry was deafening as 240 volts of electricity raged through his arm.

"Told you it would work," exclaimed Gracie with justifiable glee.

"Anyone hurt?" called Jake anxiously.

"They've ruined your jumper, Uncle Oscar," she owned, poking a finger through a hole in the sleeve. "Lucky I was taking it off at the time."

Oscar glanced towards the door, where a row of bullet holes punctured the wood.

"For heaven's sake, girl, keep low."

The echo from the shots had scarcely passed when pellets from a shotgun cartridge peppered two panes in the window, showering shards of glass across the floor.

"The blighters are bolder than I expected," groused the professor. "We can't put much faith in the glue gun when I'm sure they're dodging backwards and forwards to the car restocking with ammunition. What else have they got hidden away, I wonder? A rocket launcher perhaps?"

Oscar carefully crawled over the shattered glass. "I don't know why, Professor, but I hadn't expected a full-blown attack with guns firing. I know we talked about the possibility, but the reality of it actually happening is quite a different thing. Surely they can't want the Starlight Machine or Receptor damaged. Either way, it's changed everything. We can't risk the children. Whatever they want, we must give it to them."

"No!" shouted Miguel. "They kill me."

"That *is* a possibility," agreed the professor, wondering whether Miguel's plea would affect Oscar's assessment of the situation. "At any rate," he continued, "appeasement never works. We must man-up to anything they throw at us if we are to have any chance of getting Michael back on our terms."

"I tell truth," pleaded Miguel. "They want me. I know too much to live. But if you hand me over, they come back for machine anyway and still kill Michael."

Oscar bent low over Miguel's face, a smell of fear entering his nostrils. "Then come clean or we will throw you out to the wolves. Tell us exactly what this is about, and do it quickly?"

"Gold and other things," he replied without hesitation.

"Go on."

"For many years Michael launch space eggs and show gang boss films from Receptor machine, and gang make much money finding valuables."

"How?" enquired Oscar brusquely. "And remember, Harry and the rest are on the other side of the door."

"Simple. No brains needed. Receptor show precious things being buried in graves, or stolen paintings being hidden during war, or where robbers put coins and jewels, that sort of stuffing."

"Stuff," corrected Oscar. "That sort of stuff."

"Yes, stuffing. By looking into past, they see these things take place when originally happening. Mostly easy job to identify places and dig up. But not every time the plain sailing. Problems come when old treasure discovered to be buried under new buildings or roads. But gang still recover it by blowing buildings apart using big gas leaks and other such ways. Once, Harry put rubber cones along motorway and dig up tarmac using stolen digger. Harry say car drivers used to unnecessary road works, so nobody ask what he is doing... and they didn't, not even traffic police."

"That rings true," muttered Oscar.

"When one job finish, images later removed before start of next to get rid of evidence."

"I thought as much," said Jake. "Remember me saying that?"

"Yes, yes. But what of the present caper?" asked the professor.

"Boss getting much cross when you destroy first bit of latest image being used. But part left excite him very much as showing biggest treasure of any—Spanish sea gold. But big, big problem. Gang not get much information on where treasure go after British capture Spanish ship, so Michael required to launch new egg to find out. But, oh dear, nobody find new egg, not even Michael when breaking into cottage. At least, that is what he tells Harry."

"Did Michael help willingly? I need to know the truth."

"Every time, gun held near head."

"That's good," said Oscar, putting a comforting arm around the professor, who had begun to cry.

"Have you seen the sea battle right through?" probed Gracie, wiggling her bottom as a threat to sit on him if he didn't answer truthfully.

"Not me. I not see films, ever, I promise, except now with you. They not trust me. Harry say pictures show small rowing boat going from British boat to Spanish. One man in small boat then shooted marine colleagues when only fifteen or twenty strokes from Spanish ship. Man then throw dead bodies overboard into sea, climbs onto big ship and helps last Spanish sailors fight British."

"Butcher!" exclaimed Jake. "The traitor spy the commodore armed with two pistols."

"That may be," continued Miguel, "but Royal Navy fire on Spanish ship to warn and all ends. Man with pistols captured and put in chains. That is where picture of battle ends."

"There's nothing more?" asked Oscar.

"No more of fighting. It is not the proper finish."

"What about the Spanish gold, or the fate of the *Rosa*?"

"Oh, yes, little bit of film left, but Harry say film jumps to morning. He say film gone wrong and what happened to gold is missing. He not interested in morning, so switches off and looks no more. That is why new egg needed."

"The rotation of the Earth," shouted Jake. "It caused a break in the proceedings."

"Launching another egg could never fill the gap," added the professor, "but Harry and Tommy Brown are too ignorant to know. What do you think, Oscar?"

"I think Michael would know, but chose not to tell them. It was his way of getting back at his captors."

"Good old Michael," gushed the professor.

"You know, it's all beginning to make sense. That's why the gang was so desperate for an egg and is now ready to use any means to find out what happened. Harry knows there was gold and silver beyond measure on the *Rosa*, but not where it went."

"It also confirms why I couldn't find some of my earlier eggs—they weren't mislaid by me but stolen by them for earlier capers. Hey-ho!"

Oscar turned away to think, marching up and down the shed with his hand rubbing his chin. "Okay, Miguel, maybe you could be of help after all. If we were to let you go, would you promise to explain everything to Harry, tell him he has seen all the film there is and that the professor has found no new clues, and show him the broken bits of egg from the bin as proof there can be no more launches into space? He may then leave us alone."

"Is there no more film?"

"No more," jumped Oscar quickly before the professor could say otherwise.

"He would still think you spinning a wool?"

"A yarn, you fool, spinning a yarn," corrected the professor. "But, I guess you're right. I would think the same in his position. That's left us up a gum tree."

"But, old man, I willing to try, to keep children safe."

Gracie was suspicious and said so. "I bet you would, especially as we already know you've told him about the egg and handed over a piece as proof."

The revelation shocked Miguel, who unintentionally touched his cheek.

"You see, Uncle," she said, waving a finger angrily in Miguel's direction, "he's still lying. The question is, did he meet Harry to put him off or, as I suspect, to give him a progress report?"

Miguel shook his head. "Okay, I admit I try to send him away with news of broken egg," replied Miguel, quickly glancing towards the professor for support. "But only to be left alone for the running away. But Harry say I must come back to look at pictures with Professor, as I already get inside as friend."

"So, the letter pinned to the door days ago *was* a trick to win the professor's trust," accused Jake, not to be out-done by Gracie. "My Trojan horse theory."

"I let Harry think that, but not the case," he replied apologetically, holding out his hands in the hope of being untied.

"Not so fast, Miguel," said Oscar, forcing his arms away just as the professor pulled a pair of scissors from the drawer. "We now know the truth about the letter, but it's quite a different matter to convince me you returned from the cafe to help us, rather than obey Harry's latest instructions."

"If not to helping you, why would Harry attack now, just as you looking at pictures? He not know you tie me up."

"He has a point," agreed the professor.

"You must trust me because without me you up gum tree, and me up there too," begged Miguel.

The 3½ Musketeers swapped looks before gathering into a huddle. "We need more proof of his support before considering releasing him," whispered Oscar.

"Haven't you listened," returned Gracie angrily. "His account is full of omissions. Letting him go under any circumstances would be dangerous and stupid. We certainly don't want the gang increasing from three attackers to four."

"You know, she's right," clapped Jake. "There's no way of knowing where Miguel's loyalties truly lay?"

"At last someone is paying attention to me. But if you want more proof, ask him about the ripped cables. See if he sticks to his old excuses," suggested Gracie gleefully. "If he does, you must let me stick him to the wall."

Miguel looked sheepish when the question was asked. "I pull out wire first time to ruin Receptor, to make old man give up and sell everything for the crushing. Then I could be running away without Harry chasing me. But I not do it proper, so plan go wrong. I do it again second time, it is true, but only to stop it quickly to save us all."

"Explain why Harry is now attacking with weapons firing."

"He must think I change sides. Harry is wild man with bad temper. Without me spying for him, without new egg, without old man's help and with treasure out of reach, he now want us dead as nail in door to keep crimes secret from police."

"Kill you as well?"

"Me mostly. I was to tell him of pictures, but I have not. He will call that treason."

"How were you to get the information to him without us noticing?"

"Leave Harry's coat outside cottage with note in pocket. That is why me given coat. Sorry I first say I find it."

Oscar gathered everyone close. "Does anyone believe that load of tripe?" he whispered disparagingly. "He's not capable of telling the truth. He won't help us, that's for sure."

"Unless it *is* the truth," suggested the professor. "Let's ask him something else, something more difficult to explain... say, about the hand print in the kitchen."

"Easy," said Miguel after hearing the question. "Michael forced to break into cottage but, instead of looking for egg, he leave sign to warn. He tell me this when he certain I want out of gang."

"But we saw you check the caravan door was locked. That was hardly the act of a friend to Michael," quizzed the professor.

"You see me do that? I not know. It changes nothing. I want time to think, so I carry on as before."

"You said Michael left a warning sign. What sort?" continued Oscar as a further test.

"Hand of flour. He know I not spit on him to Harry."

"Split—split on him."

"That's right!" exclaimed the professor. "By heck, I knew it. Michael would never do anything to hurt me. My son tried to warn me of the danger. And if Michael trusted Miguel enough to tell him, I will too."

"Should I untie him?" asked Jake.

"But I haven't sat on his head yet," protested Gracie. "It's not fair."

The very moment Miguel might have been released from his bonds, another burst of automatic pistol fire rang out from the trees, making everyone's blood run cold as they jumped for cover. The bullets struck the shed in rapid succession, *crack* after *crack*, forming another long string of holes and sending tiny wooden splinters flying through the air. To the sound of dull *thuds*, the bullets buried themselves in the opposite wall. And even before the noise of the attack dwindled, a second shorter but more intense burst punctured the air, as if coming from a heavier calibre gun, followed by a third, the last striking the window and shattering more panes. Then a short pause ended with a single bullet ricocheting off a roof bracket. It knocked the glue gun clean out of Jake's hands.

"Keep your heads down everyone," shouted Oscar, staying flat on the ground. "Are you all right, Jake?"

"Yup!"

Predictably, it was some time before anyone had the nerve to look up, so horrifying had been the bombardment. And although damage to the shed was slight and the machines remained unscathed, the cost to the occupants' morale was incalculable.

The first to rise was the professor, who recklessly stood to align the holes with the buried bullets in the opposite wall.

"What the hell are you doing," screamed Oscar, his arms around Gracie and Jake. "Get down and keep low, you idiot."

"That's what they want, to scare us into doing nothing."

"They scare me," he replied.

But the professor was having none of it, finding the mathematics of the attack a stimulus to his intellect.

"Judging by the trajectory, I reckon the first lot of shots came from a point directly opposite the shed door and were fired at quite a distance. That's where Harry originally hid, so I expect he's still there. The second burst was heard but not seen, so I guess we can assume it came from a different direction, where the angle of shot was more acute and caused whoever fired to miss. Of course, as most shots struck the shed high up, it's entirely possible they intended not to hit us at all."

"Goodness, Professor," shouted Jake, "what do you want to do, thank them for not blowing our blasted heads off?"

"The third hit the window as the only low shot," continued the professor without listening, "again probably fired from the front, while the last struck the roof and bounced off. There's no telling what direction that was fired from."

"Why are you doing this?" asked Oscar, only slowing releasing his grip on the children. "It hardly matters. The only important thing is that they have lots of guns and aren't afraid to use them."

"It tells us the main attack when it comes will be from the front. I'm pretty sure the side was only a diversion to confuse us or divide our forces. That's where we must concentrate our defences."

Gracie crawled to Jake. "The professor likes the sound of his own voice, doesn't he, but his deductions are hardly rocket science. Of course they'll attack the front. It's the only place with a flippin' door!"

"Well, I don't care where they shot from. The fact is, the whole thing has got way out of hand," said Oscar firmly, now peeping around the edge of the damaged window. "Jake and Gracie have very nearly been shot, and for what? A stupid Bubble Car, an ounce of unobtainable Spanish gold and a traitor."

The professor checked the glue gun, which was found only to have a chip in the butt. "Not too bad. It will still work."

"Aren't you listening to anything I say?"

"Won't the neighbours hear the firing and ring for the police?" suggested Jake, shaken by the experience but not entirely beaten.

"I'm afraid my cottage is very remote. No, your father is right for once. I suppose the only realistic option to end this madness is to give ourselves up and hope we can convince them we won't tell anyone. The Bubble Car was going to be sold anyway."

"No! They shoot you if you do," said Miguel darkly. "I know men, and they will kill to keep secret safe. Put bullet in back of head to make you keep your tongues forever."

"Hold our tongues, you moron," jumped Oscar, "and we're not asking for your opinion."

"Hold tongues?" queried Miguel with disbelief. "You British are strange to use fingers to hold slippery tongues."

"I give up," grumbled Oscar, turning away with more important worries on his mind.

"So, what do we do?" asked the professor. "If we hesitate and they get to the window, they could shoot us like fish caught in a bowl."

The question was not easily answered. "From what Miguel says, surrendering probably won't save our lives. That leaves only one option, to fight the blighters to a standstill. The thin red line and all that."

"Then we must concentrate our firepower at the window, that is until Gracie gets a signal and the police come racing over."

"The glue gun's reservoir is half empty. What's left is probably not enough to hold them back for long. Still, I'm volunteering to give it a go," said Jake bravely, smiling towards Gracie. "And the Starlight Machine could be pushed close to the door to block it, as a back-up to the electric handle."

"No wait!" yelled the professor. "Why did it take Mr Trotter to make me see the obvious?"

"Me?" replied Oscar with eyes wide, certain he had said nothing of importance.

"We don't need to have a firefight to win. I have a much better idea. Mr Trotter, you're a blinking genius."

"Am I?"

"Don't be modest at the moment of your greatest triumph! A while ago you told me I should invoke my specials skills. Just now you said we should form a thin red line. Well, that's it. We have the answer to our prayers! Oh, and leave the car where it is. We don't want it in the way of the door opening."

Oscar was shocked. He understood nothing and for once was prepared to admit it.

"Trickery and deception, my dear fellow. There's a lesson to be learned from Commodore Bowfinger."

There was just time to put the professor's plan into action before the gang charged headlong from the trees and dashed straight for the shed, bristling over the entrance and kicking open the door with the rubber soles of their heavy boots to avoid the electrified handle. But once inside, and with the Starlight Machine in sight, they pulled-up in total terror.

Standing in a perfect line were the professor, Oscar, Jake and Gracie, all bright green and with plumes of green smoke pouring from their mouths, an empty bottle of Voice Stuff Number 8½ discarded on the floor. Each waved a stick, while the Professor chanted any old rubbish that came into his head.

"*Ripana, seguito, linguiste, fiz*," gushed deceitfully from his lips. Even he was unsure where the words came from but, what the heck, they sounded perfectly convincing.

"Devils and witches," cried Pete, dropping a pistol as he dashed from the door.

"One gone, all gone," laughed Gracie as the other two fled in his wake. Soon the trees had swallowed their presence. She turned to the professor. "That was great, but will the potion last long? I'm sort-of worried what Mum will say when I go home."

He grinned at her discomfort. "You drank an awful lot of my 8½, as did we all. I fear we will remain green for some time to come."

"Oh," she exclaimed, grabbing her phone as it rang. "The signal's back! It's Mum. What do I tell her?"

"You could ask to stay a couple more days," said Jake. He turned to Oscar, who smiled at the thought of Jake wanting Ghoulish Gracie to remain. "While she's green. That's all I meant!"

Oscar's grin spread from ear to ear. "Wait 'till I tell your mother. She will be…"

"… Horrified?"

"… Surprised. You know, I think you're growing up!"

"Stop it, Uncle," shouted Gracie. "He doesn't want a girlfriend any more than I fancy him. Anyway, we are cousins."

"Have we heard the last of the gang, Dad?" asked Jake, wanting to change the subject as quickly as possible. He was sure his cheeks flushed red beneath the green.

"I should think so," he replied, "unless they return for their firearms. Still, the police can take charge of those after we retrieve them to stop any falling into the wrong hands." Only…" His voice dropped to a pained whisper.

"Only what?" said the professor.

"We've saved our skins but not saved Michael."

The moment of triumph suddenly cooled.

"You forget me," said Miguel brightly, looking around at their glum faces. "I still wanting to help. Michael is my friend."

Chapter 23
Saving Michael

Unbeknown to the five—who retired to the cottage for a much overdue meal of eggs and hot chocolate—the gang did come back, but only to recover their car. Anxious not to be seen, they pushed it out of the garden and along the drive before starting the engine. Soon the garden returned to perfect peace.

Some time later the police arrived, their sirens wailing. The detective inspector and his sergeant were greeted at the door by Oscar, whose green face was bound to be a curiosity. The policemen were too stunned to speak and merely stepped into the lounge, where a very green professor, green Jake and green Gracie stood waiting.

"I suppose we ought to explain our colour," said Gracie quickly in response to their stares. "Um... rehearsals, yes, rehearsals for a village play. I'm the Wicked Witch of the West, Jake is the Wicked Wizard of the East, Mr Trotter is the Wicked Warlock of the North, and he is..."

"The Wicked Sorcerer of the South?"

"No, he's Professor Septimus Kneebone, genius, but you're very nearly right."

Jake was impressed by her quick thinking, but was unsure whether the explanation fell into the category of a 'little white fib' or an 'outright lie'. On this occasion, he was willing to give his cousin the benefit of the doubt.

More difficult to explain were the reasons for the attack and the weapons left behind without revealing the secret of the Starlight Machine.

"As I said, I can't say why they tried to break in," persisted the professor, handing over a spent shotgun cartridge found near the shed. "I suppose they thought I'm wealthy."

"Seems rather unlikely, sir," replied the inspector, looking around the room. His eyes stopped at the bare Christmas tree. "But, then, I hear and see many strange things in my job." He leaned towards his sergeant, who took notes. "Write down 'eccentric rich'."

"Perhaps they didn't like our acting," giggled Gracie unwisely.

"You say the pistols were fired," continued the inspector, not to be thrown off the scent, "but where is the evidence? I see no bullet holes in any of the walls. And where was the offending car parked? You must show us."

"Ah," jumped Oscar, doing his best to keep the police from inspecting the shed. "The firing was outside… into the sky… to scare us, you understand. And it did… scare us… a bit… well… quite a lot, actually… as it would… wouldn't it?"

"Add barmy, sergeant."

"Look, inspector, is any of this necessary? You have the guns we found and our descriptions of the men, and we are willing to look through mug-shots at the station, so I can't see how we can be of any further help other than to show you the exact spot where the car stopped. If you would patrol the area in case they come back, that's really enough to keep us feeling perfectly safe."

But years of experience in matters of crime and criminals led the inspector to think he had not been told the whole story. "Not so fast, Mr Trotter. I remind you that some time ago you identified a foreign gentleman at the police station, but gave us insufficient evidence to hold him. Was he among the gang who attacked you?"

Oscar answered truthfully and in a most convincing manner that the foreigner was not one of the attackers. He glanced furtively towards the bed, where Miguel was hiding from the police after being untied to eat breakfast.

Scarcely did the 3½ Musketeers know, however, that there was no chance of Miguel giving anything away. For, during the short time they stepped into the garden with the police to look amongst the trees, Miguel scrambled from under the bed and climbed out of the kitchen window. He was now running towards the road, a free man.

"Shame you touched the guns, sir," said the inspector as they came back in. "We take any crime involving firearms extremely seriously. You should've left them for us to fingerprint. Even so, my sergeant will still bag them for forensic examination, but I doubt we'll get much evidence off them now. And if you come across the shotgun that fired the cartridge, call us but please don't touch it. Oh, and while we're on the subject of weapons, what about your gun? You say it fires glue."

"It's a toy," jumped the professor, "but it scared them off."

"A toy, ah?" considered the inspector, checking the mechanism. "So this doesn't do anything much."

"No!" cried Oscar. "Don't…"

It was too late. The trigger was pulled and gunk poured out, blasting the sergeant against the wall.

"Oh, I see," said the inspector, "it's a kind of giant water pistol."

"It's great, isn't it," chimed Gracie without thinking, laughing at the unfortunate sergeant. "When Uncle Oscar fired it at one of the criminals, he…"

"Yes?" awaited the inspector with interest.

"She… she only meant to say I surprised him," interrupted Oscar.

"Uncle certainly did," agreed Gracie. "I can tell you, the bloke didn't want to 'stick around', but he did anyway, for a while after… that is… before he went!"

Fortunately, the small quantity of glue remaining in the gun was not enough to embalm the sergeant, although it made a pretty good job of ruining his uniform.

"I don't think I need to impound the glue gun," said the inspector, happy to release it back into the professor's care. "Only, I must warn you not to go around firing it in public places." He turned to the sergeant, who was scraping glue off his jacket using handcuffs. "And, Sergeant, for goodness sake tidy yourself up."

Having waved the police away, Oscar turned towards the bed. "You can come out now, Miguel."

"He's probably fallen asleep," said Gracie, crouching on all fours to look beneath. "He's gone!"

"Well, that's just great. I told you he was rotten to the core. Now he's proved it. We've been betrayed... again."

Downcast, the professor flopped into his special chair. "It seems you were right. I gave him a hundred chances to prove himself, and all along he was profiting from my good nature. Well, that's it, I've finished with him and that's an end to it."

"If only," replied Oscar.

"Meaning? Surely he learned nothing from us that he didn't already know." His stare remained fixed on Oscar, sensing something unpleasant was coming. The answer was worse than his wildest expectations.

"You're forgetting the blasted naval book, Professor. If he's fleeing back to the gang, he'll tell them all about it and how it provides a written summary of the action."

"You think they'll return for it?"

"Bound to. We left it in the shed. At least Miguel couldn't have stolen it when he scarpered, or we would've seen him from the garden."

"Jeepers-creepers, I thought the worst was over. It seems there's more to come!"

"But we're still green," remarked Gracie. "Won't that scare them off?"

"Not this time. Miguel will tell them it's only a party trick."

"I need more breakfast to help me think," grieved the professor, blindly stabbing a fork into the empty frying pan. "Oh, all the eggs are gone. And to think I shared them with that Spanish twit. I suppose a humbug will have to do! Has anyone got any?"

It is well known that gloom becomes infectious when disappointment is shared. Multiply this a thousand times and replace the word 'disappointment' with 'fear', and the true feelings of the group could be expressed. And in this melancholy nobody spoke. There seemed nothing worthwhile to say, and no safety to be had. Everyone's thoughts were as bleak as the professor's 'black menace'.

"We could call the police back," said Gracie.

"And say what?" replied Oscar glumly. "We didn't tell them the whole truth. Face it. They're more likely to arrest us than believe us if we did. Take my word, Jake and I have already experienced how their minds work. Hours could be lost proving our innocence. I think it is down to us to face the consequences of them knowing about the book. But how to start?"

"We still have the under-floor hole," offered the professor. "If they return, we could scuttle down there."

It was agreed it could be done if the situation became grave enough, although the hole was rather small for four.

"Oh, no, that's no good either. Miguel would probably lead them to it," recoiled Oscar as an afterthought, unwillingly casting a blight over the only plan they had. "He spent that uncomfortable night in the pit and is hardly likely to forget the experience."

"In that case, we must hope he was too drunk and hung-over to remember," replied the professor. "And I haven't forgiven you, Oscar, for plying him with my very best brandy."

Jake, who had lifted the trap door to judge whether four people really could squeeze in, now let it slam shut with a thud. "Attack!

If we can't defend ourselves, we must attack. Take the war to them."

"That old cherry," said the professor. "That's the second time you've suggest attacking and it's still a daft idea."

"No, it's not. We *must* attack. We still hold an ace."

"Do we?" asked the professor without conviction.

"Of course we do. We have the naval book, and I have a great idea. But you should refill the glue gun while I explain. We don't have any time to lose."

Jake rose to his full height to explain the plan. It was simple but not without risk.

"Remember when we considered showing the gang the broken egg? The problem then was we had no means of convincing them that there were no others. Well, now we can go one step better. We should find out from the book what happened to the *Audacious* and then burn it. Sorry about that, Professor, but it has to be done. After, we could dump what remains of the broken egg and the ashes from the book outside the caravan door, together with a note explaining what they are. Now, here comes the clever bit. I think we all believe Miguel has run back to the gang. Yes?" The others agreed. "Okay, so who is better placed than Miguel to convince Harry the book is a one-off? We can turn his treachery against the gang. After hearing that, even Harry would see the futility of carrying on." He looked among his companions. "Well, what do you think? Come on, tell me honestly."

Oscar stared at his son in amazement and then, without speaking, sprang to his feet and boldly grabbed the glue gun. And when satisfied the gun was fully armed, he pulled the strap over his head, marched to the front door, and was soon purposefully striding along the drive.

"Dad?" shouted Jake from the door.

"What?"

"Where are you going?"

"Isn't it obvious?" he called over his shoulder without slowing, thunder in his steps. "For your plan to work, we need to know a couple of things first."

"Will you stop for a moment and tell me what things? Dad!"

Oscar halted, but was impatient to get on. "Firstly, we must confirm whether or not the caravan is in the lay-by. Last time we saw the caravan it was being towed away. The next thing is whether Miguel is actually back with the gang. I'm going to find the answers." And, with that said, he strode on.

Jake dashed after him, finally managing to hold him back by tugging at his shirt.

"But, Dad, since then the gang has reunited and raided us. Harry, Pete and that Tommy Brown bloke don't know we're aware of the caravan and the part it plays in their misdeeds, so it's bound to be there."

"And that's exactly why I'm going. We must be sure Miguel hasn't told them to move it." He pulled Jake's hand from his sleeve. "While I'm away, Son, stay inside the cottage and barricade the door. Remember, you won't have the glue gun for defence until I get back."

Jake was flabbergasted his father would choose to go alone.

"Have you gone mad, Dad? The whole gang might be gathered inside."

The very mention of the possibility seemed to exhilarate Oscar, a reaction Jake found both baffling and disturbing. He took a step back. After cheerless looks were exchanged, Oscar turned and determinedly walked away.

"On the contrary, Jake," said the professor after being told what had happened, "it's best your father goes alone. He knows he must keep out of sight and his green skin will give him natural camouflage. He won't have freedom of movement if he's concerned for our safety."

"Yes, but…"

"There are no 'buts', Jake. Your father has spoken." He saw the disappointment on Jake's face. "There's something else on your father's mind, too. I'm sure of it."

"Really?"

"You're a fine young fellow, Jake, but your plan centred on keeping us all safe. It didn't consider the consequences to Michael's safety. I believe your father has. If the destruction of the book convinces them of the futility in continuing, what are Michael's prospects?"

"Oh! I'm so sorry," apologised Jake, feeling he had let the professor down. "What do *we* do?"

The professor, who had not followed Jake to the door but was still sitting very much where he had been left, fumbled for Annie the 40th. Watching the tiny creature crawl over his palm and between his outstretched fingers relaxed him. "We must trust your father to use his good sense."

"Oh dear, things have got that bad, have they!" replied Jake without thinking.

"Not *bad*, Jake, just coming to a crescendo. Come on, let's pop over to the shed and fetch the book. I'm interested to know what happened to the ship. And don't fret, lad. If he's not back after a reasonable time, we can always go after him."

The book proved to be a revelation. As an appendix to the description of the Cape Espiritu Santo raid by *HMS Audacious*, several pages were devoted to the personal memoirs of Commodore Bowfinger, printed from his own words.

"Ah-ha, here we are. I'll start from where Butcher climbed on board the *Rosa*."

It read:

Dismayed by the actions of the traitor, who used pistols to shoot both marines before they had a chance to set foot on the Spanish Rosa, I ordered Audacious to be manoeuvred alongside the enemy ship. We were prepared for action, having already rigged the spritsail-yard fore and aft in readiness for boarding.

The approach was made on the leeward, ready to prevent the Rosa from gaining wind should the remaining crew make a dash for port which was only some five leagues hence. We held our cannon ready but saw no reason to damage the ship. The Spanish dead or dying could be seen lying on the deck-boards, particularly on the quarter-deck. The traitor Butcher and a handful of gallant Spanish sailors returned pistol fire, forcing us to keep our heads down, but there was no hope for them. In a final act of defiance, the Spanish set fire to mats stuffed into the anti-boarding nets, which rapidly took hold.

Fortunately, the Spanish had over-reached themselves and, as their firing stopped to reload, our sharpshooters in the rigging made quick work of dispatching all but Butcher to their ancestors. It was not a pretty sight and the crew on board Audacious were crying as each Spaniard fell needlessly in the hopeless cause. Rosa became a ghost ship, whilst the mizzen mast caught ablaze to most of its height.

Once close-to, sailors from Audacious jumped onto Rosa and quickly mastered the fire by ripping away the nets and tipping the tangled mess into the ocean. The mizzen was also to be cut down and allowed to fall harmlessly overboard on the opposite side to where our ship rested. However, just as we congratulated ourselves on the prize, Rosa's mizzen suddenly collapsed of its own accord, burning ferociously. It fell upon our deck and quickly the fire spread until it threatened the gun-power room. The fire appeared great, with smoke bellowing from an aft hatch already damaged by cannon fire, but on inspection the cause was found to be exploding cartridges between decks which had set ablaze an amount of oakum. This too was quickly mastered and soon all was well.

The Spanish treasure was found to be almost three million dollars of gold from Chile and silver from Peru, as coin and *bullion, which had flowed into Phillip II of Spain's coffers, a most prestigious sum. The Spanish call dollars 'pieces of eight', but in either case, a dollar is valued as four English shillings. Thus, we had a prize worth about £560,000, an immense fortune indeed.*

Our next task was to load the gold and silver onto Audacious, as we considered our ship still to be in sufficiently reasonable condition to suffer the sea-gales and hurricanes on our homeward journey. A small crew of British sailors remained on Rosa, which was to be sold in Canton. The transfer of treasure was undertaken using the island harbour and beach.

Thus the entire voyage home, via China, was not completed until early winter, and we were much blessed to finally arrive at Spithead fairly unscathed from all that had befallen us. Unbeknown at the time, we had also sailed straight through the centre of a major French fleet of warships in the English Channel, our good fortune in not being noticed attributed only to dense fog.

And so it was that all on board Audacious profited much, with the exception of Butcher who was duly hanged. I took a commodore's share of the bounty and the value of Rosa, and thus came into my family's possession a very great fortune. One bag of gold bullion had been held back from the rest, as it had been my intention to use its value to mend and provision our ship for the return voyage, knowing the Chinese distrusted foreign coin. Yet, even in this our luck was to hold.

At Canton, Chinese officials came onto Audacious to list the number of men, cannon, ammunition and goods on board in order to raise custom duties. And thus afraid they might attempt to requisition the gold and silver, we first showed them our mighty force as a warship. The sight of hundreds of barrels of gunpowder so shocked the Chinese that they took no further interest in our ship and said they wanted us gone from the harbour as soon as could be arranged. Little did they know we had decanted much of the treasure into gunpowder barrels as a safeguard, which, as luck had it, we needed not.

Thus, the Chinese had stared at a great fortune and saw only danger from the words printed on the barrels. Needless to say, the food and other provisions necessary for our homeward leg were given free. My promotion to Rear-Admiral followed soon after we were back in England, in recognition by a grateful nation for the share in our wealth handed over to the Government.

"What a story," gasped Jake, "but where does it get us?"

The professor looked at the bottom of the page. "Ah, as I thought, there's a footnote."

It read:

*The whereabouts of the Canton bullion referred to by Commodore Bowfinger was never discovered. It was not listed in either the Admiralty's or His Majesty's Government records and, therefore, it was assumed to be lost on the homeward voyage. From his fortune, Commodore Bowfinger constructed a magnificent stately house which he named 'Golden Rosa', and upon its ramparts were placed sixty and one-half stone barrels as testament to the action.

"Lost, my Aunt Fanny," said Jake. "Bowfinger swiped it."

"That's it," jumped Gracie, "the criminal gang has been after the Chinese bullion bag, which would've been hidden by Bowfinger to stop the Government treasury confiscating it. It must be worth millions in today's money."

The professor was less certain and said so. "I can't see how that's right, my dear. We only know about the bag from this book. No, we must assume the gang wanted to find the main bulk of the treasure which, as we now know, was never buried or hidden but shared amongst *Audacious's* crew, Bowfinger and His Majesty's Government. It is as good as spent. There's nothing of the treasure left to find."

"Just because we know, it won't stop the gang coming back for the book."

"Then, Jake, you are right. It must suffer the same fate as the last egg. It must be destroyed."

While the pages of the book were being ripped out for burning, some distance away Oscar reached the lay-by. He could hardly believe his luck. The caravan was there, hitched to the Range Rover. The battered parcel van was also parked close by, its rear doors open. Clearly, it was being hurriedly loaded for a quick getaway. Yet, none of the gang could be seen.

For the first time Oscar properly understood why the gang had chosen this particular lay-by as its base; although it was on the bend of a well-made tarmac road, passing traffic was minimal. This was evident from the crushed table, smashed pallet and broken vehicle parts still abandoned by the kerb, although now heaped into a pile since Harry's flat tyre. If the police had seen the debris, it would have been removed as a risk to health and safety. But, there it remained, abandoned and unnoticed.

There was also a dark side to the assumption. If the police were actually searching for the criminal gang, as expected, they were clearly looking in all the wrong places.

"I don't like this one bit," thought Oscar as he crept alone towards the van, his stomach churning.

He moved ever closer until he reached the van's rear doors. Then, having checked he knew which way to run if he was spotted, he broke cover to look through one of the caravan's windows.

Inside were several men. Miguel and Pete were standing together at the far end. From there they had no easy way out.

"The two-faced, double-crossing rat," thought Oscar as he raised himself on tiptoes for a better look. "I was right about Miguel, the rotten swine."

Then Oscar turned his attention towards the other end of the caravan, where his worst suspicions were confirmed. Blocking the only exit was the same whisky-soaked villain he had glued to the tree. Next to Harry was Tommy Brown, the so-called cleaner from the cafe. They were engaged in a heated conversation that looked likely to turn nasty at any moment.

Armed with the knowledge he came for, Oscar was about to leave when he caught sight of a fifth man lying across the floor. He was in considerable distress, his wrists handcuffed to a metal table-leg. A length of brown tape covered his mouth.

With the criminals occupied arguing among themselves, Oscar dared tap the glass. It was just enough to catch the man's attention. The captive looked up, wide-eyed and astonished. Both men froze as their stares met. Then Oscar remembered his green skin. Yet the man showed no surprise at all. It was if he understood the cause.

Quickly, the captive turned away to keep Oscar's presence a secret, and at once Oscar knew he had found Michael.

Discovering Michael in a seriously dangerous condition now posed the greatest dilemma of Oscar's life. A quick rescue appeared essential, yet such a hazardous undertaking was not why he had come and certainly could not be attempted lightly. The odds of success were low to zero. He also knew that judgements hastily made while under pressure always brought additional risk, and in this case the wrong action could have fatal consequences to both himself and Michael. And yet, equally, he felt an obligation to the professor, and this too weighed heavily on his mind.

He needed to think and find a safe place to hide while he pondered the problem from all angles. The bushes opposite again provided the obvious sanctuary. And so, having been careful to cross the road unnoticed, it was there he reflected on what to do next.

Obviously, the safest choice was to run away to raise the alarm. But that gambled on the caravan still being in the lay-by when he returned with help. He conjured the image of Michael being held in bondage and immediately felt ashamed he even considered leaving after staring him in the face. The other option was worse. He could attempt a single-handed rescue, although without a proper weapon it was unlikely he could frighten the gang into releasing Michael. But even if the threat of being glued had some chance of working, particularly against Harry, he didn't think he had the courage to try. At once the proposition was dismissed as being far too perilous.

No, what was needed was a third choice, one which could guarantee the gang would stay in the lay-by overnight. But how could he make it happen?

Then it came to him, a good plan with two possibilities. Either offered a chance of success that, at last, outweighed the risk.

Preference would be given to the simple task of sneaking back over to the caravan to eavesdrop on everything the gang said, in what the professor would call 'intelligence gathering'. Then, if spying betrayed the gang's definite intention to stay put until morning, he could leave with a clear conscience. But, if eavesdropping confirmed they aimed to go, and soon—and certainly the open van doors indicated this was credible—he would then attempt to disable the caravan to prevent it from moving. And he had the perfect means to do it.

After taking several deep breaths to calm himself, Oscar put the plan into action.

Creeping low and in a wide circle to stay in the shadows, Oscar crossed back unnoticed to the left side of the caravan, tucking himself between the corner and the coupled Range Rover. And there he pressed an ear hard against its thin plastic wall. But the voices inside were muted and therefore unintelligible. Further along, the caravan's door hung slightly ajar. It was a tempting vantage point, and he carefully edged towards it.

At last, he could hear Harry's voice booming above the rest. Sounding chillingly close, Oscar pulled the glue gun forward to bolster his confidence.

Inside, Harry slammed a heavy fist on the worktop.

"It's no good getting angry with me. I tell you, Spanish job is done for," said Miguel bravely, talking in a steady but high-pitched voice that sounded perfectly under control. "No space eggs left, and old man see nothing in pictures to help us."

"You're lying," shouted Harry, leaning forward with his finger pointing. "The question is *why*?"

"Think what you like," asserted Miguel. "You stay, I go."

"I don't like it when other people know more than me."

"You sent me to spy, to find out things. Now I tell you all about book and green potion. Nothing left to say. It not my fault you run away from cottage, leaving weapons behind."

"Are you telling me they have our guns?"

"I not know. Police come. I was too running away to notice."

"That means they probably handed them over to the cops."

"Perhaps. It hardly matters. There's no going back."

Harry held his glare long after Miguel had stopped speaking, then leaned against the doorframe with his arms folded. Yet his manner remained as cold as steel.

Throughout Tommy Brown said nothing, observing everything but taking no active part in the confrontation. He paid Harry to do his dirty work and was content to remain an interested onlooker.

"You hurt me with nail stick and I get taken by police," continued Miguel in the same tone, intending everyone to hear, "but still I forgive you because I change mind about leaving before sea treasure found. I even tickle old man to think I am friend."

"Trick, not tickle," scolded Harry.

"Everyone rude about my English."

"Anyway, fat lot of good you were as a spy. Got yourself tied up, or so you say."

"I get away. What about you? You cry like little baby when sticked to tree."

Harry flared at the insult, fire raging in his belly. He grabbed a kitchen knife and wielded the blade at an attacking angle. But

Tommy Brown held his wrist. Slowly Harry released the knife onto the worktop, growling like a beaten dog. He twisted to spit chewing gum from the door.

Oscar, who was still listening when the door fully opened, sank below the caravan until he was lying flat on his back on the tarmac.

"Ending years of work wouldn't be straightforward," boomed Harry. "I'd have loose ends to tie up and things to dispose of. Leave no traces for the coppers to find."

"You mean Michael?"

"Among others," he said in a wicked tone. "No point in keeping unnecessary baggage."

Pete's eyes flashed between Harry and Tommy Brown, hoping he was not included among 'unnecessary baggage'. "No need to worry about me," he said in a begging voice. "I'll say nothing. You can rely on me."

"Gutless, as well as timid. But it makes no difference."

"I tell you I go, even if I have to fight my way out," said Miguel courageously. "Now police know we had guns, they will hunt us like the rabid doggies. We must hurry to coast and catch boat somewhere safe."

"Like Spain, I suppose?"

"Why not? It is my home and I have family to hide us."

"You'll get no protection in Spain," said Tommy Brown, speaking for the first time. "It's part of Europe and they'll send you back as quick as a flash to face British justice. Anyway, you're wanted in Spain for robbery?"

"Yes, I am hunted man, but rather take chance there than stay here."

"Now tell Pete the whole truth," mocked Tommy Brown, "just as you once told me."

Miguel squirmed. "I not understand what you mean."

He laughed. "I think you do. Go on, tell him the real reason you stayed in England. It certainly wasn't for the crap weather."

Harry walked forward, from where he lunged at Miguel's arm to stop him retreating behind Pete, holding him like a vice.

"I told you already. I come to escape Spanish police," and with that said he wriggled free of Harry's grip.

"I said the real reason," demanded Tommy Brown, now peering down the barrel of a shotgun he was cleaning. It had been recently fired.

"Okay, okay. I tell. I come in first place to escape Spanish police. That is true. Then gang catch me in London when I see rough stuff against Michael. I think Harry will *rub me out*. While he hold me, he talk of Starlight Machine and what gang was doing. He not care I know, as he intended to throw me in river. Then I realise how to save my life."

"Carry on, Miguel Galvez," smirked Tommy Brown.

"Galvez?" cried Pete. I've heard that name before."

"Of course you have," said Harry.

"Stop!" shouted Miguel. "I tell."

"Get on with it then, and be quick about it."

"Okay, okay. I tell Tommy Brown that, by small chance of fate, I knew interesting story of Spanish treasure ship called *Nuestra Cristo Rosa*. Captain was ancestor of mine. Many times as boy my family tell me of warship and how British kill him. I not care, as too long ago, but now I think Harry and Tommy Brown have interest in gold and silver."

"Bound to," interrupted Tommy Brown. "We needed a new job after finding the looted Russian Amber Room in a cave where the Germans had hidden it during the Second World War. You have to laugh. People are still searching for it to this day. Fools. If only they knew I have it, or rather had it. I sold it to an anonymous Ukrainian buyer for millions."

"As I say, I tell what I know. This keep me alive. So I join gang, but not much trusted. I was ordered not to tell you, Pete. As I knew date of 1743, Michael able to work out distance for egg to fly in space and exact place to look. The rest easy."

Harry laughed. "Of course we still didn't trust you, Miguel, because we knew you held patriotic feelings for Spain. We were sure you wanted to keep the treasure for yourself to buy-back your freedom. Sadly for you, Tommy and I had no intention of letting you get your hands on any of it."

"I see that now," muttered Miguel.

"Nor any money for me?" asked Pete.

"Oh, maybe some for you, to keep you interested, but not a full share," replied Tommy Brown. "A perfect crime, because I knew I could trust Harry to do my bidding by keeping him wealthy, while I could stash most of the rest in the cafe's strong-room, ready to sell bit by bit on the black market. You should see the sky-high price of gold today."

"So that's why the cafe is built like a fortress," thought Oscar from beneath the caravan.

"Why was I not told this job was Miguel's idea?" asked Pete.

"You didn't need to know," said Tommy Brown. "And, as things worked out, we were right not to trust you."

"I thought we were friends," he pleaded. "You have used me and, like the sucker I am, I was tricked by the prospect of riches."

"You're not the first."

"Did Harry kill others in gang?" asked Miguel, suspecting he already knew the answer.

"Oh, surprise, surprise, at last, the Spanish omelette gets the bigger picture."

"A broken neck from Harry or a spell in jail. What a choice for me," brooded Pete, rolling onto a bench in despair.

"No!" bawled Miguel, "not only choice you have. We escape injury and jail if we leave together, right now. My family look after you good."

"What about my money?"

"Forget money. No use in jail cell."

Pete closed towards Miguel, holding a hand over his mouth to whisper. He wore a look of pure dread.

"Maybe you're right, Miguel. Maybe it's our only chance, but I swear I'm not running first. Harry and Tommy have no intention of letting us get out alive. If we make a dash for the door and a fight breaks out, Harry will batter to death the first person he grabs, and it's not going to be me."

"I heard that," shouted Harry fiercely, and in a rapid move he snatched back the kitchen knife. "I'll plunge this into the first of you who comes near our end of the caravan. Believe me, I know how much a blade hurts." He touched his forehead.

Under the caravan Oscar shuddered as the threats escalated, wondering how his ordinary life had been turned into a melodrama of epic proportions. He felt sick, blood flowing hot and fast through his chest. Yet, despite the heightened level of danger, he was resolute not to let Michael be taken away. The only question was—could he successfully prevent it from happening without the danger of being caught? Then the answer came to him in a rush... or rather, a gush!

Wriggling forward, which was no easy task within the shallow space beneath the caravan, he manoeuvred the glue gun to a position between his outstretched legs. Then, taking aim, he fired. Glue shot out between the wheels of the caravan and the Range Rover, but fell harmlessly on the tarmac beyond. He had missed all targets. A steadier aim was required.

Frustrated, but now more determined than ever, Oscar pushed the gun further forward, allowing his feet to grip the very end of the barrel. And, with arms at full-stretch, he again engaged the trigger. Once more glue shot out at a tremendous rate, this time coating the caravan's wheels, brakes and axle in a thick layer of gunk. Within seconds it hardened into a solid mass. The caravan was going absolutely nowhere.

Meanwhile, back inside the caravan, events were at boiling point. Miguel, at last plucking up the courage to attempt a dash for the door, twisted on his heels, grabbed a cushion for protection and charged headlong into Harry, who had just enough time to swing his arm in a slicing motion that brought the knife to within a whisker of Miguel's chest. But having missed, the forward momentum of the thrust caused him to drop the knife as he fell forward in the confined space. And now, realising he too could help Miguel's escape, Michael gallantly swung his legs around to pin Harry down.

It was the chance Miguel needed.

With Harry outstretched on the floor, Miguel leapt over his back and burst out of the caravan. Moments later Pete followed. Soon both were running for their lives.

A hundred metres out, Miguel dared glance over his shoulder, surprised to see Pete far behind. Then came a terrifying cry from the caravan, as Harry broke free and vengefully stuck the knife into Tommy Brown's shoulder. The cut was deep and the wound gushed blood.

"Why?" cried Tommy Brown, falling on his hands and knees next to Michael. "I did nothing but make you rich."

"Exactly! You did nothing. You could've stopped them getting away, but didn't. Now you pay the price."

"But Harry?"

"Shut it! You're useless to me now the gang's done for." And with that said Harry jumped from the caravan to give chase, certain Tommy Brown would bleed to death before he returned.

Deep in the woods, Miguel was pleased when Pete caught up.

"Harry not catch us with bad leg from broken bottle," he panted. "But I think he try to ambush us when we go back to help Michael."

"Count me out, mate," was Pete's indifferent reply as he quickened the pace. "I'm heading for Southampton."

Miguel tried to match Pete's speed, but his muscles were fit to burst and his old wound reopened.

By the time Pete reached the edge of the forest and disappeared into the farm fields beyond, Miguel was two or three hundred metres behind and on the brink of collapsing. That was the last time they ever saw each other.

And, as predicted, scarcely had Miguel reached the woodland edge when Harry gave up the chase. He turned and stormed back to the caravan, where he looked angrily at the two men lying on the floor.

"Still alive!" he taunted as he dragged Tommy Brown by his shirt collar towards the small shower room, leaving a thick red smear of fresh blood across the laminate floor.

"What are you doing?" screamed Tommy in a spine-chilling cry for mercy, sure Harry raged with a bloodlust only his death would satisfy. "Listen for pity's sake. It doesn't have to end this way. I have money, lots of it, riches beyond imagination. I'll split everything straight and fair. Fifty-fifty." He screamed again as Harry kicked his limp legs to get him through the narrow doorway. "Didn't you hear me? I'm worth millions. Harry… Harry, no!"

In the shower room Harry dropped the body like a sack of potatoes, and then, taking hold of Tommy's right arm, he wrenched it back until it broke and flopped limply across his chest. Now he could get the door to close.

"Harry, *please!*"

"Save your breath," demanded Harry as he secured Tommy's weakened body to the toilet using strong brown tape. "I don't have to share anything. I know it's all waiting for me at the *Maid on the Lake.*"

"All right, all right, for pity's sake have everything, but for friendship let me live."

"Oh, why didn't you say so before? For friendship. That's a different matter. Now, let me think. Err, okay, I've thought and the answer is still NO," and at once he used the last of the tape to cover Tommy's mouth. "But don't worry. Because we were once friends I'll do you a favour and keep you nice and warm."

The caravan rocked as Harry jumped out, landing just inches from Oscar's face. Seconds later the parcel van doors were slammed shut.

"Once a jolly swagman camped by a billabong, under the shade of a coolabah tree…" sang Harry as he re-entered the caravan to pour petrol over the seats, floor and walls, casually stepping over Michael who tugged frantically at the handcuffs. He then closed all the windows except one, through which he intended to drop a lighted match from the outside. And, after turning the gas bottle on for good measure, he left. The caravan had been turned into a primed bomb.

With so much petrol poured, it wasn't long before it started dripping through the drain holes drilled into the caravan floor and down onto Oscar's clothes. The vapour was a familiar smell to Oscar, and at once he understood what Harry had done. Only seconds remained to get out or he would be caught beneath a flaming inferno which would then collapse on top of him. And given the level of Harry's villainy, he was certain Michael and Tommy Brown had been left inside to burn.

With panic being a stronger emotion than fear, Oscar squirmed, struggled and pushed against his heels to wriggle out, but the strap of the glue gun entangled itself on an exposed bolt. The gun had to be abandoned.

"So we meet again," gloated Harry in a horrible voice, stamping hard on Oscar's hand as he emerged from under the caravan.

Oscar looked up at the towering figure but could do nothing to prevent himself from being dragged into the open, where Harry pinned him to the ground.

"Well, well, isn't this nice. You've come to witness the end of my work and the old man's hopes," laughed Harry as he pulled a box of matches from his pocket, which he rattled provocatively. "Game, set and match to me." He took out a match and held it ready to strike. "Would you like the honour of starting the bonfire?

Oh, no, silly me, you've got petrol on your clothes. Oh well, I suppose I'll have to be birthday boy. Get ready to make a wish. This will blow your mind."

"You're totally insane," screeched Oscar, turning his head to one side to brace himself for the inevitable blast.

Then it happened, or, rather, it didn't.

A second passed, then another and twenty more, and still nothing exploded.

Oscar dared open his eyes. Above him still stood Harry, a match ready for striking in his hand, but now frozen to the spot by the melodic sound of music. His jaw hung open. Oscar twisted to see what he was staring at.

On the far side of the road was the professor, perched on top of a very high rope which was held up by absolutely nothing. He was playing the snake charmer's pipe, his loose clothes wafting in the breeze like some kind of mystical guru.

"Magic," stuttered Harry.

"What did you say?" pounced Jake, who had circled around the caravan to surprise the villain from behind. And as Harry turned, Jake landed his best right hook, leaving him dazed but still dangerous.

"How's that!" followed Gracie from the other side, striking Harry a forceful blow with a cricket bat. "Is that what you boys call a 'Six'? He's been well and truly bummered this time."

Harry dropped like a stone.

"Game, set and match to the Musketeers," yelped Gracie proudly, polishing the bat on the hem of her dress. "Anyone thought of calling the police? How about you, Prof...." She looked about. "Where's the professor?"

Jake ran across the road, where the rope lay abandoned with the pipe resting on top.

"At last, I can introduce you to my long-lost and most cherished son," howled the professor through his tears as he stepped from the caravan, a large pair of bolt-cutters in one hand.

"And in turn, let me introduce you, Michael, to the world's greatest superheroes, the other two of the three Musketeers triumphantly led by Captain Jake—boy hero."

"And Gallant Gracie, the half Musketeer," she called. "Don't forget me! After all, I thought of the electric door handle and I'm the one who swiped Harry with the bat."

"Of course, we must always thank Glorious Gracie," said Jake in a surprisingly generous tone. "The fourth *full* Musketeer."

"Hello," said Oscar wryly, "we had better keep our eyes on those two."

"Oh, Dad!"

"Behave yourself, Uncle Oscar. But we are proper friends now." She paused, looking at Jake's admiring smile. "I'm right, aren't I Jake?"

Jake nodded. She shyly walked away, but immediately wished she hadn't.

"Just the greatest friends and the best of cousins," said Jake as she twisted to look back.

Michael ran his fingers through his father's hair. "What on earth happened to you? All this white stuff."

The professor laughed as he looked at Michael's bald head. "It's a very long story indeed, Son. We'll have plenty of catching up ahead of us."

"Stand clear," said Gracie after retrieving the glue gun, which she now pointed towards Harry as he stirred into consciousness. "Do you feel lucky, punk?" Her hand squeezed the trigger until every last drop of glue had gushed out. "Probably not!"

"Was that absolutely necessary?" asked Jake.

Gracie smiled innocently, but Jake knew she had enjoyed every squirt. "Oh dear, the trigger stuck. You really must get it fixed, Professor. Gracie the Gallant Gangster strikes again!"

"My goodness, we've forgotten Tommy Brown," said Michael. "I saw him being dragged towards the shower."

"Don't worry," replied the professor, "I freed him."

"You did what?" cried Oscar. "The police will want to question him."

"Don't look so worried, my friend," replied the professor, "he won't get far. When I removed the tape from his mouth, I gave him the choice of being handed over to the police or drink a whole bottle of my Snore-Stopper. He chose the potion, the foolish man. I always wanted to know what would happen if a whole bottle was drunk in one go. My guess is, he will hand himself into a hospital tomorrow when he sees the size of his nose and, perhaps, other things! I can't wait to get the results. He can then have his arm plastered too and the cut on his shoulder properly treated. Trust me, the doctors will inform the police when they see it's a knife wound."

"And Miguel? What will happen to him?" asked Jake.

"Actually," said Oscar, "I don't really care. He wasn't such a bad bloke after all. Let's allow fate to play its hand."

"Fate *and* Jorvik," flinched the professor.

"Meaning what?" enquired Jake.

"Oh, this and that! Nothing significant for you to worry about."

But it had the greatest significance to Miguel.

The professor had decided to take Jorvik to the caravan on a strong leather lead, as protection against the gang. All the way Jorvik had pulled and chewed at the lead until finally it snapped, when the creature rushed off blindly into the woods. The speed of its escape shocked the professor, as he believed the Bloodrat would stay loyal to its master. "Still," he thought at the time, "could anyone really understand the mind of a Bloodrat?"

Now free, Jorvik used its bloodhound senses to pick up the familiar scent of a man it had once bitten. And, having tasted Miguel's blood, he wanted more. The track took it through the same trees and then beyond to a farm, where an old wooden barn stood in an open field. There Jorvik suddenly stopped, having lost Miguel's scent but instead detected the smell of other animals which seemed strangely familiar. Sniffing blindly around the barn, it eventually found its way onto the high roof.

As he ran through the last of the woodland, Miguel had heard a large animal beating a crooked path through the undergrowth. But he had dismissed it as being a wild badger, which had taken off in an unknown direction.

Minutes later Miguel also reached the barn, happy for the shelter it provided. He rattled the rickety wooden doors which, although they could be pulled and pushed to create a chink, were secured from fully opening by a tight chain. The bottom of each door was rotted where rats had chewed the damp wood, but the gaps were too small for an adult to crawl through. And so, exhausted, he slumped heavily against the doors.

It was while catching his breath that he noticed the shadow of the barn roof casting a silhouette on the ground, with the irregular shape of something standing above. Curious, he stood to take a look. And there, with its head hanging over the edge was Jorvik, its unseeing eyes but highly-developed nose pointing menacingly towards him. Miguel stepped to one side and then the other to see if the creature's head followed his every move. And when it did, he jumped back into the shadow.

Staying close to the barn wall and seemingly out of view, Miguel crept furtively to the far side of the building, comforted to look up and see the roof there was clear. But relief was short-lived. Gradually the sound of growling came closer as the Bloodrat gingerly crossed the roof until it stopped at the far edge, once more baring its needle-like teeth way above Miguel's head.

"Come, come, nice little doggy thing, let me pass," Miguel called up, sure he could win Jorvik's trust with a soft voice.

The Bloodrat remained as still as a statue.

"Okay, I no more scared," he shouted, grabbing an abandoned spade that lay beside a rusty water trough. "Jump and I smash you into next field."

Of course, raising his voice in a threatening manner was a huge mistake to the blind and mindless creature. With its mouth now wide and claws open, Jorvik instinctively flung itself from the great height, as only a Bloodrat could.

The sharp yelp of pain was terrible as a heavy whack from the spade struck Jorvik's plunging body, pitching the animal into the long grass of an adjoining field. Miguel ran over, intending to inflict a mortal blow if it so much as moved.

There Jorvik lay, stunned and wounded, its breathing so shallow that it appeared dead. Miguel tossed the spade aside and was soon running out of sight.

But this was not the end of Jorvik. Out of the barn scurried many wild rats which gathered around the disabled Bloodrat, offering protection against scavenging foxes until Jorvik recovered enough to be led into the dark recesses of the old barn.

Jorvik was never seen again. Yet, much later, rumours circulated in the village of strange dark creatures which lurked in the hedgerow. Some villagers even thought they had seen wild cats. As the rumours spread, so the animals became larger in public perception until a puma hunt was organised. Incredibly, the blind and secretive creatures even gained notoriety as the 'wild cats of Wiley's Farm'. Perhaps the professor's opinions about breeding had been wrong after all.

"You know," said Oscar, as they returned to the cottage in triumph, "you really must show me how you do the rope trick. Where do you hide the wire?"

"Trick?" replied the professor. "That was no trick, it was…"

Jake frowned. "Please don't say 'Magic'."

"My mouth is shut on the subject," the professor replied through a smile.

"By the way, what happened to Jorvik?" asked Gracie. "I saw him belt off."

"Alas poor Jorvik, I knew him well!"

"Sorry?"

"It seems you can take the dog out of the rat, but not the rat out of the dog. He's gone."

"I wish I hadn't asked," she said, turning away.

Later that evening the group sat around the professor's fire as Gracie handed out celebratory plates of sausages and humbugs.

"I didn't think we had any sausages left," said Jake as he dug in.

"Honesty makes me admit I pinched them from the fridge in the caravan when I let Tommy Brown go," said the professor shyly. "I know it was wrong, but, after all, they did eat mine."

"Actually, I'm not being ungrateful but I don't like sausages or humbugs," said Michael, pushing the meal away.

"On no," screamed the professor in an amiable manner, "I've rescued the wrong person! He can't be a son of mine."

"And these surely can't be my overdue Christmas gifts," added Michael as he grabbed the presents from under the tree and ripped the paper off. "Blimey, they belong in a museum."

"You're not too old to be put over my knee, young man," laughed the professor. "Now, who wants hot chocolate?"

By eight o'clock, Oscar was relieved to see everyone's skin tone turning pinker.

"That's good. I can take you kids home tonight after all."

Gracie groaned, as only she could. "Can't we stay a little longer? These old-fashioned games are great fun and, anyway, my mum will have my dolls ready for a tea party and I'm way too old for all that baby stuff."

"Please Dad," pleaded Jake. "After all, we are superheroes."

"Superheroes or not, Muriel will want you back." Oscar turned to Gracie. "I'm not so sure Aunt Julie would mind so much, though, if it meant she could have her nails painted."

"What about the Starlight Machine?" asked Jake. "Is it going to be broken up for scrap?"

The professor caught Oscar's eye. "You said you wanted to restore it back to its original 1960 condition. I took your money, so I'm duty bound to let you have it, if you still want it."

"Dad," begged Jake, "can't it stay as it is? There are a hundred adventures awaiting us if the professor is willing to make more space eggs."

Oscar noticed the Professor was now poking a drinking straw through the hole in his rubber boot to scratch his foot.

"Would you be willing to?"

"I could, I suppose," said the professor, "with Michael's help. But, there is one problem. I'm rather strapped for cash. That's why I was willing to sell the Bubble Car."

"What if we all chip in?" asked Jake. "I have some savings."

The professor smiled. "There has to be one condition."

"Yes?" they said in unison.

"We get in plenty more sausages for the excitement ahead. By the way, did I ever tell you about the Lost City of Atlantis?"

Chapter 24
Epilogue

Now, you might think that was the end of the Spanish gold adventure, but there was still one more surprise ahead.

After a late tea, and before the youngsters went home, the professor was persuaded to run the remainder of the images stored in the Receptor Box. Fortunately, replacing the damaged wire used in the defence of the shed took barely ten minutes, and soon the Receptor was fit for use again.

And Miguel had been right. There was only a little left to see, but what remained was… well…

It was morning, and *HMS Audacious* was once again anchored in the island's beautiful natural harbour. The great—but damaged—ship had been towed there by the *Rosa* using a skeleton crew of British sailors, and already most of the men were at work repairing the masts and mending the sails among other vital tasks to ensure a safe voyage to China and then home.

Other sailors, probably numbering fifty and comprising the men rescued from the island after the Jolly boats had been set adrift, were employed shifting the huge quantities of gold, silver and other precious cargoes from the *Rosa* to the *Audacious*.

The Spanish treasure took many forms, from gold coins to small silver statues and bars, and much in-between. A simple hoist constructed as a pyramid of three strong timbers, a pulley and a rope had been hastily erected on *Rosa* to lower the treasure onto the Jolly boats for transportation to the beach, where the white sands were used as a half-way point to repack the treasure into sixty wooden barrels which had been emptied of gunpowder. A similar device on board *Audacious* raised the heavy barrels for storage. Of course, a great many gunpowder barrels remained untouched, should the journey home encounter Spanish or French warships.

A single bag of coins was all two average men could carry at a time, lifted on a make-shift stretcher hastily made from poles and old sail cloth. And even this was no easy task. Yet, the work was happy and brisk, as each man could feel a reward coming to his pocket.

Then, the holographic images suddenly ended—the story told.

"Wow!" exclaimed Jake, "that was certainly worth seeing."

"And to think the gang didn't bother to look at it," said Gracie. "More fool them, I say."

"There was an awful lot of treasure," pondered Oscar. "Shame we won't see any of it."

The professor removed his glasses. "You're right, Mr Trotter, but never forget what you've gained from the experience. A look at history in the making. That's priceless too."

"I would rather have the gold," he replied.

Jake looked at the professor and together they burst into unstoppable laughter.

"What?" asked Oscar, confused.

"Once a salesman, always a salesman," chortled the professor.

Muriel Striker was delighted to see her precious son and Gracie return home safely. She thanked *him*—Oscar, that is—for looking after them so well.

"Are you two feeling okay?" she asked, looking from one to the other. "Car sick, I suppose. You both look a little... well... greenish."

The youngsters grinned cheekily.

"I don't suppose *he* found much for you to do," she continued from the landing, bringing the rest of Gracie's possessions downstairs. "Aunt Julie will be here shortly. She just wanted to pop into ASDA on the way over to grab a tub of beauty cream."

"No, Mum, it was pretty uneventful. I'll tell you all about it in the morning." He turned to Gracie, "… when I can explain a bit of what we did without you blowing your top!" he whispered.

"Oh, by the way, Gracie, I found your doll yesterday under the bed. I'm afraid it's horribly broken."

"Oh, that's fine, Aunty. Just bin the silly thing."

* * *

Two months later, on a quite ordinary Tuesday morning, the phone rang. Muriel answered.

"What do you want? Jake is having his breakfast. It's a school day, you know." There followed a pause. "Oh, very well, but make it quick." She left the telephone receiver on the window-sill. "It's *him* again."

"Yes, Dad?" said Jake.

"Does Mum get a daily paper?"

"No. She says she can't stand the bad news."

"Well, I do. I was trawling through the classified adverts yesterday and you'll never guess what I found. I'll read it to you."

For Sale
The Golden Rosa
An eighteenth-century mansion in need of major
restoration.
For further information, contact…

"Commodore Bowfinger's place."

"Yes! So, I went there yesterday to take a look. I took the professor with me."

"What's it like?"

"Estate Agents have a word for houses in poor repair. They call them 'tired'. Believe me, Jake, this place is not tired, it's utterly exhausted."

Jake laughed. "You didn't phone to tell me that."

"Hurry up, Jake," called Muriel, "your porridge is getting cold."

"Coming, Mum," he shouted. "Better be quick, Dad. I've got to go."

"Okay. Anyway, the roof has caved in, the windows are broken or missing, and the walls are decayed. However…"

Jake just knew there would be a 'however'.

"… However, do you remember the professor's naval book saying Bowfinger had sixty stone barrels and one half-sized stone barrel placed as decoration on the ramparts?"

"Yup."

"Well, only five remain. The rest have either fallen off over the years or been removed by builders to stop them becoming dangerous. So, I asked the Estate Agent if I could buy one of the damaged barrels dumped in a heap in the garden. He asked the current owner, who said I could take one away for a five pound note donated to charity. He didn't mind which."

"And?"

"Oh, Jake, don't you see? I chose the 'one-half' stone barrel."

"No, Dad, I still don't get it."

"How many gunpowder barrels full of treasure were loaded onto *Audacious*?"

"Sixty."

"Yet, Bowfinger had sixty and one-half stone barrels erected on his ramparts. What was the 'one-half' barrel to commemorate?"

"You don't mean…"

"I jolly well do. It was the professor who made the connection. Bowfinger spent his share of the Spanish treasure building the mansion, but nobody ever discovered what happened to the Canton bullion. Well, I now know. Bowfinger hid it in the extra half-size stone barrel, ready for recovery should he ever need it. Ironic. They say the best hiding place is the one least expected, and this barrel was in full public view for centuries. Sixty large and empty stone barrels and one small barrel full of gold."

"Gold!" cried Jake.

"A whole bag of the stuff. You know what that means?"

"Yes, Dad, and it's wonderful. We have the money to pay for more space eggs."

"Quite right, Son. The adventures have only just begun! The professor has already mentioned something about a Sunken City."

THE END—for now!